The Vatican Files

"In this fast-moving suspense thriller, the Pope dispatches a group of military-hardened Jesuit operatives to save the world against history's most evil villain. If you like a plot full of twists about Nazis and the Vatican where good and evil aren't always black and white, then this action thriller is the book for you. Filled with sci-fi elements such as UFOs, aliens, alien technology and government conspiracies, this book is a page-turner and a fun read. Enjoy!"

–M.B. Tosi, best-selling author of The Crimson Path of Honor

"A very cool trailer!"

-Gordon A Kessler, thriller novelist and author of BRAINSTORM, DEAD RECKONING & JEZEBEL

"The Vatican Files masterfully weaves UFO lore with true historical events to create a fast-moving suspense thriller! When the public gets full disclosure, will some of this book's story lines prove to be true?"

- Jeff Beals, best-selling author of Self Marketing Power and Selling Saturdays

"Jerzhy Knuteman has written a story torn from the headlines of the National Enquirer. Somewhere in that shadowy crossroads where the Da Vinci Code meets the X-files with a touch of Nazi world domination thrown in for good measure. A great read!"

- Hugh Reilly, best-selling author of Bound to Have Blood

"If you follow "Ancient Aliens" on The History Channel, if you like historical fiction, World War II, and a little "Indiana Jones" thrown in for good measure, get ready to be intrigued!"

- Doug Sasse, screenwriter of Adventures in Art Modeling

THE VATICAN FILES

A HISTORICAL SUPERNATURAL THRILLER NOVEL

Jerzhy Knuteman

Omniscient Publishing
Omaha, Nebraska

This book is a work of fiction incorporating the use of historical figures and events.

Cover art by Travis Thierstein.

Library of Congress Control Number: 2009913867

ISBN – Print: 978-1-893353-20-6
ISBN – EPub: 978-1-893353-21-3
ISBN – MOBI: 978-1-893353-25-1

Printed in the United States of America

Published and distributed by
Omniscient Publishing

www.thevaticanfiles.com

Printed in the United States of America

10 9 8 7 6 5 4 3 2 1

To the Jesuit community worldwide

and

Members of the United States Armed Forces

*"The most beautiful thing we can experience is the mysterious.
It is the source of all true art and science."*

- Albert Einstein

Acknowledgments

I owe an enormous debt of gratitude to many individuals who contributed to making the completion of this book a reality.

First, I want to thank Joe Swatek for his invaluable guidance with plot design and direction, and for his professional editing expertise. It would have been impossible to complete this project without his tremendous help and encouragement.

I want to thank my group of beta readers who located and corrected errors of historical minutiae.

I utilized Creighton University Reinert-Alumni Library to gather the majority of my background information on the Jesuits and Jesuit life, and the individuals there were phenomenally helpful. I especially want to convey my deepest thanks to David Crawford, the University archivist, who did a masterful job of locating archival information on the Missouri Province of the Society of Jesus and specifically St. Stanislaus Seminary in Florissant, Missouri. He also was helpful in identifying additional resources on Jesuit life in Omaha around 1918.

When David Crawford located the archival information on St. Stanislaus Seminary, the content was not in English, but in Latin. Adam Karnik, a Creighton graduate student identified by his professors as a solid Latinist, translated the content from Latin to English, an invaluable service that added to the authenticity of seminary life at the Missouri Novitiate.

Several faculty members at Creighton University were also instrumental in providing assistance and guidance, including Dennis Hamm, S.J., Roc O'Connor, S.J., and Gregory Bucher, PhD.

David Miros, PhD, the lead archivist at the Midwest Jesuit Archives, contributed additional background information on Jesuit life. Tom Lawler, S.J., the Vocation Director with the Wisconsin Province of the Society of Jesus, contributed heavily to explaining the requirements needed and the formal process that must be followed to become a member of the Society of Jesus.

Reverend Joseph Taphorn, J.C.L., of the Omaha Archdiocese contributed his expertise in Latin phraseology, and Laura Heimann of the Omaha Archdiocese provided astounding historical background on early parish life in Omaha from 1900-1925.

I also received valuable input from military personnel regarding covert operations. I want to thank Commander X, a retired Colonel in the United States Air Force, who requested anonymity.

My thanks go to my astronomy consultant, Michael Neece, who is the assistant director of the Morehead Planetarium and Science Center on the campus of the University of North Carolina at Chapel Hill.

Owen Conner, a curator at the National Museum of the Marine Corp, offered exemplary assistance by adding elements of authenticity throughout the book.

I wish to thank Stephanie Brennan for her expertise in formatting the book into e-book and print editions.

Finally, I wish to thank my family for their support and encouragement.

Prologue

Ancient Past
2,000,000 B.C.

AS LONG AS TIME has existed, they have been intrigued by its progress. The manipulations had started millennia ago, and little by little, with the results of each small change and mutation, a crowning triumph was emerging. But they were not satisfied.

The Nordic Ancients were wise, caring, and extremely ambitious. Sharing some common features with today's Scandinavians, both the male and female extraterrestrials were blonde, blue-eyed, and had pale white skin. The female stood a little under six feet tall, while male height could reach just under seven feet tall. They communicated telepathically with each other.

Long ago, as they traveled endlessly from universe to universe seeking new destinations to extend their dominion and test their theories of creation, a startling photosynthetic biosignature scan of a nearby planet indicating the presence of both atmospheric oxygen and the unique reflectance spectrum of plant leaves, caught their attention. Unannounced, they arrived at a basically barren land surprisingly covered with little vegetation and flora, but inhabited by the most primitive of humanoid species.

The Ancients took up permanent residence on the dark side of the planet's single, crater-filled moon. They quickly decided that the Grand Experiment should take place here, within the total solitary darkness of the planet's celestial progeny. Transport of the experimental subjects from the planet's surface to the moon's hidden laboratories would be quick and simple.

Over hundreds of millions of years, Elohim and his group of Ancients have visited, observed, and improved upon their human creation. Using bioremediation and phytoextraction techniques, they transformed the starkly void planet to one teeming with dense forests, colorful and plentiful flora, and oceans and rivers blessed with clear, blue water. Biomedical engineering trials using recombinant DNA, tubulin, blastocysts, micro-RNA, unique nucleic acid conformations, biocatalysis, and other surgical intrusions over the eons of time seemed to nudge the unique offspring toward the new evolution the Ancients deeply desired: a species in their own likeness.

Ever so slowly, the "sons" and "daughters" of the space creators were changing the face of the earth. As past civilizations flourished and then dramatically disappeared as natural disasters, random collisions with wandering, off-course celestial bodies, and advanced energy tests gone bad methodically wiped out plant and lower animal life over the course of history, the earth-bound human element, through the benevolence and watchful eyes of their creators, always remained and survived.

As the human species continued to meekly evolve on this isolated, camouflaged world, rumors were quickly spreading across the cosmic community, and Elohim and his group were no longer the sole proprietors of this universe's secret hiding place.

******

Abzu, Sumaria
45,000 B.C.

Earth now was being visited by several curious and insidious alien races from such star systems as Draco, Orion, Sirius, and Canis Minor. The most dangerous of these new races was a shape-shifting reptilian bunch called the Chitauri, led by an entity called Enki. These Reptilians also had developed a Master Plan: Move through the universe, recreate new DNA codes, and implant all unsuspecting human civilizations with those codes.

In their original form, the typical Reptilian was 6 feet to 8 feet tall, bipedal, with scaly green skin, large yellow or gold eyes with a vertical pupil, and bad body odor. When they shapeshifted into humanoid form, they were considered a race of intelligent beings with supernatural powers and a malevolent disposition.

Establishing their base camp hidden deep in the Djebel Sarhro Mountains, the Reptilians began their deceitful scheme on humankind. Through intimidating mating rituals with the local inhabitants and GMO (genetically modified organisms) and biotransformational engineering, Enki and his scientists created a black-headed race of humans to work as slave labor in their gold mines. Recent archeological findings translated from Sumerian tablets indicated that the "black-headed people" were considered slaves in the Sumerian cast hierarchy.

For thousands of years, the human experiments continued. The Egyptian, Aztec, Mayan, and early Chinese empires all had "human experiments" as leaders of their people. Enki and his reptilian race had now burrowed their "roots" deeply into Earth soil. However, they were only one of several alien races interested in imprinting their DNA on the unsuspecting human race on earth.

✶✶✶✶✶✶

Secret Underground Essene Camp
West of Qumran, Israel
5 B.C.

It was time. The young girl, only 15 years of age, had been chosen by her secret Jewish ascetic sect to be the recipient of this delicate regenerative transplantation procedure that the Nordic scientists had been attempting to perfect for over seven generations without success. This time, they hoped that the pluripotent embryonic stem cells would differentiate themselves and make in vitro fertilization less hazardous to the health of the female host.

"Has the angiogenesis run its course yet?" asked the lead scientist to his hard-working, loyal assistant.

"Yes, Doctor," she answered. "The microtubules have adhered nicely. I believe she is ready for the fertilization procedure."

"Then we need to prepare the ship to transport both subjects to the chemotaxis lab on the moon," the lead scientist stated. "We also need the sperm sample shortly."

The father donor himself was almost as young as his fertile female companion. He, too, had been specially chosen from a small group of Essenic boys who were a part of the Great White Brotherhood of the Therapeutate, an auxiliary branch of an Egyptian mystery school connected to esoteric healing traditions. His sperm samples had tested out to be one of the most compatible with the girl's regenerative reproductive system.

And so it was that Mary and Joseph were quickly shuffled from the secret subterranean location, and loaded upon the hovering spacecraft to make their way to the sterile moon lab where an immaculate conception was to be performed.

******

**Bethlehem
September, 4 B.C.**

According to ancient lore, kings and messiahs were born in September. After giving birth under the caring and watchful eyes of the anxious alien doctors, nurses, technicians, and scientists at the sterile moon laboratory, Mary, Joseph, and their newborn son were lovingly escorted to the landing pod, and gently loaded into the waiting craft along with the accompanying medical personnel to whisk all of them quickly back to Earth.

The clear, cloudless sky along with the natural shine of late-night moonbeams, turned the returning spacecraft into a glowing ball of light, which didn't go unnoticed by the shepherds and farmers tending their flocks of sheep and goats that evening outside the tiny town of Bethlehem.

"Look at that moving star," one young shepherd said to his companion, pointing out the movement of the bright object in the night sky. "It looks like it's coming straight at us!"

With their terrified watchdogs barking loudly in the direction of the moving light source, his companion answered, "Stars don't move like that. Look, it's coming down just over that next hill. Let's see what it is." At least a dozen other herders who had seen the same thing also began their walk in the direction of the steep hill, which was now cloaking the arrival of the silver-colored saucer.

Bethlehem had been chosen as the recovery and recuperation site for Mary and the baby because it was the home of Salome, Mary's sister, and her husband Simon. The location was also close to the secret Essenic base by Qumran. And Mary had insisted that she wanted to be with family, and that it was only at Salome's house that she felt safe and comfortable for her, Joseph, and their first-born son.

Upon departing the craft, the travelers found a waiting wooden cart hitched up to a donkey. Mary, her baby, and the two female nurses got into the cart. Joseph and the lone alien physician took the reins of the donkey, and began walking the short distance to the home of Salome and Simon in the slumbering town. After removing the human cargo, the craft slowly lifted off the ground and moved to a stationary location in the sky, roughly 1000 feet above the center of the town of Bethlehem, and closely monitored the steady movement of the small party traversing the pebbly road to their final destination.

Following the uneventful 15 minute walk, the group finally arrived at their predetermined location. Though deep into the night, a short knock brought an excited Salome and Simon to the door. They welcomed their visitors with hugs and handshakes, and led them to their living quarters, a back room used mainly for storage, but which had been specially prepared for Mary and the newborn. A large manger had been fitted with blankets and linens into a comfortable bed for Mary and her son.

Joseph, the two nurses, and the alien doctor helped Mary onto the bed, and put her newborn son into her arms. Exhausted by the birthing experience, flight back to earth, and the bumpy wagon ride into town, Mary quickly fell asleep. An alien nurse quietly took the resting baby from Mary's arms, and placed him in his own small cradle near the bed. Then all the inhabitants of the home found their sleeping spots, and a calming quietness spread throughout the house.

******

The baby boy appeared perfect, yet different, to the knowing eye. The end result of the adaptive experimental medical procedures fostered by the alien doctors was successful. However, the nine-month gestation period was anything but easy for the young female host.

To make this child special, countless intrusive corrective surgeries had been instigated. Many of them involved splicing procedures to fortify the baby's autoimmune system: mRNA splicing, RNA-editing, and alternative splicing. To strengthen brain development and capacity, the alien physicians initiated chromosomal rearrangement and added extra dosages of endothelin during the first three months of the pregnancy.

A synthetic mutator protein was injected into the fetus during the second trimester to lighten the skin tone. This procedure alone would differentiate the newborn infant from all other Jewish babies, and solidify his position as the "messiah of men." Neurogenesis was performed to enhance all genetic modifications in the growth factor of the nervous system.

It was always planned by the aliens that this baby, long destined to be named Jesus, would fulfill the prophecies of old. Even though alien influence did not fully immerse itself into religion or politics of the day, a decision had been mutually reached by the Essenic leaders and their extraterrestrial brethren to make this child the "savior" long sought by the Jewish people.

To make Jesus into the greatest mystical being to walk the face of the earth, the alien scientists created several biotransformational treatments to aid in the process. In one treatment, a sensory transduction protein was injected into the fetus two months before birth. The special injection of pyranosyl RNA (pRNA) was an RNA derivative that the alien doctors called their "molecule of life." The purpose of this injection was to heighten the awareness of Jesus to extracellular signals, such as light, taste, sound, touch, and smell.

To heighten awareness that would give Jesus telepathic and other metaphysical and paranormal powers during his lifetime, the alien surgeons performed an extraordinarily complex procedure that included constructing bio-based neuron circuits in the brain using concentrations of DNA nanostructure molecules located in newly-created four-strand DNA quadruplex structures. These prototypical micro-processing molecular agents were first grouped together in a test tube, underwent several chemical interaction procedures taking several weeks, and finally were stranded together into the correct combination before being implanted into the cerebellum of the resilient eight-month fetus.

Finally, in a breathtaking medical procedure barely a month before the birth that constituted a tremendous risk on the part of the alien scientists, sensitive tissue remodeling using transducers, recombinant DNA, biomedical engineering, and nanotechnology was performed during a nine-hour surgery. Mary's heart had stopped twice on the operating table during the procedure. But she was quickly revived, with no harm to her or the baby.

This tissue remodeling was extremely necessary because it created the final link for the immortality of Jesus: It would provide the alien scientists with enough human genetic material to construct a cloned replica of Jesus the man if one was ever needed.

******

It was now nearly dawn as the shepherds and herdsmen made their way over the tall hill to once again see the glowing "star of Bethlehem" sitting motionless in the early-morning sun-streaked sky directly over the little town. They continued their walk until they found themselves standing alone in the deserted center of town, directly under the "star."

"Why are we here?" one older shepherd asked no one in particular. "What are we looking for?"

"The star has led us to this place," another herdsman responded. "Something important has happened here."

******

The twelve men remained in their position as the sleepy townsfolk began to awaken and begin their daily chores. Since the town water well was located in the town square, many people began to arrive to get their daily allotment. Stories were starting that told of a late-night arrival of visitors to the home of Salome and Simon. Other stories told of a fair-skinned newborn child in that traveling party. Some even spoke in hushed tones that this child was "special" and had "messianic features."

As sunlight began to envelop the entire town, the shepherds noticed that the star had disappeared. No surprise, since all stars disappear when the sun is in the heavens. But the stories had piqued the interest of the shepherds and herdsmen, and they asked directions from the locals to the baby's location. Arriving at the door of Salome and Simon's home, the leader of the group asked if they could see the baby. Startled at the question, Salome went to Mary and Joseph to tell them of the request. Their response was positive since the prophets had predicted that the baby Jesus would be visited by "shepherds and herdsmen, coming to see the Jewish messiah." Oblivious to the presence of the alien nurses and doctor since they were disguised in traditional Jewish garb, the 12 visitors were awe-struck at the site of the fair-skinned child born of dark-skinned mother and father. They fell to their knees and proclaimed the arrival of the messiah to lead the Jews to freedom against their Roman oppressors. Mary and Joseph only smiled at the messiah reference. But deep in their hearts, they knew this special child was destined to fulfill the prophecies of their ancestors.

******

After spending a week with her sister, it was time for Mary, Joseph, Jesus, and the alien medical specialists to depart for Qumran and the Essene village. Since the land known as Nazareth in the New Testament gospels did not yet exist, the family established their homestead a short distance north of Bethany in Judaea. During her lifetime, Mary gave birth to seven more children, all natural-birth. Jesus, the oldest, had five brothers and two sisters, all of whom were very active in the preparation for the battle with Rome to free the Jews from Roman dictatorship.

Jesus was destined to lead this "holy" war. But things never seem to turn out the way they're supposed to, even for messiahs.

The Present

CHAPTER ONE

1918 – French Battlefield – 2350 Hours

CURLED up as closely to a fetal position as he could, and hugging the lower trench wall so intimately that he could taste the munitions-soaked earth, Paul Dante was literally shaking in his boots while biting on a toothpick. It was not just the awful cold weather and wet clothes that had him shivering and nervous. It was mostly the dire situation he and his troop found themselves in. For a brief moment, the young Marine was wondering what-in-the-hell he was thinking when he decided to enlist two years ago after forging his mother's signature on the induction papers.

The Marine recruiter in Omaha had told him that he would become a man, he would see the world, he would get all the cigarettes he wanted, and that everyone in his town would call him a hero.

"Yeah," Dante thought to himself, "The only world I'm seeing is this hellhole. I hate cigarettes. And no heroes are around to talk about anything anyway. That recruiter was lyin' out of his ass."

The fierce fighting that was occurring now, near midnight on a cold early October night in the Argonne forest northwest of Verdun, suddenly had ceased. The ground skirmishes with the German troops had halted suddenly when the Germans retreated following several unsuccessful attacks on the depleted American Expeditionary Force. Now Dante and 20 other soldiers from his Marine unit of the 2nd Battalion division, 5th Marines found themselves following their victory at the Battle of Belleau Wood with another battle called the Meuse-Argonne Offensive. Dante relished the quiet time, using it to reflect how lucky he was to be surviving the war.

He remembered that Belleau Wood had been a bloodbath in June. The commander of the Marine Brigade, Army General James Harbord, had ordered his troops to hold their ground instead of retreating to the rear, which their French counterparts were doing. Dante smiled when reliving his Marine Captain Lloyd Williams retorting, "Retreat? Hell, we just got here." With his bayonet, Dante and his unit had dug shallow foxholes and fortified trenches in the grain fields so they could fight the Germans from the prone position. It was a good strategy, a great one, really, Dante thought.

Unknown to Dante's unit, the Germans had also managed to dig in on Hill 142, just 600 yards east of Dante, with their machine gun nests and artillery. When it was time to attack early the next morning, Dante and his unit dispersed to cover the flanks. With the majority of the American troops proceeding straight towards the enemy position, they were easily cut down by enemy machine gun fire. However, Dante had managed to sneak his way around the unsuspecting Germans, and was able to kill several snipers, forcing the German troops to flee from their encampments.

Over the months since that battle, Dante learned that the casualties sustained were the highest in Marine Corp history, with 31 officers and 1,056 men losing their lives. The Marines now had a foothold in Belleau Wood, a crucial victory that the Allies desperately needed at the time. But the price to pay for it was very, very high, he thought.

Now, Dante found himself dispatched along with his 20 unit buddies, to fight alongside the gutless French again in a battle called the Meuse-Argonne Offensive. He must give the Frenchies some credit, though, since the French 4th Army to the west of the US 1st Army finally caught up to the American front line to fortify the area. But this had only been made possible because Dante's 2nd division, along with the 36th, had successfully captured Blanc Mont Ridge in the Champagne and were presently pursuing the German infantry to the River Aisne.

Dante was quickly snapped out of his momentary stupor by his unit commander, Sgt. Jim Hendrickson, a big Texan with a big mouth and a kind heart.

"What the hell are you doing, Marine?" he barked in Dante's face, close enough that Dante could smell the chewing tobacco and taste the dripping brown wad that Hendrickson was constantly spitting away from his mouth.

"Covering my ass, Sarge. And enjoying the quiet. We don't get a lot of it, you know."

"Well, I can't have you going spook-eyed on me, ya know. You looked like a freakin' zombie there for a while." Hendrickson then slowly slid his body to a sitting position next to Dante, and took off his combat helmet to scratch his stubby red hair.

Jim Hendrickson had been Dante's commanding officer ever since his arrival in France. He was a usually jovial, likable hulk of a man. Standing over 6'4" tall and weighing in the neighborhood of 250 pounds, Sergeant Jim was an imposing figure to the shorter, smaller-framed Dante. Early on, he had told Dante's unit that he was born and raised in Midland, Texas, a barren, tough stretch of land in west Texas known for its huge cattle ranches and quick-draw gunslingers. The Old West was still alive and well in Midland in the early 1900s, he bragged.

Farther down the trench, Dante and Hendrickson saw their fellow Marines begin to ready themselves for an imminent battle. Sporadic gunfire could be heard in the distance, and the small group of Marines knew that this could be the final battle for all of them.

The big Texan slowly pulled a religious medal from his pocket. "You believe in God, Dante?" he asked while examining the burnished silver medal with the broken chain that was tied in a knot.

"Yeah. Of course I believe in God," Dante quickly replied. "Why you askin' me that, Sarge?"

Hendrickson continued talking. "There's nothing in the Marine Corps code that says you can't pray to Him, you know." He then showed Dante his medal.

"This is my protection. We've been in some tough fights over the past few months. I've always wondered to myself how I survived all of that bloodshed. Well, I firmly believe that this medal has saved my ass countless times, and I think it has a little more magic left in it until we get back to the States."

"So what are you gonna do when you get back home?" Hendrickson asked his young soldier.

"I don't know. Haven't given it any thought, really," Dante said.

"It'll come to ya, kid. When I was a small boy, I was always buildin' tree houses, bird houses, wooden swords and such. One day, my dad says to me, 'You should be a carpenter.' He helped me get a job as an apprentice with a guy he knew. It all fell into place for me. It was just like a light bulb turned on."

No sooner had Hendrickson finished his sentence than a flare burst above their trench and the dark battlefield was now bathed in a deathly glow. All of the battle-weary Marines were momentarily mesmerized by the bright light. They were quickly brought back to reality as shell after shell began raining down around them, exploding with thunderous monotony only feet away.

Each Marine quickly pressed himself against the crumbling trench wall for protection, facing the direction of the oncoming bombs. Amidst the clamor and panic that was taking hold in the underground trench, Hendrickson tried to shove his medal back into his pocket. Being distracted, he didn't realize it had fallen to the ground below his feet.

Dante saw the medal drop, and immediately slid to the bottom of the trench to retrieve it for his commanding officer. As he was kneeling on the ground and brushing dirt off the medal, an artillery shell burst at the edge of the trench not twenty feet from where the two of them had been speaking minutes before.

Hendrickson and two other Marines were instantly blown backward, death taking them before they landed directly on top of Dante. Dazed by the sudden impact of the three bodies on his crouching frame, it did not take long for the young Marine to float away to unconsciousness.

CHAPTER TWO

**Meuse-Argonne Battlefield
0720 Hours the Next Day**

CORPORAL Timothy Edger, a medic wearing a United States uniform, a Red Cross helmet, and a Geneva Cross brassard on his left arm, was slowly trudging through the remains of German and American soldiers who had lost their lives at this burial trench the night before during one of the enemy's most bold attacks of the war. The early rising sun painted the scene in surreal tones of light.

Edger really shouldn't have been there, he thought to himself. But the Division Sanitary Inspector had ordered him to escort one group of the Corps Troops Pioneer Infantry whose primary job was to bury the dead. The role of the infantry was to follow the advancement of the combatant troops as closely as possible, and bury the dead as they found them. In many instances, the bodies were collected whenever possible into groups, and buried together in specific spots. They were supplied with picks and shovels to finish the job.

The Chateau-Thierry summer campaign where bodies of dead men and animals had littered the countryside for days had made for a terrible health hazard in the region. Decomposing bodies soon became a breeding ground for a mass of maggots and flies. This infestation had overrun the surrounding countryside, resulting in a widespread outbreak of intestinal disease. Although it was not considered life-threatening, the disease still caused severe dysentery in troops still fighting in the area.

It got so troublesome that the Chief Surgeon of the First Army Corps of the American Expeditionary Forces finally had to devise a systematic method for burial of the dead. He had decided that combatant troops should not be called upon to bury their own dead because it would hurt morale. Fighting troops cannot be removed from the line for such purposes, either, he thought. After an engagement, fighting men were often too exhausted to have to do manual labor. And so it was decided that the poor bastards of the Pioneer Infantry were chosen to fulfill this obligation in conjunction with the Quartermaster Graves Registration personnel.

Edger wasn't there to identify or bury the dead, though. He was on a miracle mission: Find American survivors. Yeah, good luck with that, he snarled to himself, as he slowly made his way from the high ground into the foxholes and then deeper into the trenches. Most of the dead on the high ground had died as a result of bullet wounds and shrapnel to the body, he surmised. As he got closer to the foxholes and then into the trenches, evidence pointed to death by bayonet. He could tell that each valiant warrior most likely died looking his killer in the eyes before mortally collapsing to the ground. There was not a slight movement or sound of anything or anyone, as far as he could tell.

As it unfolded, following a steady barrage of artillery shells and light machine-gun fire to disorient their opponents, an ambitious team of German infantrymen around midnight the night before had sprung a late-night assault on Dante's small group of exhausted Marines. Numbering close to 75 troops, the Germans had intensified their efforts to dispel of this nuisance gang of Allied fighters. For two days, Dante's small group had hampered any advancement the enemy could devise. Utilizing their superior marksmanship, the five snipers in this band of 20 had repeatedly stymied each and every thrust the Germans made. For two days, a stalemate was being played out on this battlefield in the Argonne Forest.

But Hendrickson, the ornery leader of this brave bunch, knew their time was coming when a total assault by the enemy would probably snuff out the life of each of his soldiers. He was just determined, though, to stretch that limited time as much as he could.

The battle began with a few artillery shells maneuvered into a small window of battlefield where the Marines had entrenched themselves. Used primarily to cause confusion, the German captain then sent several flares into the night sky to further disorient their enemy momentarily, and to light the way for his deadly ground troops.

The plan had worked magnificently. By the time the flares had reached the ground, the German storm troopers had descended upon the weary Marines. When the bullets stopped flying, bloody hand-to-hand combat had ensued in and above the trenches. The few Marines not affected by the shelling had fought long and bravely, taking the lives of as many Deutchland soldiers as they could before losing their lives in the battle.

It was all over within 20 minutes. All 20 Marines had gone down in a blaze of glory, and the satisfied Germans briefly scoured the scene, taking any money and cigarettes from the dead American fighters as they left. In the dark of the night, they had not noticed Dante lying unconscious below the pile of three of his dead comrades.

After Edger had gently moved each body from Dante's burial heap, he rolled Dante onto his back. The sudden movement caused Dante to open his eyes.

"Sonofabitch! We have a live one here. This one's alive!" Edger cried out.

As additional soldiers rushed to his side, Dante looked at his hands. In the palm of his right hand was the sergeant's religious medal. It was covered with dirt and blood. It had also left an indentation in Dante's skin.

"You know, there still was some magic left in this thing. The Sarge was right," Dante thought to himself.

CHAPTER THREE

THE evacuation of the wounded and dead from a battlefield was a messy, meticulous process if no fighting was going on. It was fast and haphazard at best if the fight was still being waged. Today, in Dante's case, it was the former. According to the organizational documents of medical units, the Medical Service was built upon the principle that the troops must be kept fit for service, but when a soldier became unfit to fight, he was evacuated from the field of operations as quickly as possible.

The scene that surrounded Dante was grim and grizzly. His entire unit had been massacred the night before, and in Dante's mind, he hadn't done enough damage to the German invaders as he had wanted before blacking out. He didn't remember much of what actually happened. But looking at the bloody remains of his corpsmen and the number of scattered dead Germans, he knew that his unit had fought bravely up to the end.

"What's your name, soldier?" Edger asked, observing the young Marine while he watched his stretcher carriers transport the lifeless bodies of Dante's unit to waiting motorized field ambulances. Because of the reported heroic actions of Dante's unit, Edger's commander had ordered all deceased members to be transported back to the base hospital instead of being buried in a mass grave at the combat site, which was the general burial practice at the time. From there, the bodies would be officially prepared to be sent back to the United States for proper military burial.

"Corporal Paul Dante, sir." Dante replied, still groggy and lightheaded from his ordeal. He was now sitting up, his back against the blood-soaked trench wall and his legs outstretched in front of him. Edger was kneeling in front of him, applying pressure to a head wound that continued to bleed.

"Well, Dante, I don't know how in the hell you survived this fight," Edger exclaimed. "By the looks of this head wound of yours, you took a big hit of shrapnel before your buddies here fell on top of you. You were probably out cold before their bodies smothered you. It seems like it all happened simultaneously. Their bodies hid you from the Germans. You're luckier than hell."

Edger was now applying dressing and bandages that he had retrieved from the inside of Dante's coat. As soon as Edger found Dante alive, he immediately pulled him upright and leaned him against the trench wall. He then did what he had been trained to do. He looked for the first field dressing that every soldier carried with him, sewn in the small pocket on the inner side of the lining at the left corner of a soldier's coat.

The first field dressing consisted of two roller bandages which were attached to a pad of absorbent material. When they were initially packed into the soldier's coat, the inner surface of the pad was folded so that the surface was protected from contact with the fingers when opening the package. A safety pin was held in by a single stitch to each bandage, and then was folded in wax paper to protect it. These two pads and bandages were then protected from contamination when being cut and folded, and after being sterilized, were placed in a waterproof outer covering which was sealed airtight with a gummed edge.

In addition, a small container of iodine was inserted in a small cardboard tube and placed between the two sealed packages. All of the contents were then enclosed in a khaki cloth covering, with proper instructions for use printed on top. When a soldier was wounded, he would use the first field dressing and bandages to cover the wound. If he couldn't do it, a buddy would do it for him. This is the first treatment that a soldier received. And Edger was a pro at it.

"I'll tell you, Dante, I think I've got that bleeding stopped pretty good, at least good enough to get you to the ambulance and then to the casualty clearing station," Edger stated. "From there, we'll get you on a medical train to our American hospital in Rouen, Base Hospital 21. It's the best American Red Cross hospital in France."

As Edger helped Dante get to his feet, he pulled a medal out of his pocket. "Say, I found this medal lying on the ground next to you when I pulled you up. It may have fallen out of your hand. I assume it's yours."

Dante wiped the dirt and sweat from his eyes, steadied himself, and took the medal from Edger's hand. "Actually, it was my Sarge's medal. He told me it was his lucky charm. But I think it dropped out of his hand. I think I jumped down to the bottom of the trench to get it for him. That's the last thing I remember before you touching me."

"Well, it's your lucky charm now," Edger laughed. "You better keep it with you from now on. It may have some magic power associated with it." Dante nodded as he put it in his coat pocket.

With Edger's left arm firmly gripping Dante's torso and Dante's right arm secured around Edger's right shoulder, the two men slowly made their way out of the deserted trench. Reaching the top, Edger assisted a limping Dante the several hundred yards to the waiting ambulance. With the ambulance capable of carrying four lying-down patients and two sitting patients, Dante and Edger quietly accompanied four of Dante's fallen comrades on the 20-minute drive to the casualty clearing station. Then the dead and living would travel together by rail to Base Hospital 21.

CHAPTER FOUR

NIGHT TIME. That was the usual time of arrival of the large group of wounded and dead after the long train ride from the battle zone to the base hospitals. But tonight, the arrival was even later because of the unusually high number of dead and wounded coming from Meuse-Argonne. Dante was a part of the wounded and dead French and American soldiers that filled up the entire 396 cots allotted to the hospital train on this trip to Rouen. Plus, additional time was spent at the clearing station to prepare the more seriously wounded for the long excursion.

Upon closer examination at the clearing station, one of the attending doctors found that Dante had an untreated bullet wound in his lower right calf. Dante told the doctor that he figured it was only a flesh wound when it happened since he was able to still maneuver his way in the deep forest brush with his fellow snipers during their encounter with the German troops. He had just rubbed some dirt and leaves into the area of the wound to stop the bleeding, and never thought about it again.

Dante expressed his pride that his Marine snipers had befuddled the Germans for two days with their uncanny accuracy before they ran out of ammunition and had to return to their fortified trench to regroup. That night is when the Germans mounted their deadly assault to dispose of the pesky Americans once and for all. Mission accomplished, Dante sadly conceded.

After treatment to his leg and head and labeled as ambulatory by the clearing station physician, Dante was helped aboard the train by Edger, and assigned to a cot in one of the crowded rail cars designated for the American wounded. The French survivors had their own rail car with cots. Several nurses and medical aides accompanied the wounded. For the trip to the base hospital, the wounded and dead were divided into separate rail cars.

The dead soldiers also got their own cot, with a white cloth draped over each body and their name, rank, serial number, division, and location where the body was found written on a card which was attached by string to their wrist. Individual dog tags remained around the neck of each fallen soldier throughout the trip back to the States. A Catholic chaplain often accompanied the dead, performing the sacrament of the Last Rites to the entire rail car of deceased fighters.

When Dante wasn't resting, he and Edger would strike up a conversation. Edger discovered that Dante was an Omaha, Nebraska native, and Dante learned that Edger was a surgical instruments salesman from St. Louis. Sports were the favorite topic of discussion, with baseball and the St. Louis Cardinals topping the list. Edger also gave Dante some background on Base Hospital 21, and told him of the St. Louis connection there.

The story goes, Edger began, that the Red Cross approached the Washington University School of Medicine in July of 1916 to ask them to staff a base hospital in the event that the United States would enter into World War One. All faculty members volunteered, no one thinking that any of them would have to serve overseas. When a telegram from the Surgeon General arrived, and one day later, two lieutenants from the Army Medical Corp showed up to give physicals to the hospital unit officers, things started to move quickly.

American hospital units like the one at Washington University in St. Louis had begun largely because of the efforts of a few surgeons who had taken small, volunteer surgical units to France during the first two years of the war. Through these experiences, some influential members of the American medical profession, like Dr. Harvey Cushing of Harvard University, understood the importance of having a medical staff ready on a standby basis, composed of men familiar with each other and who had undergone similar training.

Since America was not yet officially involved in the war, the Red Cross superseded the authority of the Army Medical Corp to provide volunteer aid to the sick and wounded. In essence, the Red Cross would organize the base hospitals, and the commissioned and enlisted men of the Army Medical Reserve Corps would provide the personnel.

Base Hospital 21 was one of the first six units mobilized immediately to aid the British and American fighters in 1917. The scuttlebutt in medical circles was that these six units represented the best of the medical and nursing professions in the United States. Each hospital consisted of a 500-bed unit staffed by at least 20 medical officers and 60 nurses. The

St. Louis unit, placed under the military command of Major J.D. Fife of the regular Army Medical Corps, consisted of 28 officers, 65 nurses, and 185 enlisted men.

After Dr. Fred Murphy, the American commanding medical officer for Base Hospital 21, and his entire entourage arrived in England, they were assigned to No. 12 General Hospital of the British Expeditionary Force in Rouen, France. What they weren't told was that No. 12 General Hospital in Rouen was a 1300-bed hospital, not a 500-bed hospital for which they had trained to administer, consisting mostly of tents, on the Champs des Courses racetrack, rumored to be the wettest spot in Europe. Springs and summers were great there, they were told, but winters were killers. Even though it was early October, Dante thought that Mother Nature was already tipping her hand for winter as the rail car felt deathly cold the entire trip.

Edger continued his engaging story to a dozing Dante. As soon as the American unit from Washington University arrived, the entire British hospital medical staff departed, except for a few voluntary aids and enlisted corpsmen who remained for a few weeks to help familiarize the Americans with administrative procedures of a British hospital. Ironically, Major Fife, the American commanding officer for Base Hospital 21, was considered a British commanding officer.

Medical records were kept on British forms, with each American patient having a duplicate copy on American forms. Even though the American patient load throughout the war at Base Hospital 21 accounted for less than five percent of total patient load, these unusual arrangements persisted until the war's end. In essence, the British furnished all surgical and medical supplies, plus all rations and fuel. The Americans paid the staff and personnel, while keeping their own quartermaster department and handling all military decisions and procedures.

After the monotonous five hour trip, the crowded train pulled into the station at Rouen, and the wounded, some walking and some on stretchers, were carefully transferred to Base Hospital 21. With the wounded being the top priority of the medical staff, the bodies of the deceased were later quietly and respectfully moved to a separate facility at the hospital. There each body was gently placed into a simple wooden coffin to await the sad trip home to family and loved ones.

It didn't take long for the Americans to establish new procedures, methods, and techniques to improve quality and efficiency at the hospital. In the past under the British, the ambulatory wounded, like Dante, received dressings or splints for their injuries, and then were sent to a hospital ward wearing the same dirty and vermin-infected clothing in which they had been fighting.

Under American leadership, all ambulatory wounded now entered the hospital through the bath house doors. There, they were stripped of all clothing, sanitized, bathed, and dressed in a hospital garment made of heavy blue material. Lucky for Dante, he was one of the first 100 patients to pass through the bath house this night while the water was still warm. The next 100 patients had to wait an hour while the water reheated.

From the bath house, Dante was led by a corpsman to a bed near a heated stove in Ward M, one of the newly-built medical tents placed squarely in the middle of the infield of the dormant racetrack. As the injured from the Meuse-

Argonne Offensive continued to roll into Base Hospital 21, more space was needed for the injured patients. Although not officially designated an "American" ward, it was understood throughout the hospital that all newly-arrived ambulatory American soldiers injured at Meuse-Argonne were placed here. Unofficially, Ward M was known for prettier nurses, fluffier pillows, and cleaner sheets and blankets. Dante was most appreciative of all three enticements, especially the last two. He fell asleep within seconds when his head touched the pillow and the warm blankets suffocated his broken body. He would not be disturbed for the next 17 hours.

CHAPTER FIVE

ANGELA NOONAN assertively pushed the injured soldier's right shoulder. After sleeping for almost a whole day, the sudden movement caused Paul Dante to slowly open his eyes and roll onto his back.

"Welcome back to the real world, soldier. I'm Nurse Noonan," the middle-aged American nurse said, leaning forward as she prepared to change the dressing and bandage on Dante's head wound. "It's about time you woke up. Your head wound has needed a new dressing for the past four hours, but I had specific orders from the doctor to just let you sleep and not wake you up. Who are you, some kind of Big Shot, that the doctors are covering your back?"

"Uh, no ma'am, I'm nothing special, I can tell you that," Dante muttered. "How long have I been asleep?"

"Over 17 hours, sleepy head," she chuckled. "I've been watching you closely the past four hours because that head wound of yours started leaking through the bandage. And I hate damn blood dripping on my bed sheets. It's unsanitary, it looks bad, and it makes my ward look bad.

Finally, I had enough, and gave the doctor plenty of hell that he let me wake you up to take care of the problem."

As Dante sat up in bed as ordered by Nurse Nasty, he closely examined the high-strung caregiver who had sat down next to him on the bed and was now hurriedly unwinding the blood-soaked bandage around his head. Noonan was probably in her forties, Dante thought. She kind of looked the same age as Dante's mom, same body type, too.

She was dressed in the official nurse garb of the day: a dark blue serge dress with a long, heavy, double-breasted, dark military coat. On the left coat sleeve was the white armband with a red cross on it. She had removed a dark blue felt hat when she sat down on the bed next to Dante. Her grayish blonde hair was rolled up in a ball and fastened with hair pins behind her head. Her piercing blue eyes were focused on her work.

"Whoever put this bandage on in the first place was an idiot," Noonan blurted out as she unwound the final piece of cloth covering the wound. She threw the soiled wrap into a disposal bucket that was on the floor next to the bed. While applying pressure to the wound with her left hand, she grabbed a new cloth soaked with antiseptic liquid, and began to clean the dripping and dry blood away from the wound.

Within a few minutes, she had completed this part of her chore, and the process of applying new dressing and wrapping the injury with a new sterile bandage began. Up to this point, Dante had remained silent, afraid to distract Noonan with idle chatter. Mostly, he was still in the process of waking up.

"From your records, I see your name is Paul Dante," Noonan said, breaking the silence while continuing to concentrate on her nursing duties. "You're a Marine from Omaha, Nebraska.

Hell, you're not old enough to be a Marine, are you? You look about the age of my teenage son back home in St. Charles, Missouri. I'll bet you either ran away from home, and who wouldn't if you lived in Omaha. Or you most likely forged one of your parent's signatures on the application form. How close am I with my version of the story, young man?"

Dante was caught completely off guard by Noonan's accusations. He was at once both scared and angry. First, how in the hell had she figured out what he had done to enlist in the Marines, and secondly, what right did she have for berating him and his home town? After all, he was recovering from war injuries fighting for his country.

"Ma'am, I don't mean to be disrespectful," Dante quietly responded, "but I don't feel like I owe you any kind of explanation on how I happened to arrive at this hospital. I truly appreciate all your concern for my welfare, and for taking care of my injuries. I really don't feel like talking about anything right now. But I sure am hungry."

Noonan smiled as she rose from her bedside perch next to Dante. "Son, I'm just pulling your chain," she laughed. "I give all my new boys in the ward a hard time when I meet them for the first time. I like to see how they handle it. And I can tell you right now that I'm as proud of you as I am of my own son. From the rumors going on around here, your entire unit must have done some heroic things in the battlefield. Thank you from the bottom of my heart. Now let me check that leg before we get you some grub."

Dante pulled the covers from his legs, and Noonan closely examined the bullet wound in his right calf. The bullet had completely exited through the lower leg when it had initially happened in battle. Unbelievably, no bone had been damaged, and the mud and leaf tourniquet that Dante applied had miraculously done its job. Noonan decided to repeat the same treatment on Dante's leg as she had for his head wound. Working quickly and quietly, she finished her task within 10 minutes.

After fastening the final leg bandage, Noonan called out to a nearby orderly. "Corpsman, help this young man to the mess hall for some food." She then slowly bent down and affectionately kissed the top of Dante's head.

"Take care of yourself, dear. The world needs more men like you. Semper Fi." With that, Noonan disappeared from the ward. Inexplicably, Dante would never again see Nurse Noonan during his remaining days at Base Hospital 21.

CHAPTER SIX

FOR seven days, Dante remained in Ward M of Base Hospital 21 recovering from his battlefield injuries. In his mind, he was on a quick path to returning to active duty, and back to fighting the Germans. But on this eighth day in forced rehabilitation, Dante's life was going to take a new route.

As he sat upright in bed that morning, idly reading the bedside copy of the King James Holy Bible just to kill time, he heard a commotion in Ward T, located just outside the tent and down a dirt path from his own ward. The noise included applause and the singing of God Bless America. "What in the hell is that all about?" Dante asked himself. Then he listened as heavy movement proceeded up the dirt path towards his ward, and his attention turned to the tent opening about 50 feet in front of him.

Suddenly, the heavy ivory-colored drapes that acted as the entrance to Ward M were pushed aside, and three photographers rushed in to the crowded hospital room. The eyes of the 60 inhabitants that occupied each of the 60 ward beds were now aimed squarely on the intruders. Backpedaling quickly, each photographer, holding a camera in one hand and a large flashbulb reflector in the other hand, was snapping photos of the injured bedridden American soldiers.

Following the photographers was another interloping contingent, this one including reporters and military police. Upon entering the ward, this group quickly parted into two lines, leaving an open middle space for the next visitors. First appearing was Dr. Fred Murphy, the commanding medical officer who now added the position of military commanding officer of Base Hospital 21, having succeeded Major Fife, who moved to the A.E.F. Chief Surgeon's Office. He was barking out directions and pointing in Dante's direction to the final individual to enter the tent.

General John J. Pershing was only a single stride behind Murphy. Removing his helmet and placing it firmly under his left arm, he was on a collision course straight to Dante's bed location. As the group neared his bed, a look of confusion was now changing to a look of terror on the young Marine's face. An explosion of flashbulbs made the entire tent into a simulated war zone, causing Dante to haphazardly drop his reading material to the floor beside him.

"Marine Corporal Paul Dante?" Pershing inquired in his typical booming voice, still a few strides from his destination. As his commanding officer spoke, Dante was making a pitiful effort to throw off his covers and jump to attention. "At ease, Marine." Pershing said. "Stay right where you are."

As Dante was sheepishly returning to his isolated position on the bed, he caught a glimpse of Dr. Murphy's smiling face. "What's this all about?" he silently whispered in Murphy's direction. "You'll find out in a minute, Paul." Murphy mouthed in response.

Pershing ended his march through Ward M and stopped right next to Dante's bed. He turned to one of the MPs, handed him his helmet, and asked for something. Instantaneously, he was handed a blue-colored box. He then turned to face the reason for his mission.

"How are you doin', son?" Pershing inquired while shaking Dante's hand.

"I'm doing fine, sir. Thank you, sir." Dante replied.

"Corporal Dante," General Pershing continued. "You're probably wondering about the reason for this visit."

"Yessir, I am." Dante stuttered. "Am I in trouble, sir?" That comment brought a hearty level of laughter from all those in attendance.

"No, son, you're not in trouble," the General grinned. "As a matter of fact, I'm here representing the president of the United States. He and I wish to commend you on your bravery under fire.

"The heroic actions of your entire combat unit at the Battle of Meuse-Argonne have not gone unnoticed. Keeping the Germans at bay for nearly 48 hours allowed your fellow countrymen to gain precious ground in our quest to defeat the Germans in France.

"Your Sergeant Hendrickson recommended you for the honor I'm about to bestow upon you. Although your entire sniper group was the main reason the Germans could not advance in your sector in Meuse-Argonne, your commander wrote in his report that you were the primary individual having the most success in your role as lead sniper. For such a young guy, where did you learn to shoot so accurately?"

"My dad used to take me hunting with him when I was little," Dante replied. "I suppose that's the biggest reason, sir."

"Yes, well, your dad must be very proud of you, Corporal." Pershing stated.

"My dad is dead, sir. But, yessir, I believe he would be proud." Dante answered.

"I'm sorry to hear of your loss, son," Pershing continued. "But let's get back to the reason I'm here."

With that, he lifted the lid on the blue box, and began his practiced, yet sincere, speech. Gazing straight into the eyes of the young Nebraskan, Pershing stated, "Marine Corporal Paul Dante, in the name of the United States Congress, I present this Distinguished Service Cross to you, for extraordinary heroism involving risk of life while engaged in action against an enemy of the United States. God bless you, son, and God bless America."

Pershing then lifted the shiny bronze cross from its blue case, and gently placed it over Dante's head, the red, white, and blue-striped silk service ribbon snugly adhering to the back of Dante's neck. Pershing's medal was now the second medal Dante wore around his neck. When he had completed his work, General Pershing stepped back from the bed, and saluted Dante. He then quickly stepped forward again to shake Dante's hand. A beaming Dr. Murphy followed Pershing in congratulating Dante on the prestigious award. *It was a day of tremendous honor for all the doctors, nurses, and aides at Base Hospital 21*, Murphy said to himself. Not one, but two Distinguished Service Cross recipients in their midst.

During the presentation ceremony, many of the ward occupants who could get out of bed made their way to Dante's area. After the presentation, the entire room burst out in thunderous applause. Then, spontaneously, the entire crowd began singing God Bless America, with Dante's voice rising above the others. Surprisingly, the entire ceremony was over within 10 minutes.

Pershing wasn't through with Dante just yet. Moving closer and bending down to where he was only a few feet from Dante's face, he delivered another quiet message that completely took Dante by surprise.

"Marine, I have some additional information I want to pass along to you before I leave," he said. "Son, you're going home. We can't have one of our bravest Americans getting himself killed after receiving the Distinguished Service Cross for bravery. It would kill troop morale, and frankly, would do more harm than good for our cause. So take as much time as you need to fully recover from your wounds. Dr. Murphy will then be responsible for honorably discharging you from your service duty with the United States Marines. Thank you and God Bless You, son. Have a great life." After shaking Dante's hand for the last time, Pershing received his helmet back from the young MP, and while returning it to its official position atop his head, whirled around and was through the ward doors in the blink of an eye, Murphy and the MPs in close pursuit.

After the rousing rendition of God Bless America, the ward well-wishers began to slowly return to their beds in the huge tent. As soon as the area around Dante's bed had cleared, the reporters and photographers covering the ceremonies quickly engulfed Dante to get his personal comments that would accompany their stories.

"Well, kid, what do you have to say for yourself?" asked the short, balding reporter with the cockney accent from the *Westminster Gazette*, Britain's daily newspaper. "This is quite the honor, isn't it?" As he was talking, his photographer was moving in to get a close-up shot of the American hero.

Before Dante could answer, a towering figure with wire-rimmed glasses moved closely to the bed. "Corporal Dante, I'm William Rasmussen with *Stars & Stripes*, the official newspaper of the American Expeditionary Force in Europe. Can you describe how you were able to keep the Germans at bay so expertly for two days in such miserable fighting conditions?"

Dante could only say that he was lucky to have found a well-camouflaged hilly area a couple hundred yards from the German camp. His fellow Marine snipers had found similar cover on the perimeter, he said, so that the band of five marksmen encircled the exasperated enemy patrol. And for a couple days, they harassed and killed any Germans trying to leave the camp to fight the phantom Americans. Then each sniper seemed to run out of ammunition at the same time, and they had to quickly return to their fortified trench. They were planning to resume the sniper positions the following morning when the group was attacked late that night.

The last reporter then stepped forward. "Bill Grimsley with the *New York Times*. I'm sure the folks back in Omaha are eager to hear about their war hero. Tell us how your dad taught you to be a crack shooter like you are."

Dante was getting weary from all the questions and blinding light bulbs of the cameras. But he found a way to answer the guy from the *Times*.

"My dad was around animals all his life. He grew up on a farm in Italy before moving to the States when he was a young boy. Hunting was about all he did for fun. When he got his job as a buyer at the Stockyards, he used to take me along on short trips to look at cattle on people's farms. He was always checking out the cattle before they made it to the yards. The best cattle went for the best price, and my dad's commission would be better if he spotted the best cattle before the other cattle commission companies did.

"Anyway, he'd always carry a BB gun with him to shoot at rabbits and squirrels and birds. He let me start shooting when I was six. My mom gave him hell for it because she thought I was too young to be handling a gun at that age. But I got better as I got older.

"I was eleven when my dad died. But I never stopped shooting. He was the greatest teacher in the world, my dad. I owe everything to him."

"Nice story, kid," quipped the British reporter. "That should sell some papers back home." All three reporters laughed together.

After the reporters were satisfied that they had gotten enough information to file their stories, they asked Dante to pose with his Distinguished Service Cross for one final picture. Sitting up in an American hospital bed in Rouen, France, Dante smiled sheepishly as he lifted the medal off his chest and toward the cameras. As he expected, the combined flash from the three cameras momentarily blinded him.

"Hey, kid," Grimsley called out as he was walking away, "What's the name of the Omaha newspaper? I'm going to send them a copy of the article and picture. I'm going to make you a hero in your home town."

"I think it's called the Omaha *World-Herald*," Dante yelled. With that comment, all the hoopla surrounding his award ceased in Ward M. Once again the room was quiet, devoid of flashing light bulbs, pesky reporters, intimidating MPs, annoyed doctors, impressed nurses, respectful Colonels, and one very proud commanding officer.

It didn't take long for an exhausted Dante to close his eyes to the world. With the Distinguished Service Cross still clinging to his chest, Dante pulled the blankets up to his neck, and settled in for a long, well-deserved nap. After the war was over, Dante would learn that he was one of a handful of Marines among the 6,185 recipients awarded the Distinguished Service Cross.

CHAPTER SEVEN

WHEN Dante opened his eyes after his two-hour respite, he was startled to see a tall, lanky officer with smiling green eyes staring down at him from beside his bed. Dante thought the stranger looked about the same age as Dante's dad would have been if he were still alive. Rubbing his eyes and trying to focus clearly, he sputtered out, "Can I help you, sir?"

"I was just admiring that medal you have around your neck," the officer said with a heavy Irish brogue. "Not that bright gold one, though. That old silver medal peeking out from under the new one."

As Dante began to pull himself up in bed, he noticed the gold cross that dangled from the neck of his visitor. He immediately recognized he was in the presence of a Catholic chaplain. "Forgive me, Father, I didn't recognize the cross until I got a closer look."

"I didn't mean to disturb ya," he said. "I'm sorry if I woke you up."

"No, Father, I was just waking up myself," Dante said. "Say, I'm pretty hungry. Would you like to join me for lunch? We can talk along the way." Before leaving, Dante took off the

Distinguished Service Cross, placed it on his bed, and put on his walking robe and slippers. He didn't disturb the religious medal around his neck.

During the long walk from Ward M to the mess tent, Dante learned that his visitor was Father Francis Duffy, a Catholic chaplain attached with the 165th Infantry Regiment from New York City. His group called themselves *"The Fighting 69th"* because they were members of the 69th New York National Guard Regiment that had been federalized again to fight in the war. The regiment was made up primarily of New York Irish immigrants and the sons of Irish immigrants. When the unit moved up to the front in France, Duffy accompanied them as their military chaplain. He was visiting some of his wounded soldiers at Base Hospital 21.

Duffy told Dante that one of the soldiers in the New York unit had been awarded a Distinguished Service Cross. When he found out that a second American soldier at Base Hospital 21 had also been awarded the same honor, he made it a point to look up the soldier and congratulate him. He had arrived just moments before the young Marine rolled over and opened his eyes.

After about 10 minutes, the two men finally arrived at the mess tent. Dante received a rousing ovation from the diners as they entered. He politely smiled and waved. Duffy filled his tray from the food in the mess line while Dante waited to receive his special meal of pancakes. One of the perks of being an award honoree was your choice of food items. Dante's choice each meal was pancakes and whatever dessert was available. They then sat down on opposite sides at the end of one of the bare wooden tables at the back of the tent. Dante immediately started eating while Duffy recited a silent prayer before picking up his knife and fork.

"It's quite an honor when your fellow soldiers recognize excellence," Duffy stated while starting to eat his meal. "That must make you feel very proud."

"Actually, it's very embarrassing. I was just doing my job," Dante countered, looking up from his tray. "My entire unit is made up of heroes. Not just me. I was the lucky schmuck who survived. My body should be in a wooden box just like my friends on their way back home."

"Now, son, you shouldn't be so hard on yourself," Duffy exclaimed. "God must have a plan in mind for you." Without pausing, he continued his talk with Dante.

"That religious medal you're wearing really caught my eye," Duffy continued his conversation with Dante. "It's quite a rare one. Do you know the image on it?"

"I'm embarrassed to say I don't know, Father," Dante stated apologetically between bites. "It was my sergeant's medal. He said it was his lucky medal during the war. He was showing it to me right before our unit was attacked. It fell out of his hand, and I was knocked out when I tried to retrieve it for him. The medic who found me said I had it in my hand when he found me during the burial unit's recon work. He told me there must be some magic in it because it must have saved my life. The chain was broken, so I got a new one and decided to wear it around my neck.

"I am a Catholic, Father. You probably figured that out from my name. I went to Catholic grade school, so we learned the catechism and we went to church every day. I was an altar boy. My dad was and my mom still is real religious. But I don't consider myself to be a religious person, although I believe in God. I think I'm more superstitious than religious. I've made it through a lot of fighting and bloodshed. I think the medal is a good luck charm. That's probably why I wear it."

Duffy laughed out loud. "Paul, there's nothing wrong with being superstitious. Hell, my entire unit is superstitious. They're Irishmen, for God's sake. What else would you expect?" He paused a moment to eat some of his food, then he resumed his talk.

"That religious medal you're wearing has on it the image of St. Ignatius Loyola. Do you know of Ignatius?" Duffy asked.

"Not a clue, Father. Was he a superstitious guy, too?" Dante responded.

"That I am not aware of, Paul," Duffy grinned. "But you and he have much in common." He set his knife and fork aside, leaned forward with both elbows firmly planted on the table, and faced Dante. "Let me tell you a little about him. He was a young soldier just like you."

Dante nodded in agreement as he continued to eat his meal. Every once in a while he would raise his eyes to Duffy as the chaplain told his story.

"Inigo Lopez de Loyola, that was his full name, was born at Loyola, Guipuzcoa, Spain in 1491. His parents were Spanish nobility, and he had 11 siblings. He was actually a page in the Spanish court of Ferdinand and Isabella. As was the practice of the day, he was given a military education, and entered the army, serving in several campaigns.

"Then, at the siege of Pampeluna in 1521, he was wounded in the leg by a cannonball. To keep himself occupied during his recuperation, he read the books that were handy. There were only two books accessible to him. One was *The Golden Legend*, which was a collection of stories on the lives of the saints. The other book was the *Life of Christ* written by Ludolph the Carthusian. Well, the time spent reading the books and contemplating on them changed him enough that he converted to Catholicism.

"When he was fully recovered, he shocked his family by declaring he was leaving the military to live his life as a devout Christian. He self-imposed a vow of chastity, hung his sword before the altar of the Virgin Mary of Montserrat, and lived in a cave for a year.

"In 1523, he took a pilgrimage to Rome and the Holy Land, working to convert the Muslim population. After five years, he decided that he could be a more effective preacher by actually becoming a priest. So he began studying theology in Barcelona, Alcala, and ended up in Paris, where he received his degree and was ordained in 1534. His meditations, insights, visions, and prayers led him to form the Constitutions of the Society of Jesus that same year."

Dante listened intently to the gabby chaplain between slow bites of his apple pie for dessert. Duffy seemed to be on a roll, Dante surmised, so there was no use in stopping him to ask a question.

"As many powerful teachers naturally do," Duffy exclaimed, "they attract a group of students who believed in the message and way of life. And Ignatius surrounded himself with a solid core of friends, including James Lainez, Alonso Salmeron, Nicholas Bobadilla, Simon Rodriguez, Blessed Peter Faber, and Saint Francis Xavier, who, of course, wasn't a saint when he started following Ignatius, but later went on to establish his own identity within the Catholic Church with his mission work and gained sainthood."

Dante had finished his meal by now, and was wiping the excess food around his mouth with his napkin. After setting the napkin aside, he plopped a toothpick into this mouth, and decided it was time to comment on Duffy's story.

"Father, so you're saying the guy on my religious medal is the guy who started the Jesuit order?" Dante asked. "The way you told the story in such detail, I gotta ask, are you a Jesuit?"

"To answer your questions: Yes, Ignatius Loyola was the founder of the Society of Jesus, or Jesuits. Interestingly, the term 'Jesuit' was coined by one of the opponents of the society as a demeaning joke. Ignatius had never used the term until that time.

"And, no, I am not a Jesuit," Duffy responded. "Some of my best friends in the clergy are, though. Because of my many discussions with them over the years, I think my religious convictions are similar to the Jesuits. But technically, I'm not."

"So what makes the Jesuits so appealing to you?" Dante queried. "What's so special about them"?

Duffy took a few bites of his cooling meal to gather his thoughts on how to answer Dante's questions. After taking a sip of his lukewarm coffee, he set his cup down and began his response.

"Many in the Catholic hierarchy regard the Jesuits as the "bad boys" of the Catholic Church," he stated. "Actually, the head of the Society of Jesus in Rome is disturbingly referred to as the Black Pope. "Black" meaning "on the dark side or rebellious" I guess. When Pope Paul III officially recognized the order in 1541, there was much outcry from the Pope's inner circle that the group could not be trusted to follow the true spirit of Catholic doctrine. Even though the main objective in the Jesuit constitution is complete obedience to the Pope, the order has fallen out of grace with the Papacy on several occasions because of its progressive thinking and idealistic concepts, especially toward education.

"Education has always been at the heart of Jesuit life. From the beginning, Jesuits have always been teachers. Even though the Jesuits concentrated on educating the middle and upper middle class of American society, it has not prevented them from teaching the poorest of the poor in all societies worldwide. But because of their progressive thinking on education matters, it has spilled over sometimes to where this progressive thinking has affected doctrinal matters as well. And any differences in matters of doctrine do not go over well in Rome, as you would expect.

"The Jesuits have always been practical, creative thinkers. They're always willing to do what it takes to make things work. But they're an ironic bunch, too. Even though the order has been built on a militaristic model of discipline and obedience and rules, they very rarely follow national guidelines regarding the formation and administration of their schools."

"Even when those directives come from Rome?" Dante interrupted.

"Especially if those directives come from Rome." Duffy smiled.

"So you're saying you're kind of a "bad boy" priest, too?" Dante laughed.

"I wouldn't say "bad boy," but I'm completely opposed to the so-called anti-modernism movement that's coming out of Rome these days," Duffy stated.

"What do you mean, Father?" Dante asked.

"Let me tell you a little bit about myself, and then I'll give you an example of where I think Rome is making a big mistake.

"I'm a Canadian by birth, and an alumnus of St. Michael's College in Toronto. After college, I came to New York City, and taught at the College of St. Francis Xavier and earned my Master's degree there. I was ordained as a priest of the Archdiocese of New York in 1896. After ordination, I was asked to serve on the faculty of St. Joseph's Seminary in Yonkers. I taught Philosophical Psychology, which basically was a course on human development. At the same time, I was named the editor of the *New York Review*, which at the time was the most scholarly and progressive Catholic theological publication in America.

"Well, a little more than 10 years ago, Pope Pius X issued an encyclical against modernism. With it, he began a purge of all seminaries to modern thinking, even discouraging and forbidding seminarians from reading secular books, newspapers, and periodicals. This even affected the everyday Catholic, too.

"The papacy was now claiming power over people's minds as well as the spiritual souls of Catholics. Intellectual curiosity was discouraged. And American seminaries were now becoming puppets of Vatican thinking. As you can expect, the Jesuits revolted against this kind of thinking.

"At the same time, many Catholic Biblical scholars and clergy were writing articles in the *Review* that questioned this line of thinking. When some of them fell under suspicion of heresy of Modernism, Archbishop Corrigan, the leader of the New York diocese, broke up the faculty, shut down the *Review*, and reassigned us to other work. Although it was never confirmed, I firmly believe that order came directly from Rome. "

"So you experienced the heavy hand of the Vatican personally, too, huh?" Dante replied. "Since you're a progressive thinker, I can see how you would empathize with the Jesuits."

Duffy nodded in agreement as he took his final swallow of coffee. The two men slowly rose, took their empty trays back to the dishwashers, and began their trip back to Ward M.

As they sauntered back, Duffy resumed his conversation with Dante. "Paul, I hear you're being discharged shortly. What kind of plans do you have when you return home?"

"I haven't really given it much thought, Father," Dante said. "My mom is alone with my brother and sister, and I've been sending her my paycheck each month for support. My dad was a part of a cattle commission firm at the Omaha Stockyards. I didn't graduate from high school, so maybe I'll try to get a job there."

"Have you ever thought of the religious life as something you may be interested in?" Duffy asked. "You know, you'd make a good Jesuit. You're a leader among men, you're adventurous, you know about sacrifice, and you've developed a masculine toughness about you.

"The Jesuits only take the best of the best. It's a very tight-knit group, with a lot of prestige associated with the order.

They know a thing or two about surrounding themselves with benefactors who can assist them in the political and business worlds, too. They take care of their own. Your family would be very proud to have a member of the clergy in the family. It's a great life, son. You can help a lot of people. Give it some serious thought."

As they neared Dante's bed in Ward M, Duffy turned to shake the young Marine's hand before leaving. And he also made his final recruiting pitch at the same time.

"It was just splendid meeting and talking with you, Paul. You are a true American hero. Don't sell yourself short with feelings of guilt. You are representing all of your fallen comrades with the award. That should make you feel better," Duffy stated. "Again, congratulations on your Distinguished Service Cross, and thank you for inviting me to lunch with you.

"Now don't forget about our little talk about the religious life being your destiny, son. Before I go, I'm going to give you the name of a good friend of mine who happens to be the Provincial Superior of the Jesuits in St. Louis. His name is Father Alexander Burrowes. Great guy. Funny guy. He's submitted some articles to me for publication in the *Review*. Brilliant thinker. He's a very strong proponent of bringing Jesuit colleges into harmony with outside academic standards. He's a mover and a shaker. He's the top guy for the Jesuits in the Midwest, which is where you would attend seminary training. I'll talk to him about you. When you're ready to commit to becoming a Soldier of Christ, you contact Al and tell him Frank Duffy personally recommended that you get in touch with him. He'll take care of the rest."

After handing Dante the paper with the contact information, Duffy had him kneel to receive a blessing from the departing chaplain. Placing his left hand on the top of Paul's head, he recited a short prayer invoking St. Ignatius to give the young man strength when seeking excellence and commitment to a worthwhile deed in his life.

He completed the ritual by making the sign of the cross using his right hand, and closed the blessing with the common priestly words, "*Benedicat te omnipotens Deus, Pater, et Filius, et Spiritus Sanctus. Amen.* God be with you, my son." He then ceremoniously kissed Dante on the top of his head.

Dante quickly got to his feet, and thanked the charismatic priest for the special blessing. They shook hands, and Dante watched as Duffy stopped at several beds on his way out of the tent, providing abbreviated blessings to those soldiers who asked for one.

"That guy is some talker," Dante smiled to himself. Getting back into bed, he placed the Distinguished Service Cross on his bedside stand, and read the note that Duffy had left him. He then picked up the reading material that had fallen to the floor when Pershing's group had arrived, and started reading just to kill the boredom. The note would serve as a bookmark when Dante finished reading his Bible verses for the day.

CHAPTER EIGHT

Bavarian Countryside
Spring 1926

IT was a glorious late May afternoon in a large clearing on the southern edge of the Bavarian Forest, a wooded, low-mountain region that geographically shared the same mountain range with the Bohemian Forest, extending along the Czech border in Bavaria, Germany. The Bavarian Forest was a fragment of the Hercynian Forest, an ancient and dense forestland that stretched eastward from the Rhine River across southern Germania in Roman times. The blue cloudless sky filled with an endless supply of drenching sunlight made a stunning picture for the group of young revelers.

This was a day of celebration for the followers of Adolph Hitler, the 37-year-old leader of the National Socialist German Workers Party, known widely as the Nazi Party. Only a few months earlier, Hitler, having finished his ambitious political monograph, *Mein Kampf*, had declared his intentions of returning to party affairs. Fresh out of prison because of his involvement in the Beer Hall Putsch, a misguided attempt to overthrow the national government in Berlin, Hitler had gathered 60 of the Nazi Party's top activists to a meeting at Bamberg, where he delivered a passionate two-hour speech criticizing the political agenda of the "socialist" wing of the party. For Hitler, the real enemy of the German people was always the Jews, and not the capitalists.

This day was a respite for Hitler and members of his own private army, the Sturm Abteilung. The SA was commonly known as the Brownshirts because of their distinctive uniforms. These storm troopers wore gray jackets, brown shirts, swastika armbands, ski-caps, knee-breeches, thick woolen socks, and dark, heavy combat boots. The brown khaki shirts, intended for German soldiers fighting in Africa, had been purchased in bulk from the German Army by the Nazi Party.

Recruited mainly from private armies that had flourished during the period following the First World War, Hitler desperately needed a tight-knit group of thugs who could disrupt the meetings of political opponents and protect him from revenge attacks. This present group was the best and most violent he could find, and they were lavishly enjoying themselves with fresh-baked breads and meat, the best liquor the Nazi Party could steal, and the presence of the most flirty and beautiful young members of the League of German Girls.

There were several small groups congregating along the 100-meter-long expanse of the grass-covered clearing. Hitler was standing on the far north side of the opening with one of his newest converts, Joseph Goebbels. They spoke in rapid, hushed tones, animating their conversation with wildly swinging arms and finger-pointing. A few daring and drunk soldiers had hijacked some willing girls to take into the brush for sexual favors. But the majority of the picnic-goers were groups of three to six men and women, scattered about the rolling lawn, some sitting on colorful blankets, engrossed in their own worlds of gluttony and perversion.

One distinct group of obnoxious henchmen stood laughing at the far south end of the clearing, near the dirt road where the cars they used to reach the picnic were parked. Dorf, Bert, and Falk were all in their mid-twenties. All possessed the prototypical body type for the kind of work they did. Falk and Bert were a little over six feet tall, with broad shoulders and dark straight hair combed to the side. They wore a day's worth of scratchy whiskers on their faces. Their ski-caps were crumpled inside the back pocket of their knee-length pants. They each had a bottle of confiscated whiskey in one hand and dangled a newly-lit cigarette from their lips. They were having a good time.

Dorf, the third man in the triad, stood out from his two party companions. He towered over his friends by a half foot. His massive chest pushed the buttons on his brown shirt to the breaking point. His hands were like small anvils, and his piercing blue eyes were unobstructed by his short-cropped blonde hair. His square jaws were free of any facial hair. He was not smoking, but he held a half-empty whiskey bottle in each gigantic hand. He was doubled over with laughter.

"Did you see that tiny man run away like a scared little girl when I threatened to shove his campaign flyers down his throat?" Dorf asked no one in particular.

Bert followed Dorf's comment with one of his own. "He should get used to running away if he's going to back the Weimar Republic."

Falk interjected, "He's like all those old men. They don't want change. They're content with a second-class Germany.

That's why we need a real leader with a vision, like Adolph."

The other two men nodded in agreement.

Facing the forest, Dorf raised the almost-empty bottle in his left hand to his parched lips for one final gulp when he noticed a bright light that appeared in the late afternoon sky above the tree line about a quarter mile from where he was standing with his two equally-drunk comrades.

Pointing to the sky, he asked, "See that? What is that?"

Falk responded, "It must be a dirigible with a spotlight."

Bert shot a disgusted look at Falk. "Are you *ficken* nuts? Dirigibles don't have lights that powerful. And where's the dirigible? All I see is a light."

Without listening to either Falk or Bert, Dorf turned his attention to another group of four Brownshirts who were standing nearby.

In a drunken stupor, he again pointed to the sky where he had seen the light, this time asking the new group, "Hey, you see that light up there? What the hell is that?"

The new group turned their attention to where Dorf was pointing, but saw nothing.

"Have another drink, Dorf," one of the men blurted out. "It may help you see prettier Fräuleins instead of stars." The four men laughed.

Dorf was not used to getting laughed at, especially by members of his own organization. In a gruff, pleading tone, Dorf exclaimed, "There was a bright light in the sky. I know what I saw."

In the same instant, Dorf curled a tight fist in his right hand, and menacingly motioned to the group of four, "I can fix it so you see plenty of bright lights, you assholes."

"Ooh. That threat will keep me awake at night," the first Brownshirt answered, still laughing from the previous comment.

A second Brownshirt from the group chimed in. "Why not? The sight of Dorf's face kept his mother awake at night." That caused the four to laugh even harder.

While the banter and cajoling continued, the mysterious light zoomed back into view, and now the second group also saw it.

"See. I told you." screamed Dorf.

"What is that?" one of the "asshole" Brownshirts asked.

The light now drifted down below the tree line and into the heavy foliage below.

"Let's go take a look," Bert said. "Except for Dorf. He's too scared." Everyone laughed, except for Dorf.

Some of the men unbuckled their side arms and checked the chambers for bullets. The men without guns began to look for anything to use as a weapon as they all slowly turned their attention to the dazzling white light now pulsating among the dense forest trees roughly 250 meters from where they stood only moments before.

<u>CHAPTER NINE</u>

THE high-pitched screams echoed suddenly throughout the picnic area.

A completely naked short blonde woman carrying her undergarments in one hand and her high-heeled shoes in the other, bolted into the grassy opening, her arms flailing as she ran. Immediately behind her followed a completely naked man, carrying nothing in his hands, but yelling at the top of his voice as he quickly passed the woman in his flight from their conjugal hideout in the woods.

The sudden commotion startled Hitler and Goebbels from their conversation, and they both turned to face the direction from where the noise emanated. Hitler smiled as he watched the horrified young woman running away from the forest, her nubile and huge breasts bouncing heavily with each step. He barely noticed the naked young man as he sprinted past Hitler and Goebbels to crouch behind Hitler's shining new red Mercedes Benz, parked 20 feet away. Within seconds, the young woman also passed Hitler to join her heavy-breathing lover behind the vehicle. Goebbels stood frozen, his eyes wide and his mouth agape.

Hitler hurriedly walked to where the man and woman were hiding behind his new sedan. Both were now huddled together, holding each other in a tight embrace, a look of sheer terror on their faces. When Hitler inquired as to what caused their present state of emotion, both looked up at him with blank expressions. They remained speechless as Hitler again interrogated them.

"What did you see?" Hitler demanded. Blank eyes stared up at Hitler.

Without notice, gunfire broke out beyond the far south entrance to the clearing. Hitler turned to see his legion of protectors one by one running wildly into the forest, yelling obscenities and waving their guns. A few women had joined the gunmen as they hurried to join the other Brownshirts already engaged in battle. The remaining women, however, had turned in the direction of Hitler and Goebbels, and were now racing toward the two naked individuals to both take cover and to ask what they had seen.

Hitler quickly broke away from the group of fleeing women and the young naked couple to begin walking quickly toward the south end of the clearing. As he passed Goebbels, he motioned to the shorter man to follow him. Goebbels, unaccustomed to being around gunfire, snapped out of his stupor, and speedily limped to catch up with Hitler, his deformed right leg dragging clumsily along the ground.

Dusk was now descending on the area as Hitler and Goebbels reached the far southern edge of the grassy knoll and entered the dense forest region, a few late-arriving Brownshirts falling in behind them. The soldiers quickly passed the two walkers as they ran with guns drawn to where the gunfire was heaviest. As the fighting got louder, Hitler stopped along the path where the Brownshirts had traversed. As gunfire faded in the distance and feeling that the members of his special private army had taken care of the problem, Hitler cautiously marched up the winding brush-lined path to near a clearing in the woods. Goebbels was almost 20 feet behind Hitler, desperately trying to shorten the gap between himself and his political idol.

As Hitler inched closer to the large opening in front of him, someone from behind grabbed his left arm. Thinking it was Goebbels, he spun around to see that it was Falk who was hanging on to him.

"Don't go out there, Adolph," Falk pleaded. "It's too dangerous. It's too unbelievable."

Hitler looked disgustingly at his young Brownshirt, then became angry and pulled out of the grasp of his henchman. He said nothing, and proceeded to the entrance to the clearing.

What he saw before him made him catch his breath and stop in his tracks.

CHAPTER TEN

THE carnage was spectacular by military standards. Hitler noted that there were still a handful of Brownshirts crouched behind trees with their guns pointed toward the clearing. But the deafening gunfire had ceased. The scene that opened up in the killing clearing was mind-boggling.

Within steps of Hitler lay the dead bodies of Dorf, Bert, and dozens of other Brownshirt guardians. But they weren't just dead. It was how they must have died that puzzled Hitler.

Dorf's body had been sliced in two at his waistline. His upper and lower torsos were right next to each other, but they were separated in equally severed parts. From a general glance at Dorf, it looked like he was simply lying on his back, albeit dead. But upon closer observation, Hitler could see a lethal cut had traveled cleanly through his entire body just above his belt line. There was plenty of blood, but it seemed like the fatal cut had also cauterized his wound and made the loss of blood minimal. It was truly a frightening picture. Yet from a physiological point of view, it mesmerized Hitler's mind.

Whereas Dorf's execution seemed like a work of art to Hitler, the bodies of Bert and the others within the short viewing distance were straight out of a horror novel. It looked like Bert's body had exploded…from the inside. There was a huge, gaping hole where his chest had once been. His internal organs were splattered about five feet in front of him. His face carried the visage of terror and wonder that a man expresses before his untimely death at the hand of a superior enemy. Bert never knew what hit him.

A cursory glance to his right and left gave Hitler more examples of death by an unconventional weapon. Some of his young warriors lay motionless with burn marks still hissing on their shattered bodies. Other corpses were contorted, with severed arms, legs, and heads lying next to their owners. Still others had mercifully died, body intact, but their eyes continued to bulge out of their sockets, blood streaming down their youthful cheeks to the soggy earth below.

Hitler then refocused his gaze to the most remarkable sight he had ever seen. Roughly five hundred meters directly in front of him stood a silver metallic object that was resting on four landing gear legs. It looked like it was 100 meters long and 10 meters high. There was a row of square windows about a meter in diameter each roughly half the way up the craft with blinding white light shining out from the inside.

The dying sunlight at dusk was bouncing off the craft to make it appear like a golden glowing orb. There seemed to be a steady mechanical hum surrounding the object. Even though Hitler thought himself to be privy to all secret military experiments being conducted by German scientists since the First World War, he was not familiar with what he was watching here. This was something completely new. This all seemed so unreal, yet very exhilarating. His heart was pounding in his chest. But he needed a closer look.

As Hitler surveyed the surreal scene, his attention was drawn to some short odd-shaped figures standing close to the craft, some kind of smoking weapon dangling from their hands. They seemed to be dressed in a kind of grayish coverall, but what in God's name was on their heads? In the dimness of the forest opening, Hitler's eyes opened widely in astonishment and wonder when he realized that it wasn't something that was on their heads. It WAS their heads! They were misshapen and ghastly.

As Hitler was about to walk toward the craft to get a better look, he heard another voice behind him. He knew it wasn't Falk again, and then he surmised that it was Goebbels. During all the excitement, Goebbels had hidden behind a set of sturdy trees, frozen with fright at what he was watching. Suddenly, when he realized Hitler was about to confront the unknown, he vacated his safe haven, and put an arm out to stop him.

"Wait, Adolph. Let me try this." With that, Goebbels took out a white handkerchief from his pocket, and tied a corner to a tree branch he picked up off the ground. He offered it to Hitler. If it had been any other ignorant Brownshirt, Hitler would have shot him dead where he stood. But Goebbels was a loyal follower, and Hitler softened his reply.

"I do not accept the idea of surrendering," Hitler pontificated to Goebbels.

Goebbels countered. "Just long enough to see who...or what...they are. We'll fool them."

Hitler grudgingly nodded in agreement, and side by side with Goebbels, the two Nazis crept into the clearing, the white flag held prominently in front of them. The other cowering Brownshirts and terrified women who had stumbled into and survived the deadly encounter remained behind the cover and protection of nearby trees and rocks. They all stared intently as the two solitary figures moved slowly away from the tree line and into the forest clearing, stepping over and around dead comrades as they inched their way closer to the strangers and the strange vehicle.

CHAPTER ELEVEN

THE sun had almost completely disappeared below the towering evergreens that made up this part of the forest. You could still see daylight peeking through sparse patches of foliage. But as Hitler and Goebbels ambled farther away from their Brownshirt protection detail waving their white flag ahead of them, the ensuing darkness quickly enveloped them and they were no longer visible to their group.

Looking over his shoulder, Hitler realized he was out of the view of his Brownshirt protectors. But his curiosity was stronger than his fear of the unknown at this point. And even though he knew Goebbels would be worthless if any physical attack commenced, his adrenaline level had never been higher. He hastened his pace toward the group of truly ugly beings in front of him.

As the last remnants of sunlight melted into the countryside, Hitler and Goebbels found themselves within twenty meters of their destination. As they neared, they forced their eyes to acclimate more quickly to the darkness surrounding them. When their night vision improved, what they saw made them stop and rub their eyes. This could not be real, Goebbels exclaimed. But to Hitler, the scene unfolding in front of him was a dream come true.

In 1919, when Hitler became the seventh member of the newly-organized German Workers' Party, he was also quietly initiated into the Vril Society of Germany, a secret enclave of individuals who believed that a source of universal power was available to a special class of humanity. His two mentors in the society, Karl Haushofer, professor of Geopolitics at the University of Munich, and the drunken poet Dietrich Eckart, taught him that the accumulation of this inner energy would prove bountiful in the real world.

They repeatedly told Hitler that this universal power created an animal magnetism within the enlightened person, and that this force had the potential to control others, to control events in the physical world, and to establish lines of communication with superhuman or alien entities. This drama playing out in front of him, Hitler told himself, validated the teachings of his secret mentors, and proved that he truly was endowed with this universal power. This scene unfolding before him, though subconsciously expected, still caused a conscious shudder of terror.

A mystifying glow was still present around the silver stationary object. Within that glow, Hitler could now vividly observe what had been a blurry image only a few minutes ago. Standing 10 meters away, Hitler saw five of the most hideous creatures he had ever seen. They were all very skinny and exactly the same height, probably around four to four and a half feet tall. Goebbels stood barely five and a half feet tall, and he towered above them. Their skin was a grayish color, which matched the color of the jumpsuits they were wearing.

Their thin arms hung almost to their knees. There were no identifying marks to make them male or female.

Hitler quickly noticed the hands and feet. They wore no shoes, and below their skintight one-piece jumpsuits, they only had four toes instead of five. The skin seemed very taut and scaly on their feet. There were no toenails on their appendages. The hands below their jumpsuit resembled the feet in the same weird way. There were only four fingers instead of five. And they looked bony and skinny as they wrapped them around the weapons they were holding at their sides. They had no fingernails either. They made no sound and didn't move an inch as they gazed back at the two interlopers.

And then Hitler found himself staring directly at their heads. He instantly realized these were not earthbound beings by any stretch of the imagination. They couldn't be. Not even the worst outcome of a botched German scientific experiment could turn out like this, he concluded to himself. He stood there, mesmerized by what he was seeing.

The heads were round, elongated, and twice the size of a normal human being. But it was the eyes that made these visitors so distasteful. They were bulbous, bulging, and egg-shaped, with vertical pupils running from top to bottom in their sockets. They didn't blink. They had no hair. They had no eye lids. They had only openings where the ears should be. They had no nose, only a slit between their eyes. And they had no mouth or lips. Again, they possessed only a slit where a mouth should be. The entire scene made Hitler momentarily shiver. Goebbels was so unnerved that he became visibly nauseous, using the white handkerchief on his flag to wipe away the vomit that covered his mouth and boots. Hitler sneered in disgust at his putrid ally.

As this mind-numbing scene was unraveling before the two men, there was a clicking, hissing sound. Suddenly, an opening appeared on the side of the craft, and a flat metallic ramp five meters long began to lower to the ground. When the ramp had completed its descent, three additional figures, all identical to their brethren standing outside, arrived at the entrance of the ramp.

In single file, and with an awkward gait, they traversed down the 45-degree pathway to the bottom of the ramp. The first figure took a step to the right, the second figure took a step to the left, and the third creature followed his two escorts to end his stroll about three meters in front of the entire eerie group of visitors. He held some kind of device in his right hand. This "leader" now stood only two meters from Hitler and Goebbels, the repulsive eyes gazing directly at Hitler. A slight breeze touched Hitler's face, but the night was deathly still.

And then it got even more bewildering.

Inexplicably, as Hitler, adrenalin-induced sweat pouring down his brow, stood stiff at attention before the band of unsightly creatures, he heard a voice in his head. He snapped his neck in the direction of Goebbels, thinking his cowardly accomplice was trying to communicate something to him. But Goebbels was still hunched over, viewing the vomit pit he had just created. Realizing the voice was not coming from Goebbels, he glanced back to the vision before him. Then a conversation erupted in his head.

"Adolf Hitler, wir beobachten Sie in einem Abstand für viele Ihrer Erdenjahre. Wir kennen Ihre Ziele. Wir sind hier,

um Ihnen helfen, diese Ziele zu erreichen. Wir kommen als Freunde. "

"Adolph Hitler," the ethereal voice announced, "We have been observing you at a distance for many of your earth years. We know of your ambitions. We are here to help you attain those ambitions. We come as friends."

Hitler was momentarily stunned by this incredulous mental invasion he had just experienced. He no longer stood in wonderment. To bolster his ego and diminish his fear, Hitler decided to feign anger with these unworldly new-found "friends."

"What in the hell are you things?" he angrily cried out. "What is this craft? Where do you come from?"

In his typical animated fashion, Hitler continued his discourse.

"And you say you come as friends? You're goddamn monsters. How fucking stupid do you think I am?" He turned around and motioned to the dead and dismembered bodies of his loyal group of Brownshirts that lay in the darkness beyond their view a short distance away.

"Friends don't fucking kill innocent strangers for no apparent reason. And what the hell are those weapons you used to destroy my men? How do they work?"

Goebbels, still doubled over, now swung his attention toward Hitler. Amidst his continued feelings of nausea, he asked Hitler to whom he was talking.

In a hushed tone, he asked, "Adolph, who are you talking to? I hear no other voices speaking. There was dead silence, and then I heard you screaming."

Hitler, now distracted away from his primary target of retribution, looked with frustration at his slumping cohort.

"What are you talking about?" he stammered. "Don't you hear the bullshit this bug-eyed asshole is telling me?"

Goebbels, a quizzical look on his face, sheepishly answered Hitler. "Why no, Adolph, I didn't hear anything. But from your tone of voice, it's obvious that you are hearing something."

He continued his brief conversation with the Nazi leader. "Adolph, what we are experiencing here is truly amazing. This entity somehow is telepathically connected with only you. My God, you are the Chosen One, Adolph. These other-worldly visitors even know of your greatness. That's why they must be here.

"Hear them out. Get as much valuable information from them as you can. Learn about these hand weapons. These fantastic weapons can be of great help to our cause. You definitely need to find out more about this unbelievable flying machine. Can you imagine the power that someone can possess with a flying machine and advanced weaponry like we're seeing here?"

After listening to Goebbels's speech, the staged anger dissipated from Hitler. But his sense of invincibility had only been fortified. His disabled convert had made a strong and lasting point. Of course, he thought, the appearance of these creatures proved what his Vril masters had been telling him for years: only the Chosen Ones with the universal power within them can attract communication with alien entities. And the best part, he concluded to himself, was that they possess technology above and beyond anything German scientists were creating these days. *If they want to help me attain my destiny*, he thought to himself, *why shouldn't I let them?* With that, he turned his attention back to the otherworldly entity.

"I apologize for my outburst," he addressed the leader. "I am honored that you are here to help me. I am humbled by your presence. Please tell me more about your race, and why you have chosen me."

The alien leader transferred his thoughts again to Hitler.

"Ich bin glücklich, dies zu tun," the alien leader telepathically replied in Hitler's native tongue. "I will be happy to do so."

Hitler immediately assumed a military stance, feet shoulder width apart, arms behind the back, and hands clasped together. Goebbels found himself sufficiently recovered from his short-lived, terror-induced sickness to copy the body language of his political hero. Hitler was eager to contemplate what he was about to learn. And the best part was that he alone would hear this fantastic tale.

CHAPTER TWELVE

WITH the feet of both Nazis firmly planted in a locked standing position in front of him, the otherwordly leader started the telepathic transfer of an incredible story that would both captivate and embolden Hitler's spirit.

"We are communicating with you in your language to put you at ease and make our mental connection readily understandable by you alone," the alien leader stated, prefacing what he was about to tell Hitler.

"My name is Tehlri," the alien leader proclaimed. "I am the leader of a nomadic group of star travelers from what your people call the Ophiuchus constellation in outer space. We are one of several star groups who have settled on your planet, and have had a presence here for tens of thousands of earth years.

"To avoid contact with the inhabitants of this world and to ensure the secrecy of our presence, we established a base camp deep below the surface of the mountains of snow and ice of the desolate land you call Antarctica. Our primary mission is one of peace and observation. Yet, when confronted in a hostile fashion by the earth inhabitants as we were today, we can take defensive measures to preserve our own lives. Since our technology is vastly superior to those of any nation on this planet, it was quite simple to defuse the problem. We do regret that we had to take such action against your people. But frankly, we did not have any chance to avoid the conflict with your inexperienced fighters. They fired their weapons first."

While Hitler was intrigued by what he was hearing, Goebbels had a look of disinterest since he was not hearing any part of what was being divulged to Hitler. The story unfolded further.

"Over millennia, the human race has been in contact with the vast majority of space visitors. Through the evolvement and disappearance of multiple earth civilizations, these encounters have been documented and discovered during the recovery of ancient manuscripts and curious religious artifacts throughout time. There have been some groups whose plan it was to breed with the local citizenry simply for the sexual gratification it enhanced. The offspring, however, were almost always killed immediately following birth because of the grotesque result that was produced. However, some creatures depicted in your early Greek mythology actually existed because these outlaw alien groups failed to manage their hideous experiments properly.

"Other space groups ran multiple scientific tests on the local Earth fauna to produce a bigger and stronger animal. Your dinosaur period on earth was the outcome of mismanaged genetic mutations that simply evolved out of control for millions of years. The presence of these wild beasts did nothing to help the intelligence-impaired humans of the time. The only way to eradicate the problem was to destroy the creatures. Contrary to the belief of many of your theorists that a collision with the earth by a cosmic boulder caused the extinction of these creatures, the space visitors responsible for the initial problem simply injected a mutating virus that eventually annihilated each species of these nonproductive animals.

"Very little contact has been made among the multiple space visitor groups that populate this planet to this day. However, we all know of each other's presence and are well aware of the contrasting philosophies regarding contact with your human race. Unfortunately, there are some groups that are out to harm the human race. Thankfully, there are other benevolent groups like ourselves who have made it a point to ensure no unnecessary harm comes to the inhabitants of your planet. After all, the Primordial Manifest of all interplanetary visitors is to allow the human inhabitants of each planet to evolve on their own terms. We believe we are your strongest ally. "

Hitler was enjoying the storytelling ability of his gruesome host. Up to this point, he often found himself nodding and commenting in wonderment at what he was hearing. Goebbels, on the other hand, was falling in and out of consciousness in the cool evening dampness that had fallen on the area. He found himself dozing off standing up until he was abruptly brought back to his senses when he heard Hitler expressing surprise and bewilderment at the story he was being told.

But Hitler was getting tired of hearing the history of the world according to Tehlri. His maniacal ego was making him anxious to find out why these aliens had chosen him to be their friend. Unfamiliar with how this telepathic mumbo-jumbo worked, he nevertheless interrupted the tale by blurting out a question of his own.

"Herr Tehlri, I am overwhelmed by what you have told me thus far. But, if you don't mind, I would like to know something about your craft and weapons and why you have chosen me to tell this fantastic story."

Expressionless, Tehlri silently sent his answer to Hitler.

"Yes. You display your impatience. The end of the story is near. Then I will tell you of your importance to us."

Hitler dropped his eyes, and nodded his acceptance, feeling once again like a child being admonished by his superiors. Tehlri continued his thought transmission.

"Since our arrival to your planet, my group has constantly watched the evolution of your primitive species. In particular, we have been most interested in certain human members …your smartest, your strongest, and most importantly, the most intellectually adaptable. Over millennia, we have visited, communicated with, and in some instances, given guidance and direction.

"The great thinkers, writers, and scientists have demonstrated the most intellectual adaptability. We have been most intrigued with individuals such as Plato, Socrates, Pythagoras, Copernicus, and Homer. King Solomon, Sir Francis Bacon, Isaac Newton, and William Shakespeare all received visitations from us.

"Great historical religious leaders have also caught our attention because we consider them some of the most inspiring individuals to walk the earth. We have spoken with many of these earthmen, including Abraham, Moses, John the Baptist,

Ezekiel, Mohammed, Buddha, Confucius, and Gandhi. We gave counsel to Martin Luther and Thomas Aquinas. It was also Brigham Young, and not Joseph Smith, that received our help. Ignatius Loyola, the founder of the Jesuit order, received contact from us.

"Interestingly, our deepest fascination surrounds men and women who have demonstrated military dominance. We are most drawn to the group of individuals who have amassed the strongest armies of the world, and commanded fear and respect from their countrymen and enemies. Warlords you know by the names Constantine, Alexander the Great, Attila the Hun, Napoleon Bonaparte, Genghis Khan, Charlemagne, William the Conqueror, and Hannibal. Joan of Arc and Julius Caesar received frequent visits from us, as did the Indian warrior Sitting Bull. In secret letters to his commanders, George Washington gave us credit for assistance during crucial Revolutionary War battles. We have been around to see all of these inspiring military men and women control their worlds because of our influence and intervention.

"It is now you, Adolph Hitler, who commands our attention. Your country, Germany, has shown itself to be a leader in technological and scientific advancement. No other country on earth is anywhere near your present state of scientific inquiry and testing. Your scientific experimentation methods are quite simpleminded, but the thirst for superior knowledge is impressive. And we see your steady rise to political power as a certainty that you will soon earn your ascent to the highest level of authority. Your driving ambition to be a world leader has caught our attention. We can help you towards this end. This is why we approached you…to build a partnership… that will benefit both of us."

As Hitler was beginning to join his dozing companion during Tehlri's diatribe on the smartest and most intellectually adaptable humans, he instantly perked up when the story about military leaders was presented. And when his name and the name of his beloved country were mentioned in the same breath, his pride overflowed into joyous commentary.

"I had no idea my beliefs and life story had made such an impression upon you," Hitler effused. "And I have no doubt that my country is a world leader in technology and science. But you can help me even more, can't you?" He pointed over Tehlri's shoulder to the flying craft and weapons that were still in the hands of the alien fighters.

Hitler continued. "You have proven that you are a powerful emissary to Earth. Your weapons are vastly superior to our own. I am in awe of your presence. I am such a small piece in Germany's rise to world preeminence. So, yes, I would be honored to join you in a partnership that will help me, uh… us... attain our mutual goals."

By this time, Goebbels had snapped to attention from his drowsy state as Hitler started yet another conversation with the ugly alien. He noted Hitler's pride in the words he was now communicating back to the alien leader. Noting from his wristwatch that the time was nearing nine o'clock, he was immensely envious that only Hitler was the recipient of the telepathic connection that had lasted well over an hour. He wanted to speak to Hitler, but he knew any kind of interruption at this point would draw distain from the Nazi leader.

Tehlri's response was not what Hitler initially wanted to hear.

"Your enthusiasm toward our ship and weapons is understandable. All earthlings respond in awe to our advanced technology. You will have the opportunity to gain the knowledge surrounding our technology at a later time. At this time, however, I wish to offer you a gift to solidify our growing friendship."

Hitler inquired, "What kind of gift?"

With that, Tehlri raised his arms and offered a small square blackish-green box that he had carried from the craft and had held throughout his telepathic conversation. Hitler had noticed the object as Tehlri had descended from the craft. But then he had dismissed it when the mental discussions commanded his total attention.

Once in Hitler's hands, the object was roughly four inches square and about two inches thick. It fit easily in the palm of his right hand. The object had a nonreflective surface and looked like black steel. There were no connecting pieces to it. It looked like one solid smooth mass.

On the top was a clear plastic bubble about an inch long and inch thick that seemed to be pulsating light from beneath the surface. There were no noticeable dials or lights on the outside surface anywhere. Hitler also noticed some kind of yellowish hieroglyphs that circled the width of the object. He didn't recognize any of it, though. But it was extremely light in Hitler's hands, weighing less than a pound. So it couldn't be steel, he thought.

"It's so light to the touch," Hitler told Tehlri. "What is this thing?"

"This is a communication device that will allow you to summon us at any time," the lead alien planted in Hitler's mind. "The blinking light indicates that we are within 100 meters of the device. If you have any requests for information or wish to ask a question or need our assistance, you can accomplish all of those by simply holding the object in your hand and touching the top bubble. When the light begins to pulsate, you are assured that we have heard the call and are near. It's that simple."

What Tehlri transmitted to Hitler about the communication device was only half true. One function was indeed that of a communication device with the alien beings. The untold truth was that the device also acted as a listening transponder. Wherever Hitler took or placed the device, Tehlri would always know what was being discussed within a 100-meter radius.

Hitler turned toward Goebbels and proudly showed him the strange object he had just received. Goebbels reached out to touch it, but Hitler quickly pulled it away from his grasp.

"Only I can hold it," he admonished Goebbels. "It's only for me."

His outward exuberance with the gift was suddenly brought back to reality by what Tehlri was now passing along to him in another telepathic sermon.

"This gift comes with a request from us. We ask that you allow us to continue our effort to improve the physical and intellectual capacity of the human species, especially your German troops and people. We know your ambition is to make your Aryan race the most powerful on earth. We can help you attain that ambitious goal. To perfect our technique, we will need to conduct scientific experimentation on human subjects. Both our scientists and yours will take part. We hope you can help us acquire those subjects as you rise to power."

Hitler was still basking in the euphoria of his new personal toy when he briskly responded to Tehlri.

"Unfortunately, I'm in no position to help you with your request at this time," he stated curtly. "But if what you tell me about my future turns out to be correct, then I just may be able to provide you with large numbers of the kind of experimental subjects you're looking for. Now, tell me about your ship here and how I can get some of those weapons that easily overpowered my young soldiers."

CHAPTER THIRTEEN

HITLER was absolutely giddy with delight as he and Goebbels made their way away from Tehlri and his group. The night was still and peaceful, with a cool breeze tickling their faces. As they hurried in pitch blackness back towards the grisly combat scene, they turned to observe the light fade from inside the craft as the rising door soundlessly closed behind the space visitors. In an instant, the silver ship elevated off the ground, the four landing pods disappearing magically into the bottom of the craft. In a blink of the eye, the craft slowly rose without making a sound, and then it was gone, zooming high into the clouds and becoming just another shooting star to the casual night sky observer.

Goebbels pressed Hitler for the privileged information he had just received from Tehlri.

"Adolph," he sang out, "what did he tell you? What did you learn? Who are they and what do they want? Did he tell you anything about the ship and weapons? What is that thing he gave you? Will we see them again?"

The questions rolled off Goebbels' lips in rapid fashion. Finally, Hitler raised his right hand to signal a halt to the inquisition.

"Joseph, take a breath for Christsake," Hitler exclaimed. "Pull yourself together, man." He continued. "I know you were not able to hear anything that I was told. Just remember that the information was meant for me alone. That is why you heard nothing. I will share pieces of it with you as time goes on. What I learned was unbelievable. I'm still having trouble comprehending the information I was given." The corner of his mouth morphed into a sly smirk.

Within a couple minutes, Hitler and Goebbels had retraced their steps and now stood amidst the dead combatants, the few surviving soldiers, and the sobbing women who had accompanied them to this spot in the forest. At the sight of the two brave men returning from their clash with the unknown, the unharmed sprung to their feet and pounced on the two heroes.

Questions came rushing from the lips of every living person in the clearing. "Adolph, what happened out there?" "Adolph, what were those things and what did they want?" "Adolph, why weren't you and Joseph killed?" "Adolph, what are you carrying in your hand?" One question echoed off another to where Hitler couldn't comprehend any specific query. But he didn't care. He wasn't staying around to answer any questions from these losers. He had things to do.

As Hitler moved methodically through the crowd, pushing away pleading arms and reaching hands and ignoring all interrogation, Goebbels was stopping every few feet to provide an answer to a question posed to him. But every answer was the same. "I don't know" was repeated again and again by the short, crippled man.

On Goebbels' third stop along the dark path back to the cars to answer queries from the still-shaken men and women who had survived the firefight, an exasperated Hitler stopped in his tracks, wheeled around, grabbed Goebbels under his right armpit with his open left hand, and jerked him ahead of the pack. Hitler grunted but said nothing as he increased the quickness of his pace along the thin woody trail while practically dragging Goebbels alongside.

The pace quickened as Hitler and his crippled hostage burst from the thick brush into the picnic clearing. With the alien communication device vicegripped in his right hand, they continued their steady march straight towards Hitler's red Mercedes as the group of women and the now-clothed lovers left their protected position behind the car and started running toward Hitler and Goebbels, questions flying from their mouths.

Arrogantly ignoring all contact and questions, Hitler forcefully pushed through the oncoming crowd of inquisitors, and ran the final ten feet to his car, Goebbels in tow. When they finally reached the car, Hitler aggressively opened the driver-side door and tossed Goebbels behind the wheel. He ran to the passenger door, frantically opened it, jumped in, and slammed the door hard enough to cause the vehicle to shake for a moment.

"Drive, you bastard," Hitler screamed to the still struggling Goebbels. "Get us the hell out of here now."

After catching his breath, Goebbels reached down and turned the ignition, and the red Mercedes convertible roared to life. After turning on the headlights, he frantically reversed the car from its isolated picnic position, narrowly missing a wounded Brownshirt who had been limping behind the fleeing Hitler. He then put the surging sedan into gear, and the swift departure began. The speeding car accelerated towards the entrance to the clearing, leaving behind all the dead, wounded, limping, and shocked. In a matter of seconds, the getaway was complete.

As Goebbels was navigating the winding road snaking through the sleepy, moonlight-soaked forest, surrounded by the calming effect of nature's invisible sounds, Hitler closely examined the communication device, rolling it around and over in his hands, looking discreetly at all angles and sides. He was mesmerized by not only its feel, but by the power that it represented.

Goebbels glanced toward Hitler, smiled, and waited a moment before speaking.

"Adolph, now no one can prevent you from becoming Germany's leader. The creatures have given you the power because they recognize what you can do. They've chosen you. It's like you believed all along. The Aryan race is superior."

Hitler looked at his thoughtful chauffeur as the complimentary words disappeared into the thin night air. Not a word was spoken between the two men as they drove away from the most horrendous and life-altering picnic either had ever attended.

CHAPTER FOURTEEN

Berlin, Germany
Spring 1933

ANIMAL MAGNETISM. Hitler was certain that he possessed it. His occult training confirmed it. He believed it was the key to his rise to power, and the major reason why he would lead his Aryan nation to world domination. His little alien friends, frankly, were a disappointment to him at the moment. As he rode through the streets of Berlin in the back seat of his black convertible staff car with the custom-made gold swastika hood ornament emblematic of his new leadership position in Germany, he silently recalled the many events in his life that played a critical role to his ascendancy to the position of Chancellor.

He first remembered the derision and threats he received from his father Alois when he told him he would rather be an artist than follow his father's footsteps in civil service. He remembered fondly his kind, loving, and gullible mother, Klara, who valiantly tried to intercede on his behalf during the many heated arguments with his father. Since she spoiled him unapologetically all his life, he remembered being devastated by her death from cancer, much more than when his father died. He would carry her picture with him at all times in memory of her gallant spirit.

He vividly recalled that his obsession with returning Germany to its former glory began at a young age. He remembered he was around 15 years old when he told one of his closest childhood friends, August Kubizek, that he was destined to lead the German people, the purest of the Aryan race, to world dominance.

He fully recalled his many days in 1908 spent with Dr. Walter Stein and feeling empowered while viewing the Spear of Destiny, the relic in possession of the Hapsburg Dynasty for 250 years and on display in the Hapsburg's Treasure House Museum in Vienna. The spear was also known as the Holy Lance, which in Christian tradition, was the spear that the Roman soldier Longinus thrust into the side of Jesus as he hung on the cross.

Each time Hitler viewed the holy artifact, it became the single driving force of his ambition to conquer the world. Hitler discovered that as many as 45 emperors had owned the lance, including Frederick the Great of Germany. According to legend, whoever claimed the spear and solved its secret held the destiny of the world in his hands for good or evil. Mesmerized by the thought, Hitler swore to himself that he, too, would possess the spear in due time and would extract the secret powers within it to overwhelm his enemies.

He callously remembered his destitute days living in Vienna posing as an art student after having his applications rejected from the Vienna Academy of Art and the Vienna School of Architecture. Humiliated by these rejections and determined to make up for his educational deficiencies, he delved into the study of the occult legend of the Holy Grail while reading Wolfram von Eschenbach's 13th-century Grail romance "Parzival." He felt eerily strengthened to have met Guido Von List, the spiritual mentor to the infamous Blood Lodge, who guided Hitler in his quest for esoteric and mystical power.

He angrily remembered the disrespect he received from the German army commanders during World War I. Even though he was forced into service, he knew he had performed bravely in his position as a dispatch runner, winning five Iron Cross medals because of his "fearless activity" to get important messages through to the front lines. He even endured temporary blindness from a British mustard gas attack, for God sake. Yet the highest rank he attained was that of corporal, the reason given was that his eccentric and odd behavior would make it impossible for others to obey his orders. Those unhappy days would never happen again because he was now the leader, not the follower.

As his car moved smoothly along its route, Hitler would idly acknowledge waves and shouts from citizens walking nearby who recognized their new chancellor. His mind, however, was still processing memories as he smiled, nodded, and waved to the masses as a result of his newfound fame.

He silently laughed at the fluke encounter he experienced with Anton Drexler and the newly-organized German Worker's Party in 1919 while spying for the German army following the signing of the Versailles Treaty. The reparations from that treaty following World War I had depleted Germany of 38% of her national wealth. While looking for communist links within the organization, Hitler had surprisingly found himself agreeing with the message of anti-Semitism and German nationalism. But he thought the entire group was badly disorganized and in need of direction. And it must have been fate, he surmised, that caused him to impetuously stand and proselytize his disagreement with a statement that had been made by a member. So impressed was Drexler with Hitler's oratorical abilities that he invited him to join the party. A failure no more, Hitler had now found a platform to display his nationalistic passion and to begin forming his political aspirations.

Playing on a socialist theme that was popular following the war, Hitler proudly recalled how he was able to manipulate his nationalistic ideology and hatred of the Jews to form the National Socialist German Worker's Party, or Nazi Party, in 1920. He was even more proud of how he was able to displace Drexler as the party leader in 1921. He only regretted that he was sent to prison for three months for inciting riots and acts of violence towards those politicians not in sync with his beliefs.

Following his incarceration, Hitler decided that he needed personal protection. So with the help of Hermann Goering, a former German Air Force pilot, he formed his own private army called the *Sturm Abteilung*. Made up mostly of former German soldiers, hooligans, and common criminals, these storm troopers became known as the Brownshirts. They did an admirable job for a while, he thought, of protecting him from revenge attacks and disrupting the meetings of political opponents.

But Hitler knew he needed a much more foreboding and intimidating secret police unit than what the Brownshirts could accomplish. That's why, in 1929, he allowed another loyal follower and poultry farmer, Heinrich Himmler, to assemble and lead his new personal body guards, the *Schutzstaffel* (SS). Supposedly using the Jesuits as his organizational model, his hierarchy ranged from lay brothers to father superior. Himmler had been magnificent, Hitler added, in his ability to recruit the good "Aryan" types to populate this elite group of soldiers that had grown in strength to nearly 52,000. And, Hitler noted with pride, he greatly approved of Himmler's decision to dress his SS police in all-black uniforms. Nothing was more intimidating to the common citizen than a Death's Head secret police authority figure dressed in all black, Hitler grinned.

As Hitler was rising up the political ladder in Germany, he never forgot his obsession with the occult. Striving for mystical powers, he happily remembered being indoctrinated into the two most powerful secret societies operating in Germany: the Vril Society and the Thule Society. His presence among the elite leaders of each sinister group indicated to him that he, too, was an elite member of German society. He had fought his way from being a high school dropout to being a man to be feared because of his knowledge of esoteric matters.

He amusingly recalled the flattering and narcissistic deathbed words in 1923 of his mentor with the Vril Society, Dietrich Eckart, who prophetically stated, "Follow Hitler. He will dance, but it is I who called the tune! I have initiated him into the 'Secret Doctrine', opened his centers of vision and given him the means to communicate with the Powers. Do not mourn for me for I shall have influenced history more than any other German." No, my dear Dietrich, Hitler smirked, I will be the German who will influence history the most.

The smirk quickly turned to a frown as Hitler recalled the events leading up to his prison sentence for his failed takeover of the German government in 1923. Feeling invincible with a large band of almost 3,000 armed supporters, his group was quickly met with resistance by Munich police. When 21 people were killed and another hundred wounded during the skirmish, he ran and hid, knowing there would be hell to pay for his ambitious actions if he was caught. Which he was. Three days later.

With a possible death penalty awaiting him, Hitler remembered succinctly how he orchestrated his trial into grand theater. What fools the judge and jury were, he thought, his mockery heavy with vitriol. His impeccable oratory rallied his sympathizers among jury members, he thought. The outcome was a triumph of sorts, he told himself, because instead of the death penalty, he got sentenced to only five years at Landsberg Castle in Munich.

In spite of being allowed to walk the grounds freely, wear his own clothes, and receive gifts from visitors, Hitler often entertained suicidal thoughts during his imprisonment. He read voraciously, especially books dealing with politics and German history. Two books took on a special meaning, though. He was enamored by American car manufacturer Henry Ford's autobiographical publication called *My Life and Work* and a second text called *The International Jew*. In the latter, Ford had written about his claim that there was a Jewish conspiracy to take over the world. Hitler also agreed with Ford's adverse position towards communism and trade unions.

During those trying days at Landsberg, Hitler fondly recalled Max Amnan, his business manager, insisting that he stop reading and start writing his autobiography. Feeling very awkward with his lack of writing skills, Hitler remembered taking Max's suggestion to dictate his thoughts to a ghostwriter. He remembered what a joke it was when Emil Maurice, his chauffeur, was first given the task. His writing skills were worse than Hitler's. Plus, Hitler couldn't convey his passionate voice and quirky body movements in print like he could during a speech.

The job finally fell onto the shoulders of a young Munich University student named Rudolf Hess. He tried his best, but the prison product still turned out to be a rambling, repetitious, and confused piece of writing. Hitler thought his publisher did him a favor when he changed the title of the book from *Four Years of Struggle against Lies, Stupidity, and Cowardice* to *My Struggle (Mein Kampf)*. At the heart of his political philosophy was the superiority of the Aryan race, the need to keep the race "pure" from intermarriage contamination, and the elimination of the Jewish race, which Hitler believed to be a group of lazy individuals who had contributed little to the civilized world.

Ah, and then there were the women in Hitler's life, he mused. So many of them. He liked them young, he liked them beautiful, and he liked them dumb. He grimaced if any woman wanted to talk politics with him. *"A man should take a primitive and stupid woman"*, he told himself often. Most often using his new red Mercedes as a magnet, he attracted mostly the young and flirty girls that he could exploit easily.

He recalled his first involvement with 16-year-old Maria Reiter. For a man in his thirties, any kind of association with a teenage girl made for delicious scandal, he smiled. She was so despondent when Hitler tossed her aside, she attempted suicide. How boorish, he told himself.

Then there was his infatuation with his 20-year-old niece, Geli Raubal. When she moved into Hitler's house to assist her mother, Angela, with housekeeping duties that Hitler had asked his half-sister to perform as a favor to him, there was an instant spark of sexual tension between the two. Hitler recalled that his infatuation quickly turned to obsession with the girl. He remembered that they would steal away to out-of-the-way locations to be alone. It got so intense, Hitler remembered, that when Emil, his chauffeur, began to show interest in Geli, he fired him on the spot.

For two years, Geli lived with Hitler, but things didn't turn out well. They argued incessantly, mostly about Hitler's wandering eye and controlling behavior. When Hitler became enamored with a 17-year-old blonde named Eva Braun and began driving her around in his Mercedes, it seemed to push Geli over the edge. After a heated argument with Hitler, and his quick departure to Vienna, she pulled out a pistol and shot herself through the heart. Poor, poor girl, Hitler told himself. He felt somewhat responsible, but obviously, the girl was not strong enough emotionally to handle Hitler's absence. So this really was the best thing to happen…to him and to her, he deduced.

After his release from prison in 1924 after serving, unbelievably, only one year of his sentence, Hitler remembered jumping back into the political arena. His extremist views on ridding Germany of Jewish/Marxist influence, expanding German dominance by acquiring other countries, and appealing for an anti-democratic form of government, mostly fell on deaf ears. While moving to Berchtesgaden to live in the Bavarian Alps and recharge his tiring political ideas, his chance encounter with the aliens strengthened his resolve once again. But these little bastards weren't living up to their end of the deal, he argued.

Hitler wrinkled his brow as his thoughts now swung to his little gray alien friends. He graphically recalled the calm spring night seven years ago in the Bavarian forest when he and Goebbels first laid their eyes on Tehlri, the saucer, and the weapons. After that eventful night, Goebbels' continual begging and cajoling over the years to share knowledge of the device he was given had finally taken its toll on Hitler. Today, only Hitler's inner circle had seen and was briefed on the communication device he was given by the alien leader.

Those damn aliens had yet to deliver on their promises, Hitler complained. Despite several communication attempts from Hitler utilizing the alien device within the first month of his possession of it, Telhri never showed up. Hitler wanted some of those laser weapons as Telhri had described them. He wanted one of those flying saucers, too. When Telhri did answer Hitler's summons, he told Hitler he would receive everything in due time.

For years, he had impressed upon his inner circle how the presence of those technologically-advanced alien devices would be the centerpieces of the rise of the Third Reich. As Hitler would stockpile this advanced technology, there would be less of a need to keep the alien presence around, he thought.

As Hitler got what he wanted, he figured, he would no longer need the unreliable aliens.

These weren't outrageous requests, Hitler believed. But since Telhri wasn't giving them to Hitler, it was as if the alien leader was reading his mind of the devious plot to eventually break away from the alien influence. Unknown to Hitler, Telhri was monitoring Hitler's deceitful conversations through the communication device, which Hitler had disguised and placed strategically on the upper bookshelf in his executive office.

CHAPTER FIFTEEN

Lower Tisza Plain – Szeged, Hungary 1935

"**I** did not sign up for this shit," muttered Konrad Wolff, knee-deep in mud, mortar, and soot at an abandoned farm house in the middle of nowhere in southern Hungary. Himmler had definitely gone off the deep end with this expedition, he grumbled. For a moment, Wolff forgot the reason why he and his team were ordered to this godforsaken piece of earth.

Wolff was an Obergruppenfuhrer, a General of the Ahnenerbe branch of the SS and leader of the Institute of Scientific Research and Recovery (ISRR), one of 50 different research branches named "Institutes" within the organization. Himmler, along with two Nazi ideologists with deep pockets and deep roots in the occult, founded the Ancestral Heritage Research and Teaching Society, or Ahnenerbe Society, as a private non-profit organization commissioned to research the Aryan race and provide scientific documentation to support the Nazi dogma. Secretly, the Ahnenerbe was a part of Himmler's long-range plan for the systematic creation of a Germanic religion to replace Christianity in Germany following the war.

Regarded as a politically-motivated academic association, the group made itself attractive to scholars who wanted to join the academic elite of Nazi Germany.

Barely a year into the job, Wolff already had grave doubts about what he was doing. *"Don't ever allow yourself to be recruited in a bar when you're drunk on your ass,"* he reminded himself often. Which is exactly how Wolff got himself into his present predicament.

Konrad Wolff had been the Boy Wonder in the Department of Geosciences during graduate school at the University of Munich. Graduating at the top of his class while earning a doctoral degree in Archeological Anthropology, Wolff pretty much thought he had the world by the balls. Anything was possible. The sky was the limit.

After graduating in 1931, he accepted a post-doctoral teaching assignment within his department at the University of Munich. For the next three years, he happily taught undergrad and graduate students the many intricacies of the world of archeological anthropology. He was engaged to a wonderful girl he had met while teaching her in a graduate course.

But then his world suddenly and inexplicably collapsed. Following the tragic death of his father, he got burned out teaching, broke off the engagement when he caught his fiancé with another man, found himself wallowing in self-pity, and frequented Munich bars into the early morning hours.

He remembered clearly the night he was duped into joining the Ahnenerbe. Sitting alone at a table in Kafer Schanke, a tiny cafe and liquor store located at Prinzregentenstrasse 73, he was startled to see Professor

Walter Wűst, the dean of the University of Munich, enter the door and walk directly to his table.

Stumbling to his feet, Wolff addressed his former boss. "Good evening, Dr. Wűst," Wolff slurred, extending his hand, "What brings you to this fine dining establishment?"

Wűst shook Wolff's hand, and sat down across the table from the drunk former teacher.

"Konrad, it's good to see you," Wűst began. "How has life been treating you since you left the university?"

"Just peachy, sir," Wolff stammered. "Couldn't be better. Would you like to join me for a drink?

With a stern look, Wűst declined the offer. But he continued his conversation while Wolff yelled his repeat order to the bartender. "Sorry, sir," Wolff apologized. "You were saying…"

Wűst leaned forward in his chair and looked Wolff directly in his eyes. "Konrad, how would you like to resume your prestigious career, doing all the fieldwork you ever dreamed of doing, leading scientific expeditions all over the world, earning a hefty paycheck, and having an unlimited source of funding at your disposal?"

"Say what again, sir? Wolff stuttered. "Did you say unlimited source of funding?"

"Why, yes I did," Wűst answered. "And did I mention the hefty paycheck?"

Suddenly, Wolff was fighting to get his mind less foggy, forcing himself to sober up. "I'm interested, sir," Wolff said. "But it sounds too good to be true. What's the whole story, and not just the good part that you just told me?"

Wüst sat back in his chair, folding his arms in front of him. He then proceeded to tell Wolff the entire story.

"Are you familiar with the Ahnenerbe Society, Konrad? It is a nonprofit think tank that Heinrich Himmler is forming to draw the best academic minds in Germany into one special organization. It is a grand plan to conduct cutting-edge research to prove that the Nazi political agenda is built on solid scientific facts. I have accepted Himmler's invitation to become the executive administrator of the society, and he has instructed me to find the best and brightest of Germany's intellectual elite to join this noble cause. That's why I am here with you tonight.

"I understand that you have never been enamored with political agendas, but the society is adamant in not bringing politics into the picture. Himmler is strictly interested in scientific results. Plus, by joining the Ahnenerbe, you avoid military service because your work will be considered 'war essential.'"

"There's got to be more that you're not telling me, sir," Wolff replied. "This still sounds too good."

Wüst squirmed in his chair as Wolff continued to press him on the issue.

"You will need to wear a military uniform," Wüst whispered, knowing how Wolff would react. "But your salary will be 90,000 marks, plus you will be in charge of your own institute."

"Wear a military uniform?" Wolff screamed. "Are you shitting me? I'd rather be dead than wear a Nazi SS uniform." But the 90,000 marks sounded good, he thought.

"I knew you'd be most unhappy with the uniform request," Wüst answered. "So I pulled some strings to get you the highest rank I could. And that would be Obergrupperfuhrer. With that level of rank, you will be included on the same security level as most of Himmler's top aides. You would have access to all high-level security areas and be considered a part of the Inner Circle of Himmler himself. Now, doesn't this sound good to you?"

Without answering, Wolff leaned back in his chair to ponder the proposal that he just received from Wüst. Upside, he thought, included the salary, worldwide expeditions, being in charge of his own institute, and unlimited funding. Downside was definitely wearing the uniform, and, oh yeah, hanging around military-types.

"What institute would be under my direction?" Wolff asked, resuming the conversation.

Wüst perked up with excitement upon hearing the question. "Your responsibility would be the Institute of Scientific Research and Recovery, the ISRR. You would have under your command a secretary, a female research assistant, three non-commissioned officers, and 15 soldier/laborers."

"And where would my offices and laboratories be located? Wolff inquired.

Wüst now moved in to close the deal. "Why, the many institutes would be located around Germany, mostly in Berlin, Munich, and Hamburg However, because of the importance of your special group, Himmler has requested that you join me at the SS headquarters at Wewelsburg Castle, located between Lippstadt and Paderborn in Alma valley. Do you want to make a difference in the lives of Germany's citizens, Konrad?"

Wolff figured he could do this for a few years to embellish his work resume. And he wouldn't have to worry about being forced to enlist in the army. Moving a few hundred miles to the northwest and starting his own institute sounded especially inspiring for a guy who needed a fresh start.

Through squinting and bloodshot eyes, Wolff's world took an unexpected turn as he accepted the enticing offer from Wűst. "I accept your offer, Doctor," Wolff said while shaking hands with his former boss who suddenly became his current boss again. "When do I report?"

"In one week, Konrad. Report to the main desk at Wewelsburg. I'll be there to meet you and set everything up for you. By the way, start thinking about the scientific expeditions you want your institute to conduct."

CHAPTER SIXTEEN

*"**WHY** again am I knee deep in mud, mortar, and soot at a deserted farm in No Where, Hungary?"* Wolff kept repeating to himself. *"Oh, yes, I'm looking for the fucking Holy Grail, for Christ sake,"* he muttered. *"I can't believe I'm doing this."*

This scientific expedition, if you could call it that, continued the long list of questionable directives he received from Himmler. The very first one he was ordered to organize and complete a year ago, although a bit on the strange side, at least fell into his field of expertise. The order was to travel to Tibet to establish diplomatic relations between Nazi Germany and Tibet, and to search for documentation of a lost Aryan race hidden on a Tibetan plateau. Himmler believed that this group may be the last remnants of the original Aryan tribes, the forefathers of the German race. Himmler was also told that, supposedly, these people were endowed with supernatural powers that could help the Nazis rule the world.

Using information from local tribesmen and research he had conducted on his own, Wolff and his team was able to locate a plateau hidden among towering trees at the base of Mount Jomolhari, a part of the Great Himalayan Range on the northwest border of Tibet and Bhutan. After climbing a couple hundred feet up the west slope, Wolff noticed what looked like an aberration in the ground formation. Upon closer examination, he identified it as an ancient burial plot.

For 10 days, Wolff and his team excavated the area and recovered nearly 300 skulls and skeletons. After measuring and documenting the remains of each discovery, the bones and skulls were carefully wrapped in sturdy sackcloth and packed snugly into wooden crates to be sent back to Wewelsburg Castle for closer scientific examination.

As word got back to Himmler regarding the discovery of the skulls, he quickly sent word back to Wolff that he should also take head and body measurements from the local tribesmen and women. If he found any similarities between the measurements of the local tribesmen and the ancient remains, Himmler gave Wolff explicit orders to talk to the tribal leaders about any secret rituals or incantations that they used to conjure up powers from their ancestors. Unfortunately, Wolff found no anthropological similarities between the living and dead, so he never asked about any secret rituals or incantations.

Upon further examination of the ancient skulls and skeletons in his laboratory at Wewelsburg, Wolff concluded that the Tibetans were ancestors of Mongols and European races. No Northern Race or Aryan race. The expedition and laboratory work that lasted nearly five months had produced no scientific data to aid the Nazi cause, much to Himmler's dissatisfaction.

Himmler then gave Wolff two weeks of preparation time before he sent the ISRR team to Central America in search of a crystal skull that was reportedly found in a Mayan ruin near the city of Lubaantun in British Honduras. Wolff again was amazed by both the location of the mission and the object of importance. Central America was such a long trek to be chasing some rumors. And going to a British colony was very risky for a Nazi expeditionary group. But the possibility of procuring a skull made of crystal got his scientific juices flowing again.

Upon arrival late at night in the Central American village, Wolff's team was briefed by the local agent working undercover for the Nazis. He was informed that the skull was indeed real, but that local authorities had shipped the valuable artifact to the city of Belmopan that housed the Archaeology Museum where the icon would be under constant surveillance and protection. The museum was the resting place for 3000 years of Mayan discoveries and exhibits.

The next day, the entire group traveled to Belmopan. Masquerading as a European tour group, the Nazi interlopers visited the museum to view the objective of their trip. Wolff was in total awe of the crystal skull. It was real, and it was magnificent from a scientific and artistic point of view. His agent wasn't lying when he talked about the security surrounding the exhibit.

The skull was enclosed in a steel-enforced square glass case roughly three feet square that was fastened to a concrete base by four tamper-proof padlocks. There were also eight armed guards positioned 24 hours a day around the exhibit which was cordoned off from the public by four-foot-high steel fencing. Truth be told, you couldn't get within 10 feet of the skull.

Following a strategy discussion in their hotel room, Wolff quickly realized that the research and recovery portion of this trip was going to have to become a snatch-and-scoot mission. But who was he kidding? He had no background or experience in espionage. A few of the soldiers assigned to his team told him they were familiar with the art of breaking-and-entering. But that was it from a skills standpoint among the entire group. The local agent gave his assessment of the situation. Against his better judgment, Wolff was finally persuaded to give the desperate mission a try.

After watching guard movement and switching times for five days, it was decided that a late night invasion would have the best chance of success. A diversion would need to be executed to lure four guards away; then an armed rush would need to capture the remaining four guards. The local agent would snap the padlocks with iron clippers, and Wolff would raise the glass box, grab the crystal skull, place it in a burlap bag, and everyone would depart the way they had entered.

If the plan sounded like it was conceived by a group of amateurs, the actual event turned out even worse. In reality, the plan didn't advance past the luring part of the scheme. On the appointed night, the local police surprised the group by adding a third set of security personnel outside the museum. When the three soldiers assigned to cause a disturbance arrived at the museum, they were instantly arrested on the spot. With the first part of the plan in shambles, the rest of the group returned to the hotel to discuss how to get their comrades out of jail the next day.

While in custody, the three soldiers begged the forgiveness of their captors, saying they had been out drinking the night before and impetuously decided to come to the museum to take additional pictures as souvenirs. The young British sentries were not convinced by their tale, and took the three to the local jail to stay overnight and to face a judge the next morning.

When Wolff and the local agent arrived at the jail the next morning, they discovered that their three members had been moved to the local courthouse. They quickly found their way to the courthouse and to the room in which their men were being arraigned. Wolff took the lead in persuading the judge to allow the three men to leave with only a fine to pay. Wolff also promised that his entire group would leave the city that same day. Wanting the matter to be over, the judge agreed. Wolff paid the fines, and all of the men exited the courthouse.

Understanding they had failed the mission miserably, Wolff was happy that no one had been hurt in the scheme. Knowing they would feel the wrath of Himmler upon their return to Germany, Wolff believed that being caught in any kind of lie would meet deadly retribution from Himmler. So he did the one thing he thought most prudent: Tell Himmler the British scuttled their plot, and they escaped to fight another day. But if there was another mission to Central America, an entirely new espionage team would need to be sent. Again, Himmler was not pleased with Wolff's work.

But now Himmler had Wolff and his team on another wild goose chase: looking for the Holy Grail in Hungary. This was probably karma being enacted upon Wolff and his team for failing the crystal skull mission, Wolff thought. But goddamit, this is not what I signed up for, Wolff complained again.

For this mission, Himmler's contacts had told him the Holy Grail was supposedly buried deep under the false floorboard in the barn of this isolated farm. With rain pounding down steadily through the broken roof shingles, Wolff was watching as his team members were searching futilely for any kind of false floor boarding. They had dismantled the entire barn floor and had found nothing.

As Wolff was ready to call the mission to a close, one of his soldiers yelled that he found a padlocked box buried under four feet of dirt under one of the cow stalls. Tired and unimpressed, Wolff trudged his way through the mud to where the soldier was kneeling with the large black box positioned in front of him.

"Let's open this sonofabitch," Wolff ordered. With that, the soldier used his shovel to break off the padlock. When opened, all the members of the ISRR team sounded his version of "wow".

"Holy shit!" "Jesus Fuckin' Christ!" "God damn it!" "Can you fuckin' believe it?" One after another, the obscene phrases kept coming until everyone had his say.

In the box was not the Holy Grail; that was for sure, Wolff said. But the value had to be close to that of the Grail, he thought. What he did see was a hoard of coins, paper currency, and jewels. The coins were old, very old, Wolff deduced. Maybe thousands of years old. The currency was not German, either. Mesopotamian, possibly? Wolff would need to examine them more closely in his lab. But the jewels were what took your breath away. Rubies, sapphires, diamonds. Some connected to form necklaces and brooches. Some adorned rings. Finally, Wolff exclaimed, he didn't know why the bounty was buried there, or who it belonged to, but they finally had something to take back to Himmler.

But then bedlam broke out. Each young soldier began grabbing handfuls of the precious jewels and stuffing their pockets with the loot. "No way that bastard Himmler is going to get all of this booty," one young soldier cried. "We've been doing Himmler's dirty, crazy work for a year now. Our wages are putrid. We deserve a piece of this."

Wolff was quick to respond. "Jesus Christ, are you idiots out of your fuckin' minds? I agree all of us are most worthy of a piece of this treasure. And there certainly is enough treasure in this box to where a few pieces would not be missed. But you boys are going way overboard with what you're grabbing here.

"But listen to me. The consequences of what would happen if Himmler or Wûst discovered the real truth would be deadly for all of us. You all understand that. Simply put, we would all be executed on the spot. There would be no explanations. There would be no excuses. There would be no trials. We would be shot for cause.

"As much as I think Himmler is a lunatic with what he has been commanding us to do with our expeditions thus far, I do not want to risk our deaths, or the future of ISRR. I believe we have a lot of solid scientific work ahead of us. I will ask Wûst to raise your wages since we are delivering a treasure of enormous value to the Nazi cause. I know you're not satisfied with my reasoning right now, but I'm just thinking what's best for all of us."

Despite some grumbling, Wolff's team knew he was acting wisely as their commanding officer. Cursing loudly, each team member emptied his pockets, watching their future falling back freely into the wooden box. After viewing the treasure one last time, Wolff closed the box. They slid a long plank through the two handles on each side of the box, and four of them carried the treasure out of the barn.

Upon the team's return, Himmler and Wūst agreed that the treasure was the most awe-inspiring sight they had ever seen. Wolff's team was treated like war-time heroes by every person at SS headquarters. Wūst complied with Wolff's request for added wages for each member of his team. Wolff called in additional experts to identify the source of the coins, currency, and jewels. His initial conjectures had been correct. The final tally for the treasure chest exceeded 28 million Reichsmarks. Before Himmler personally delivered the treasure chest to impress Hitler, he removed 30 pieces of treasure and placed them in his secret vault. He wasn't going to give Hitler everything, he thought.

CHAPTER SEVENTEEN

**Vatican Garden
Spring 1936**

MONSIGNOR Paul Dante was deep in sleep when he heard the frantic knocking on his wooden apartment door. Clumsily, he arose, put on a tattered wool robe that was hanging near his bed, and while rubbing his eyes, shuffled off to see who the intruder could be this early in the morning.

"I'm so sorry to be disturbing you this early, Monsignor, but your presence has been requested immediately in the Vatican Garden."

The "intruder" was none other than Father Luigi Bellavista, the young Italian upstart priest who was trying to make a good impression on Dante while serving as his personal secretary. Cardinal Eugenio Pacelli, Dante's mentor for three years after his arrival at the Vatican four years ago, had assigned the energetic Bellavista to assist Dante in whatever way Dante needed him. Waking Dante up in the middle of the night was NOT one of those assignments, he thought.

"Well, if it's not my dear Father Loogie. Who else could it be who would wake me up from one of my best sleeping nights since I came to the Vatican?" Dante stammered after opening his locked door. "This had better be good, my friend."

Bellavista, trying to hide his dislike for the crude nickname that Dante had invented for him, quickly informed Dante that Cardinal Pacelli was personally asking for him because of some pressing Vatican business that had suddenly presented itself to the Holy Father. Because of the urgency, and because the request had come to Pacelli straight from Pope Pius XI himself, Dante knew that something important was happening. Pacelli wanted the meeting to take place in the Vatican Garden near the statue of Saint Peter.

"Go. Tell Cardinal Pacelli I'll meet him in 10 minutes." With that, Dante quickly closed the door, and returned to his bedroom.

Ten minutes later, an exhausted Dante, still buttoning his black cassock, came sprinting into the Vatican Garden where Pacelli was standing alone. In the darkness, Dante could not see the beads of sweat on the forehead of the future Pope Pius XII.

"Papa Gino, I came as quickly as I could after I got your message. What is so urgent that you've called me here in the middle of the night?"

Dante had arrived at the Vatican in the spring of 1932 to continue his studies at the Gregorian University following his ordination into the Society of Jesus. The intense, devout Pacelli, himself one of the most powerful figures in the Vatican hierarchy, had taken an instant liking to the outgoing young American after their chance meeting. Following Dante's heroic act at the Basilica that saved Pacelli's life in 1933, he quickly named himself the mentor for Dante during the remainder of his stay in Italy. "Papa Gino" was Dante's heartfelt nickname for his kind mentor, Paul's unique way of once again gaining a father figure into his life.

Pacelli had been responsible for Dante's rapid promotion to the title of Monsignor within three months following the heroic deed. The new rank held very little meaning for Dante, but Papa Gino had insisted that the added prestige was necessary for someone working as close to Pacelli as Dante was. Pacelli also used his influence to have Dante appointed as a member of the world's most exclusive Vatican fraternity, the Gentlemen of His Holiness, or Papal Gentlemen, the ceremonial ushers of the papal household. As a part of Dante's "remuneration" package for his unwanted ascension up the hierarchical ladder, Pacelli had assigned the eager Bellavista to assist Dante.

Pacelli, looking very disturbed and nervous, said, "My son, a great evil has been perpetrated against the Vatican, and His Holiness has assigned the task of righting this malicious wrong to me alone."

Dante, looking surprised, responded, "Papa Gino, what sort of malicious act has caused His Holiness so much pain?

With his voice rising in the darkness of the garden, Pacelli, slowly and methodically, stated, "We were just informed by our loyal contact in Istanbul that a deceitful act of brazen thievery has occurred at one of the Vatican's secret archives located in that city. An ancient manuscript was stolen, the contents of which, if made public, can cause not only tremendous world panic, but also the total collapse of the Catholic Church itself."

With concern in his voice, Dante exclaimed, "Jesus God Almighty, what is this document and who is responsible for this theft? Did your contact give you that information?"

Then Pacelli, calming himself with a deep breath, continued. "The document is called the Nestorian papyrus. It is one of many parts of *il libro dei segreti del papa*, the Pope's Book of Secrets. The bandits are supposedly members of a group that call themselves the Illuminati, a secret sect that has long been at odds with the Vatican."

Dante, still wanting more information, queried his friend. "I have heard stories of this group, the Illuminati. But I thought they were just rumors, and there was nothing much to it. We can discuss them later. But I need to know what is so valuable about this Nestorian papyrus that it carries the potential doom of the Church. And there really is such a thing as the Pope's Book of Secrets?"

Pacelli motioned to Dante to take a seat on a nearby stone bench. After seeing Dante comply with his request, the Camerlengo of the Roman Catholic Church eased himself down next to his young protégé.

"Sit down, my son. Because of what I need to ask you to do, which is most dangerous and may cost you your life, I feel it is only fair that I tell you some of the most guarded information in the Vatican. This information is known only at the highest levels, meaning only His Holiness, and a few of his inner circle. I am one of those individuals. And this information is most embarrassing to divulge."

CHAPTER EIGHTEEN

Hagia Sophia Museum – Istanbul, Turkey
1936

IT couldn't have worked more perfectly for the two Illuminati thieves. The plan for the heist, a major quest within the secret society for centuries, was conceptualized two years earlier when Turkish President Mustafa Kemal Atatürk announced that the glorious mosque of Hagia Sophia would begin renovation work in 1935 to convert it into a museum. Once considered the most beautiful Christian Church in the world, it served as a Roman Catholic cathedral during the Latin occupation of Constantinople from 1204-1261. The Byzantines recaptured the city in 1261 until the Turks conquered Constantinople in 1453, converting the church into a mosque.

Damaged over millennia by earthquakes, the building had been restored and repaired on numerous occasions by Ottoman architects. The most extensive work had been performed in the 16th century by Mimar Sinan, considered one of the most famous architects in history. He was responsible for adding structural supports to the exterior of the building, replacing the old minarets, and adding Islamic pulpits and art.

Sitting majestically atop the hill at the tip of the historic peninsula, surrounded by the waters of the Sea of Marmara, the Bosphorus, and the Golden Horn, this massive structure was both an architectural wonder and the secret repository of the most controversial historical religious document ever discovered. Every pope since Stephen III in 754 A.D. knew of its existence. The Illuminati became aware of its existence in 1710. And almost by accident, the secret organization discovered the true LOCATION of the document only 10 years ago. But every attempt to steal it had been thwarted or botched over the years. Until now.

The Nestorian papyrus, as it was known within archeological circles, carried with it a reputation of mythical proportions. Was it real? Was it a hoax? Was it really written by Jesus himself? Did it prove Jesus was not the Son of God? It all seemed much too fantastic to interested academics, and much too ridiculous to religious leaders. But to the Illuminati, the discovery and theft of such a document would prove to be the ultimate downfall for the group's hated rival, the Roman Catholic Church.

It was so simple for the Illuminati to plant a mole within the organizational team responsible for the conversion of the mosque into a museum. The logistics of such a project was overwhelming to the common man. A working group of almost 2,500 people were needed to complete the huge task. To say there would be controlled chaos during the actual process was an understatement. Using chaos, incompetence, and the huge number of people involved during the conversion as the diversion tactic, the Illuminati leaders picked their most accomplished thieves and chose the exact moment to swipe the precious artifact.

To art historians, the architecture of Hagia Sophia was wondrous. Built on a northwest-southeast axis, one entered from the northwest through an outer and inner narthex. Once a visitor entered the inner narthex, he realized it was twice the size of the outer narthex. Passages attached to both ends of the inner narthex gave access to the gallery. The entryway to the southwest served as the ceremonial entrance for emperors. A pair of ornate bronze doors welcomed the royal visitors.

Nine doors lead from the inner narthex into the nave. The nave measured roughly 74 meters long and 70 meters wide. A stately dome rose 56 meters above the floor. To the northwest and southeast, semi-domes were spaced evenly around the majestic dome. The combination of the central dome and semi-domes was unprecedented at the time of the church's construction. Flying buttresses were added to the northwest facade around the 9th century.

Marble panels formed the floor of the nave, with porphyry and verde antico columns dotting each aisle. Decorative cornices separated the aisle, gallery, and clerestory levels and helped add lateral support to the structure. Finally, wrought iron chandeliers, stained glass windows, famous mosaics, frescoes, and imperial portraits were the final pieces of the restoration projects over the centuries.

The basement level of the building, however, was the main reason why Atatürk recommended the conversion to a museum. The aged, dusty floors were lined with majestic pieces of statuary from centuries past. Elegant cobwebbed paintings from some of history's most accomplished artists dotted the walls and overflowed the bulging storage bins. This magnificent assembly of the world's greatest art treasures had been estimated to be worth tens of millions of dollars. But it did no good just lying unnoticed and gathering dust, Atatürk thought. The world deserved to experience these treasures.

As much as the main floor dazzled its visitors over the centuries, the floors below the basement were meant to bewilder and confuse anyone foolish enough to enter this domain. To descend to this secret level, one needed to lift and remove a five-foot square piece of heavy marble flooring located in a deserted storeroom in the southeast corner of the basement. Climbing down an eight-foot wooden ladder brought the individual into a stuffy, darkened ten-foot-square chamber.

After lighting two oil torches that were attached to the stone walls nearby, an explorer instantly noticed two four-foot wide dirt corridors with five-foot high mahogany ceilings snaking in opposite directions through the lower floor. Walking down either corridor presented him with locked wooden chamber doors appearing magically around each dark corner. There were nearly 50 such chambers spaced evenly throughout the lower floor.

The location of the Nestorian papyrus was even more secluded and camouflaged. Over the centuries, the mythical religious artifact was moved deeper and deeper within the bowels of the church by members of a select group of protectors called Watchers. It was the responsibility of the Watchers to make sure the artifact was never found. During the three major renovations of the church that took place over the millennia following earthquake damage, sub-chambers were cut out of the floors of the subterranean rooms. These sub-chambers were protected by false floors and booby-trapped walls. If an intruder didn't know where he was going, he ended up dead.

Through intense research, bribery, and guile over the past decade, the Illuminati finally were able to pinpoint the exact location of the papyrus. But they knew that many lives would be lost in order to secure the document. Each unsuccessful foray to steal the artifact in the past had left behind one or two dead bodies. The Watchers would leave the corpses as a reminder to future robbers, but would quickly move the papyrus to another location deeper beneath the church. But with the confusion surrounding the renovation of the church into a museum, the watchers became temporarily distracted with all the activity taking place in the church basement and beyond. For just a few hours, there was an open window of opportunity for the brazen group of Illuminati thieves.

CHAPTER NINETEEN

THE cloudless azure sky and abundant sunshine made this day in Istanbul one for the gods. The busy workers were making excellent progress converting the mosque of Hagia Sophia into a world-class museum. Now only weeks away, thousands of volunteers were laboring around the clock to meet the June 1936 deadline for the opening of Europe's newest and most magnificent art and history museum. The physical activity was frantic in most areas of the church, particularly upstairs on the main floor. Ninety feet below the basement, more frantic activity was taking place.

Around mid-morning on this glorious day, five bearded men, one in his late forties and the others in their early thirties, had nonchalantly left their designated work stations and weaved their way to an abandoned storage room in the southeast corner of the basement. The room had been one of the first to be emptied of its contents during the renovation. All that remained were empty wooden bins that were discreetly placed around one special piece of flooring. No regular workers were within fifty yards of the abandoned room.

Once there, the men quickly removed the large marble flooring that would give them access to the secret, deserted chambers below. The final man through the opening returned the displaced flooring to its original position. At the bottom of the ladder, the two oil torches were lit, and the older man pulled out his map that would lead the group to their glorious place in Illuminati history. Taking a few minutes to acclimate themselves to the dark, musty environment and to warn each other of traps and pitfalls along the way, they quickly grabbed the torches and dashed down the corridor to the left. Time was of the essence.

The five-foot ceilings caused each man to slump slightly as they rushed down the dirt corridor toward their first destination. As they dashed by each unopened wooden door, they yelled out the number before moving on to the next door. Following the twenty-second door, the group slowed as they reached chamber door number twenty-three. This was their first stop. The leader pried open the ancient wooden door with a steel tool bar each man had brought along for such purposes.

As the first man rushed through the open door, there was a scream, and he suddenly disappeared from view. The second man through lowered his torch to see his comrade desperately clinging to a piece of the floor that had collapsed under his feet. The second and third man through quickly grabbed each arm and pulled the frightened trespasser to his feet. Once all were safely inside the room, the group gathered around the map once again, but not before the old man lectured his young assistants to be more alert to danger.

Through the flickering light, this room, barely large enough to contain the five criminals, was supposed to possess a secret opening that would take the group to yet another lower level. Quickly pounding on floor and wall boards, one man finally heard a shallow thud on the lower right wall. Two of the men hammered the wall with their steel bars until the wooden boards collapsed outward, revealing another opening with another wooden ladder leading into the blackness below.

Slowly entering the opening, each man cautiously grabbed the ladder and began a descent that seemed to travel into endless darkness. Roughly fifteen feet down, there was a slight cracking sound as the group scurried down the ladder. Then it happened. The second man down started falling into black space as the ladder rung shattered on contact with the weight of his body. Yelling and clutching futilely to the sides of the ladder, it was only a split second before his feet collided with the head of the man below him, and both men and one torch light were sent hurtling downward into the black abyss, their deathly screams fading away from the remaining three climbers. It was not difficult for the others to hear the ghastly thump as the two bodies ended their terrorizing freefall at the bottom of the dark chasm.

It took another five minutes for the remaining Illuminati to harmlessly reach the end of their descent. This ladder had taken the interlopers 40 feet deeper from the room above. It had also taken two lives without remorse. Ironically, the torch was still burning, surviving the 25-foot drop. When the three anxious men finally touched ground, the glow from the fallen torch displayed a grizzly scene. The stench of death was overwhelming. There was a pile of dead bodies, one atop another. Joining their two dead comrades in this frightful burial heap were three fully-clothed skeletons, a prophetic reminder of past failed Illuminati attempts to snatch the mythical papyrus. The layout of the bodies seemed to indicate each died in the exact same way, a long fall from above. Over the centuries, the Watchers simply replaced the same broken rung with a slightly cracked one. The results were identical each time.

It didn't take long for the shock to wear off from the sudden demise of their associates. Grabbing the second torch, the three men quickly discovered they were in a circular chamber that seemed to be cut out of solid rock. Each man also shivered simultaneously, as the air in the chamber was not only colder, but their situation seemed to have hit a dead end. The two younger men gave their older leader a look of futility and loudly cursed their predicament.

The Illuminati leader ignored the disgruntled shouts, and pulled the map from his coat pocket. "We're getting close, my friends," he smiled as he focused the torch light on the map. "We need to look for a piece of rock that has the mark of a cross on it."

To give themselves more room to examine the walls of the deathly stone chamber, the men carefully moved the remains of the dead Illuminati to the middle of the room, laying them side by side. The color of the stone in the chamber was reddish beige, the result of oxidization and heat pressure from past earthquakes and tremors. The glow reflecting off the red walls and dead bodies gave an impression that the mercenaries were working close to the gates of Hell. It also seemed ironic for them to be looking for a religious symbol so close to Satan's boundaries.

For nearly 45 minutes, they painstakingly examined every inch of the chamber, from top to bottom. With the torches gradually running out of oil to keep them burning, a sense of panic and urgency fell over the group. They needed to find that cross immediately, or this mission would fail just like the others.

As the tired leader leaned against the wall, he once again focused his attention on a small section of the wall next to him. Rubbing his eyes trying to bring more clarity to his vision, he noticed a marking that looked more like an X instead of a cross. Better than nothing, he thought to himself. Crouching down to get a closer look, he felt the stone where the X figure appeared. The stone lines had indentations in them, something you wouldn't notice from a standing position. He put the fingers of his right hand into the indentations and pushed. Immediately, there was a creaking sound from across the chamber. A piece of the wall was now slowly opening, revealing a dark passageway beyond.

The two younger men gasped in amazement as the great stone wall was presenting an opening to the wayward villains. As the younger men eagerly rushed to enter the new passageway, the leader shouted to them to wait while he again studied the map.

"The map indicates that the passageway runs about 30 feet ahead of us, and then comes to an opening containing two ladders. One ladder keeps us on the correct route, and one will take us to our death," he said. "The map doesn't indicate which one to use after we get there. Hopefully, we choose the correct one."

The three men walked to the opening and shined their torches into the black corridor that awaited them. Seeing no obstacles, they slowly stepped through the stone door and began counting out their paces to reach the next set of ladders. Upon arrival, they found, to their astonishment, that the two ladders did not go down, they were HORIZONTAL, and they went in opposite directions. The ladders now became the actual footpaths to continue the journey.

"God damn it," growled the old man. "Those frickin' Watchers. That goddamn Catholic Church. But I will defeat you today. Your God will not stop me." He was shouting and shaking his two fists in the air. The younger two just stared at their leader, stunned at the misfortune they kept finding along the route.

"Which way?" one man asked the leader. "Which way is the safe way?"

"Let me look at the map again," answered the old man, "Maybe there's a clue that I overlooked."

With one torch ready to extinguish itself, the leader pulled the map from his coat pocket and extended the flame to as near to the map as possible without burning it. He searched the map for any indication on which ladder to follow. Which way, he kept asking himself. Finally, he noticed that, beyond these ladders, the path would turn to the left.

"This one," he said, pointing to the ladder to the left. "This is the correct way to proceed."

"How do you know for sure?" the other man asked. "We are blind in either direction."

"The map seems to point in that direction," the leader growled in reply. "We're losing time and our one torch is ready to go out. Just do as I say. Let's get on with it."

He motioned to the man closest to the left-side horizontal ladder to begin the adventure that would mean either success or failure at this juncture of the quest. The man got down on his hands and knees, wedged the torch tightly under his left armpit to light the way, and grudgingly crawled a few feet out from the side before suddenly stopping. Without saying a word, he turned around to notice the other two men had also gotten down to their crawling position and were waiting for him to continue. Despite the tension tightening in his hands, neck, legs, and back, he pushed on.

The horizontal ladder started swaying slightly from left to right when the full weight of the three men was upon it. Inch by inch, the group moved farther away from the safety of solid ground. Sweat poured down the face of each man despite the cool temperatures in the cavern. From a distance, the slow movement of the men teamed with the two glowing torches made for a very unusual sight. It seemed as if some magic yellow lights were dancing eerily against a sheet of solid nothingness. To the crawlers, it was nothing less than sheer terror.

And then it happened. The lead torch bearer was so self-conscious of his precipitous predicament that he didn't notice that the flame was growing exceedingly dimmer as they moved along the unstable ladder-path. Then there was a shout. Startled, all three men stopped in their tracks.

"My torch is out," the lead crawler yelled. "But I think I see ground just up ahead."

The old man, positioned directly behind the talker, spoke in a subdued tone. "Drop that torch and keep moving. I can see we're only a few feet away from the landing."

Cautiously, the three men quickened the pace to reach the end of the ladder. After all three were safely on solid ground again, they turned to surmise how far they had crawled along the horizontal ladder. Lifting the remaining torch and extending it over the ladder, they were amazed to discover that they had only moved about 10 meters from their last starting point.

"At least we know how far it is when we return," the leader stated. "Let's see where we need to go now."

He again pulled the map from his coat pocket and the new torch bearer gave him some fresh light. "The map says we're 20 meters from a door along this path. Inside that door, my fortunate friends, is the papyrus. Let's get that cursed artifact and return with haste."

Leading the way, the new torch bearer started running toward his destination, with the two others in quick pursuit. In less than a minute, the three Illuminati thieves were standing directly in front of the door at the end of their journey. A small Knights Templar white cross was painted on the dusty wood panels.

"This is it. Open that damn door now," the old man grumbled. "But keep your eyes open."

His young associate hastily complied with the order. With one powerful kick, the shattered door swung open. Before the three men could rush into the room, three arrows came zooming from out of the darkness, aimed squarely for the heart of each intruder. Screaming in fear, the three men dived to their left, the arrows narrowly missing their intended targets.

"Those Watchers are creative bastards. I'll give them that much," sighed one of the young men. "But we outsmarted them this time."

Getting to their feet and gaining their composure, the three exhausted, but excited men moved slowly into the room. Once inside, the torch bearer waved the fire in a circular motion to examine the layout of the room. Seven meters directly in front of the door frame stood a makeshift platform that housed three upright bows, with a trip wire attached to a lever connected with the doorknob on the inside. The two younger men moved closer to examine the contraption that almost cost them their lives. The old man's attention went elsewhere.

"You see how this thing was constructed?" one of the young men asked. "It's pretty ingenious, if you ask me. It looks like the trip wire was on a little delay mechanism. If the door had been opened more slowly, all three of us would have been in the doorway when the arrows were released. I think by kicking in the door, the delay mechanism got messed up, and the arrows fired too early."

"Yeah, thank God for brute force," laughed his partner in crime.

Their short conversation was interrupted by the leader. "Bring the light over here. Check out the corners of the room. That book is somewhere in here. I'm sure of it."

It didn't take long to discover an old wooden chest in the far left corner of the room. The three men walked to its location. It can't be this easy, the old man thought. They wouldn't make it this easy after what we've gone through to get here.

The three men examined the box more closely. It measured about two meters across and one meter high. It wasn't made of wood, but bamboo. The lid needed to be lifted off. "Open it," the leader ordered. The torch bearer lowered the flame to light up the working area.

As the leader stood by watching, the other younger man slowly lifted the lid from the box. No sooner had the lid been removed than a King cobra reared up into the man's face, poised to bite the person who had disturbed its quiet, dark resting place. Terrified, the man shrieked and quickly took two steps back.

The snake hurled itself into the air, targeting the landing spot somewhere on the man's body. Still holding the lid in his hands, he used it as a shield against the soaring reptile. The snake hit the lid and fell harmlessly to the ground. Reacting quickly, the other two took out their steel bars and beat the snake into submission. Once dead, the leader kicked the snake out of the torch light and into the darkness of the far side of the room.

"Son of a bitch. Don't these guys ever give up?" the young man asked no one in particular. "There's probably another one around here somewhere."

The leader quickly refocused everyone's attention to the box. "Get that light over here to look into the box," he stated.

As the light was placed over the box, they looked inside, and all responded with a collective "shit." The bamboo box was empty. Angrily, the old man kicked the box away, and put his hands over his face in disgust. But his grief was quickly softened by what he heard next.

"There's a piece of floorboard underneath the box," the torch bearer cried out.

The old man stood aside as the young men pushed away the dirt from the covering. When the wooden floorboard was completely cleared, the three Illuminati again saw a white Knights Templar cross painted on the panels. "I'm sure we've found it," cried the leader.

Using their steel pipes to remove the second painted panel, they quickly noted the presence of yet another smaller bamboo box inside the hole in the ground. Swearing they wouldn't be fooled again, they prepared for the worst as they began lifting the smaller bamboo lid. And they weren't disappointed.

Lying inside on top of the contents of the box was a saw-scaled viper, the deadliest snake known to man. It didn't move, and initially looked asleep. In the blink of an eye, the snake moved into attack mode. Before it could react, the three men mercilessly drove their steel pipes through the head and body of the snake, killing it instantly. The leader picked up the remains and again tossed them into the far dark corner of the room. All three took a deep breath to calm their nerves.

Putting the flame close to the floor opening, the leader looked inside to see what the Illuminati had been dying to claim for millennia. What he saw didn't take his breath away. In fact, there was nothing special about it. It looked like a common leather pouch of some sort.

"Take it out, and give it to me," the leader told his young assistant. The young man lowered his hands into the hole, brought out the package, and handed it to the old man.

"Let's see what makes this thing so special," the torch bearer said.

The black leather pouch was bound with two leather strings, one wrapped vertically and one horizontally, connecting in a knot at the center. Untying the knot and removing the leather strings, the leader opened the container, pulled out the contents, and handed the empty pouch to his associate.

In his hands was a short pile of aged, but remarkably well-preserved papyrus sheets. He recognized the language as Hebrew. He read the first sentence, and his eyes opened in wonder. "I, Jesus of Nazareth, am writing this account forty years after my crucifixion…"

The old man smiled as his body shivered with delight. He quickly returned the sheets to the pouch, tied it as he found it, and dropped the valuable packet into an old burlap sack that he brought along just for this purpose.

"What did it say?" asked the torch bearer.

"Yes, was it worth all the bloodshed today and through the years?" asked the other thief.

Without giving an answer to either question, the old man simply said they had successfully completed their mission and it was time to leave. As the torch bearer began to make his way to the doorway with the leader closely behind, they both heard a deathly scream from their comrade.

Turning quickly, they saw the young man sprawled on the ground, crying out in pain and holding his left ankle. What they saw next made them gasp in horror. Still attached to the man's left arm were the poisonous fangs of a Malayan krait that had been lying in wait in the shadows, ready to spring at the last man out the door. The covert attack had caught his prey unaware. There would only be two men returning from this mission.

"We've got to leave now," yelled the old man. "He's dead where he lays. The venom takes effect immediately. He won't suffer long."

With that, the two men raced from the room and retraced their route until they reached the piece of flooring in the basement of the church. Their journey had lasted three hours, and they had lost three men. The Watchers may have taken their pound of flesh, the old man, thought, but it didn't disrupt their success. With the proof that would guarantee the demise of the hated Roman Catholic Church securely in their possession, the two remaining Illuminati thieves quickly melded into the massive group of renovation workers and walked out of the church into the bright Turkish sun. It couldn't have worked out more perfectly.

CHAPTER TWENTY

**Berlin, Germany
Summer 1936**

IT was a rare moment for Wolff's ISRR team. Instead of being half way across the world chasing after another ancient artifact that Himmler thought contained occult power that would help the Nazis become world rulers, the entire team was nestled comfortably in a private dining room in the back of the Steigenberger Hotel in downtown Berlin. The hotel was built only a few years ago, and was the most elegant of Berlin's lodges. The cuisine was also considered the best in the capital city.

They were celebrating the end of the summer Olympic Games that had been hosted in Berlin at the newly-built Deutsches Stadion. The Olympic torch, carried by 3,000 relay runners from Olympia in Greece to the main stadium and which had burned brightly throughout the event, was extinguished only a few hours ago, signaling the end of the Games. The torch run, an innovation created by the German Olympic Organizing Committee during preparations for the event, was seen as a symbolic act linking past and present Olympiads.

The two-week world athletic extravaganza was a crowning triumph for Hitler and his propaganda machine. When Berlin received the official bid in 1931 to host the 1936 Summer Olympiad, Hitler made sure that the spectacle would be a gigantic Nazi showpiece to the world. He directed that $25 million be spent on constructing the finest facilities, providing the cleanest streets, and assisting in the temporary disappearance of any state-run anti-Jewish campaigns.

He made sure there were more Nazi swastikas than Olympic flags waving in the stadium. Even though Germany led the gold medal count with 33 compared to the United States count of 24, most were in the more esoteric events such as horse-riding, gymnastics, and rowing. However, that didn't stop Hitler from proclaiming each German success as a victory for the master race.

"We showed them damn Yanks who the best athletes in the world were," slurred one of Wolff's young captains, standing and raising his beer stein high above his head in recognition of Germany's 89 total medals topping the American total of 56. "Except for that black bastard Owens. Nobody could catch that sonofabitch."

He was talking about Jesse Owens, a black sharecropper's son from Alabama who won three individual gold medals and added a fourth in the 400-meter relay. Hitler had made it a point to leave the stadium before Owens received his recognition at the medals ceremonies. Owens was living proof that shattered the Nazi theory that the black races were inferior to the Aryans. And Hitler despised him for it.

The evening at the hotel was proceeding splendidly according to Wolff's plan. The food and drink had been plentiful and satisfying, and the soft lighting and soothing distant melody provided by the engaging hotel orchestra in the upstairs ballroom combined for an intimate setting. Wolff thought it was the perfect time and place to begin his quest to romance Olga, his newest young buxom blonde research assistant.

Wolff dismissed his rowdy group of soldiers and junior officers so that he and Olga would find themselves alone in the secluded dining facility. After the men shuffled out of the room, Wolff and Olga took their glasses of cognac and left their dining table for the velvet-covered couch located in front of a fireplace at the far end of the room. Even though it was a summer evening outside, the kitchen manager still kept a gentle flame flickering in the fireplace.

"You look ravishing tonight," Wolff whispered, allowing his eyes to fall from Olga's cherubic face to the abundant cleavage exposed from her low-cut black and red dinner gown.

"Thank you, General," Olga responded. "I'm glad you like my dress."

"You can call me Konrad tonight," Wolff continued. "We don't need all the formalities like we have to follow in the office." He moved closer to her, and put his left arm around her shoulder.

Olga snuggled closer to Wolff, and their lips were ready to meet in a passionate kiss when a sudden movement and voice from outside the room interrupted their path to ecstasy.

"Oops, sorry to interrupt your almost-lucky moment, Wolff," quipped Captain Hardinger, Himmler's assistant chief of staff, as he entered the room. From the very beginning of their association at the Castle, Hardinger never addressed

Wolff by rank, believing that Wolff's rank of General was not only absurd, but a disgrace to the Nazi uniform. He thought the best way to denigrate Wolff would be to call him by his last name only. Wolff hated Hardinger for the lack of respect.

"What do you want Hardinger?" Wolff snapped. He removed his arm from Olga's shoulder and sat back on the couch. "This had better be good, for your sake."

Hardinger only laughed at Wolff's insinuated threat. "You've been given a new directive from our fearless leader. From our contact in Istanbul, we've learned that a valuable religious artifact has been stolen from a secret Papal archive located in one of the city's churches. A group that calls themselves the Illuminati supposedly pulled off this heist.

"Since it's an important document to the Pope and Catholic Church, Hitler wants you to find the document and deliver it personally to him. He wants to have some kind of leverage over the Pope, and having this artifact in his possession supposedly will give him that."

Wolff had been listening to Hardinger's long-winded speech, and was trying to ignore the dwarfish messenger's annoyingly high-pitched voice.

"So what am I looking for exactly?" Wolff interrupted. "What is this valuable artifact, another one of those energy-charged things that will make Hitler into a god?" Wolff smiled at his own insubordination.

"The thing is an ancient manuscript called the Nestorian papyrus," Hardinger interjected. "According to legend, Jesus jwrote the thing himself almost 40 years AFTER his crucifixion. So this is a huge assignment for you and your R & R boys. Don't screw this one up, too, like your other failures,

Wolff. You ship out early tomorrow morning. Better get your ass moving."

With his final words, Hardinger rushed from the room. Wolff and Olga looked at each other with sad eyes. No words were spoken as the two arose from the couch and walked out of the room.

CHAPTER TWENTY ONE

Istanbul, Turkey

"**AW,** piss on it, Paul," replied Brother Geno Ferrelli to Paul Dante's repeated sarcastic pleas to Ferrelli to stop flirting with the barmaid. Dante loved to antagonize his seminary buddy just to hear his crude response. This was their little insider repartee that started when they began their novitiate studies in Missouri. That seemed like a lifetime ago for both Jesuits. They were now sitting in the shadows in the back room of a decrepit café in the heart of Istanbul with the Vatican's local sworn agent, who happened to be the Watcher in charge of protecting the invaluable Papal artifact.

When Papa Gino directed Dante to pursue the Illuminati thieves and retrieve the stolen Nestorian papyrus, he told him all Vatican resources were at his disposal. He also told Dante that he could fill his team with whomever he wanted, as long as they were all Catholics, in addition, of course, to Father Loogie. Dante wasn't thrilled that he had to include Bellavista on his recovery team. But he wasn't about to disobey Papa Gino's directive. So he was going to have to live with Loogie's presence. Papa Gino wanted him around Dante for some reason. Dante was dumbfounded as to the reason why.

When Dante returned to his room after his nocturnal meeting with Papa Gino, he quickly began to formulate a plan and to think about the team members he would need. He knew he needed someone with a background in covert operations, possibly someone with military experience in undercover search and seizure operations. He needed a pilot. He needed a weapons expert. He needed a translator. He needed someone familiar with the area they would be searching. He could pick up a guide once they reached Istanbul, he thought. He also needed someone with knowledge of this Illuminati group.

Ferrelli was the first person he contacted. Before accepting Paul's invitation to join the most secret team within the most secret organization in the world, Brother Ferrelli had been head of discipline for six years at a Catholic boy's high school in an underserved part of south Cleveland. A former Navy pilot during World War I, the six-foot airman had been convalescing in an American field hospital in France from an injury when a fast-talking Irish Catholic chaplain from New York recruited him to join the Jesuit order. Told him it was all set up, and all he had to do was report to this isolated, camouflaged location in the boondocks outside Saint Louis, Missouri. That's where he met Dante, and the rest was history.

For the covert operative for the group, Dante chose Father Jimmy McPherrin. He found him in the same place he had last seen him: The library at Gregorian University. A former soldier like Dante, six-foot-four, 220-pound "Jimmy Mac" had specialized in covert operations in Europe during the First World War. Adept at bomb-making skills and also having the uncanny ability to infiltrate an enemy location, McPherrin had met Dante while completing post-graduate work at the

Gregorian University in Rome. Before being transferred to covert operations, he had entered the war as a member of "*The Fighting* 69th" New York National Guard Regiment. He told Dante he had been recruited to the Jesuits by his regiment's Catholic chaplain, Father Francis Duffy. Dante had laughed heartily when he heard Duffy's name during the conversation.

Dante had little trouble finding his weapons expert. All he needed to do was call home. Upon being ordained into the Jesuit order, Father George Ramirez had been given his first official assignment back in his hometown of Omaha, Nebraska, that being assistant chaplain at Saint Joseph's Hospital in downtown Omaha. Three years younger than Paul, Ramirez had attended South High School, and like Dante, had been recruited into the Marines by Sergeant Gomez. He built a solid reputation as a weapons expert during World War One. On his trip back to the States from Europe following his honorable discharge, Ramirez had sat next to a priest from New York who sold him on the glamorous life as a Jesuit priest. George and Dante had built a strong relationship over the years utilizing all the commonalities that surrounded them. Dante found him with one phone call, and he explained his need for George's skills. After Ramirez agreed to join the group, Paul's next phone call to Pacelli had Ramirez on his way to Rome.

"How in the hell did this happen again?" Dante questioned the Watcher. Dante and his team had just returned with the Watcher from a trip to the underground vaults and passageways below the museum of Hagia Sophia. Paul needed to see for himself what kind of effort was needed to accomplish the theft. He was impressed with all the precautions and traps that the Watchers had devised over the centuries to keep the sacred manuscript untouchable. However, he was more impressed with the relentless pursuit the Illuminati had displayed in this criminal act against the Vatican. During the underground trip, he instantly recognized that loss of life was not a big factor to the Illuminati; that in fact, it was expected.

"Monsignor Dante, I am so sorry this terrible act has taken place," lamented Aji Ralabi, the head Watcher for the past 15 years. Enouncing his English words slowly to be understood by the group, he continued his mea culpa.

"I have truly failed His Holiness. Our group of Watchers has safely guarded the manuscript with our lives for almost 1,200 years. We learned the Illuminati discovered the existence of the artifact in the early 1700s. We were not aware that they knew about Istanbul. And we had absolutely no knowledge that they actually knew the exact location below Hagia Sophia.

"No one in our group would ever confess this location, under any condition. We would die instead. The information must have come from an insider, possibly even at the Vatican. There is no other explanation."

Dante finished listening to Aji's difficult interpretation of his story, and took another sip of his warm beer. He actually felt sorry for the guy. The group of Illuminati may have found a sympathizer within the walls of the Vatican over the centuries. But discovering the leak wasn't the mission. Recovery of the manuscript was the mission.

"First of all, Aji, don't call me Monsignor, or any kind of religious name," Dante stated. "We don't need anyone putting names and titles together during this job. It's not safe to any of us, and it's certainly not safe for the Vatican. Just call me Paul, like everyone else. Except you, Loogie. You can call me Boss." Bellavista bravely nodded his acceptance of the order, while Ferrelli, Jimmy Mac, and Ramirez smiled and shook their heads in mock derision.

"It's getting late. We've done enough for today," Dante said. "Let's get some sleep and meet at Aji's house early tomorrow morning. There we will examine all the resources we have and determine our plan to find the thieving Illuminati bastards and get the manuscript back before it falls into another enemy's hands."

While everyone began to rise from their chairs, Dante overheard Bellavista talking to Aji in his native language. "Loogie, are you talking to Aji in Turkish?" Dante asked.

A startled Bellavista responded, "Yes, Monsignor. Uh, I mean Boss. I was only telling Aji that I would be more than happy to assist him with the idiosyncrasies of the English language and the new phonetic variant that the Turkish Language Association initiated in 1928."

Dante inquired further. "And what phonetic variant would that be?"

"The Latin alphabet, Boss," Bellavista answered. "In 1928, one of President Atatürk's first reforms in the early years of the Republic of Turkey was replacing the Ottoman script with a phonetic variation of the Latin alphabet. The Turkish Language Association was trying to westernize the language by removing Persian and Arabic loanwords in favor of native variants and coinages from Turkic roots. It may all sound quite confusing to you, but actually Aji is doing quite well with his adaptations."

Dante had trouble comprehending Bellavista's mini diatribe. But he continued to probe his young ass kisser. "Just how many languages do you know, Loogie?"

"Nine, Boss. English, Latin, Turkish, German, Italian, Russian, Polish, Spanish, and French," Bellavista rattled off in quick succession.

After hearing the impressive list, Dante now realized why Papa Gino insisted on Loogie being a part of his team. Wherever the group may find themselves anywhere in the world, it's a good chance that Loogie would be able to speak and interpret the local language. *"I guess I just found my interpreter,"* Dante thought to himself.

Sunset was rapidly approaching as Dante and his team exited the café via a back entrance, and followed the winding alleys until they came to the intersection of the main street in downtown Istanbul. As Dante and his weary team walked slowly toward their hotel located a block away, his attention strayed to the other side of the street. He noticed another group of men, larger in number than his, all dressed as local residents, walking in the opposite direction. For an instant, Dante locked eyes with the man at the front of the group.

As the distance between the two groups widened and the sunlight quickly disappeared behind a horizon of tall buildings, Wolff casually looked over his shoulder to take a second look at another group of outsiders that looked like they had a secret reason for being there, too.

CHAPTER TWENTY TWO

"JESUS Christ, Loogie, can you please hurry the hell up," Dante yelled at his young interpreter. After a restless night of sleep in their Istanbul hotel, Dante and his covert Vatican recovery team were hastily finishing their packing for the trip ahead of them. It was a few hours before dawn, but Father Luigi was not moving as quickly as Dante wanted.

"Come on, Loogie. You're holding up the show here," Dante exclaimed. "Remember, Aji is picking us up to take us to the plane. Hell, you don't have anything to pack. What is taking you so goddamn long?"

"Well, you know, boss, our trip could take us to several countries," Loogie began. "So I'm just packing additional maps of cities and topographical maps of the terrain. Plus, I'm making sure I'm updated with the current language of the area we'll be traversing. You always want us taking care of the 'little details,' and these are what I consider to be the "little details" that are very important to our cause."

Dante just shook his head. But in his mind, he knew Loogie was correct in his thinking. He was actually proud that the little kiss-ass was listening to him as he addressed the group the previous day.

Dante was now moving room to room to quicken the pace of the group's departure from the hotel. Since Geno, Jimmy Mac, and George were all ex-military, they were familiar with quick exit strategy. He poked his head in Geno's room first.

"Geno, we ready to go?" Dante asked. Ferrelli answered in the affirmative.

"Yeah, Paul, I'm all packed and ready to go. I can't wait to get to the plane and into the cockpit again. I can't fucking believe the Pope actually bought that thing for us."

"That thing" was a Douglas DC-3 DST, the newest American fixed-wing propeller-driven airliner manufactured by the Douglas Aircraft Company that had just come off the assembly line less than a year ago. The "DST" part of the designation was for Douglas Sleeper Transport, meaning that the plane contained seats and sleeping berths, which was the perfect combination for travelers like Dante and his team.

The transaction had happened quickly. When Ferrelli had jokingly recommended to Paul the most dynamic and expensive plane on the market, Paul added it to his list of primary supplies he gave to Pacelli. After that, all it took was a papal directive from Pacelli delivered to Amleto Giovanni Cicognani, the Vatican Apostolic Delegate to America, who personally contacted Donald Douglas himself about the purchase. Priced at $79,500, the Vatican didn't blink when informed of the cost. *There is no price too great to pay when the survival of the Church is at stake*, the Pope had told Pacelli. When Pacelli had informed Dante that ALL Vatican resources were at his disposal, he didn't think it came with carte blanche on expenses. But he was happy it did.

Jimmy Mac met Dante in the hallway with his duffel bag over his shoulder. "All ready to go here, Paul," Jimmy told Dante.

"You got everything you need, Jimmy?" Dante asked, continuing his questioning before Jimmy could answer. "Geez, Jimmy, we're carrying a boatload of explosives with us on that plane. Is the shit safe on the plane with us?"

Jimmy just laughed. "Yeah, Paul, it's all safe. Then he hesitated and thought for a moment before he said, "Unless we crash. Then everything blows. Oh yeah, and if we get shot out of the air, that would make the shit go off, too."

He smiled as he continued. "Man, I can't believe how easily the Vatican got their hands on some of this stuff. I mean, a lot of this was simply from post-war inventories, like the black powder, EC Powder, the dynamite, and TNT. Easy to find. Easy to get. But the penthrite, picric acid, mercury fulminate, and lead azide? Man, those are not easy to find. But the Vatican seems to have their ways of getting things, don't they?"

As Jimmy Mac strode away from Paul down the hallway, Dante stopped into Ramirez's room, just in time to see George pack the final assortment of guns into his bag. "You gotta admit, George, you fucking love this assignment," Dante laughed. "Just like a kid at Christmas. You got everything you ever wished for."

Ramirez, dressed in his local Istanbul clothing, chuckled at Dante's assessment as he rose from his kneeling position on the floor. With his arsenal bag full of weapons, he took one final glance around the room. Seeing nothing out of place, he gripped the handle of the bag, and he and Paul exited the room, closing the door securely behind them.

Walking briskly down the hallway, George began to tell Paul the extent of the types of weapons they will have at their disposal.

"You're right, Paul. I'm in seventh heaven with what we've got here. Jesus, I can't believe I got my entire wish list," he stated. "But, I mean, not only did I get everything I wanted, but the Pope's supplier gave me some other things I never expected."

Paul's curiosity got the better of him. "What do you mean by 'never expected'?" Dante asked. George then began to rattle off the name of the weapon and the country that manufactured it.

"Most of our handguns are American-made, as you'd expect." George stated. "We've got Colt M1911s and Smith & Wesson Model 10s. I've got some in my bag here, but most of the weapons are stored on the plane.

"You'll like our rifle collection, too, Paul. We got that M1918 Browning Automatic Rifle, some Winchester Model 1907s, and that Remington Model 8. We've also got Vickers machine guns, Browning Auto-5 shotguns, some F1 grenades, some Stokes mortars, and some Mark I trench knives. And, of course, we have plenty of ammunition to go with these guns."

As both men descended the stairs from their second-floor hotel rooms, George looked at Paul with raised eyebrows. "But the Vatican supplier also threw in some German Lugers and Wechselapparat flame throwers. But that's not all. He also gave us a Mauser anti-tank rifle and some Flachmine 17 land mines."

With an inquisitive expression, George asked Dante, "Now why in the hell do you think the Vatican guy gave us the German weapons, too? He must have had a reason."

Dante replied, "You know, George, I'm not sure why he'd give us German weapons, too. Maybe because they're as good as American-made? But Papa Gino told me that there would be several different groups of people searching for the artifact. Maybe the Germans are one of the groups most likely to try. But for what those German weapons were designed to destroy, he may be preparing us for the unexpected, too. One thing I'm certain of, though. I'm sure they won't go to waste."

At precisely 4:30 in the morning, as planned, Aji arrived at the hotel in his 1926 Morris Oxford Tourer car to gather the Vatican team and transport them to their waiting airplane inside an abandoned hangar at Sabiha Gokcen airport. As the group piled into the old car, they found that there wasn't much space to place their bags in the back seat, so Paul and Loogie kept theirs in their lap.

"Good morning, everyone," Aji exclaimed. "It's a great day to help Holy Mother Church." All five passengers mumbled their inaudible polite responses in return.

As Aji slowly drove away from the hotel, Paul noticed the same large group of men he had spotted the night before on the other side of the street going in the opposite direction from their hotel. They were starting to gather on the street corner in front of another hotel.

"You see those guys back there?" Dante asked. "I saw them last night." As the others turned around to look, Paul continued, "You know, they remind me of us. They're not locals. They're only dressed as locals. Plus, about a half dozen of them had on combat boots. That definitely doesn't make them locals. You know, I think we have ourselves another response team on the same trail as we are." Wolff's gaze met the focused eyes of the departing car's occupants as the vehicle vanished into the pre-dawn darkness.

CHAPTER TWENTY THREE

AS Aji sped toward the airport on the lonely, isolated dirt road, he broke the early morning silence in the car by addressing Paul and his group. "Paul, you are correct in your thinking about that group of men we just saw on the street corner," he began. "They are a highly successful German search and recovery team, a part of a secret group that supposedly answers to Hitler himself. Their job is to hunt down curious items of tremendous value that gives Hitler leverage and power over his enemies."

"Where did you get this information, Aji?" Paul interrupted. "We only saw these guys yesterday evening when we left the bar. How were you able to get that kind of information so quickly?"

"I was surprised, too. But we have an asset hidden within the German ministry of defense," Aji replied. "When I returned home from our meeting last night, our telegraph operator handed me a coded message. It told me that our asset had heard that a special German undercover team was sent by a high-ranking Nazi official to search for and recover an ancient artifact that would cause much damage to the Catholic Church. The message stated that this artifact had been stolen from a secret location in Istanbul by some renegade group called the Illuminati. This group was to start its assignment in Istanbul. So your gut feeling was right, Paul. You will not be alone in this quest."

Aji reached the airport in 15 minutes. It took another five minutes to guide his vehicle to the isolated hangar that housed the Vatican plane. Painted an exterior dark gray color per the instructions of the Vatican purchaser, there were no visible markings anywhere on the fuselage or wings that would identify it in any way to the Pope. Per the guidelines set up in 1919 by the *Commission Internationale de Navigation Aerienne*, established as part of the Paris Peace Conference immediately following World War I, the plane was legally mandated to carry an international aircraft identification number on the back tail section.

To meet this requirement, Pacelli had ordered the identification mark **IP-3276** to emblazon the vertical rudder. The "I" identified the country of the plane's owner as Italy. The "P" designation meant that the plane was a private aircraft. Finally, "3276" was the month, day, and year of birth of Papa Gino: March 2, 1876.

Upon reaching the plane, all six occupants hurriedly exited the car. The Vatican team began unloading their valuable baggage from the car and on to the plane. Aji assisted them to quicken the pace. Dante and Loogie were the first two travelers up the mobile stairs and into the aircraft. Following close behind was Ferrelli, who took a quick left when he entered the craft, and headed toward the cockpit to begin his pre-flight routine. Ramirez ran up the stairs with his loaded knapsack on his shoulder. The last of the Vatican team on board was McPherrin. He had deposited the remainder of his arsenal into the plane's lower storage area before climbing the stairs.

The interior of the plane was stunning in appearance. As part of the purchase agreement between the Vatican and Douglas Aircraft, Pacelli had directed the company to extensively modify the seating area and sleeping berths. Regular cloth-covering on the seats was changed to rich black leather with extra padding on the bottom, arms, and back. The foam-filled mattresses in the sleeping berths were replaced with high-quality down-filled mattresses and pillows. He also requested military-grade wireless telegraphy for communication.

But the most remarkable part of the plane was the back of the fuselage. It had been refurbished into a small kitchen area. In addition to containing a pantry for canned goods and bread, Pacelli requested a new General Electric "Monitor-Top" refrigerator and a high-end propane gas stove from Sweden called the AGA cooker to be installed. Dante and his team members were flabbergasted when they entered the airplane the first time after Ferrelli picked it up from the Douglas Aircraft production plant in Oklahoma City and flew it to Rome within a week's time of the theft. The extensive redesign of the interior of the plane along with the five-day rush-job order had tripled the price of the plane. But Pacelli wanted his warriors to be self-sustaining throughout this venture. *The added cost for convenience and comfort for Dante and his team was a small price to pay for the importance of their mission,* Pacelli thought.

When Aji entered the plane, he carried with him a brown leather pouch that contained the newest information from his network of secret Vatican operatives in Europe. All six men sat at a large round table at the back of the plane that had been installed as part of the special interior design requested by the Vatican. Aji pulled out a colored topological map of Europe, unrolled it on the table, and began to address Dante and his group.

"Paul, here is the latest information my wireless radio operator transcribed from our many contacts in Europe," Aji said. "When the theft was discovered, I first contacted Rome, per protocol. But immediately after, I began transmitting an urgent message to all of my Watcher contacts around Europe, asking for their assistance in catching the thieves and recovering the artifact. I contacted my Watcher brothers in Bulgaria, Yugoslavia, northern Italy, Spain, and France. Unfortunately, no Watcher uncovered any specific leads, only a few rumors from amongst the people in their villages. So from what little information I received back, here is my best guess on how you might conduct this mission."

Ferrelli fired the first question. "Jesus fuck, Aji, you mean with all the money and contacts the Vatican has around the world, you weren't able to get any kind of solid leads for us to follow?" He just shook his head in bewilderment.

Dante responded. "Geno, Aji is not our problem. He's just going with his gut on this. Let's hear what he has to say."

Aji bowed his head toward Paul in respect for Paul's defense of his position. He resumed his dialogue. "I believe the infidels wish to return their prize to their leaders as quickly as possible. So that means they're probably taking a direct route back. I'm sure they're well aware that the Vatican would not be the only group trying to retrieve the papyrus."

George chimed in. "Aji, just where do the Illuminati work out of? Where is their home base? Surely the Vatican has been able to identify their home turf by now since this has been going on for, what, a thousand years or more?"

Aji welcomed the question, but had no definitive answer. "The Vatican has identified the location of Illuminati headquarters over the centuries. Greece, the British Isles, Portugal, even France. Now the belief is that it is in Spain somewhere. No one knows for sure. But as quickly as the location is identified, the building is always empty when the papal mercenaries arrive to destroy the occupants and its contents. Then, as today, they've always been able to stay one step ahead of us. Then, as today, it seems like they have someone on the inside of the Vatican assisting them."

Dante looked at Jimmy Mac. He could tell the big fella had something on his mind. "What do you think, Jimmy? As a guy who worked covert ops, do you think the thieves are making a bee line home?"

"Yes and no," Jimmy answered. "I believe they want to deliver the goods home as quickly as possible." He hesitated momentarily before resuming his idea. "But I think their delivery system is going to be a little more complicated to follow."

"What do you mean, Jimmy?" Ferrelli asked the question that was on every man's mind.

Jimmy explained his theory. "I mean that the guys who actually stole the thing will not be the guys delivering it home. I think they'll use several sets of couriers, probably exchanging the artifact quite a few times along the route. I'm sure by now that they've forged some fake documents just to throw off the pursuers. They need to keep changing couriers in case some of them are identified and caught by the Vatican Watchers or the Germans. So I think we're chasing two sets of thieves. One set with fake documents and one set with the real McCoy. We have to hope we catch the guys with the real documents."

Dante exclaimed, "In other words, Jimmy, we're really looking for fucking needles in a haystack, right?"

Jimmy nodded in agreement. "Yes, Paul, we are literally on a goddamn wild goose chase, as far as I'm concerned. But that's the fun part." The four Americans laughed. Aji forced a smile. Loogie spoke up.

"There is nothing funny about this," Father Luigi interjected, his voice rising. "We are fighting for the survival of the Catholic Church. We are on a divine mission from God."

"For Chrissakes, Loogie, will you please fucking lighten up a little?" Ferrelli said. "We know the importance of this mission. We're not going to let the Pope down on this. Just let us do it our way, OK? We're the experts here." Ferrelli then rose from his chair and directed his next comment to Dante. "I'm going to complete my pre-flight inspection so we can get the hell out of here," he said. "I should be done in less than 10 minutes."

With Dante's imminent departure only moments away, Aji again took control of the conversation. "Paul, here is a list of my Watcher contacts throughout Europe, along with their wireless radio contact frequencies," he said while handing Dante the first sheet of paper. "And this paper here contains the secret inscription that will help you identify the document as genuine when you find it." He handed Dante a second sheet of paper, yellowed by time. "Guard this information with your life." Dante nodded, folded both sheets of paper, and put both of them into the zippered pocket of his jacket.

As each team member rose from the table and headed to his padded leather seat to await takeoff, Aji continued his rushed conversation with Dante. "Each Watcher has his own wireless radio operator, too." Aji told Paul, "So you can communicate with each man when you need his assistance in the search. I will notify each one that you are beginning your search immediately. You keep this map, too. You're going to need it."

As Aji departed the plane, he turned around and shook hands with Dante. "Your first stop is the city of Sophia in Bulgaria. I'll contact my Watcher and tell him to expect your communication." Aji then tightly gripped Paul's hands, and looked directly into his eyes. "Good luck, my friend. May God be by your side during this journey."

With that, Aji turned and quickly descended the stairs. When he reached the bottom, he turned and lifted the attached stairway, pushing it upward into the open doorway, sealing the Vatican team inside. When he heard the door lock inside, he darted away from the plane as Ferrelli cranked the starter, and the twin-engine propellers came to life.

The plane slowly taxied to the long grass runway a short distance from the hangar. When Ferrelli received clearance from the airport tower, he turned in his seat and gave a thumbs-up gesture to Aji. The wheels on the gray Vatican plane carrying the team of Jesuit warriors on their mission to save the Catholic Church lumbered down the runway, rapidly gaining the necessary speed to lift off. Within seconds, the former Navy pilot had the plane off the ground and soaring into the light cloud cover and early morning light, westward bound for Bulgaria's national capital.

After watching Dante's team depart, Aji released several sighs of relief as he rushed back to his car. His work was done for the moment. He gave Dante all of the important information that Pacelli had instructed him to give. He, too, was in awe of the opulence of the Vatican plane. As he hastily drove out the airport entrance, he met two other vehicles moving swiftly toward the airport gate. As they sped by, he recognized them as the elite German squad that Hitler had unleashed to find the papyrus. *Stay a step ahead of these men, Paul,* Aji told himself. *They look determined, too.*

CHAPTER TWENTY FOUR

BULGARIA from 10,000 feet in the air looked a lot like every country in Europe, Dante thought to himself as Ferrelli yelled from the plush cockpit that they were 20 minutes from landing at Sofia airport. When he and the other members of his team weren't resting comfortably in their seats, planning strategy at the big table during the seven-hour flight, or being forced to listen to Loogie regale them with stories about the uncommon history of everyday things, their personal viewing of the terrain showed them an abundance of snow-capped mountain peaks, rugged tree-covered mountain ranges, bountiful grassy farmland, and thousands of patches of barren brown earth. But as the plane began the slow descent toward Sofia, the capital city, Dante quickly realized how colorful and vibrant the area beneath him looked.

But Dante's thoughts were once again assaulted when Loogie started his "Did you know?" stories. During the flight, the group had already heard *"Did you know that the 'cross-my-heart-and-hope-to-die' saying really originates from making the sign of the cross?"* and *"Did you know that shrugging your shoulders is a gesture passed down through vertebrates for millions of years?*" and "*Did you know that the skull and crossbones sign dates back to the bubonic plague of the mid 1300s?*" Now the story turned to praying hands.

"Did you know that hands joined together when people pray was not the way early Hebrews and Christians worshipped?" Loogie asked. "And it's not imitating the steeple of a church either, as many people believe." As Loogie took a breath to continue his amazing story, Dante looked across the aisle at Ramirez, who was mimicking his own death by self-strangulation, his hands firmly clamped around his neck, and his tongue hanging out from his mouth.

"Loogie's absolutely killing me with these stories, Paul," Ramirez complained. "Instead of killing myself over this useless information, maybe I should just strangle Loogie to death. How would that be?" He laughed at his own joke. But Dante was thinking the same thing.

Loogie continued preaching with fervor. "You know, joining hands in prayer is not mentioned in the Bible anywhere. Actually, the gesture can be identified with the bound hands of prisoners. Greeks and Romans ceremonially bound their hands as a symbolic way to show they were binding the devil. To us Catholics, though, tied or shackled hands are symbolic of a worshipper showing humility and submission to God's will." When he finished, Loogie proudly gazed around the plane, waiting for the expressed approval of his fellow warriors. Jimmy Mac answered for his fellow Jesuits. "Goddamn it, Loogie. That's the last goddamn story I ever want to hear from you, do you understand?" Dante and Ramirez clapped their hands in agreement with the assessment.

With only minutes to go before touchdown, Dante and each member of the Vatican-sponsored response team readied himself for the danger and adventure that awaited them. Each man holstered a loaded pistol under his jacket, even Loogie. "Goddamn it, Loogie," Dante had bellowed when Luigi had repeatedly refused his order in Istanbul to carry a pistol during the hunt. "You're hurting everyone else's safety if we have to look after you. I won't have you jeopardize the success of this mission because you're too selfish." Being shamed by his boss and feeling the steely glare from the others, Loogie ultimately relented. To prepare Loogie, Dante had asked Ramirez to give him a crash course on how to shoot. Sofia would be the first test for Loogie if such an occasion arose.

In addition to the hidden guns under their coats, the four Americans also clipped to their ankle a sheathed trench knife. The specialists packed their valuable supplies. Ramirez loaded his bag with extra ammunition and guns. McPherrin gathered the necessary materials to create any explosive devices that may be needed. Dante double-checked his jacket pocket to make sure he carried the verification code to identify the true artifact when they found it.

Ferrelli guided the luxury plane to a bumpy landing on the dirt runway, swiftly taxied to a nearby hangar, and skidded to a stop. After killing the engines, he completed his post-flight check within seconds, and quickly left the cockpit, locking the inside door behind him. When the plane arrived at its designated spot and parked, Dante kicked open the door, and the six-step stairway fell easily toward the ground. The five revitalized Vatican warriors rambled down the stairs, carrying their loaded bags. When all had exited,

Dante pushed the stairway back into the doorway, hearing the locking mechanism snap shut.

"Our contact should be here in a couple minutes," Ferrelli told the group. During the flight, he had radioed Aji's Bulgarian Watcher and negotiated landing times with pick-up times at the Sofia airport. As the group milled around their locked plane waiting, they noticed a dark car racing toward their position. As the car neared their location without slowing its speed, the anxious group began to scatter in all directions.

When the vehicle was within 10 feet of the parked plane, the driver quickly maneuvered a left turn. When he did so, the right front and rear tires left the ground momentarily. Half of the vehicle was now airborne. The car, still moving in a semi-circular motion, landed firmly on the ground after performing a 180-degree spin, and came to a screeching halt.

The driver kept the engine idling as he jumped from the driver's seat. "Welcome, my Papal emissaries!" the jolly man exclaimed in his Bulgarian-accented English, his arms raised high as he began to run toward his perturbed passengers. When the heavyset man realized that he had five gun barrels pointed directly at him, he stopped his advancement with a jolt.

"Now just take it a little easy there, big fella," Dante said, still aiming his pistol at the driver's head. "My friends and I don't take a liking to someone who tries to run us down." The conversation went silent, but the five guns remained pointed at their target.

"Oh, dear God, I am so sorry for my hasty and erratic arrival," the man stated apologetically. "My driving seems to get away from me sometimes. I am Kosta Nayden, the Vatican's

Watcher in Bulgaria. I am honored to meet your acquaintance, but not under the present conditions."

Dante and his men lowered their weapons after Kosta's introduction. "Kosta, it's a pleasure to meet you, too." Dante extended his right hand and shook hands with the big man. Paul then began introducing his team members to Nayden.

"This is Geno Ferrelli, our pilot. He's the one you were communicating with on the radio." Ferrelli stepped forward and shook hands. Geno quipped, "For a minute there, Mr. Kosta, I didn't know your intentions. I'm glad it worked out, though."

McPherrin, Ramirez, and Bellavista rounded out the order of introduction. After everyone had a chance to shake hands, Kosta sprang from the group, and raced to his car, calling out in his wake, "You must hurry. I have been tracking two suspicious foreigners for the last day. They have been meeting up with others at Patriarh Evtimii Square. Quickly, into my car, please."

Dante and his team dashed for the car, following Kosta's direct order. They had barely squeezed into the vehicle when Kosta floored the accelerator and the car lurched into motion. Kosta cleared the airport entrance in minutes, and drove directly to Tzarigradsko Shose, the major boulevard leading from the airport into the city. As Kosta zoomed past slower moving vehicles, Ramirez barked out, "Jesus Christ, Kosta, you trying to get us killed in the first 10 minutes of our arrival in Sofia? Slow the hell down!"

The big Bulgarian turned in his seat, taking his eyes off the road momentarily. "My good man, speed is of the esse..." Before he could finish his sentence, all five passengers shouted in unison, "Look out!" Kosta quickly directed his attention back to the road, only to find a large truck barreling down the road directly at his car. Kosta jerked the steering wheel to the right, sending the car careening to the other side of the road, and into a small ditch. He adjusted the steering column and regained the primary roadway. "Sorry about that," Kosta stuttered.

Since the adrenalin was running high for all six men in the speeding vehicle, Dante decided to probe the Vatican Watcher for details regarding Kosta's supposed suspects.

"OK, Kosta. Tell me about those foreigners you're talking about. How did you find these guys, and what made you suspicious of them?"

Kosta cleared his throat, and began his explanation. "Mr. Paul, I have four additional men on the Vatican payroll working with me in Sofia. When Aji informed us about the theft and who was responsible, we immediately set our recovery plan into motion.

"We figured there were only three ways into the city. One is by rail. One is by air. And one is by car. We figured out that flying was too expensive and noticeable for anyone trying to stay hidden. So we staked out the train station and the main roads coming from the east."

Stopping his story momentarily, and not feathering the brakes at all, Kosta swung the speeding car left on to Eflogi Georgiev Boulevard, the quickest route to Evtimii Square.

Kosta continued his story. "The Illuminati historically have used men of Middle Eastern ethnic origin, both young and old, as their mercenaries, so I instructed my team to concentrate on those identifying points. Then two days ago, my Watchers at the train station noticed two Middle Eastern men, one younger and one older, depart a train that originated in Burgas, our gulf city on the Black Sea."

Jimmy Mac was listening intently, and interrupted the tale with his question. "Were these two guys carrying anything with them? Like walking canes, or leather pouches, or small boxes? Maybe even a bigger-than-normal flower pot?"

The question surprised Kosta. "Yes, the older man used a walking cane, and the younger man was carrying a tall pottery vase. They looked like all passengers stepping off the train, except for their Middle Eastern complexion. Why do you ask?"

McPherrin answered the inquiry. "Thieves like to hide things in plain sight. They need to blend in easily with their surroundings. No one notices anything unusual because the deception is concealed. Documents can be easily hidden in a hollow cane. You can hide documents underneath the dirt in a pottery vase. So even though your men noticed the dark facial complexion right off the bat, they were observant enough to notice the cane and vase. I think we're on to something here."

Kosta made a right turn at breakneck speed on to Graf Ignatiev Street. "We're only moments away from the Square," Kosta instructed. "When we arrive, I'll park a short distance from the entrance. My men will be waiting. The meeting yesterday took place at the northwest corner with two younger men. Both groups usually enter from opposite directions, meet, and then move away from the crowds."

Dante assumed his leadership role. "Oh, yeah, thanks for the enjoyable ride over here, Kosta," Dante said sarcastically. "We now know no one will ever outrace us in a vehicle if you're driving." The Vatican members smirked at the comment.

"Here's how we'll attack this, men," Dante began. "Kosta, since you and your men know what these guys look like, one of my men will team up with one of your men. That will give us five sets of eyes on the area. We'll set up in a circular area around the meeting location, making sure we stay close enough to see, but far enough away not to be noticed. I'm sure these guys are a little paranoid and jumpy. Meeting in a crowded public square probably eases their minds a little bit. On my signal, we'll move in on both groups."

When Kosta turned on Graf Ignatiev Street, Patriarh Evtimii Square loomed ahead. Known as "Popa", which coincidentally translates to "priest" in the local language, the immense square played the role of major traffic hub, open market, and preferred meeting place for Sofia residents. As he approached the southeast section of the square, Kosta darted to an open parking spot, nearly hitting three screeching girls who hurriedly jumped to the curb away from the decelerating car.

"Nice job, Kosta. Nothing like having three screaming girls announcing our presence," Dante said sardonically as he and the others quickly exited the car. Within minutes, Kosta's four associates met up with the group.

Even though sunset was a couple hours away, the immense square was bustling with activity. Loud vendors in their colorful attire hawking cooked food, raw food, clothing items, books, and artwork stretched as far as the eye could see. Hundreds of individuals, partaking in animated conversation in small groups, milled around the concrete square. Small children ran about freely, much to the chagrin of their parents. The scene reminded Dante of a South Omaha carnival atmosphere.

Dante asked Kosta if his men had spotted the targets. "No, Mr. Paul, they have not," Kosta answered. Dante hurriedly matched his men with a Watcher, making sure that he and Kosta stayed together in the final group.

"Let's start walking toward the northwest corner," Dante ordered. "Split up so we're at least 20 yards apart from each other. We don't want to draw any attention to ourselves by staying together. When we get to the area where Kosta saw the men yesterday, let's circle the area, again staying 20 yards apart. When any of you notices the arrival of the targets, raise your hand, but just lay low until all targets are in the vicinity. We don't want to spook them into running."

Snaking through the cumbersome crowd to get to their appointed area a few hundred yards away proved a challenge for the group. Every few yards, each pair would be accosted by an assertive vendor, thrusting an item into their faces, and desperately trying to begin a sales negotiation. On every occasion, it was the Watcher in the group who aggressively pushed the vendor away. Dante was thankful that Kosta's men took this job seriously.

The conjoined forces finally arrived at their appointed area and took up their assigned positions. It didn't take long for McPherrin's watcher to raise his hand, and nod in the direction of the two young unaware targets as they emerged from a group surrounding a jovial vendor displaying a table loaded with large raw fish. They carried nothing in their hands.

"Shit, they're not carrying anything. That means the next two have to be our couriers," Dante said to Kosta. "Now we wait." Kosta nodded in agreement.

The two young men, dressed in local garb, unknowingly stopped squarely in the middle of Dante's invisible web of papal rescuers. Occasionally, each would glance around the area, seeking the gaze of any stranger that might cause them to hastily flee. Dante worried only about Loogie, noticing that his excitable interpreter never took his eyes off the two targets.

Fifteen minutes later, Loogie's Watcher raised his hand, and nodded in the opposite direction of the first two arrivals. Walking slowly toward the two young men were two middle-aged men, one using a cane, and the other man carrying an old leather satchel. The four men made eye contact from around 10 yards away, and quickly embraced when they came together.

Dante could read the body language of his team members. He could tell they were eager to pounce on the four suspects. He kept moving his head side-to-side, indicating that the time wasn't right. But then it happened.

Loogie suddenly broke away from his Watcher companion, and started moving quickly through the crowd toward the four suspected thieves. When he was within a few feet of the four men, he drew his pistol, and started shouting at the men. "I know you've stolen the precious Vatican icon from Istanbul," Loogie screamed in Russian dialect to the four surprised men. "All of you, stay where you are. You, with the satchel, give it to me now!"

When they saw Loogie break away from the Bulgarian Watcher, Dante and Kosta began running frantically toward the escalating scene. "Oh, shit," Dante kept repeating to himself as he fought his way through the market crowd. "Aw, piss on it," Ferrelli was saying as he and his Watcher came sprinting from opposite Dante and Kosta. But all of them were too late in their arrival to remedy Loogie's error in judgment.

The moment when Loogie had pulled the pistol from inside his jacket, a woman standing nearby with her two small children began screaming and pointing at Loogie. "Gun, gun, gun!" the frantic woman yelled to anyone who could hear. Pandemonium was quick to erupt around Dante and his team. The hundreds of bystanders who had been demonstrably talking within their groups now became a herd of thundering animals, running in all directions, and demolishing anything in their way. The vendors in the area desperately tried to save their products as the stampeding crowd ran over and through the tiny shops.

As panic set in around the square, the four men of interest saw the dramatic distraction as their chance to escape and dashed away from Loogie. Fearing their capture, the four divided up and ran separate ways, disappearing easily amidst the chaos. Loogie's Watcher dove at the feet of one of the fleeing men, trying to tackle him. He was unsuccessful.

Instinctively summoning their military experience to adapt to the situation, Dante, Ferrelli, Ramirez, and McPherrin started chasing the closest suspect in their vicinity. Kosta stopped to assist Loogie, who had been pushed to the ground and was being trampled by the frightened throngs as they tried to distance themselves from the perceived danger.

"My friend, you have caused quite a commotion," Kosta said to Loogie as he pushed people aside and pulled the short cleric to his feet. "And I might add, Mr. Paul was not very happy when he saw what you did."

"Oh my God, Kosta, what have I done?" Loogie asked, still dazed, bloodied, and bruised from his brush with death. "The boss is going to send me packing right back to Rome after this terrible mistake. My anger with those men just overwhelmed my judgment." He took a deep breath. "I've ruined everything, haven't I?"

The large Bulgarian Watcher, almost twice the size of Loogie in both height and weight, began to laugh heartily. "My dear man, you haven't ruined anything. The eight men chasing those four targets are trained in just this kind of pursuit. Don't worry. None of those men will be able to escape the clutches of the Vatican."

Kosta's words of encouragement, however, were premature at the moment. Not one target had been caught yet.

Ramirez and his Watcher were the first of the four pursuer groups to capture a target. When the chase began, the older suspect with the satchel had thrown it to one of the younger men before he backed away from Loogie and began running westward toward the outer edge of the square. Ramirez, caught in the onrushing crowd about twenty yards away from Loogie, determined his angle of pursuit once he saw which direction the older man was running.

"I've got you, you sonofabitch," Ramirez kept repeating to himself as he knifed his way through the maddening crowd. Within minutes, he found himself running parallel with the target. Ramirez motioned to his Watcher to take a path behind the fleeing suspect to stop any retreat that might occur. He continued his diagonal approach, timing it perfectly when the older man had reached the outer edge of the square, and turned around to see if he had escaped safely.

"Going somewhere, cocksucker?"

The startled older man turned quickly to find Ramirez's right fist aimed directly at his left jaw. The powerful blow instantly drove him downward on to the pavement. "I think you've got some 'splainin to do, asshole," Ramirez quipped. He quickly jerked the man to his feet, bent the man's arm behind his back, and started to lead him back to where all the commotion began.

Ferrelli had taken aim at one of the young targets as the kid began a northward evasion route. "Aw, piss on it, and piss on you, you little fucker. You ain't getting away from me," Ferrelli told himself as he weaved past the bodies being thrown in his path. Unlike Ramirez's target, who didn't know if he was being chased until he was grabbed, the young man knew Ferrelli was hot on his heels. In his effort to escape, the young suspect took to throwing unsuspecting victims into Ferrelli's path, trying to detain the pursuing Jesuit. And at the moment, the escape strategy was successful.

Unknown to both Ferrelli and the fleeing suspect, Kosta's assigned man to Geno had started his chase to intercept moments before. As the suspect's attention was placed solely on Ferrelli, the young man had no idea that his flight of escape was to come to a crashing end.

"I'm gonna rip your fuckin' head off, you bastard!" Ferrelli screamed at the fleeing suspect. But as Geno's tired legs started to slow him down, he started to fall behind his prey. "You can't escape from me," Geno yelled as the distance between him and the younger man widened.

Satisfied with the distance he had put between himself and Ferrelli, the younger man started to smile. He no longer needed to throw unsuspecting victims into Ferrelli's path. As he saw the edge of the public square come into his view, the young Illuminati increased his speed. He knew that once he made it to the outer edge of the square where traffic was heavy, he would be able to quickly slip among the passing cars and disappear into the surrounding alleys across the street. But he forgot about his second pursuer.

Suddenly, Kosta's Watcher broke free from the scurrying crowd, and tackled the young man with a vicious hit from behind. The Illuminati tried to break his fall by locking his wrists when he came in contact with the ground. But the massive force behind the hit caused both wrists to break instantly upon contact with the hard pavement.

"My wrists! You broke my wrists," the young man cried, looking at both hands dangling loosely from his lower arms. When his wrists had collapsed, the young man's face also met the hard surface, bloodying his nose, chin, and forehead. The Watcher showed no sympathy for the runner as he dragged him to his feet.

"We got ourselves a thievin' bastard who's crying over some broken hands," the Watcher snarled at his prize. "Ain't it a cryin' shame."

By this time, Ferrelli had caught up to the action. "Nice job, buddy," Ferrelli said to his companion. "I guess I don't have that old acceleration I used to have." Both men smiled as they secured the young thief's hands behind his back, and directed him back to where the action had started.

Dante and Jimmy Mac were not as fortunate as their teammates, as their prey had eluded them after a desperate chase. But now two suspects were standing in front of Dante and Kosta, away from the disappearing crowd, both of them bloody, bruised, and broken from the collisions they had with flying fists and the hard pavement of the public square.

"Let's not interrogate them here in the open," Dante told the group. "Kosta, do you have some private accommodations we can use?"

"Yes, we have a deserted warehouse a short distance from here," Kosta replied. "It will work perfectly for what you have in mind."

CHAPTER TWENTY FIVE

DANTE, Jimmy Mac, Ramirez, and Ferrelli directed their prisoners to Kosta's vehicle for the short drive to the vacant warehouse. Loogie was ordered to join Kosta's associates in their trip to the covert destination. "Loogie, I'll deal with you later for starting all this," Dante threatened as both groups split up.

As the small group of vehicles arrived at the designated location ten minutes later, Dante quickly realized that the deserted warehouse was an ideal site for their purposes. Blocks away from any pedestrian foot traffic and hidden among an area of similarly dilapidated buildings, their presence at the broken warehouse would not be noticed by any of the local populace. The diminishing daylight added to the dark scenario that was about to take place inside.

After parking their cars next to the decaying building, the bloodied suspects were jerked from the back seat of Kosta's car. They all entered the barren facility and Kosta closed and locked the creaking door behind them. The manacled suspects were lead to a solitary wooden table in the middle of the room. Two chairs were gathered from against a far wall, and the prisoners were forced into their seats. With no electrical lights operational, the only brightness in the room was provided by the hazy dusk light seeping through the broken glass of some second-floor windows.

The Vatican hunters surrounded the ill-begotten pair, and Dante ordered Loogie to ask the prisoners if either of them spoke English. Bellavista stepped forward and stood directly in front of the forlorn men. Luigi began his questioning in Bulgarian first. When there were no responses, he asked in Italian. Again, no response. He tried in Russian. Nothing. Finally, he tried Spanish. Suddenly, the younger man responded. "I speak English," he spit in the direction of Loogie. Bellavista jumped away from the vile projectile headed in his direction. The young prisoner laughed in derision at Loogie's reaction.

From a standing position across the table and directly facing each suspect, Dante leaned down and began the interrogation. "Gentlemen," Dante addressed his group while looking directly at the young man, "our young guest here thinks this situation is humorous. He is sorely mistaken."

When Dante calmly spoke his last word, he slammed his fists down on the man's two broken wrists which had been tied together and lying limply on the table, causing a bloodcurdling scream from the suspect. "Do I have your attention now?" Dante asked. With his eyes welling up with tears, the young thief nodded his agreement. Loogie cringed at the sight and sound that befell the room. The others didn't flinch.

Dante continued questioning the young man. "Are you working for the Illuminati?" When there was no initial response, Dante looked first at the man's eyes, and then shifted his attention to the man's crippled hands. Understanding that he could not endure additional pain, the young man turned his head toward his fellow captive, and with sympathetic eyes directed at the older man, answered Dante's query. "Yes." The older man remained stoic.

"What was the purpose of the meeting in the square?" This time the question was fired by Ferrelli.

"We were there to act as the next set of couriers," the young man responded. Hearing that response, the older man pursed his lips.

"Couriers for what?" Ramirez chimed in to the conversation.

The young man didn't take his eyes away from his partner's face. "Father, what shall I do?" he pleaded with the old man.

"You fool!" the old man screamed. "You are so weak. I'm sickened by your cowardice to pain. You have betrayed our noble cause. You are no son of mine."

"So you do speak English, you old geezer," Dante exclaimed.

McPherrin now assumed the role of lead inquisitor. "Where's the leather bag and cane?" he asked the young man. Neither of the items had been retrieved when the two suspects were apprehended, and a subsequent brief search of the area had turned up nothing.

"I don't know. But hopefully far from here," the young man retorted, his head bowed from the verbal abuse previously directed at him by his father.

"Ah, yes. The cane and leather bag," the old man repeated McPherrin's words. "Very observant of you to notice the cane since it is such a common companion to an old man."

Kosta could curb his passion no longer, and blurted out, "Aha, so you were carrying the stolen manuscript with you, not in the obvious leather pouch, but hidden within the lining of the cane. You conniving bastard." Kosta shook his head with incredulity.

"You will never find your precious artifact," the young Illuminati pawn suddenly declared, looking defiantly around the room at each member of Dante's team. "You may have caught us, but we're more intelligent than any of you. We made sure we had another outlet if trouble occurred. And I welcome your torture. Pound my hands again and again if you must."

The old man, startled by his son's renewed courage, smiled his approval to his injured warrior's resurrected boldness. He knew they both would meet death following this secret interrogation. But he promised himself that he would not allow his son to experience any more pain at the expense of these Vatican heathens.

McPherrin turned his new focus of questioning to the young man's comments. "So you had a Plan B ready to go?" He noticed Dante's heightened level of interest, and pursued further explanation from the captive father and son. "Tell me how you've outsmarted us."

Before his son could utter a hasty response, the old man proudly proclaimed the brilliance behind the Illuminati deception plan. He knew he and his beloved son were at death's door, and he wanted to die knowing he had beaten the Vatican at their own game.

"You all are such puppets to the Holy See," the old man stated, accusing his captors of replicating the history of how the Vatican eliminated its enemies. "You fear the real truth behind your religion that is buried deep away from the eyes of your blind followers. Without conscience, you easily justify death, destruction, and intimidation to bury your Pope's enemies and preserve the hypocritical history of your religious dogma. You are the spineless infidels on this earth, not I or my son or our group."

The old man continued with more vigor. "Yes, we did have a Plan B, as you call it, for every facet of our flight with your precious hidden artifact. The Illuminati have been at odds with your leadership for millennia. For so long, we grew weary of the lies and deception that the Catholic Church has propagated on its members and the world." For an instant, the old man felt a loneliness of separation from loved ones that accompanies death's appearance. But the elegance of the moment provided him another shot of adrenaline to continue his accursed diatribe.

"Our history parallels those of the early Christian movement, you know. We, too, had leaders that believed in Jesus Christ and his message. But then the Vatican as an institution became evil incarnate. The religion of Christ changed to a religion of corruption, power, greed, and treachery."

Luigi Bellavista could take no more of this slanderous blasphemy. "You lie, you miserable piece of shit," he cried out. A look of shock, then accompanying smiles, adorned the faces of Dante's group when they heard the devout Catholic priest spew his venom toward the old man. "Everything you say is a lie. The Illuminati are the sewage of this earth."

The old man ignored the interruption. "The Vatican became a haven for false popes, began a quest for world political domination, and invented the justification to use murder and torture to strike the fear of God into non-believers. And as more historical proof surfaced that the Catholic Church's most sacred precepts and doctrines were false, the deeper these secrets were buried away around the world in closely-guarded hidden vaults."

The old man was beginning to tire from his verbal onslaught, but he again found the inner strength to continue. "I proudly proclaim that I was a member of the initial Illuminati team that stole the ancient artifact from its hiding place in Istanbul. After hundreds of years of searching, our institution finally discovered the exact hidden location of this volatile document around 20 years ago. It took us a generation to conduct our surveillance of the church and determine where the vault was hidden. We lost many brethren in the process."

The sunlight had long disappeared inside of the warehouse as the old man disseminated the role of the Illuminati in the confiscation of the valuable Vatican artifact. Darkness enveloped the barren room as he looked over at his son, who seemed mesmerized by his father's story. He stretched out his right arm and gently squeezed his son's shoulder, a look of love and admiration emanating from his face. As unbelievable, and undoubtedly hyperbolized, as the story seemed to be, Dante, Kosta, and the others were impressed by the depth of the confession of the conspirator. But they still needed an answer to McPherrin's question that had been asked almost an hour ago.

"That's a nice story, old man. But we're still waiting to hear how Plan B fooled all of us," Dante said. "Give me that story now."

A look of inevitability surfaced on the old man's face. He knew when he finished his story, that the life of he and his son was finished, also. So he told Dante what he wanted to hear.

"I know the precious moments together that my son and I are sharing are quickly coming to an end. But we have fought the good cause, and we understood from the beginning that losing our lives was part of the deal. I will tell you what you want to hear, fully believing that your best efforts will not be able to derail our plans to destroy the papacy and what it stands for."

"So let's hear it for Christ's sake," Ferrelli interjected. "Get this show on the road."

"You don't have to tell them anything, father. You know that," the young man responded. "We will die as heroes regardless. I'm proud of you. I'm sorry I was so weak and terrified of the pain of my broken hands that I disgraced our family before. But I welcome death because I know you and I will be crossing over together."

Tired of the delay and eager to end the interrogation, Kosta drew his curved knife from the scabbard under his jacket, and slowly moved to the side of the young man. "Tell us the illustrious Illuminati plan to deliver the manuscript to your leaders now, or I'll cut a finger off your son's hands one at a time," he directed at the old man.

Kosta aggressively pressed his left hand down on the badly bruised right hand of the son, pinning it to the table. He began to direct the blade to the young man's thumb when the old man begged him to stop.

"Stop brutalizing my son, you bastard. I'll tell you the whole story now. Just back away and leave him alone." Kosta looked at Dante for approval to move away. Dante nodded his consent.

"Tell us quickly, old man. We're tired of hearing your voice," Kosta snarled.

"We, indeed, carried the true artifact with us to the exchange this afternoon," the old man stated. "The true manuscript was hidden in the cane. An intricate forgery was inserted into the leather satchel. The plan calls for a new carrier for both the forgery and the authentic document during each exchange. It shouldn't be a satchel or cane again."

"Are there always two couriers during an exchange?" Ramirez asked.

"Yes, and no," the old man replied. "Yes, in that two people always carry the two documents, and two people are involved in the exchange in a public, highly-crowded location. No, in that after the initial exchange, there will be a second exchange in the same city before the couriers swiftly move on to the next exchange in a different city."

"So you're saying another exchange will take place in Sofia?" Dante remarked excitedly. "Where and when will that exchange take place?"

"You see, it already has," the old man answered confidently. "The second exchange was to take place outside the public square immediately after the first exchange. When your little friend here disrupted the first exchange and caused the ensuing chaos, the disarray of the situation allowed the two couriers that escaped your attempt to catch them to exchange the documents with the second team.

"As you were chasing the other two Illuminati couriers, they had already made their exchange during the chase. Fortunately for them, they escaped. If you had caught them, they would not have been carrying anything with them anyway," he laughed heartily. "Our mission is still active, and you'll never find the artifact because you'll never find our couriers."

"To what city are the couriers heading to now? Dante demanded. "Your life hangs in the balance of your answer."

"I do not know. My responsibility ended when we made the exchange here in Sofia," the old man replied. "Only the new couriers know their destination. We are of no good to you anymore." The old man smiled at his son with sad eyes. The teary-eyed son returned the smile.

"Shit," Ferrelli said as he looked around the room and saw the disgusted looks on the faces of Kosta and his associates. "What do we do now?"

Dante was about to respond to Ferrelli's summation when Kosta charged up to him. Talking in a muffled voice so that the captives would not hear, Kosta spoke to Dante.

"We should kill them now, Mr. Paul. The old man is correct in his thinking. If his story is correct, and it sounds plausible, they need to be silenced. I've got direct orders from Rome that no Illuminati that we capture and pressure into giving us useful information is to stay alive. These terrible thieves need to be taught a lesson."

"No, we don't need to kill them," Dante told Kosta. "We know how they're moving the artifact now. We can still find it. We almost got them today if Loogie hadn't fucked things up for us. The worst case that can happen is that they report to their leaders that a Vatican team is hunting them. They already knew that would happen." Dante added, "We're lucky we got to them before that Nazi team."

Prepared to die, the father and son remained motionless at the table as Dante huddled with the Vatican team to decide how to proceed. The father and son clasped hands when the huddle broke and Dante walked toward the Illuminati thieves.

"Where is the headquarters of the Illuminati located?" Dante asked the pair. The blank look on the face of the young son told Dante he didn't have the answer.

"I asked…where is the location of the Illuminati headquarters?" This time Dante spoke to the old thief, bending low to look the man directly in the eyes.

"I will take that knowledge with me to the grave," the old man answered indignantly. "Even the death of my son before my eyes today will not sway me to tell you."

Dante and his team had surmised that the old man would not give up the location of the Illuminati headquarters, but he needed to try to extract that information.

"Get these assholes out of my sight," Dante shouted. "We've got enough solid information to find the original manuscript. I've had enough of them."

Kosta moved forward and cut the binding rope that had secured the hands of the suspects during the interrogation. As two of Kosta's associates grabbed the back collar of the pair's coats and lifted them forcefully from the chairs, Kosta made sure that he squeezed the broken wrists of the young man to leave a lasting remembrance of the pain the Vatican is capable of inducing in its enemies.

With Kosta delivering a swift kick in their asses, the two Illuminati conspirators found themselves outside the warehouse, lying on the ground. As the father and son rejoiced in their good fortune, they arose, and quickly disappeared into the darkness of the evening. The old man felt contentment because he had withstood the rigors of the interrogation without giving up the location of the cities the couriers would be traversing before they reached the home of the Illuminati: Paris, France; Belgrade, Yugoslavia; and Milan, Italy.

Exhausted and hungry from the activities of the day, and noting the lateness of the evening, Dante and Kosta agreed to meet the next day to analyze the information captured from the Illuminati thieves, and formulate a new plan of action to find the stolen Vatican artifact. They exited the abandoned warehouse, climbed wearily into Kosta's car, and began the trip to their Sofia hotel for the evening.

On the way to the hotel where Dante's team was staying, Kosta made a side trip to his favorite café and ordered food for the weary Vatican travelers to take to their rooms. As Ferelli, Ramirez, and McPherrin munched on their food in the comfort of their small hotel rooms, Dante was in Bellavista's room for half an hour vehemently chastising the little priest for the trouble he caused that day. Feeling he had made his point, and noting the tears of embarrassment and shame rolling down Loogie's cheeks, Dante left the room, telling the impetuous Bellavista that he would remain a part of the team for the time being. But any new problem would send him packing back to Rome.

CHAPTER TWENTY SIX

THE next day, unknown to Dante and Kosta, Wolff's Nazi team, dressed in local garb, quietly arrived in Sofia, met up with their local investigator, discovered the identities of the Illuminati thieves, and hunted down the old man and his son, forcefully kidnapping them from their own home as they sat down for noon dinner. Putting hoods over their heads, the father and son were dragged from the house, dumped into the back seat of an idling car, and delivered to an empty warehouse that mirrored the one used by Dante the night before.

In less than 30 minutes, Wolff's interrogators had extracted the same information that took Dante's team almost two hours to gather. In addition, the Nazi team, through the use of diabolical torture methods, was also able to gather the names of the cities in which the Illuminati couriers would travel, although not in the order of the planned flight. The old man was pleased he guarded that privileged information within him. He also refused to disclose the location of the Illuminati headquarters despite the intense beating he took from his Nazi captors.

This was Wolff's first official assignment that did not call for his team to hunt down mythical items of interest to the Fuhrer. Very seldom did Wolff and his team interact with the general population during official assignments. It was also the first assignment in which intense interrogation and distasteful information extraction methods were employed. He despised the tactics, but he knew many of the soldiers under his command welcomed an assignment that justified the use of force to gain information. He surmised this horrid scene playing out in front of him was actually a morale booster to his troops. That realization sickened him even more.

As Wolff watched in silence from the back of the smoke-filled room and cringed during the questioning and treatment of father and son, he was extremely displeased and horrified with the amount and degree of torture his men inflicted upon the two helpless men. Reaching his limit of tolerance to allow further pain and feeling his men had gathered the needed intelligence, Wolff stopped the interrogation.

"That's enough, sergeant," Wolff interjected as he walked from the back-room darkness into the mid-afternoon sunlight pouring through the broken windows that dotted the perimeter of the warehouse. Then he addressed the two Illuminati conspirators.

"I apologize for the lack of restraint on the part of my men," Wolff began. "I really do. But you leave me no choice because you haven't been as forthcoming as you need to be. I want to complete this mission as quickly and painlessly as possible. Unfortunately for you, it has not been painless.

"From what you both have told me today, you sustained many of your injuries yesterday at the hands of a team of Vatican soldiers, is that correct?" The old man and his crippled son nodded in the affirmative, their faces streaming with blood from the cruel pounding of the Nazi questioners.

"I do not care what beliefs you carry as a member of this Illuminati group," Wolff continued. "As a matter of fact, I'm intrigued by the information you've given us. I really don't care about the Vatican or the Catholic Church either. But I do care about retrieving that ancient document that Hitler believes will give him some advantage over the Pope.

"My group has built up quite a favorable reputation within the German military," Wolff stated proudly. "And I intend to keep our record flawless by tracking down your friends, gaining possession of the valuable artifact, and returning to Berlin once again hailed as heroes."

Although not a trained soldier, Wolff's men had grown to respect the young officer's leadership and decision-making. They, too, enjoyed the internal fame and fortune the group had established over time. This was just another challenge that would pay handsome dividends, they thought. If there was some collateral damage involved along the way, so be it. And the stubbornness portrayed by this old man and his son made them worthy candidates as victims of collateral damage.

"I think I've heard enough to discern that your friends are on their way to Belgrade on their serpentine trip back to Illuminati headquarters to deliver the artifact to your leaders," Wolff addressed the two prisoners. "We have spies in every locale in Europe. We'll catch them. And when we do, we'll tell them it was because of your assistance. Your presence is no longer needed, gentleman." Following his final comment, Wolff ordered the release of the two disabled men. But his sergeant had different plans in mind as he ran up to confront Wolff.

"Sir, I don't believe releasing these two men is the right thing to do," the sergeant stated, leaning in close so the prisoners would not hear the conversation. "Releasing them will cause us a lot of headaches in the long run."

"I'm listening." Wolff responded.

The sergeant continued to explain his reasoning. "Even though we have left our mark physically on these conspirators, allowing them to go free will not free our consciences of any guilt, sir. In fact, freeing them will hurt our reputation."

"And how is that?" Wolff queried his soldier.

"Simply put, these men have seen us. They will report to their leaders who we are and what we look like. Every Illuminati courier will be on notice for our appearance. We will not have the advantage of a covert presence any longer in this hunt. And when word gets back to Himmler and Hitler, our reputation will be diminished because of our lack of foresight and inability to take corrective action." He paused before delivering his final thought. "They must disappear, sir. That is our only option."

Wolff was dismayed following the sergeant's convincing speech. He may not have the stomach to eliminate the father and his son, but several of his foot soldiers would relish the opportunity to permanently silence the pair. *There are always victims of war, and maybe the death of the two Illuminati couriers was inevitable*, Wolff internalized. "What do you have in mind, sergeant?" Wolff asked.

"It's probably best that you don't know, sir," the sergeant responded. "It's for your own good.

"This just doesn't sit well with me, sergeant. Murdering them in cold blood is not the way we do things in this unit. And I don't want to start now." Wolff said.

"But if things turn on us because of our lack of fortitude, it will be your ass on the line with Himmler," the sergeant argued. "Your ass, sir."

For a moment, Wolff remembered back when he and his unit were assembled and the strange missions they were given. He remembered the derision he and the unit sustained within the rank and file for their perceived lack of combat worthiness as Nazi soldiers. He also enjoyed the fame gained and jealousy grown within the rank and file for the major successes the unit had experienced. He didn't want to lose any credibility with Himmler or Hitler.

"Don't take long, sergeant. We leave for Belgrade in a couple hours." Wolff nodded his approval, setting in motion a decision that would haunt Wolff's every dream for the rest of his life.

The sergeant separated himself from Wolff and approached two members of the team. "Wolff signed off on this. We do a simple body dump outside the city," the soldier explained. "We'll drive them to the outskirts of town to where the forest begins. Then after they are eliminated, we can easily bury them where no one will find them. It's clean and it's foolproof. Let's go."

The sergeant approached the two injured thieves who could barely stand after two successive days of torture and bodily assault. "You are releasing us as your commander stated, right?" the young man asked. "He said you don't have any need for us anymore," the old man repeated Wolff's decision to the sergeant.

"Yes, you *finken* thieves, we are releasing you because we don't need you any longer," the sergeant stated with a grin. "We're going to take a ride and release you outside the city." The father and son exchanged gazes that displayed terror in their eyes. They realized they had been lucky the previous night with the Vatican team. But their good fortune was coming to an end with the ruthless Nazis.

The sergeant and two additional soldiers of Wolff's retrieval team drove the battered father-son Illuminati team to a remote area of the Bulgarian countryside, handcuffed their hands behind their backs, and marched them inside some dense forest a few hundred yards off the deserted road.

"You lying bastards," the old man cursed. "No man escapes damnation for cold-blooded murder. You'll burn in the fires of hell for this."

Reaching a secluded spot, the Nazi foot soldiers forced the pair to kneel down on the soft pine needles that covered the area. The father and son, bloodied and maimed, stole a final respectful, loving glance, and awaited the finality of their lives.

"We will burn in the fires of hell," the sergeant laughed as he pulled the revolver from inside his jacket. "But you two will beat us there."

The sergeant walked slowly to the back of the prisoners. He raised the barrel within six inches of the back of the old man's head, and calmly pulled the trigger. Blood and brain matter exploded onto the clothing and exposed skin of the Nazi soldiers. "Shit. Standing too close," the sergeant quipped as he wiped blood from his eyes.

As he watched his father's lifeless body tumble to the ground beside him, the young son screamed in agony. This time, the Nazi killer took a step back and fired a single shot from point-blank-range into the head of the son. Silence overtook the sounds of the forest for a split second.

"We gonna bury them now?" asked one of the soldiers.

"Nein," the sergeant answered. The three Nazis strode away from the scene, leaving the bodies exposed. "The animals will take care of them," the sergeant told his comrades.

Wolff did not ask for details when the three Nazi foot soldiers returned to the warehouse, despite the amount of blood on the sergeant's jacket. He did not want to relive the decision he made a short time ago. But Wolff swore to himself that he would never allow another cold-blooded murder.

CHAPTER TWENTY SEVEN

Secret Anenerbe Warehouse – Berlin, Germany
1937

OTTO RATHMAN, the jovial curator of all things strange and wonderful for the Nazi regime, completed his meandering walk, weaving from his office to Section 13 of the warehouse. The nondescript, but oversized, warehouse, cleverly buried within the central warehouse district of downtown Berlin, was the secret Nazi repository for all items recovered by Anenerbe teams from expeditions around the world. Some things were of a scientific nature, some were of esoteric value, and others were just crap.

Unknown to Hitler, a special department in the cramped basement of the warehouse was used to manufacture much of this crap. Whenever word got to Otto that an expedition had failed its mission, Otto and his highly-skilled technicians and craftsmen would produce some kind of meaningful object to appease the Fuhrer. Otto was most proud of the faux Ark of the Covenant, with its electrified walls and shattered remnants of supposedly the stone tablets containing the "10 Commandments." Hitler could never tell the difference between what was real and what was faked, Otto joked to himself. But Hitler wanted all of these "treasures" in one location. And this monstrous cavern of a warehouse was where everything was shipped or delivered.

When he arrived at his designated location in Section 13 reserved for ancient written documents, he deposited into a small locked airtight steel box a very old manuscript that he had received from the captain of a Gestapo covert recon group. The sergeant told him that his undercover agents had confiscated the item from two foreigners outside a bar in Paris.

"Yeah, these two young Middle Eastern guys were drinking heavily and boasting about stealing something secret from a church in Turkey," the captain told Otto. "Supposedly, they weren't the ones who stole it, but were part of an organized secret team transporting it to their headquarters in Spain. They kept shouting that the book would destroy the Catholic Church. They kept twirling this old burlap bag above their heads, taunting everyone in the bar.

"When they finally left late in the evening, they were so drunk, they could hardly walk. My agents followed them for a couple blocks. When they turned into a dark alley, my men jumped them. For being as drunk as they were, they certainly put up a fight. We eventually shot and killed both of them and took the bag. It took us a little longer to get back to Berlin, but I knew I needed to deliver this to you.

"I took a short look at the book when we got it. It's not really a book, but just loose pages that are really fragile. It's written in a language I don't understand. But since it's supposed to hurt the Pope, I thought it might be valuable to the Fuhrer. Make sure you mention my name when you show it to him. I want full credit for finding it."

Otto smiled and told the captain he would certainly provide his name to Hitler for recognition. After the captain left the warehouse, Otto emptied the burlap bag, and spread the crumbling written pages on his table. He, too, didn't recognize the language. But the thing did look authentic at first sight.

It may look authentic, Otto told himself, but it's probably just some more crap when someone actually interprets it. To be on the safe side, Otto decided that an airtight box would lessen any damage to the fragile contents. So he carefully reassembled the pages to their original order, put the contents back into the burlap bag, placed the bag into the airtight steel box, and secured it with a padlock.

The box blended in quite well with all the other items on the massive shelving in Section 13. While retracing his steps back to his office, Otto made a mental note to contact his friend Konrad Wolff about the manuscript. Within two days, he forgot about his mental note.

CHAPTER TWENTY EIGHT

St. Louis, Missouri June, 1925

THERE was a buzz of excitement at Vacanti's Tavern on this sunny 26th day of June. Downstairs, proprietor Salvatore, wife Mary Catherine, and Sal's mother Rose were preparing to host not one, but two, special groups for dinner this evening. Upstairs, a different kind of excitement had climaxed.

"God, Luce, I love those big tits of yours," sighed Vincent (Vinny) Vacanti, the 16-year-old son of the tavern owner. "They're so soft and your nips get hard as rocks when I touch them. I can just play with them all day long." Young Vinny, still panting from his orgasmic fondling session, was reclining on both elbows on his bed as he pleasantly watched his girlfriend position her heavy breasts into her undersized brassiere, and put on her best white school blouse for a second time.

Vinny's small bedroom was located in the farthest west room on the second floor of the family's living quarters. This location was almost 50 feet away from the master bedroom where Lucy's high school girlfriends were readying themselves for the night's festivities. Privacy was at its peak here, and helped make Vinny and Lucy feel more comfortable exploring their Catholic teenage obsession with sex.

Lucy Vincenzo, the 17-year-old paramour of young Vinny, and oldest daughter of the biggest bootlegger in St. Louis County, was buttoning her white blouse as quickly as she could because she knew she was going to be late in getting downstairs to help serve the guests. Lucy loved when Mrs. Vacanti would call her to gather a group of 10 teenage girls from St. Elizabeth Academy to serve as waitresses at special dinners at the restaurant. This was her parent-free chance to see Vinny and take their sexual thirsts to the next level.

The girls always wore their school uniforms to these affairs. Mr. Vacanti liked the short navy blue pleated skirts with the snow-white short-sleeved blouses. He thought they looked "appealing" in a nice way for the customers. Each girl was given a Vacanti's Tavern red and green apron to wear over the uniform while they were serving. They all ate a free dinner after cleaning up after the last guest left the building. All the flirtatious girls agreed, though, that the best part of the job was the lipstick and rouge that Mr. Vacanti requested. The nuns at the strict all-girls Catholic high school they attended allowed no such devilish face paint during school hours and church functions.

"Vinny, you better get moving," Lucy urged. "You're supposed to be downstairs before I get there, remember? If I arrive first, your mom and dad are going to suspect something is going on." She quickly applied her make-up, brushed back her long dark curly hair a couple more times, straightened her blouse and skirt, took one final glance in the mirror, and raced out of the bedroom, blowing a kiss at her still-gawking boyfriend.

Vinny smiled as the streaking brunette left the room, and quickly ran to his closet to change his underwear and pants, still wet from his milky discharge. "Man, that was great!" he laughed. "I just love these big dinners, too." He was downstairs within two minutes, making sure he quickly got to the steaming kitchen before his dad arrived. He could always count on Grammy Rose to cover for his absence.

******

Less than a minute later, another smaller figure squirmed out from under Vinny's bed and ran from the room, giggling and punching his small fists in the air. *Yeah, I really love these big dinners, too, Vinny!* smiled Joey Vacanti, Vinny's 12-year-old brother.

Joey decided months ago that in order to learn how to talk to girls, he needed to learn how his older brother did it. It seemed to him like Vinny always had the pretty girls hanging around him. He wasn't going to learn any of this in his seventh grade class at St. Ann's Elementary School. And in order to learn from his experienced brother, he needed to watch it up close and personal. And that meant being in the room at the same time as Vinny and Lucy were there. And for someone five feet tall and less than 100 pounds, the safest place with the best view was from under the bed.

The first time he saw Vinny touch Lucy's breasts over her shirt, he gulped hard. Each private session following that, Joey saw more of Lucy's clothing coming off. And then today, he saw what he had only pictured in his dreams. Lucy allowed

Vinny to take off her brassiere this time. When she turned around to face Vinny, Joey captured a quick glance of both completely exposed breasts. He gasped so hard, his head jerked upward and he hit the box springs of the bed. He was sure that Vinny and Lucy heard him. But the two lovebirds were too consumed with their momentary passion to notice the bulging pair of green eyes peering out from under the bed.

As Joey ran to his room to dress for the night's festivities, he realized that he never really heard Vinny say very much to Lucy except that he loved her big tits. And he was positive that he couldn't go up to a girl and say anything like that to her. But he was sure of one thing: He needed to watch a lot more of Vinny and Lucy from his secret viewing position under Vinny's bed. *You can learn a lot by just watching*, he told himself.

******

The friendly neighborhood eatery, nestled on the bottom floor of a two-story brick structure at 3701 Sullivan Street, also happened to sit right across the street from Sportsman's Park, home of the National League St. Louis Cardinals and American League St. Louis Browns, two of Major League baseball's best franchises. And today was the day that the Vacanti clan had been awaiting for months.

"Mary, for Christ's sake, where are those extra waitresses?" bellowed Sal Vacanti, a short, gentle soul in his mid-30's with a booming voice that left no doubt who was in charge of this establishment. "It's almost 4:30. Some of those guys are going to start showing up pretty soon." He was busy rushing between the confectionery store at the front of the building and the back dining room that would be hosting two groups of players and dignitaries totaling 41 men. Fifteen were Cardinal players, 22 were Jesuit seminarians (11 from Florissant and 11 from St. Louis), two were priest administrators from St. Stanislaus Seminary in Florissant, Missouri, and two were representing the archdiocese of St. Louis, including the archbishop himself, John Joseph Glennon. The small restaurant was well-known for home-cooked Sicilian meals, and tonight was going to be a grand showcase for the Vacanti family.

"Sal, dear, don't be so antsy. The girls from St. Elizabeth's are upstairs combing their hair and putting on their aprons," answered Mary Catherine Vacanti, Paul's attractive, overworked, and frenzied wife of 17 years. "I told them they needed to look extra special because of who they will be serving tonight. So settle down. They'll be downstairs in a minute." After completing the short conversation with her harried husband, Mary continued to put her best silverware next to her best dishes, coffee cups, drinking glasses, wine glasses, and cloth napkins on the specially-decorated tables. The Vacanti's were preparing their humble café as if the Pope himself was coming to dinner.

"Okay, honey. Sorry about that. I'm just a little more nervous tonight because we've never had so many ball players and church people in here at the same time," he stated. "It sure was nice of the Cards to let the seminarians play their annual game at Sportsman's Park instead of at St. Stan's like they usually do."

Sal was talking about the annual baseball game between the younger Juniorate seminarians at St. Stanislaus Seminary in Florissant and the older Regency seminarians associated with St. Louis University. Dante remembered vividly the butt-whipping the regency team had put on his Juniorate teammates during his time at St. Stan's. He could tell then, as he did today, that the game was played for much more than bragging rights. There was a much deeper sense of pride among the older seminarians to win the game. Even though Dante's teammates today were in the prime of their lives physically, each player knew that his time in the spotlight was slowly fading as the endless 13-year march toward Jesuit ordination kept on its focused course. For Dante, it was his final game in this annual rivalry since his next three years would take him out of the state, working as a teacher in a Catholic high school in Illinois.

The game was usually played at the seminary this time of year. But in January, an invitation was extended by the Cardinal's front office to both groups to play their annual bragging-rights contest following a 1:00 o'clock game between the Cards and Chicago Cubs on this date. The Card's 3-2 win over the Cubs had lasted a little less than two hours, and the seven-inning game between the two Catholic seminarian teams concluded around 5:00, with the Paul Dante-led St. Louis University seminarians dominating their younger St. Stan's counterparts by a 12-4 score. Sal Vacanti was thinking the bulk of the two groups would begin arriving around 5:30 that evening, with some Card's players arriving earlier since their game ended before the exhibition game began.

Sal ended his brief conversation with his weary wife and hurried towards the kitchen to check on tonight's fabulous meal. The heavenly smells coming from behind the wooden swinging kitchen doors enticed Sal to quicken his pace.

******

Entering the aromatic kitchen, Sal first spied his son, Vinny, dicing up the lettuce for the dinner salads at a side table cutting board.

"Vinny, how ya doin', son?" Sal asked his oldest son, slapping him on the back. "Did you have a chance to see Lucy yet?"

"Oh yeah, dad. I've seen Lucy already," he answered, head lowered to both hide his snickering smile and show his father how hard he was working. "She's looking really nice tonight, just like you want all the St. Lizzy girls to look for these special meals."

Sal nodded, and then headed toward his mother Rose, the chief cook and menu maker for the restaurant, who was diligently monitoring the progress of food simmering on the stove, items baking in the oven, and young Vinny's cutting skills with the lettuce. She did all this while slowly sipping on a glass of red wine.

"How ya doin', Ma?" Sal asked his 57-year-old energetic and head-strong mother while leaning over to plant a light kiss on her left cheek. "Everything smells great. How's that farsumagro comin'?"

"*Gesù christo*, Sal, how in the hell do you think it's coming?" she answered sarcastically. "This is a work of art, for Christ's sakes. I'm going into the Holy Mother Mary Hall of Fame for sure when I die because of this meal. I mean, this meal is to die for. It's by far the best I've ever made. We're going to build up a lot of holy indulgences with the Man Upstairs after those priests eat this meal."

"Say, Ma, how many glasses of wine have you had already? Cuz it sounds like you're talking like a crazy woman," Sal laughed. "Are you going to make it through the dinner alright?"

He loved giving his mother a hard time because of her love of the vino. She was raised on it in southern Sicily where she had met Sal's father. Both of them had grown up together in the same small village where every family owned their own vineyard. It was an arranged marriage, she had always told Sal. They had married very young, and had two sons before she turned 20. Wine is what brought the two of them together. But it also drove them apart. Sal's father had been a mean drunk, and often abused his wife and young sons before falling asleep in a drunken stupor.

One day, Rose decided that she and her young sons had endured enough physical and emotional pain. She realized her husband wouldn't change his ways, in spite of pleadings from her and his family. While her husband was working in the fields, she quickly packed one small suitcase, bundled up her young sons, and left the old country for America, settling in the coal mining region of southern Illinois. She found out later that her husband had died when the ship he was sailing on to find her in America had sunk in the Atlantic Ocean after a violent storm. After Sal and Mary were married and the family moved to St. Louis, Rose moved in with them. And Sal was happy she had, because she was a fantastic cook.

"Tell me again what we're serving tonight, Ma," Sal said. "I want to make sure I've got it straight when the guys ask me about it." Then he stepped back from his mother to listen to her forthcoming colorful description.

"Well, Sal, I'm only going to say this once. So make sure your *grossa testa* absorbs what I'm telling you, *capisce*?" she said, taking another gulp of her dark beverage.

"The farsumagro is simmering in these two pans right here. I just added the wine, oil, and tomato paste a few minutes ago. By the time we serve around 6:00, this meat will melt in their mouth.

"Of course, we'll open with the lettuce salad. After Vinny's done cutting that lettuce, I'll have him dice up some black olives and tomatoes to top off the salad. I'll put a dish of vinaigrette on each table, and they can spoon on as much as they want. Plus, I've got bread baking in the oven that we'll put in a covered basket on each table.

"Since those players love meat dishes, I made my famous lemon chicken, too. That's baking next to the bread. Then I made a fish dish, too," she said, taking another sip of her wine. *Holy shit, I can't believe I got 'fish dish' out without slurring it. I AM good*, she thought to herself. "Salmon with agrodolce sauce. Oh my God. It's just heavenly."

"What are we doing for vegetables, Ma? We gotta have vegetables with this meal," Sal whined.

"*Maledizione*, Sal! Do you think I was born yesterday, for Christ's sakes?" Rose retorted. "We're having your favorite side dish, caponata, you idiot. And before you ask me which one, it's the one with mashed eggplant, onions, tomatoes, anchovies, olives, pine nuts, capers, vinegar, and olive oil."

"And dessert? What's for dessert?" Sal asked.

"I'm really glad you asked, Sal, because this is the final item on the menu, and the final thing I have to tell you," Rose responded with a smile. "It's Mary's favorite. The cassata.

You know, the one made with sponge cake with that ricotta-chocolate filling.

"Now get out of my kitchen before I throw you out! This bread has to come out of the oven right now. Come tell me when the men start showing up, especially the Card players. I kinda like that Rogers Hornsby character," she grinned.

Vinny chuckled as Sal quickly exited the kitchen after hearing his mother's idle threat. He was amazed how Grammy Rose could cuss out his dad in Italian like she did, and his dad wouldn't respond with any of his usually funny comebacks. *I guess that shows how much he respects her*, Vinny thought. He went back to his job of cutting up the olives and tomatoes.

Meanwhile, Rose swallowed her last sip of wine, set the glass down near the sink, grabbed her hot pads, opened the oven, and began to earnestly remove the steaming loaves, not stopping until all 20 of them were placed on a side table to cool. In 15 minutes, she would cut each loaf into 10 pieces and place them in the small brown baskets that were lined with a white napkin that would neatly fold over the bread to keep it warm at the tables. Then it was Joey's job to deliver a basket to each of the 10 round tables that would be in use tonight.

******

"Nice game today, Dante," said Specs Toporcer, the Cardinal's starting shortstop, as he entered the dining room around 5:30, and sat down at the table next to Dante. "For a goddamned priest, you can hit the ball pretty good," he kidded the young Jesuit. Specs was in a group that included first baseman Jim Bottomley, left fielder Ray Blades, right fielder Chick Hafey, and second baseman Rogers Hornsby.

Rose Vacanti just happened to be the person delivering the fresh-baked bread to Hornsby's table, elbowing young Joey out of the way when he tried to leave the kitchen to complete one of his important tasks this evening.

Dante, who had arrived five minutes earlier, laughed, and raised his beer to salute the major leaguer's profane comment. Even though Prohibition was five years old, Sal Vacanti always had a few cases of ice cold beer for special occasions like this. His supplier of the illegal brew was none other than Lucca Vincenzo, Lucy's bootlegger father. Lucca was a big Cards fan, and the local police seemed to bypass their official inspection of local taverns around the ballpark. Sal had heard that the police chief was a big fan of Hornsby, too. And because Hornsby liked his beer, Sal's place was one of only a couple taverns that police would look the other way when enforcing the law prohibiting the making, selling, or distributing of the illegal drink. For those not drinking beer, there was a plentiful assortment of legal red and white wines that Rose and Sal had made themselves.

Paul Dante was feeling good about himself. He was proud that his body had grown from a scrawny five-foot-seven inch, 140-pound frame when he entered St. Stan's seven years ago to his present physical dimensions of six-foot-two and 200 pounds. His combed-back dark hair had grown a little shaggy in the back, quite different from the required butch haircuts he wore while at the seminary long ago. He felt comfortable wearing his layman's clothes today instead of his priestly garb. He liked the "respect" from the major league ballplayers.

Dante was also proud of his production at the plate this afternoon. He accomplished the rarest of baseball feats:

hitting for the cycle. He doubled to right-center field in the first inning, homered over the 353-foot fence in left field in the second inning, singled to left in the fifth inning, and hit the most-difficult-to-earn-in-a-cycle triple off the 430-foot center field wall in the sixth inning. At game's end, he had driven in seven of his team's 12 runs. He also performed flawlessly at shortstop, committing no fielding errors while recording seven putouts, including an unassisted double play in the third inning. *This beer tastes mighty fine right now*, Dante told himself.

Geno Ferrelli, Dante's second baseman this afternoon, was sitting across the table from Paul, busily flirting with the young, nubile waitress who had volunteered for the back room duties tonight for the two groups of players and church dignitaries. The professional players she knew from their frequent visits to Vacanti's following games that season. *They always handled themselves with class*, she thought. But she was fearful of this second group of players. And they were supposedly Jesuit priests? *Goddamned pervert*, Lucy told herself, glaring at Ferrelli as she rushed away from the table.

"For Christ's sake, Geno. You're scaring the poor girl," Dante blurted at Ferrelli. "Give the poor kid a break." Dante motioned with his raised bottle to the closest server that he needed another cold beer.

"Aw, piss on it, Paul," Ferrelli retorted to his friend, taking another swig of his beer. "I was just being nice to her, you know. But they always get the wrong impression of me for some reason."

"I can tell you the reasons, dumbshit," Dante responded. "It's a combination of your lustful eyes, your groping hands, and the worst come-on lines in the history of mankind. Add on top of that that you're a fuckin' Jesuit, and your picture now resides in every dictionary next to the word "pervert." Dante tried to keep a straight face as he stared down Ferrelli after delivering the deprecating comments to his best friend.

Ferrelli reciprocated with his own version of "the glare" towards Dante, contemplated his friend's insightful bullshit, and responded with his customary rejoinder, "Aw, piss on it again, Paul." Both men laughed heartily at their feigned seriousness of the moment.

******

The procession of dignitaries into the backroom restaurant began in earnest around 5:45 that evening. Every Cardinal player and seminarian jumped from their seats when they spied Archbishop John Glennon striding into the room. The fiery Irish leader of the city's Catholic population cast a large shadow in the St. Louis community. Both revered and feared, Glennon nodded in modest approval at the respectful applause that greeted his grand entrance. As he headed toward his reserved table nearest the kitchen door, he suddenly stopped at Dante's table.

"Paul Dante," Glennon said as he took Paul's hand and began a lengthy, gripping handshake. "If you keep up that kind of exhibition that you demonstrated today, I'm afraid that professional baseball is going to seduce you away from Holy Mother Church." He started to smile as Dante struggled with his response to the compliment. Before he could open his mouth, Glennon continued his praise.

"That was as good a piece of hitting as I've ever seen from a Regent in this game," he stated. "I knew of your reputation from past games, but how in the hell did you come up with that kind of game today, son?"

"Your Eminence, I think I was inflamed with the power of the Holy Ghost today," Dante stated, straining not to burst out laughing from his extemporaneous comment. "I felt the Lord was telling me what every pitch was going to be. And the ball looked like a slow, lazy watermelon coming to the plate every time. It must have been Divine Intervention for me, your Eminence. Divine Intervention."

Glennon had released his grip by now, and slowly looked around the room to view the response from the other players to Dante's sarcastic answer. The wide-eyed Juniorates from St. Stan's were all nodding their heads in agreement, basically thinking that it had to have been divine intervention for an old guy like Dante to hit the ball like he did today. The Cardinal players were just smirking and shaking their heads, amazed at the level of bullshit that Dante would actually give his boss, for Christ's sake. Dante's fellow teammates could only smile in silent jealousy that Dante could get away with talking to a superior in this fashion. Geno Ferrelli could take the silence no longer.

"Your Eminence, may I be the first to apologize for my friend's total disrespect for your kind comments," Geno exclaimed. "You see, our young Paul here has taken humility to the extreme. What he really wanted to tell you was that he was the best and toughest sons-a-bitch in that ballpark today."

Upon hearing Ferrelli's profane diatribe, Glennon threw back his head and started a long, howling laugh that filled the room. His laughter was soon drowned out by the sudden din of noise, laughter, and tasteless commentary from the rest of the attendees. Glennon quickly gave Dante a pat on the back and a quick wink of his eye as he departed for his table, accompanied by his limousine driver for the night, a young diocesan priest who worked in the chancery.

Following quickly behind Glennon were two people Dante was very familiar with from his days at St. Stan's. Father John Mathery, the rector of the seminary, was the first to stop in front of his former star pupil. He eagerly grabbed both of Dante's hands and held them tightly.

"Paul, my son, how incredibly nice it is to see you experiencing such homage from His Excellency the archbishop," exalted Mathery, the rector at St. Stanislaus Seminary since August of 1915. "And it is so well-deserved. Your baseball prowess was at the height of its proficiency today." He kept smiling and didn't release his death grip on Paul's hands. You could tell he was very proud of his past student.

Effortlessly loosening himself from Mathery's enthusiastic paternal handshake, Dante, too, was thrilled to see his former seminary leader. "Father John, thank you very much for your kind words, and thanks, especially, for coming to the ballpark today. I didn't want to let you down." He then gave the jovial Jesuit a big hug. Ferrelli just rolled his eyes at the sight.

Mathery continued his conversation. "I hear you're heading for Illinois to teach at a high school next year. You will be a marvelous teacher. Do you want to do some volunteer coaching at the school, too? You know the faculty there would welcome your expertise on the diamond."

Dante laughed at the suggestion. "No, Father, I don't think coaching is in my future with the Jesuits. I don't know which direction it may take me, but coaching high school baseball is not something I aspire to do. But thanks again for the kind words.

"You don't want to keep the Archbishop waiting now, Father. Plus, the food is just about ready to be served after the Archbishop gives his blessing. I'll keep in touch."

With his closing words, Dante again hugged Mathery, holding him closely for an extended period of time. He then smiled sadly as Mathery walked away to take his place at Glennon's table.

The next visitor following Mathery to Dante's table didn't stop as he briskly brushed his way past Paul and Geno, turning to leave an evil stare wrought with hate and envy at the two young seminarians. There was no love lost between Dante and Father Joseph Beiler, the Dean of Students at St. Stan's during Dante's years at the seminary. Dante returned Beiler's glare with one of his own. Only his stare took on more of a mocking sneer, indicative of his negative feelings for the man.

Ferrelli watched Dante closely as Beiler strode past the two of them. Geno was very aware of the bad blood between the two men. He, too, had experienced some heated arguments with Beiler behind the closed doors of the dean's cramped office. He knew exactly what was going through Paul's mind.

"Hey, Paul, you really didn't expect that cocksucker to actually stop and talk to you, did you?" Ferrelli asked. "You know that was never going to happen."

"Oh, no. I certainly didn't expect that to happen," Dante replied. Both men began to sit down at their dining table. Geno spoke first.

"I'll never forget the way he treated you from Day One when you arrived at St. Stan's," Ferrelli began. "That bastard had it in for you from the beginning. No Distingished Service Cross winner was going to have any influence at the seminary during his watch. He was going to dig his heels into you every chance he got. He was going to show you how powerful he was. He disobeyed Mathery's orders all the time when it came to you. I'm sure all of that was running through your head just now."

"Oh, yeah," Dante answered. "All of those bad memories just started flooding my brain when I saw his face." Dante bowed his head as the Archbishop began his invocation to bless the meal. But as the silence in the small backroom restaurant overtook the surroundings, Paul Dante began to remember his early days in Florissant, Missouri.

CHAPTER TWENTY NINE

St. Stanislaus Seminary
Juniorate Year, 1920

"WELL, if it's not my two biggest pains-in-the-ass again," sneered Father Joseph Beiler, the hated Dean of Students at St. Stanislaus Seminary, barely lifting his head while sitting behind his large oak desk, as Paul Dante, S.J., and Geno Ferrelli, S.J., were ushered into his office by Julian Maline, the main supervisor of the evening meal this day. "Thank you, Brother Maline, I'll take it from here." Maline nodded, turned, and left the room silently.

Dante and Ferrelli had recently reached the Juniorate level of training after completing the first two years of Novitiate training at St. Stanislaus. To reward the aspiring seminarians, the society allowed each candidate to use the venerable symbol "S.J." after their names. Each student ascending to Juniorate status also received a black biretta, a stiff, square hat with three ridges on the top, which was to be worn at meals, Mass, and other communal occasions. Dante and Ferrelli arrived at Beiler's office without birettas.

Leaning back in his large, leather-padded chair, Beiler removed the dark-rimmed glasses from his face and glared at his two Jesuit misfits. He began his usual method of interrogation with a condescending diatribe.

"God Almighty, you two no sooner receive your dignified birettas and your "S.J." designation, and here you are standing before me because of more code violations. Why are you two still here at St. Stanislaus anyway? You take nothing seriously, yet you pass your classes with relative ease. You are the antithesis of Jesuit life, yet your fellow seminarians don't hesitate to cover for your transgressions. I would have thrown your unfit asses out of here long ago if the rector didn't always overrule me," Beiler complained.

"And thank God Burrowes is gone. He treated you dipshits like royalty while he lived here for that year. He thought your presence would bring prestige to the Jesuit cause, and increase vocations among young returning war veterans. The number of initiates increased in our region last year, but I'm convinced you two had nothing to do with it. You both think your shit doesn't stink because of your military backgrounds and hoopla surrounding your arrival here. But I don't care who you are, and I'm going to continue to make your lives a living hell while you're here."

Dante and Ferrelli stood rigidly in front of their nemesis, absorbing the insults and preparing to receive more vitriol from Beiler. The momentary silence in the musty-smelling, dimly-lit room was broken as the inquisitor began to systematically list the code violations that the two young men had accumulated today.

"Violation of silence. Obeying with reluctance. Carelessness in the observance of obedience. Not doing things at the proper time. Criticizing new undertakings while refusing to support them. Want of punctuality. Violating the rules of the library. Ridiculing culpas. Not wearing your birettas to dinner. How in God's name can anyone acquire these many code violations in one day?" Beiler asked rhetorically. He wasn't waiting for a response from these two hooligans.

"At first bells at 5 o'clock tomorrow morning, you will report to Father Bronsgeest at the cattle barn where you will shovel manure until Mass and Holy Communion at 7:30. You will be expected to be clean when you arrive at the chapel. That should knock a little humility into the both of you. Now get out of my sight." Beiler's emotions exploded with his last comment as he suddenly rose from his seat, and pointed to the door. The humbled pair bowed their heads respectfully, turned, and departed the room without saying a word.

Once outside Beiler's caustic chambers, Dante and Ferrelli stood silently for a couple minutes in the dark hallway, then walked briskly to the front door of the Old Rock Building and exited into the warm evening. Contemplating the verbal tongue-lashing they had just received for what seemed like the hundredth time during their time in Florissant, they finally turned and faced each other.

"All right!" Ferrelli exclaimed. "That played out just the way we wanted it, Paul. Beiler can just piss on himself."

"Yes, it did," Paul responded. "Well played, old buddy. That asshole still hasn't figured us out yet. He thinks shoveling shit at the cattle barn is our worst punishment. Man, let's make sure he never finds out why it's our favorite punishment."

Beiler's growing anger with Dante and Ferrelli mirrored the frustration he felt with his own life. The 65-year-old balding and heavyset man was in his 34th year as a Jesuit and in his eighth year at St. Stanislaus, the first five years as a Latin teacher and last three years as Dean of Students. As Dean of Students, he also had the final word on disciplinary matters, which he enjoyed tremendously. His lofty position also allowed him to both hide and satisfy his homosexual lifestyle within the small secluded community. But he could only exploit the weak seminarians. He hated Dante and Ferrelli because he could never break their willpower.

Most of the seminarians believed that Beiler enjoyed his role as chief disciplinarian of the seminary because he had been bypassed so often for promotion within the Jesuit hierarchy. He never could attain the top leadership position wherever he found himself. He was always second-fiddle to some inept bastard, he thought. It was he who should have been named rector of St. Stanislaus, not John Mathery, he complained. Mathery was just a simple, good-hearted soul with no administrative experience to lead a teaching seminary. It was he, Joseph Beiler, who was the true leader, he told himself. When Mathery was named the rector of St. Stanislaus in August of 1915, his first official announcement was naming Beiler as his second in command, with the position of Dean of Students and chief disciplinarian as a part of his job responsibilities.

Both Mathery and Beiler, however, took a back seat to senior leadership when Alexander Burrowes, the Provincial Superior, took up residence at St. Stanislaus at the same time as the arrival of Dante and Ferrelli in 1918. During his short one-year stay in Florissant, Burrowes had extolled Dante's leadership ability and took a personal liking to the boy hero from Nebraska. The Provincial Superior predicted a quick climb up the leadership ladder for Dante if Paul remained committed to the long process of becoming a Jesuit priest. When Dante and Ferrelli realized they were kindred spirits, it was Burrowes who helped cement the bond between the former Marine and Navy pilot. Paul and Geno both fought back tears when Burrowes was relieved of his provincialship in 1919, and sent to Brooklyn, New York to serve as a master of tertians within the Jesuit community. But it allowed Burrowes to hook up again with his lasting friend, Frank Duffy, the master recruiter who had secured both Dante and Ferrelli to St. Stanislaus.

Dante and Ferrelli understood that their two years of Juniorate-level training would be indicators of how they would progress within the stratification pattern of the Society of Jesus. By the end of Juniorate training, students were directed to become either a Priest-in-Training or a Temporal Coadjutor. The Priest-in-Training candidate would be exposed to a long course of academic study with the purpose of developing fully-professed Jesuits in major leadership positions. The alternative life path would be training to become "spiritual coadjutors", a position in which the candidate is ordained with the powers of the priesthood, but which would be subordinate to candidates in leadership positions. A Temporal Coadjutor would take a less taxing academic load, and concentrate on chiefly manual labor positions, with the long-term purpose of becoming a Jesuit "brother."

Surviving the first two years of Novitiate life had been challenging enough for Dante. *Oh, those goddamned bells,* Dante moaned every morning at 5:00 A.M. when the bell tower on top of Old Rock would wake the slumbering students with its crescendo of booming gongs. Then the bells sounded almost hourly during the day to announce the end of one activity and the beginning of another. Dante easily compared the Jesuit's bell system to the bugle serenade during basic training for the Marines. *I'll take that bugle any day to these damn bells*, Paul commiserated.

Dante recalled his day in the life of a novice. Every day for two years, he followed the same schedule. It was indelibly inscribed in his brain.

5:00 A.M. – Rise with bells

6:00 – Morning Community Chapel with all students

6:30 – Meditation for one hour

7:30 – Mass and Holy Communion

8:30 – Culpas and hearty breakfast

9:00 – Daily conference with Master of Novices

9:15 – noon – Duties/classes/exercise/recreation

12:00 P.M. – Culpas and dinner

12:45– Meet in chapel for prayer

1:00 – 4:00 – Duties/classes

4:00 Haustus – late afternoon snack

4:15 – 5:00 – Duties/classes/exercise/recreation

5:00 – Litany recited before supper

6:00 – Culpas and supper

7:00 – Chapel for prayers

8:00 – 9:30 – Personal time

9:30 – Lights Out

At this secluded wilderness outpost, the oldest and largest seminary in the Midwest, friendships and formations of cliques were formed early during novitiate training. Famous, ordinary, rich, poor, timid, assertive, athletes, bookworms, city kids, farm kids, religious, worldly, sexual, chaste, obedient, rebellious, innovators, followers, good, bad, and eccentric. There were difficult and quirky personalities to assimilate. Everyone at St. Stan's was there for a reason, either running toward or away from something. The Jesuits accepted them all if each candidate made the Society of Jesus stronger in some visible way, or if the generous donation to the Jesuit coffers came with specific stipulations. To the public, the Jesuits liked to be viewed as superhuman. At home, behind the mythology, they were just men, with foibles and frailties that helped build the lore of the community.

The vast age discrepancy between teaching faculty and students made rebellion a common daily occurrence. With the founder of the Society of Jesus himself a former member of the military, seminary life was organized and driven by strict daily schedules, codes of conduct, and ethical behavior in order to control all aspects of the student's lives. A curriculum heavy on humanities training didn't allow for anything except rote memorization of facts. Recrimination and punishment were swift to those who broke and bent the rules.

Seminary life also meant experiencing ironic behavior from superiors. The Jesuits took great pride in being known within the Catholic Church as practical thinkers and unafraid to go against the status quo when needed. The first quality that the Society expected in its stratus climbers was leadership. With that in mind, idiosyncrasies and incidental deviations in conduct were accepted if the individual was considered a fast riser within the Jesuit community.

Absurdity and redundancy of rules were commonplace. The confession of bogus culpas (faults) before meals became a time of comic relief for the harried scholastics. Two favorite "faults" were "making a fool of myself by imitating the actions of superiors" and "arguing too long that the truth might appear." The laughter quickly subsided when the perpetrator of such frivolity was suddenly snatched from his seat by the hall supervisor and delivered to Dean Beiler's office.

The list of "permissions" in the rule book was insane and impractical. The Dean's permission was needed in order to practice music and have more than three library books at a time. A Rector's permission was needed to write letters. Finally, a Minister's permission was needed to take long walks, use the telephone, and be dispensed from speaking Latin after supper. For Dante, the quest was simple: survive, and have some fun in the process.

Dante's simple method of acclimating himself to a new environment and remembering names included assigning each new person he met with a unique nickname. He commonly did this back home in Omaha, and it always proved helpful to him. In some cases, he also discovered that nicknaming someone was a way of enamoring yourself to that person. So when he arrived in Missouri, he was quick to put names with faces at Florissant.

Father Clement Martin, in charge of the orchard, became "Fruitman." Father Anthony Geyser, the chicken ranch proprietor and chief cook, became "Cluck." Father Andrew Ganss, supervisor of the wheat fields and the person responsible for providing firewood for all housing, became "Fire Guy." Father Jacob O'Meara, the master of the vineyard, became "Vino." Father Francis Nebrich, the butcher and assistant cook, became "Knives." Father Robert Manning, in charge of the dairy and creamery, became "Teets." Father Francis Hillman, baker extraordinaire, became "Sweetsmells." Finally, Father Henry Bronsgeest, supervisor of the cattle barn, became lovingly known as "Shovelshit."

Dante also tagged each administrator at the school. Provincial Superior Alexander Burrowes, Dante's first mentor at St. Stanislaus, became "Alexander the Great." Father John Mathery, the seminary rector who took over for Burrowes both as a leader and mentor, became "The Big Guy." Finally, Father Joseph Beiler, the dean of students and chief disciplinarian, was named after Evil Incarnate, "Satan", in addition to other curse words.

It took only a few days for Paul Dante and Gino Ferrelli to realize they were kindred spirits. And it was a simple act of justice that drew them together. During a late-afternoon haustus during the first week of novitiate, the overwhelmed students were enjoying their 15-minute rest and snack break when a large group of rich city kids surrounded a small group of farm kids, and began to bully them for no good reason except intimidation. The two faculty supervisors, talking on the other side of the small, cramped room, saw what was developing, but stood solemnly in their tracks, arms folded across their chests. They either didn't care what was transpiring, or they were waiting to allow the disruption to escalate before intervening.

Dante, who had grown nearly six inches since his Marine induction day over two years ago and now stood over six feet tall, was standing alone in a corner devouring one of

Sweetsmells's donuts and washing it down with a glass of chocolate milk. He was viewing the troubling scene as he took another frosted donut from the serving tray next to him.

The leader of the intimidation group was a taller guy with short blonde, flat-top hair. The intruder resembled some German soldiers that Dante had shot during the war, Dante thought. The leader of the target group was a little shorter than his counterpart, with short red hair that matched a red, cherubic face that had seen plenty of time in the sun. The shorter man was standing toe to toe with his aggressor, not giving an inch. When the intimidator stuck his finger into the chest of his shorter adversary, a scuffle ensued between members of both groups. Still, the supervisors did not budge from their positions. Dante felt he has seen enough. *All right, let's restore some order here before somebody gets hurt*, Dante figured, cramming the last bite of his third donut into his mouth as he snaked his way through the mingling group to the commotion.

Across the room, Geno Ferrelli had also been observing the scuffle and decided the situation needed his presence. Two years older than Dante, the former Navy pilot in World War I gobbled down his last piece of chocolate bar, and began making his way toward the fracas. *Aw, piss on it. Those idiot supervisors over there don't have the balls to step between those fellas. Stand back and let the men handle this*, Ferrelli surmised.

Dante and Ferrelli arrived at the uprising at the same time. As the flailing arms and swinging elbows intensified, and the pushing and shoving escalated, Dante bearhugged the tall blonde and pulled him away from the pile of bodies as Ferrelli grabbed arms and shoulders of the other combatants and started flinging them backward and away from the action. Within a matter of minutes, both groups had been separated with no blood shed, but the hard feelings remained.

"This isn't over yet, farm boy," yelled the tall blonde as he shook himself free from Dante's grasp. "If your buddies here hadn't shown up, we would have wiped your asses all over the room."

"Not a chance, rat face," the redhead countered. "We would have wiped your asses all over the room. We don't need help from anyone to do that."

As the snickering blonde sauntered away and the redhead re-assembled his group, the two room supervisors made their way toward Dante and Ferrelli.

"Why don't you two come with us," the first man said. "Father Beiler wants all the troublemakers to be brought to his office." He motioned to Dante to begin walking toward the door. The second supervisor had corralled Ferrelli and pointed him in the same direction.

"What's this about? We're the ones who stopped the fight," Dante protested. "Why are we being brought to Beiler's office? We didn't do anything wrong."

Ferrelli was outraged. "Where were you two gutless wonders when everything started going south?" he questioned the two supervisors. "Paul and I had to do your work for you, you two pieces of sh.."

As Dante interrupted Geno's colorful description of the two supervisors, the room full of seminarians began to loudly protest how Dante and Ferrelli were being wrongly accused. A few jumped in front of the foursome to inhibit the progress toward the door, while others shouted their disapproval of what was transpiring. Sensing another uprising, this one directed towards THEM, the two supervisors increased the grip on their prisoner's arms, and hastened their movement to the door.

After Paul and Geno were delivered to Beiler's office, the dean took the two supervisors aside and spoke softly as to not be heard. "My little ruse worked. I knew those two would try to play heroes, and I'm sick of heroes. Thank you for bringing these two to me. My directive continues. Any time we can catch them being a part of a contrary scene, bring them to me. I don't care how popular they are with their peers, I will humiliate them enough to get them to quit the seminary. That will teach Burrowes a lesson. I have the power, not him," Beiler bragged.

Following a severe verbal tirade, Beiler assigned Dante and Ferelli to his favorite form of punishment: shoveling manure at sunrise in the cattle barn under the scrutinizing eye of Father Henry Bronsgeest, the barn's supervisor. Being a native of Philadelphia, Beiler had deduced early upon his arrival at St. Stan's that shoveling manure had to be the most humiliating of all punishments for all students. He had continued to employ this disciplinary tactic since his first day as dean of students.

When Dante and Ferelli reported to Shovelshit the following morning, Bronsgeest informed them that a few head of cattle had wandered off during the night. "I need you two to find those cattle and bring them back. Do you understand?" Bronsgeest said. "We can't afford to lose any livestock with the appetites of everyone at this seminary. So instead of shoveling this morning, go find those cattle. They've been branded with "STS" on their hind quarters. That stands for St. Stan's. I think they may have gone that way." He finished his order by pointing to the northwest. The two young war veterans smiled at each other, dropped their shovels, and began their quest to locate and return the cattle to the barnyard.

A little over two miles down the narrow road that led to and from the isolated seminary, Dante noticed a large group of cattle in a distant pasture. "Hey, Geno, look over there. Maybe some of our cattle are mixed in with those," Dante said. "Let's take a look."

As they drew near the grazing herd, both men saw that the grassy pasture was located a short distance from a white farm house with a bustling farm yard. The dawning sun was slowly rising above the grove of trees behind them as the early rays of the day spotlighted feverish activity around the farm. Bodies seemed to be moving in all directions. But it seemed like controlled chaos to Dante.

As they slowly walked up the lane toward the house, a man in his mid-50s approached them. "What can I do you for, gentlemen?" he asked cordially. "Running away from the priest farm, are ya?" He smiled as he wiped the sweat from his brow, waiting to hear their reply.

"No sir," Dante responded. "We are from the priest farm, but we're here to locate some of our cattle that wandered off during the night. We saw the large herd, and wanted to ask you if we can take a look if any of them are ours. They're branded, so it should be easy to identify them. By the way, I'm Paul Dante, and this is Geno Ferrelli." Both stepped forward and shook the man's hand.

"Thomas Murphy. Glad to make your acquaintance," he answered while returning the handshake of the two young men. "You two must be in trouble at St. Stan's if you were sent out to look for cattle at daybreak. But Father Hank must like you since you aren't shoveling manure in the yards. Am I right?" He chuckled as Dante and Ferrelli exchanged inquisitive looks.

"I'm just messin' with ya," Murphy laughed. "I've known Hank Bronsgeest all my life. We grew up together. His family lived just a few miles to the west of here. We went to country school together. Then he went off to high school and then joined the Jesuits. They assigned him to St. Stan's right after ordination, and he's been there ever since. I stayed here to help my dad run this place. When he passed, I inherited it, and now my whole family is a part of the operation.

"Hank always stopped by every week to talk and catch up on things. His folks died about 10 years ago, and they sold the farm. But he used to tell me what he did at the priest farm. Since he grew up farming, the rector put him in charge of the cattle yards. It also didn't take him long to figure out that the crazy dean over there punished the kids by having them shovel manure at dawn. He told me he worked out a system that the kids who really deserved the punishment did the shoveling, but the kids who got railroaded by the dean got to go out and fetch the lost cattle. Late at night, he'd open the gates and let a few head wander off. So, yeah, I assume some of your cattle are over there with mine. They seem to find their way here with no problem. Kind of like homing pigeons, you know." He laughed again.

While Murphy was telling his story about him and Bronsgeest, Paul and Geno couldn't help but notice that the farmer had three very beautiful daughters. They also noticed three young men. All six were busy completing their early-morning chores, moving quickly from the chicken coop to the dairy cows to the haystack in the barn to the machine shed located next to the outdoor latrine. The girls were carrying buckets of eggs and creamy milk to the house as the men attended to their work in the barn, shed, and pasture. Once in a while, Dante would make eye contact with one of the siblings, smile, and nod his head. The men always responded with a nod. The girls all turned up their noses.

"Tell you what, boys, why don't you two go down there and find your cattle and separate them from my herd. Then come in and join us for breakfast." Murphy didn't wait for a reply as he turned and waved as he moved toward the house. Dante and Geno turned in the opposite direction and headed for the herd. It took them five minutes to locate the branded seminary cattle, and set them apart from Murphy's. They then raced the 50 yards to the house, a little winded as they knocked on the screen door.

"Come in, boys," yelled Martha Murphy, Thomas Murphy's wife of 32 years, as she continued to fry eggs and country ham on the wood-burning stove. "Your two spots are right over there between Laura and Bonnie. Don't worry, they don't bite." She giggled as her two embarrassed daughters rolled their eyes and protested meekly. Dante and Ferrelli walked to the vacant chairs, pulled them out, and sat down, Dante with Laura to his right and Ferrelli with Bonnie to his left. After all were assembled, Thomas led the group in saying grace before the food started being passed around the table.

Over the next hour during a fabulous country breakfast, Paul and Geno learned the names and ages of all the siblings: 27-year-old William, 25-year-old Janet, 24-year-old Russell, 23-year-old Ben, 21-year-old Bonnie, and 20-year-old Laura. The two young seminarians also told the Murphy's about themselves and why they had chosen to come to St. Stanislaus. Thomas and Martha were impressed that the young war veterans chose a religious life for a career when so many other opportunities were thrown their way. The Murphy boys were eager to test their shooting skills with Paul and Geno. Janet and Bonnie just cursed Holy Mother the Church for seducing two eligible bachelors away from them. Young daughter Laura yearned for a life of adventure and excitement that Paul and Geno had experienced at so young an age.

For the next two years, Dante and Ferrelli plotted successfully on how they could get assigned to Shovelshit duty so they could sneak away to visit the Murphy's farm. It didn't hurt that Father Hank liked both men, and enjoyed perpetrating the ruse upon Beiler. *Martha's cooking was the best*, the two interlopers told themselves after each tasty meal. After conducting their usual shooting games with Bill, Russ, and Ben, and assisting with chores around the farm, Paul and Geno would end their clandestine visits with short walks and innocent conversation with Bonnie and Laura.

Two years of casual walks and conversation eventually morphed into deep and lasting friendships for the two young couples. Platonic feelings suddenly became more intimate. As the relationships deepened, so did the feelings of guilt. Paul and Geno felt they were betraying their Jesuit vows, and were falsely leading the girls to a place they couldn't take them. Bonnie and Laura felt guilty about "stealing" the seminarians away from their stated path with God. Deep down, though, the girls hoped that Paul and Geno would choose them over God to complete their life's journey.

But one fall afternoon, everything changed for the Murphy family. Geno was helping Bill and Russ in the machine shed, while Paul was with Thomas and Laura in the pasture feeding the cattle. Suddenly, Thomas felt a sharp pain develop in his left shoulder and traverse down his left arm. His chest began to hurt, and it felt like his heart was ready to explode. He called out as he clutched his shirt and fell to one knee. By the time Paul and Laura arrived, he was lying on the ground on his back, gasping for air.

Laura was screaming for her mother as Paul knelt down next to Thomas. "What's wrong, Mr. Murphy?" Paul asked while lifting the father's head to put his rolled-up shirt under his neck for a pillow. "How can I help you?"

"My chest. It feels like it's going to explode," he stammered. "I can't catch my breath, either. What's happening to me?"

Dante's military mindset immediately kicked into high gear. He needed to stay focused and calm. Thomas was most likely having a heart attack as they spoke, he thought. But his military training never prepared him to deal with a medical situation like this. He felt helpless.

"We're going to call a doctor for you, Mr. Murphy. Just hang in there," Paul said with a soothing voice.

Laura's screams had caught the attention of everyone on the farm. Martha and Janet came rushing out of the house. Bonnie dropped the pail of milk she was carrying and began running to the pasture. Geno and the brothers dropped their tools when they heard the screams, and made their way to the doorway of the machine shed.

Laura was now on both knees on the other side of her father, holding her father's left hand. Sobbing uncontrollably, she was begging God to save her father's life. Paul kept his focus on Thomas.

Without warning, Thomas grabbed Paul using his right hand and raised himself a few inches off the ground. Looking Dante straight in the eyes and with his final breath, he said "Take care of Laura, Paul." Upon uttering his last words, Thomas Murphy gasped one final time, closed his eyes, and fell heavily to the ground.

Within a minute, the entire Murphy family and Geno arrived at the pasture. Laura continued to cry and began to slam her fist into her father's chest, hoping to awaken him from his deathly sleep. Martha knelt down next to Paul and grabbed her husband's right hand, a look of desperation and sadness clouding her face. Everyone else just stood motionless, viewing the horrific scene silently.

Seeing that Laura was frantic with grief, Martha turned her attention to Paul. "Oh my God! What happened here, Paul? Is my husband dead? Wake up, Thomas! You can't leave me like this!"

Dante, exhausted from the ordeal and now sitting on the ground next to the body, looked up at Martha with tears in his eyes. "There was nothing I could do. It happened so fast. He just collapsed. He said his chest felt like it was going to explode and that he had trouble breathing. I am so sorry, Martha. Not even my military experience could help me in this situation."

Martha began sobbing softly. With streams of tears cascading down her cheeks, she gently stopped Laura from trying to pound the life back into Thomas.

"Laura, dear, please stop. There is nothing you can do for your father anymore. He's gone. He's in a better place." She pulled Laura close to her, the embrace lasting for several minutes. Mother and daughter were sharing their disbelief and sorrow in the best way they knew at the moment.

After releasing Laura, Martha again turned to Dante. "Paul, did Thomas say anything else before he died? What were his dying words?"

Dante shot a quick glance at Laura to see her reaction to the question. During all of the commotion with Thomas, Dante could not tell whether Laura had heard Thomas's last request to Paul. When Paul and Laura locked eyes this time, however, he could tell that she had indeed heard the request from her dying father.

He knew he couldn't tell Martha the truth. *What did Thomas mean by "take care of Laura"?* he asked himself. *Marry her? Financially support her?* Paul had no idea, and now wasn't the time to discuss it. He knew, though, that he and Laura would need to talk about it later.

"No, Martha, there were no last words except that he had trouble breathing," Dante lied. Martha just nodded her head, accepting Paul's answer. But Dante felt sick to his stomach for not being honest with Martha at such a vulnerable moment for her.

Martha asked Father Hank to conduct the funeral mass at the little country church that Hank and Thomas had been baptized in and had attended all their lives. Hank requested that Dante and Ferrelli assist with the mass, and Mathery gave his consent. After mass, the burial took place in the small graveyard located behind the church. Five generations of local families had members buried there. Martha felt that Thomas was with departed family members in the next life. She knew that Thomas would always be watching over his family from beyond the grave.

During the traditional luncheon held in the small church community room following the funeral, Dante and Laura sat alone at a secluded corner table, holding hands. Martha noticed the pair, and figured they were coping with the grief in their own way. In a way, she was right.

Laura spoke first. "Oh, Paul, I know you're worried about what my father asked you to do before he died. It was just the ramblings of a scared, dying man. He didn't mean anything by it, and I certainly don't hold you to anything he said. So please don't feel you have an obligation to fulfill because you don't." She smiled as she squeezed his hand to confirm her feelings.

Paul returned the smile along with his interpretation of Murphy's dying plea. "You know, Laura, I feel very strongly about the wishes of a dying man. I experienced dozens of them during the war. And most of them were simple requests. "Tell my wife I love her." "Pay Sarge the twenty bucks I owe him." "Tell my family I love them." "Ship my body home. Don't bury me here." These were all very easy to accomplish. But with your dad, I feel a lot different."

He took a deep breath, and looked Laura in the eyes. "I saw the look in your father's eyes. I felt the grip on my arm. I heard the message. To me, I really think he meant what he said."

He continued. "You have become a special part of my life. I do want to take care of you. But I don't know how I can do it. I'm committed to finishing my journey with the Jesuits. Even though I have a long way to go, I know there will be an end to the training and schooling.

"But you also have a life to live. I can't give you marriage. I can't give you a family. I can give you my love and emotional support. I don't want you depriving yourself of happiness. I want you to find the love of your life, settle down, and be the great mother and wife you will be. I should have never let our relationship evolve beyond friendship. I feel very guilty about it. It was very selfish of me, and I apologize for it."

Laura squeezed Dante's hands even harder when he finished his thoughts. She now looked him straight in the eyes. "Maybe I have found the love of my life. But maybe MY selfishness allowed the relationship to cross the line. This is the sin that I must atone for. I challenged God's intentions for you, hoping my dreams would defeat God's plan for you. I was wrong to hope for such things.

"I'm very proud of you. I've never been happier since you came into my life. You will make a great priest. I apologize for thinking I could have you instead of God. I will live my life, but I won't ever forget you."

Following the funeral, Dante and Ferrelli never again returned to the Murphy farm. Not that Geno didn't want to. He and Bonnie had consummated their love for each other many times. But there was no chance of coming back to the Murphy farm without Paul. *Aw, piss on it,* Geno stated often to himself. They were a team. And he knew that he and Paul needed to reconcile their feelings of lust and desire with the discipline of becoming a Jesuit priest. Plus, they had Beiler to keep driving crazy.

After much thought and prayer, Paul finally concluded that the best way for him to comply with Thomas Murphy's dying request to take care of his daughter was by staying away from her so that she could live her life.

CHAPTER THIRTY

Vatican City – Pope's Secret Radio Room
1937

THE secretly coded cryptic message arrived from the Vatican's spy who had infiltrated deep within Hitler's Nazi organization in Berlin. Dante and his team were still investigating in Milan when Pacelli was sent the disappointing news. Stressing the importance of the scope of the message, the wireless communique was delivered by Sister Pascalina Lehnert, Pacelli's long-time secretary and confidante, who traveled from Pacelli's personal residence to the Pope's secret radio room, hidden deep within the Vatican Archives, to retrieve the message for Pacelli.

The message was short and devastating:

Mission failed. Satan holds package. Please advise. E

Upon reading the shocking message, Pacelli immediately sent word via Ferrelli's radio on the plane to notify Dante to return to Rome with his recovery team. *"Your mission is over, Paul,"* the coded message read. *"The enemy prevailed this time. Return home. Need new plan to attack evil."*

The secret radio room was of invaluable assistance to Pacelli. Historically, Pope Pius XI was credited with the founding of Vatican Radio in 1931. In the process of developing plans in 1925 for the establishment of a wireless communication station in the Vatican, the concept to establish a secret radio room known only to members of the inner circle of the pope was the brainchild of Jesuit Father Giuseppe Gianfranceschi, the Director General of Communications for Vatican City at the time. Before assuming his Communications position, he was professor of physics at the University of Rome and the rector of the Gregorian University. It was his belief that the political climate in post-World War I Europe could easily explode into another world conflict, and the Vatican needed to be ready to communicate secretly, if needed, with its hierarchy of bishops, priests, and the Catholic Faithful in the affected countries.

The man chosen in early 1927 by Gianfranceschi to assist and mastermind the covert and overt aspects of the Vatican Radio project was Italian scientist, Marquis Guglielmo Marconi. The 1909 Nobel Prize in Physics winner for his contributions to radio communications, the Catholic and Fascist Marconi was very interested, but he needed a little extra incentive from the Vatican Jesuit.

"Father Giuseppe, it's such an honor for you to consider me for this bold and brazen quest to project the word of the Holy Father to the entire world," Marconi stated upon his initial meeting with the Director General in the official Communication Center office within Vatican City. "Your idea of constructing the secret radio base shows much foresight on your part. It can be accomplished, but for my part in this hidden plot, I ask for two small favors in return."

"Why, yes, of course," the dark-haired Gianfranceschi replied, a look of puzzlement on his face. "How may the Vatican be of service to you?"

Marconi laid out his terms. "First, Father, I wish to speak the first words when the radio station goes on the air. I wish to be the person to announce that His Holiness will be addressing the Faithful of the world. Can I do that?"

Gianfranceschi was quick to reply. "I believe I can inspire His Holiness to grant you that request. He is a humble man whose ego does not need to be placated. What is the second item you wish me to consider?"

Marconi got the impression that Gianfranceschi was beginning to feel undue pressure. But the Jesuit's reply to the second item was paramount in Marconi taking on the project. It was more than a request. It was a demand.

"As you may have been reading in the papers, the divorce with my wife Beatrice was not a cordial separation," Marconi claimed. "In fact, it has been filled with great malice on her part. In addition, she married Liborio Marignoli, the Marquis of Montecorona, less than three weeks following the divorce, which was quite humiliating to me.

"In the interlude, I have met a wonderful woman to fill the void and sting left by the divorce. Her name is Maria Cristina Bezzi-Scali, the daughter of Count Francesco Bezzi-Scali. But there is one problem, Father Giuseppe. In order for me to legally marry her in the Catholic Church, my first marriage must be annulled."

"How long was your marriage before the divorce?" Gianfranceschi asked.

"Almost 20 years, Father," Marconi stated, his head bowed in embarrassment.

"My son, an annulment is impossible within the guidelines of the Catholic Church," the Jesuit stated resolutely. "Annulments are given quite infrequently in the first place, and they usually occur within the first year of marriage. You're asking to annul your first marriage after 20 years? I'm sorry to disappoint you, but I don't believe that can happen."

Marconi straightened up in his chair, and leaned forward to address Gianfranceschi.

"It's not a request, Father. To buy my expertise is secondary to binding the confidentiality of the covert aspect of this project."

Marconi continued, "Combining your knowledge with mine, we can easily cover the installation of the secret radio room while constructing the public radio station. But you must guarantee me the annulment of my first marriage."

On April 27, 1927, roughly two months following the veiled threat to Gianfraceschi, Marconi's first marriage was officially annulled by the Catholic Church. On June 12, 1927, Marconi married Maria Cristine Bezzi-Scali, with Fascist Dictator Benito Mussolini serving as the best man at the wedding.

Around 4:20 in the afternoon of Inauguration Day of Vatican Radio, February 12, 1931, trumpets announced the arrival of the Holy Father, and Pius XI made his way to the Radio Transmission Station. With Marconi and Father Giuseppe accompanying him, the Pontiff moved to the Generator Room where he steadily moved the controls which activated the power.

With the Pope having completed all operations necessary for the first Papal transmission, Marconi spoke his historical first words of introduction: *"I have the highest honor of announcing that in only a matter of seconds, the Supreme Pontiff, Pope Pius XI, will inaugurate the Radio Station of the Vatican City State. The electric radio waves will transport to all the world his words of peace and blessing."*

Following the announcement, Pius XI sent the first worldwide radio message ever given by a Pope. The message was heard in Italy, and stretched as far as London and New York City. Catholics around the world huddled close to their radios to hear the encouraging words of the Holy Father.

The world was now aware of the existence of the Vatican Radio. Only the inner circle of papal confidantes knew of the existence of the secret radio room, which Pacelli would utilize throughout his tenure as pope. The foresight of Jesuit Father Giuseppe Gianfranceschi, and his adept handling of the fragile negotiations involving Marconi, proved prophetic when Hitler began to formalize his European invasion plans.

CHAPTER THIRTY ONE

Mittelwerk Underground Factory
Nordhausen, Germany – 1938

"**MUTTER FICKEN!**" sighed young Nazi rocket engineer Peter Wegener as he climaxed on his final thrust into his *heimliche Geliebte* Emma Salzberg. "Yah, mother fuck," Salzberg repeated softly, the sweat dripping from her brow and escaping semen seeping from her naked torso onto the sawdust-covered floor. The engineer and the riveter met in the isolated fuel supply room each day during lunch. The menu? Assorted sex positions that can take place in 15 minutes in a six-foot-square unlit damp storeroom.

Today's "lunch special," as Wegener playfully called it, was a *Kama Sutra* position that had both lovers standing upright with female entry from under and behind. Salzberg had to work the hardest to find an elevated resting position for her left leg that would allow maximum penetration and pleasure. During this exploratory time, Wegener busied himself by standing behind his partner, putting his hands under Emma's blue work shirt, releasing her heavy breasts from her sturdy undergarments, and groping the twin mammary glands until both lovers simultaneously discovered the magical fornication position and Wegener began his rhythmic upward thrusting motion. It didn't take Wegener long to "finish."

As the two *sexbesessenen* Germans quickly dressed and readied themselves to return to their work posts, they were startled by a loud booming sound. And then another. With startled looks, they darted from their lover's lair, and began running in the direction of the noise. As they neared the immense fortified underground laboratory that housed the secret alien airship, they saw a disaster in progress. Explosions were erupting everywhere, with balls of fire and construction materials whizzing in all directions.

"Mutter ficken!" screamed Peter Wegener as he watched a raging stream of fire snake along the fuel-saturated ground and slowly engulf the alien space craft. The safety of the craft was his responsibility, and he saw his life going up in flames in front of his eyes. He realized he was a dead man walking when Hitler would arrive shortly to receive his report on his attempts to find a way to enter the craft. The craft had been in his possession for a week, and his team had failed in every effort to locate an entrance. He knew Hitler would not listen to his explanation. He would shoot him on sight.

When Emma saw what was happening, her instincts sent her off in search of the fire retardant foam that was used to fight such blazes. It was uncommon NOT to have a fire of some sort break out each day since so much incendiary materials and flammable liquid fuel and chemicals were in abundance throughout the secret underground laboratory. But having the spreading flames in the most secret and secure laboratory chamber containing Hitler's most prized possession was truly a catastrophic event that would have dire consequences for Peter, she thought.

A large group of workers had arrived with fire-fighting equipment when the first explosion occurred. But the chemical-induced fires burned so hot that most of the rescuers could not extinguish the flames that were threatening the alien craft. Two workers had died instantly when their heads collided with flying debris as they neared the craft. When Emma returned, she carried two 25-gallon steel containers of retardant with spraying attachments. She gave one container to Peter, and both of them sprinted toward the flames engulfing the airship.

"Emma, we've got to put these flames out!" Peter yelled at the top of his lungs. "Try to get as close to the craft as you can." He then furiously aimed the fire retardant foam at the flames that were inching their way toward the craft. He made sure he stayed within visual range of Emma to document her progress.

Emma methodically inched her way to the large silver oval object, spraying a path clear to the craft. As she looked back, smiled, and waved to Peter, championing her victorious assault on the fire, a five-foot piece of lead pipe that was hurling through the air buried itself in her left temple, slowed as it slid through her brain matter, and exited out her right temple, a brain-and-blood-saturated two-foot section protruding from both sides of her impaled skull. She was dead before she hit the ground.

Incredulously, Wegener watched the grisly scene unfold in front of him. The tragedy happened so quickly that he was still smiling from Emma's heroic fire-killing march to the airship. The shock of seeing Emma's lifeless body collapsing on the cold cement floor caused Peter's body to go numb.

His body began to shake uncontrollably as a loud guttural scream exploded from his throat. He wanted to run to Emma's side, but his legs wouldn't move. Tears welled up in his eyes. Vomit found its way out his mouth from deep inside his stomach. His knees buckled, and he fell awkwardly to the floor. But he needed to get to Emma's side, to cradle her head in his arms one last time.

With newfound courage and strength, Wegener slowly rose from his knees, and started to stumble toward his dead lover. Upon reaching her, he dropped to his hands and knees and gently moved her bloody and brain-splattered head to his lap. He stroked her hair, letting his tears fall onto her face, still lovely in death. Only moments before, he had felt the sweet dampness of her womanhood. Now, he felt her warm, lifeless blood trickling from her head wound onto his pants. It was over. She was gone. And he felt like he had caused her untimely death.

As the fire intensified around Wegener, Emma, and the alien craft, additional scientists, engineers, and laborers were frantically dousing flames as they quickly made their way to rescue Peter. Another young rocket engineer and Peter's best friend, Wernher von Braun, was the first to arrive to aid his crestfallen friend.

"God Almighty, what the hell happened here?" von Braun yelled into Wegener's face as another explosion ripped through the top-secret chamber. As smoke and flames continued to spread quickly to all corners of the enormous work room, von Braun finally noticed the gruesome sight of Emma Salzberg.

"Mutter finken, Peter. I'm so sorry about poor Emma," von Braun lamented. "But we have to get you away from these flames. Let's pull Emma away from the flames, too."

As Wegener struggled to rise, von Braun grabbed Emma under her shoulders and pulled her safely away from the fire. When Wegener was upright, he and von Braun carried Emma's body to an adjacent room and away from further danger. As they left the body and walked slowly to the doorway of the room, they were amazed at two sights: The damage to the room was very extensive. Work stations were leveled to the ground. Barrels of rocket fuel and chemicals had disintegrated. But, miraculously, the alien craft showed no signs of damage at all. Not even any signs of heat erosion or soot marks from smoke. Even more amazing to both Wegener and von Braun was the pristine condition of the outer shell of the craft in spite of several horrendous collisions with airborne steel and lead rocket parts that had arrived at hundreds of miles per hour during the explosions.

"Jesus Christ, Wernher, that *finken* airship doesn't have a scratch on it," Wegener gasped. "How in the hell do you explain that?"

"I have no idea, Peter. But thank God it survived this catastrophe," von Braun stated. "Hitler will still go absolutely berserk when he sees what happened here. He considers the technology behind that craft to help Germany win the war. And, you know, it's my ass and your ass on the line here, buddy.

"Your team has the responsibility of finding a way into that ship. My job is to discover how it flies, back-engineer the technology, and install it into one of our flying disks. I know you've tried everything short of dynamiting your way in. But there's got to be a simpler way. I know you'll eventually find it. I'm not sure, though, that Hitler will be patient enough to let us do our jobs."

Another glance into the cavernous laboratory saw the final blaze being extinguished. Although it seemed like the explosions and subsequent fires and flying debris had lasted for hours, it actually lasted only 20 minutes. But the toll had been great: 10 dead. Five research work stations demolished. Six-hundred gallons of rocket fuel and chemicals eradicated. Thousands of pounds of experimental building materials annihilated. Not to mention the scorched walls and ceiling of the chamber, and the hundreds of liquid pools of fire-retardant foam that was scattered everywhere.

After he finished talking with von Braun, Wegener returned to Emma's corpse to plant a final kiss on her bruised and bloody forehead. "Goodbye, my love," he whispered into her mutilated ear.

Then Wegener became incensed. "Who is the incompetent bastard responsible for this disaster? When I find him, I'm going to kill him!"

Walter Dornberger, another brilliant engineer recruited from the private sector into the German Army to research aerodynamic shape at the secret underground factory, overheard the angry plea and ran to deliver the message Wegener wanted to hear.

"I was told that dumbshit Amsdel was using the hydraulic hammer on the underside of the craft to try to get inside," Dornberger said. "I understand your team hasn't had any luck in finding a way into that piece of shit aircraft yet. I think he may have gotten tired of you trying to use your heads to find a way in. He probably decided that brute force was the only answer. If you had been around here within the last hour, you would have seen the idiot.

"Well, there was so much friction from the blasting that one of the sparks flew into a small puddle of rocket fuel next to the craft. Before he realized it, the small explosion escalated into a massive destructive force that ended up in the dismal and dramatic scene you see before you."

"Where is that little cocksucker Amsdel?" Wegener yelled while spinning around to locate the young laborer who was hired only a week ago and mysteriously assigned to Peter's group. Supposedly, the kid had some connection to one of Hitler's powerful inner circle of confidantes, and that's how he got the job. Wegener thought the kid's mom was probably screwing the high-ranking Nazi. That's the only way a kid could have gotten a position in such a top-secret facility and assigned to the most delicate and intricate job there.

Dornberger pointed in the direction of an assembly of scattered body parts about 100 feet from their position. The head, torso, and left arm had been severed from the lower body. The bloody legs and dismembered right arm, still clad in the required blue work shirt and pant, lay nearby. "There's Amsdel over there. At least what's left of him."

Wegener quickly ran to Amsdel's remains, and kicked the dead man's lifeless head, shouting profanities at the same time. He was ready to run to the rolling head and kick it a second time when von Braun grabbed him around the waist from behind and pulled him away.

"For Christ's sake, Peter, leave him alone. He's already dead." von Braun bellowed. "He's already paid for his ignorance. Kicking him won't bring Emma back. That was an act of God. Just walk away. You're making a scene, and people will think you've lost control. And you don't want to give people that impression."

Wegener struggled to free himself from von Braun's iron grip. "God dammit, let me go, Wernher," he demanded. As he freed himself, Peter caught a glimpse of the hundred sets of eyes watching him closely.

"What are you looking at?" Wegener shouted in the direction of the onlookers. "We've got to get this place cleaned up right now. Hitler will be here any minute. And if I'm going down for this *finken* accident, I'm taking as many of you down with me as I can," he sneered.

The crowd of emergency workers dispersed quickly, many shaking their heads in derision regarding Wegener's phony threat. But von Braun heartily agreed with his friend. Peter Wegener was going to take the full fall for this catastrophe.

CHAPTER THIRTY TWO

MITTELWERK was an architectural wonder. Hitler firmly believed that it was the perfect location for several reasons - to hide the space craft, back-engineer its advanced propulsion system, construct a similar circular version of the outer shell, and insert the alien technology into the new Nazi craft. Upon a successful completion of the project, world domination was inevitable, Hitler boldly proclaimed to his inner circle.

The first reason making Mittelwerk the perfect military research and development facility was the underground location. Since it was not detectable to enemy airborne missions, work could be accomplished without fear or disruption of bombing raids.

A second reason was the vastness of the facility. Stretching for miles, the tunnels were segmented into areas that offered both secrecy and flexibility for its technicians, diagnosticians, scientists, engineers, and laborers. The laboratory to recreate the flying disk was over a half-mile in diameter, with a ceiling stretching almost 150 feet above the dirt floor.

A third reason was convenience. Mittelwerk was also the location for testing and manufacturing the V-1 and V-2 rockets that would cause havoc and horror to the citizens of Great Britain during the height of the war. Fuel, chemicals, raw materials, and design and manufacturing facilities were all available to the scientists and engineers working to decode the mysteries surrounding the saucer.

The final and most compelling reason to make Mittelwerk the solitary location for the flying disk research and development was the number of laborers available to Hitler and his scientific teams. Those "laborers" were available because they were chosen from the thousands incarcerated into concentration camps since 1933. The Jews were Hitler's favorite outcast group to inhabit the camps. But he also populated the camps with political prisoners, criminals, homosexuals, gypsies, and the mentally ill. His master plan was to eliminate all inferior human groups and replace them with only those individuals of true Aryan descent. The inhabitants of the concentration camps were also the "subjects" that Hitler had promised to supply to Telhri for human scientific experimentation. As far as Hitler and Telhri were concerned, both sides were keeping their end of the deal.

The creation of the Mittelwerk underground factories began as a result of a spectacular secret internal political plot instigated by Hitler and his inner circle just weeks after Hitler's swearing in as Chancellor of Germany. Buoyed by the election and confident in his long-range plans of world domination, Hitler understood the need to begin building vast networks of underground factories and facilities in preparation for a second world war. But he needed thousands of laborers to accomplish his goals. He needed scapegoats, and he needed the sympathy of the German citizens to justify his actions. So the plot to stage the Reichstag fire was born.

As much as Hitler hated the Jews, he hated communism more. As much as he liked the Jews to be the scapegoat, he was coaxed by his inner circle that it was politically expedient to make a communist the scapegoat for the fire. Hitler's SS agents identified a Dutch insurrectionist, Marinus van der Lubbe, as the prime target. Spewing a communist agenda and unemployed from his bricklayer job, van der Lubbe had just arrived in Germany to eventually carry out his political activities. The SS infiltrated van der Lubbe's group, with the covert Nazi agents convincing van der Lubbe of the grand scheme to set the Reichstag building ablaze.

The arson attack began as planned on a cold Berlin evening on February 27, 1933. The Reichstag building was chosen for the assault because it was the assembly location of the German Parliament, the seat of political power of the country. Disguised as janitors and maintenance personnel, van der Lubbe's group waited until the last person exited the building, and then fervently began to strategically place bundles of flammable material throughout the quietly abandoned premises. At precisely 9:47 P.M., the bundles were set afire, and the Communist perpetrators quickly dashed from the blazing building.

The Berlin Fire Department received a message at 10:00 P.M. that the *Reichstag* was on fire. Ninety minutes later, the blaze was extinguished. Hitler, having dinner at Joseph Goebbels' apartment, was notified of the fire, and he, Goebbels, Vice-Chancellor Franz von Papen, and Prince

Heinrich Gunther von Hohenzollern were taken by car to the *Reichstag* to view the damage.

According to Hitler's impeccable plan, Hermann Goering met the group there and quickly proclaimed that evidence had been found linking the fire with the Communist Party. Van der Lubbe, along with fellow Communist party members Ernst Torgler, Georgi Dimitrov, Blagoi Popov, and Vassil Tanev were arrested and indicted on charges of setting the *Reichstag* on fire.

The Leipzig Trial was widely publicized and broadcast on the radio. At the conclusion of the trial, only van der Lubbe was convicted, while his fellow defendants were found not guilty. In 1934, van der Lubbe was beheaded in a German prison yard. But the damage to the Communist Party as a result of the trial allowed the Nazis to increase their share of the votes in the German Parliament from 33% to 44%. This gave the Nazis and their allies, the German National People's Party, who controlled eight percent of the vote, a majority of 52% in the *Reichstag*.

With the voting majority now in his favor, Hitler easily sold the *Reichstag* fire to the German populace as the beginning of a Communist revolt to overtake the German government. With the proclamation that German national security was at risk, Hitler decisively engineered quick passage of the Enabling Act, which gave Hitler the right to rule by decree. So with support of the right-wing German National People's Party, the Catholic Centre Party, and several fragmented middle-class political parties, and with the Social Democratic Party members (the only group that would vote against the Enabling Act) under-represented due to arrests and intimidation by the

Nazi SS, the measure passed easily on March 23, 1933. When the measure went into force on March 27, 1933, it effectively made Hitler dictator of Germany.

With supreme power firmly established in his domineering grip, Hitler and his inner circle of Nazi Party officials commenced their grand plans to obliterate the Jews, create the perfect Aryan race, and become the dominant world political and military power.

CHAPTER THIRTY THREE

"**THOSE** ugly little bastards finally did something right," Hitler gleefully exclaimed as his official military car raced toward the secret subterranean Mittelwerk rocket facility in the heavily-forested Harz Mountains. This would be his seventh visit in seven days, because this was the location of the large silver flying disk that Telhri had finally delivered to him after years of relentless begging, pouting, and cajoling his space buffoon. The flying craft arrived a week ago, but with a catch. Telhri didn't tell Hitler how to fly it, or how to get inside it. It was up to Nazi scientific ingenuity to figure out how to enter and how to back-engineer the craft to see how it operated. Hitler really hated the little alien leader for making things so hard for him.

On this trip, Hitler brought Hermann Goering, the newly-appointed head of Germany's armed forces. The Mittelwerk facility was now under his jurisdiction, so he was as eager as Hitler to learn of the progress of the highly-skilled German engineers as they probed their way around the outside shell of the craft, looking for an entrance.

Goering and Hitler had a history together, going back to 1923 when Goering heard Hitler speak at a National Socialist German Worker's Party meeting. Admitting that it was "political love at first sight," Goering quickly became a trusted member of Hitler's early inner circle.

"I hope that imbecile Wegener finally figured out the secret of entering the craft," Hitler shouted to Goering, both men peering out the side car window as Hitler's military driver sped through the exterior security gate of the secret mountain stronghold into the sprawling interior of the monstrous underground research, development, and manufacturing plant. "He was the one person that could get the job done, I was told by Herr Nebel, my most experienced scientist. But the young man has been nothing but a disappointment so far."

Upon entering the underground facility, Hitler's driver lowered his vehicle speed, bypassed several busy work stations addressing highly-classified projects, and came to a stop at the entrance to the huge cavern housing the large alien disk. A crowd of nearby workers followed the Nazi-flagged car into the clandestine room, and assembled together to watch how Hitler would react to the fire that had damaged the room's interior, nearly scorched the bottom of the craft, took the lives of several responders, and had only been extinguished moments ago.

Hitler and Goering noticed the unusually high number of gawkers as they exited the vehicle. Hitler's ego always told him that his presence at any location would always draw an admiring crowd. Goering was angry that people were not at their work stations, creating and developing the advanced munitions and weaponry that would help Germany win the war. Then both of them smelled the smoke-filled air, and saw the remnants of the quick-spreading fire.

Hitler was livid. "What happened here? Where's Wegener, that worthless bastard? What did his incompetence result in here?" He kept looking around and shouting at the top of his lungs, his arms flailing in the air. Goering joined Hitler in his visual search for Wegener, as both leaders quickly made their way to the alien craft to inspect the damage.

Several of the gathering gawkers smirked when they witnessed Hitler's tirade directed toward Wegener. Many of them were present when Wegener claimed that he wouldn't be the only one punished for the fire. They remembered his searing threat that he would take down as many people with him as he could. All were now present and eager to see if Wegener's self-fulfilling prophecy would occur.

Peter Wegener slowly made his way into the huge working room amidst the sound of Hitler's voice and humiliating accusations pointed toward him. Wernher von Braun also entered the room, keeping a comfortable distance behind his fellow engineer and escaping into the growing crowd of workers. Arriving where Hitler and Goering now stood alongside the craft, Wegener began his rehearsed speech.

"Mein Fuhrer, the scene you see in front of you was caused by an incompetent fool named Amsdel," Peter claimed. "The idiot was trying to jackhammer his way into the craft when a spark ignited a small pool of rocket fuel. The small fire escalated into tiny explosions that sent debris and loose building materials flying across the area. Several responders and innocent bystanders lost their lives because of this fool's insubordination."

Before Wegener could continue to build his case against Amsdel and shift blame away from himself, Goering cut him off. "Dr. Wegener, you say this was a case of insubordination. But where were you when this travesty occurred? How did this blaze get out of control so quickly? You are the expert when it comes to preventing and extinguishing all forms of chemical and fuel fires that break out here on a daily basis. Why did you react so slowly when you knew the safety of the alien craft was at risk?"

Wegener was momentarily stunned by Goering's line of questioning. As Hitler listened intently for Peter's response, a look of increased frustration and anger overwhelmed the Fuhrer's face. Wegener could sense that Hitler did not care what his answers would be. He also sensed that his life was probably coming to an ignominious end.

"Reichsmarschall Goering, I took immediate action when I saw the extent of the flames and the damage that might cause harm to the alien craft. I was swift and decisive." Peter boasted.

"Obviously, your response was not swift and decisive because several people lost their lives," Goering countered. "Where were you when the fire broke out, because you certainly were not in this work area?"

This was the one question Peter did not want to answer. He swallowed nervously, and his mouth suddenly got dry. His hesitation to answer the question only fueled Goering's curiosity and Hitler's anger.

"I was called from the room by a worker to answer a manufacturing question," Peter blurted out. "I was gone only momentarily. I returned immediately when I heard the first explosion and smelled the smoke permeating the complex."

Wegener thought his answer was adequate, and felt proud of his response. But without warning, another voice dispelled Peter's story.

From the back of the standing crowd, a female voice was painting a different picture of Peter's alibi. "Wegener, you lying bastard," the voice shouted. "You were off screwing Emma Salzberg in the chemical supply room, just like you did every day at lunch. I know because Emma always told me everything the two of you did."

Hitler, Goering, and everyone else turned in the direction of the accusatory voice. Hitler spoke first.

"Show your face, woman. I want to see who's making this serious accusation," Hitler demanded.

The crowd parted, and a short young women with flaming red hair tied into a long ponytail, began walking toward Peter, Hitler, and Goering. Peter noticed that she had the same work uniform as Emma. Peter did not know who she was, which made the entire scenario a very dangerous one for him.

As she approached the group, Wegener raised his right index finger and pointed it straight at his accuser. "You're a liar. Emma and I were only friends. We were not lovers." Peter stated.

"And you're a bigger liar, asshole, because Emma told me about that Kama Sutra shit you did today. You just used her. Just used your influence as a Nazi scientist to get inside her pants. You make me sick," the woman exclaimed.

Hitler had heard enough. He raised his left hand, squelching any immediate retort from Peter, and quieting the red-haired woman. He then walked quickly to Wegener, and looked him straight in the eye. "How can you defend yourself against these accusations?" Hitler demanded. "Who can vouch for your whereabouts when this disaster started?"

A small bead of sweat started to form on Wegener's brow. He was starting to panic when he blurted out, "Wernher von Braun. Wernher von Braun saw me here fighting the flames. Tell them, Wernher. Tell them you saw me fighting the flames."

Nestled inside the noisy crowd of workers, von Braun just rolled his eyes in disgust. He was flabbergasted that Wegener had drawn him into this *he-said, she-said* argument. He knew one thing: he wasn't going to lie to protect Wegener's ass. Plus, Goering knew who von Braun was, making the final decision to assign von Braun and his weaponry expertise to Mittelwerk.

Goering called out to the crowd. "Dr. von Braun, would you be so kind as to step forward to substantiate Dr. Wegener's claim." When Wernher arrived, he gave Peter an angry glance.

Hitler again took control of the conversation. "Dr. von Braun, did you see Wegener here in this room when the fire began?"

Without hesitation, von Braun responded to Hitler's query. "Mein Fuhrer, I did see Dr. Wegener in this room fighting the flames when I arrived. But I arrived a few minutes after the fire began."

Hitler continued with his questions. "So you saw Dr. Wegener in the room when you arrived, is that correct?" von Braun nodded his head in agreement. Peter's shoulders straightened and his survival mode brightened when he saw von Braun's nonverbal communication to Hitler. He figured Wernher had just saved his ass. But Hitler continued to probe.

Hitler now cast his attention back to the red-haired woman. "I understand this Emma Salzberg is one of the fatalities here," he stated. "When did she tell you about her meeting with Wegener this afternoon?"

The woman turned away from Hitler, and instead directed her response toward Peter. "Emma told me when she was running to get the flame retardant containers to help fight the flames.

"She said her body was just starting to feel normal again since the Kama Sutra position she said dipshit here put her into to screw had made her uncomfortable. She kept yelling that she had to get the retardants to help Peter fight the flames, because she said Peter was afraid that Hitler would shoot him if he found out Peter wasn't around when the fire broke out." Upon completing her final sentence, the red-haired woman turned back to face Hitler. Hitler immediately swung his gaze back to Wegener.

Wegener was now sweating profusely. All eyes in the large cavern were now directed straight at him. His head was spinning. He started to get nauseous as the pressure of lying to Hitler was taking its toll. He kept looking at von Braun, a look of desperation painting his face.

"I swear, Mein Fuhrer, the accident was not my fault. Emma and I were valiantly fighting the blaze when she was killed. It was a freak accident. I didn't want her to get in harm's way, but she heroically fought the flames to make it safely to the craft, and then she was extinguishing the flames closest to the craft when a pipe flew out of nowhere and slammed into her head. She died a hero." Hitler laughed at the thought of a woman acting heroically.

Growing more intolerant, Hitler addressed the crowd of onlookers. "Is there anyone here who can tell me if Dr.

Wegener was not in this room when the fire began? I'm tired of wasting my time with this bullshit," he screamed. All eyes in the room began their own personal scans. Finally, someone spoke.

"Dr. Wegener was not in the room when the fire began. In fact, he didn't arrive until the flames had reached the flying disk, which was around 20 minutes after the blaze started." Again, all eyes were seeking the speaker.

"Who's telling this story?" Hitler demanded. "Get out of the crowd and into my line of vision."

Walter Dornberger now made his short walk to Hitler. As Dornberger approached, Peter was outraged. As a fellow scientist, Wegener believed that scientists should always cover the back of a colleague. This was blasphemy. This was a flat-out betrayal, Wegener surmised.

"Who are you?" Hitler addressed Dornberger. "How do you know for sure that Wegener was not in this room?"

Dornberger identified himself as the chief German engineer in charge of back-engineering the propulsion system of the craft once entry into the craft was finally achieved. He told Hitler and Goering that he entered the room from a nearby work station when shouts and explosions were sounding at the same time. Amidst the chaos, Dornberger told Hitler that he, too, was looking for Wegener because this was Wegener's workplace and job responsibility.

For a long moment, Hitler said nothing. Wegener was now in a full body sweat. The red-haired lady stood nearby, sneering at Wegener and hoping for his quick demise. Dornberger concentrated on avoiding eye contact with

Wegener. Von Braun also stood by, thinking how stupid and unprofessional Peter had acted following Emma's death.

Finally, Hitler spoke directly to Peter. "You cannot deny this man's story, can you?"

Without listening for Peter's answer, Hitler abruptly called Goering to his side.

"Escort Dr. Wegener off the premises and make sure he doesn't return," Hitler commanded, his voice at a fever pitch. "His presence is not needed any further. His actions have been disgraceful. He put personal lust ahead of his job. I will not tolerate such insubordination. Get him out of my sight!"

As Goering held Peter's arm while leading him away, Wegener suddenly broke away from Goering's grip, and started running. Wegener knew what Hitler meant when he told Goering to make sure Peter didn't return. He was going to kill him. Peter decided that he wasn't going to die without trying to escape. And, besides, his fertile mind had instantaneously created a brilliant escape plan.

Peter thought he would be safe if he started running through the crowd of workers. They would act as shields to any bullets that might try to be finding their way into his back. When he exited the crowd, he would make a quick dash toward the barrels of rocket fuel that stood near the entrance to the room. Certainly, Goering wouldn't fire at Peter, knowing that a stray shot could find its way into an explosive fuel target. And any kind of explosion could harm the craft.

Peter continued to sprint through the crowd, throwing people aside in hope that Goering's line of vision would be compromised in the chaos. As Wegener broke free from the crowd of workers, he began running in a zigzag motion to make it more difficult for Goering to find his target. Peter was feeling free. Free from Goering. Free from Hitler. Free from the scorn of his fellow workers. Free from his responsibility to get into that *finken* space craft.

Wegener turned briefly to see how much distance he had put between himself and Goering. He was delighted to see that Goering was standing hundreds of yards behind him, only staring at his fleeing figure. He saw Goering raise his arm, as if waving goodbye, Peter thought. *You bet your ass I'm out of here*, Peter thought. *Goodbye and good riddance.*

When Peter turned to continue his mad dash to freedom, he heard a loud noise. Without having any reason to stop, Peter suddenly realized he wasn't moving any more. In fact, he saw the vast room starting to tilt to one side. He quickly reasoned that he must have tripped over an object that got in his way, and he was falling.

Trying to correct his balance and continue his retreat from Goering, Peter felt a burning sensation in his chest. He put his right hand on his chest to locate the warm spot. Looking down, he was amazed to see a dark red substance on his hand and shirt. The burning sensation felt more severe to him now. But he could fight through the pain, he thought. He just needed to get back on is feet. But he couldn't.

Peter found himself on his back, his gaze starting to blur as he looked at the ceiling of the cavern far above him. His breathing had become difficult, and his strength was leaving his body.

"What the hell is happening to me?" he wondered. And then he saw the Nazi soldier standing over him, his black rifle aimed at his head. As Peter stared in bewilderment at

this curious situation, and as he struggled to get up off the dirt floor, the young soldier put a bullet directly between the scientist's eyes. Peter's world went black.

Hundreds of Mittelwerk laborers stood in shocked silence. Only minutes before, they had watched Peter Wegener elude Goering's grip, and begin his futile run away from his accusers. Some of them felt angry at the fleeing suspect. Some of them felt sorry for him. Some of them internally cheered him for his brazen act of defiance toward Hitler. But they all knew how this scene would end. Peter didn't have any chance of escaping. There were too many armed guards in the facility. Peter's death was inevitable.

After viewing Peter's pitiful death, Hitler turned to the crowd of onlookers, and bellowed out, "You foolish idiots, get back to your jobs. This is what happens to liars. This is what happens to fornicators. You don't want to disappoint me, because what you've just witnessed is the way you will die for your incompetence."

Within seconds, every worker returned to their work stations, and hurriedly resumed their duties to the Third Reich. Peter's bloody dead body was dragged away from the expansive room and ignominiously dumped into a deep hole that had been dug to house the victims of the fire. At the bottom, Peter's lifeless body rested next to a young woman with a lead pipe through her head.

Back in the secret chamber, Hitler and Goering turned their attention back to the reason for their visit: the progress on finding an entry point into the flying disk. Goering invited von Braun to join them, and informed the young scientist that he now was responsible for Wegener's job. Hitler agreed with Goering's decision, but sternly warned Wernher that he would meet the same fate as Wegener if he wasn't successful.

Wernher von Braun was now the man in charge of Germany's most secret weapons project. "*Finken*" was the only word that Wernher could think of to describe his feelings toward his new work assignment for the Fuhrer.

Vatican City – Government Palace
March 1939

THERE was an air of high tension and fear in Vatican City on this cold March day. Pacelli was barely a few days into his papacy following the death of Pius XI when he received a special communique from Germany. Adolf Hitler was sending notice to his old friend that he would be arriving to congratulate Pacelli on his selection as the new pope, among other unnamed topics of discussion. This was not a request for permission. It was a subtle demand for the new Pius XII to be ready to greet the German Fuhrer with open arms.

"He has arrived at the gates, Your Holiness," the pope's personal secretary announced to the 63-year-old pontiff as he waited within the Vatican's official office within the Government Palace to receive political and religious visitors. "Thank you, Father," Pacelli replied.

For this quietly-publicized and highly-classified Vatican meeting, Pacelli surrounded himself with his most trusted aides. The first person he requested to be with him was Monsignor Paul Dante, who was dressed in his black and red priestly robes. Rounding out the small intimate group was the Cardinal Secretary of State, Luigi Maglione, who, too, was only days into his official duties.

"What do you think he wants to address?" Maglione asked Pacelli. "You know this is not a social visit."

"I have a feeling that blackmail is going to be in the conversation," Dante blurted. "Hitler is a sick bastard who wants to rule the world. He's already marched into the Sudetenland and Czechoslovakia. Maybe he's going to tell us he's marching into Vatican City."

Pacelli disagreed with Dante's comment. "No, Paul, that is not going to happen," the politically-astute Pacelli answered. "There would be worldwide sympathy for us and public outrage toward Hitler. It would be a public relations nightmare for him. But I do agree with your idea that we may be blackmailed so that Hitler can continue his quest for world domination."

A moment later, Hitler, dressed in full military uniform and holstered pistol, and his armed entourage marched quickly into the meeting room, ignoring the weak plea to stop by the papal Swiss Guard, and bypassing the pope's secretary, whose job it was to formally announce him before entering.

"I'm so sorry, Your Holiness," the personal secretary apologized to the new pontiff. "He just marched right by me, not stopping when I pleaded with him to allow me to announce his arrival." Pacelli just nodded his acceptance of the apology as the secretary closed the door.

"Hello Eugenio," Hitler sang out as he entered the large open room. Removing his hat and putting it under his left armpit, he quickly moved toward Pacelli, and grabbed both hands of the diminutive bespectacled leader of the world's

Roman Catholic Church. "My, it's so good to see you again, my old friend. What's it been, almost six years since you and I signed the concordat in Berlin? By the way, your security is quite feeble with those Swiss Guards you employ. Such dreadful uniforms, too. Quite pathetic, if you ask me."

Pacelli allowed the German leader to shake his hands instead of the traditional kissing of the pope's ring, which he knew Hitler would never agree to do. He also didn't respond to the sarcastic comment regarding Vatican security.

"Hello, Chancellor. I'm a little surprised to see you," Pacelli answered. "Now, exactly why did you request this meeting?"

Ignoring Pacelli's question for the moment, Hitler quickly added, "So sorry to hear about the death of your brother, Francesco. When was it, a few years ago? Anyway, he did such a splendid job for your previous pope negotiating that Lateran Treaty with Mussolini that made this small piece of land you call home into a politically sovereign country. Amazing. Just an amazing job of negotiating."

Hitler continued without taking a breath. "But all of that hard work must have taken a toll on his health, didn't it? Alas, he died too soon. But I'm sure he's living a grand life in the afterlife because of his work for the Vatican. Popes and their employees all get special treatment in the afterlife, don't they, Eugenio?" Hitler smirked at his self-perceived cleverness.

Pacelli's facial expression began to turn to anger, but he refused to dignify such an ignorant statement with a personal response.

Hitler slowly moved away from the pontiff, completely disregarded Maglione's presence, and proceeded to approach Dante.

"And who might you be?" Hitler asked Dante.

Pacelli intercepted the inquiry. "This is Monsignor Paul Dante. He is one of my top advisers. Now, why again have you traveled to Rome to personally speak with me?"

Laughing, Hitler responded. "Before I tell you, allow me to introduce Konrad Wolff. He is one of my youngest and brightest officers." Hitler did not introduce the two soldiers wearing side arms who were acting as Hitler's personal security detail for the trip.

Dante knew exactly who Wolff was. He had seen Wolff and his men countless times during the mission to rescue the Nestorian papyrus. Wolff stepped forward, removed his hat, and kissed Pacelli's ring, a look of disgust adorning Hitler's face as he observed the ritual. Wolff then shook hands with Maglione.

When he came to Dante, a smile creased Wolff's face. "Hello, Monsignor Dante." Then leaning more closely to Dante, he whispered, "You look different in your priestly attire." Dante did not respond as he shook Wolff's hand. Before Wolff could continue the private conversation with Dante, Hitler began speaking again.

"Eugenio…Excuse me, Your Holiness…I am not just here to congratulate you on your selection as pontiff," Hitler began. "I am truly happy for you. But there are more worldly things I need to discuss with you. Shall we sit down?"

All individuals moved to an open chair surrounding a large round mahogany table in the sparsely, but opulently, decorated room. Pacelli, Dante, and Maglione sat together on one side of the table, while Hitler and Wolff sat together across from the Vatican hierarchy. The two German guards lined up in tandem a few feet behind Hitler and Wolff.

Hitler began his announcement. "As you know, the Munich Agreement was signed last September by Germany, England, France, and Italy. In essence, I got what I wanted, a legal declaration stating that I can occupy other country's land, and no one is going to stop me."

He laughed as he continued. "Chamberlain was so skittish about keeping England out of another World War that he would do anything to appease me. And Daladier is such a coward, as are all the French, that I don't worry about any of France's involvement in my political proceedings. And, of course, Mussolini is right here in Italy, waiting for a chance to spread his Fascist regime."

Pacelli interrupted Hitler's ramblings. "Just what are you trying to tell me with this gratuitous, long-winded speech?"

"My dear little man, I'm telling you that I'm going to begin invading any European country of my choosing within a few months. I am building an unstoppable army with advanced weaponry to dominate the world. And the Vatican is not going to do or say anything to get in my way."

Maglione was quick to interject his thoughts. "You're going to start another World War? That's insane. Germany is still recovering from the last war. Your people don't want another war. You're leading them to slaughter."

"But you're so wrong about the German people," Hitler snapped at Maglione. "They are solidly behind me. They are tired of being humiliated in the world's eyes. They believe they are the strongest race of people on earth." Wolff nodded his agreement with Hitler's statement.

"For years now,' Hitler continued, "I've been cleansing German society of the Jews and other weak links. I'm building the pure Aryan race that is destined to rule the world. And you, Eugenio, you, too, hate the Jews. You made your position very clear while you were assigned to Berlin. You said you believe that the Jews were responsible for the death of Christ."

Pacelli took a moment to collect his thoughts before responding to Hitler's accusations. "You are wrong in your simplistic assessment of my views of the Jews. But you are simply rounding them up and killing them and others because you enjoy killing. How can you possibly justify killing innocent women and children, regardless of ethnicity?"

"I do it in the name of progress, Your Holiness," Hitler sneered. "Inferior and weak people only hinder the progress of the great people. I am doing society a favor. I'm eliminating the worthless people that drag down society. Anyway, I'm only building my empire like the Catholic Church built its."

Dante exploded from his chair after hearing Hitler's comment. "I'm sick of your blasphemous statements regarding his Holiness, the Vatican, and the Church. Don't you dare compare your hedonistic beliefs to those surrounding the principles of the Catholic religion."

Hitler's full attention was drawn to Dante's bellowing response. "Why Monsignor Dante, have I touched a sensitive subject of yours?"

"You damn right you have," Dante answered, momentarily noticing the look of anguish on Pacelli's face. "All we're hearing are the ramblings of an insane person." Maglione nodded his approval once again.

Hitler's face became beet red, and he slammed his fist on the hard mahogany table. "Insane person, you say?"

Accentuating his loud outburst by pointing a finger in Dante's direction, Hitler screamed, "I say YOU failed your History of Catholicism class during your seminary studies, Monsignor Dante."

Hitler continued his manic diatribe. "The Catholic Church was built around a culture of violence, and I'll use world history to prove it." Hitler proudly began his historical lecture.

"First, in 380 A.D., the Catholic Church was made the official religion of the Roman Empire. That doesn't happen unless the Roman emperor declares it. And all the people who didn't comply with the emperor's wish were quickly killed. Thousands upon thousands were slaughtered in the name of God. So there's blood on the hands of the Catholic Church from the very beginning."

Pacelli jumped into the conversation. "Every new religion has its growing pains. The Vatican had no control over what the emperor did. You're exaggerating the situation."

"Am I now?" Hitler asked. "Shall we talk about the Crusades? That was just a power ploy by the Vatican to gain more power, riches, and land throughout Europe and the Middle East. The pontiffs at the time called them 'Holy Wars'.

"In actuality, the Crusades were only attempts by the Vatican to impose its religious will upon anyone who dared to get in its way, including Jews, Orthodox Christians, heretics, and Muslims. And the Popes were more than happy to send their holy warriors off to kill the infidels."

It was Maglione's turn to disrupt Hitler's ranting. "Mr. Chancellor, much good came from the Crusades. Catholicism solidified itself as the people's religion."

Hitler exploded with laughter. "Yes, the People's Religion, as you call it, was rammed down the throats of the people, whether they liked it or not. Again, the Vatican became stronger and bolder in its quest for world domination."

"You can stop this overbearing revelation of your take on the history of the Catholic Church," Pacelli verbalized, his voice rising in frustration. "We've heard enough. We don't need to hear any more derogatory comments from you."

Hitler quickly rose from the table. "Oh, but hear me you will, Eugenio. I'm not done making my point."

Walking around the table with his arms clasped behind his back, Hitler continued to impress himself with how much in common he believed his quest for world domination paralleled those of the Vatican.

"Your Pope Gregory VII, back in 1081, boldly stated that the Roman Pontiff alone had the power to make and depose kings, declare religious writings as true or false, and make laws to rule all lands." Hitler's hand gestures became more pronounced as he quickened his pace.

"Gregory was pompous enough to state that the Roman Catholic Church was infallible, that kings should kiss the feet of the Pope, and that the Pope was above the law, and can only be judged by God himself. Such outrageous comments for a religious leader, don't you agree?" Hitler asked no one in particular.

Dante began to again rise from his chair in protest, but Pacelli grabbed his arm, and pulled him down. Leaning in, he whispered in Dante's ear, "Let him finish what he has to say. Any interruptions on our part only prolong the agony of his presence." Dante looked into Pacelli's eyes and nodded his agreement of the pontiff's request.

Now in a self-induced manic daze and oblivious of his surroundings, Hitler continued his bellicose denigration of Catholic history.

"Ha ha, let's talk about the Inquisition," Hitler shouted. "That was another excellent example of Papal abuse of authority." Before he could continue, Pacelli shot up from his seat.

"Enough," demanded the new pontiff. "You are in my house, and I dictate how much I will allow my guests to extrapolate about the flaws of the Catholic Church. You have surpassed my degree of patience."

Brought back to reality by Pacelli's protest, Hitler regained his focus and addressed the new pontiff with renewed vigor.

"You have surpassed my degree of patience with your Catholic insolence," Hitler screamed. "The Office of the Papacy is just an excuse to keep your followers subservient to your lies and threats. If your followers only knew the truth behind the supposed foundation event of your religion, there would be no organized Catholic religion as we know it today."

"You may attempt to bully me into submission, but the Catholic Church is too powerful to be bullied," Pacelli announced to Hitler. "Our faith will never bend to the demands of a tyrant. No one will ever believe anything you say because of your biased rhetoric."

"Oh, people don't need to believe what I tell them," Hitler laughed. "But they will believe when they SEE what

I am capable of doing. Germany will rule the world. I've got a higher power assisting me, and I don't mean your meaningless Trinity."

"You know that I will use the full political power of the Vatican to stop you," Pacelli warned.

"No you won't, little man. Because if you do, I will expose the Vatican for what it is, a political organization racked with hypocrisy, ego, pride, greed, and corruption. The Catholic Church has been built on lies from the beginning of its existence, and you perpetuate those lies to keep your believers in tow.

"You use the power of your Church laws to keep your people subservient," Hitler continued, his voice rising to a shrill. "You intimidate your faithful followers with the threat of eternal damnation in the fires of hell if they deviate from the belief in your ridiculous teachings."

Pacelli again forced his way into the conversation. "Why are you doing this, Adolph?" the pontiff asked. "You are a baptized Catholic, as are all your henchmen: Himmler, Goebbels, and Goering. You've all lost your souls trying to reach your goal of world supremacy."

Pacelli advanced his position. "Political power does not follow you into the afterlife. Being a dictator on earth does not buy you any favors when you are judged at the gates of heaven. But all of your horrible deeds will follow you. And because of them, you can surely expect to burn in the fires of hell for all eternity."

Hitler was quick to counter Pacelli's logic. "Your religion is built on a tremendous lie," he shouted. "Your crowning moment of glory in the Catholic Church is the death and supposed resurrection of Jesus. But I have in my possession the vital document of antiquity that proves that Jesus did not die on the cross. My expert translators tell me he survived his crucifixion, and lived in France for another 40 years with his wife, Mary Magdalene, and their children. And Jesus wrote all of these words himself."

Hitler's eyes were ablaze with the look of conquest. "But you already know this, Eugenio. The Vatican has been hiding the truth for centuries."

In Hitler's warped mind, he felt he had now completed his mission to Rome. "I alone possess the document that will tear apart your hypocritical religion at its core. If you try to stop me, I will expose you and the Vatican for what you really are: Corrupt political leaders who will stop at nothing to stay rich and powerful at the expense of the poor and destitute."

Before any individual on the Vatican side of the table could respond to Hitler's religious bigotry, the impatient Fuhrer abruptly turned, and began to briskly walk in the direction of the closed office door.

"In 1515, your Pope Leo X stated the position of the Vatican quite eloquently when he said 'It has served us well, this myth of Christ'. Nice talking with you, Eugenio. I'll show myself out."

After taking only two steps toward the door, Hitler quickly spun around, pointed his right index finger squarely at Pacelli's face, and hurled his warning once again, "Don't try to stop me, or I'll destroy you. You know I will." Within seconds, Hitler and his group exited the room, and disappeared down the long hallway.

Dante was the first to speak. "Papa Gino, we can kill him after he leaves the physical boundaries of Vatican City. I can have my men in position to eliminate him on his trip back to the airport." Maglione nodded his approval of the improvised plan.

Pacelli pondered the option momentarily, but then offered his response to Hitler's threat to expose the Vatican and its many indiscretions.

"No, Paul, killing the most evil man alive right outside the gates of Vatican City is not the answer to our dilemma," Pacelli stated. "What we need to do is silently call to arms our vast network of undercover spies and fight this villain covertly. We will bring about his demise long before he brings about the demise of the Catholic Church."

Turning away from Dante, Pacelli now addressed Magione. "Cardinal Maglione, as Vatican Secretary of State, you wield heavy influence with the leaders of the world. I need you to quickly devise a plan to begin secretly housing Jews here at the Vatican and at Castel Gandolfo.

"In addition, contact convents and friaries throughout Italy and Europe and inform them of the plan. Finally, through discreet political channels, inform the leaders of Great Britain, France, and the United States of Hitler's plan for imminent invasion of Europe." Maglione nodded his approval of the new assignment, bowed before the Pontiff, turned, and quickly left the room.

When Maglione had disappeared out the door, Pacelli addressed Dante. "We need to find out what that vile scoundrel meant when he said he had assistance from a higher power. Get your team ready, Paul. You've got another important mission ahead of you."

CHAPTER THIRTY FIVE

Office of the Schutzstaffel (SS) – Berlin
1935

"**ELISE,** get in here. What in the hell am I looking at?" Heinrich Himmler, the leader of Germany's secret police, the Schutzstaffel (SS), was puzzled by what lay in front of him on his large wooden work desk. Upon hearing the order, Elise hurried into the room to help her boss.

A look of concern turned to a grin on Elise's face. "Herr Himmler, it's a book of poems to give to your wife. You know tomorrow is her birthday. You told me to get her something nice. You didn't forget, did you?" asked the bright, young secretary.

"Jesus Christ, you saved me again, my dear," responded Germany's most feared police official. "What would I do without you?"

"I wanted you to see what I had gotten her before I wrapped the gift," Elise stated. "If it meets with your approval, I'll wrap it right away."

Himmler responded with a quick nod of his head. As Elise bent down to gather the book, Himmler quickly stole a long glance down the blouse of his attractive aide. Elise was very aware of Himmler's compulsion of looking at her breasts. That's why she always dressed as provocatively as possible in the office. She needed to make sure that Himmler never fired her.

Elise Kaufman possessed 100-percent German ancestry. She was also young, beautiful, blonde, and a college graduate. She fit the perfect profile of the perfect Aryan female that Hitler would build his world empire around. When she applied for a secretary's position within the German Chancellery after graduation, she was quickly chosen by Himmler himself. *"I've got to have young beautiful women around me in the office,"* Himmler told himself when he hired Elise.

But Elise held a secret that she would take to the grave with her. She lived in constant fear of being discovered. But she enjoyed, even craved, the thrill of the adrenaline rush that surrounded her life.

She was a spy. Not for England. Not for the French. Not for the Americans. She was a spy for the Vatican. And her interesting story started several years ago.

CHAPTER THIRTY SIX

Office of the Secretary of State – Vatican City
1934

WHEN Dante first met Cardinal Eugenio Pacelli at the Vatican in 1932, Pacelli was acting in his official role as Vatican Secretary of State for Pope Pius XI. As Secretary of State, it was his responsibility to negotiate concordats, or political agreements, between the pope and leaders of secular European governments that would guarantee the Catholics in those countries would be treated fairly and would be able to practice their religion without fear or harassment from local judiciaries. It was an important job for Pacelli, and he thrived on the challenges.

He was also astute enough to recognize the volatility of European politics, and he decided that the Vatican needed to protect itself from outside political and military intrigue. During one spring afternoon meeting with Dante, Pacelli informed the young American of his plans.

"Paul, I need you to find some friends of the Vatican, and recruit them to be our eyes and ears within their communities," Pacelli said. "I'm especially worried about the political climate in Germany these days. A man named Adolph Hitler is rapidly ascending up the political ladder."

"Of course, Papa Gino, I would be happy to do that for you. So you're looking for spies for His Holiness, right?" Dante asked.

"His Holiness does not think along these lines, but I do," Pacelli grinned at Dante's *tell-it-like-it-is* question. "As Secretary of State, it's my job to protect the leader and the sovereign domain of Vatican City.

"We cannot be blindsided if and when Europe explodes into another world war. We need to know what is going to happen BEFORE it happens. Do you understand my position?" Pacelli queried his American aide.

"Yes, I understand." Dante replied. "But how will I locate these people? And what do we promise them for their service? This is very dangerous work."

"How does guaranteed entrance into heaven sound following death for them and their family members?" Pacelli seriously offered the idea to Dante.

Papa Gino displays a strange sense of humor at times, Dante thought. "Well, you would certainly have my mother's attention with that benefit," Dante laughed. "But I think money would do the trick."

"Yes, of course. But we would need to deliver it very secretly. We couldn't afford to have the money traced back to the Vatican. That would be disastrous," Pacelli stated.

"So when do I begin?" Dante asked.

"Immediately, my son. We have identified a young lady in Switzerland who is eager to assist the Holy Father. Her name is Elise Kaufman, and she's waiting to meet with you."

Pacelli continued. "I've made all the arrangements for you already. You will leave on a commercial flight to Zurich in two hours. Father Lukas Joost from Saint Francis Church will be your contact. He will pick you up at the airport, and transport you to the meeting. He will divulge all the details you need to know."

Pacelli rose from behind his desk, and walked around to the standing Dante. Grabbing Dante's hands, Pacelli held them tightly while giving Paul some final instructions.

"This is an extremely important and delicate mission, Paul. The Vatican cannot be implicated or identified in any way. You and Father Joost will not wear any kind of religious clothing that would identify you as Catholic priests. You must make this meeting seem like you're meeting a casual friend. I'm counting on you to successfully complete this mission for the Vatican."

Upon closing the conversation, Pacelli gave the young soldier-priest a kindly hug, and ushered him from the room.

"Good luck, my son. Don't let me down." Pacelli thought as he returned to his cluttered desk.

CHAPTER THIRTY SEVEN

Old Botanical Garden – Zurich, Switzerland

FATHER LUKAS JOOST was a gentle soul with a hidden death wish. After picking Dante up at the Zurich Airport, carrying his luggage to his waiting car, and making small talk, Dante got the impression that the soft-spoken Swiss priest would make Paul's ride to the meeting with Elise a leisurely one. He was wrong.

"Hang on, Paul." was the only warning Joost gave to his unnerved passenger. As Dante gave his host a quizzical look, he was thrust back in his seat as Joost put the car in gear, gunned the engine, and raced from his parking place. Quickly gaining speed, Lukas began a dangerous route of lane-weaving once the car reached the main street of Zurich.

"Jesus Christ, Lukas. Are you trying to kill both of us before we even get to the meeting?" Dante yelled at his chauffeur. "Remember, we're not supposed to draw attention to ourselves."

Joost just smiled at Dante's plea as the car zoomed down the narrow streets of downtown Zurich. Since it was late afternoon, employees were leaving their work locations for their next destinations. Both foot traffic along sidewalks and vehicle traffic on the public streets were increasing. At one crowded street corner, an unaware female bystander was startled to see a dark-colored car moving swiftly toward her as she began to cross the street. She lunged back to the sidewalk just in time as the car zipped past her, never decreasing speed as it went by.

"Goddamn it, Joost. You better fucking slow this car down before I strangle you at the wheel myself!" Dante screamed at the manic-eyed cleric.

When hearing the un-priestly vulgar threat escaping Dante's lips, Joost quickly realized that his improvised driving pattern did not meet with Dante's approval.

"I'm so sorry, Father Dante," Joost apologized as the car slowly decelerated. "I thought you Americans love the speed when driving. I should not have assumed that thought."

Finally able to catch his breath and calm his nerves, Dante took a moment to collect his thoughts before addressing Lukas Joost, aspiring race driver.

"Listen, Lukas. My first car was a brand new Chevrolet, and for all practical purposes, I drove it like a race car," Dante said. "And I enjoy driving fast as much as you do, but not to the point where we may harm others and ourselves. And what you're doing here is just that. You might hurt us and other innocent people."

By the time Dante had finished his lecture, Joost was pulling into the parking area of the Old Botanical Garden, located just off Talstrasse Road. The meeting with Elise was scheduled for 5:00, a time when people would naturally be hooking up at the garden to make plans for the evening.

Elise Kaufman was told by Father Joost to be sitting on a wooden park bench near the middle of the garden. That is where she would meet with Paul Dante, the Vatican emissary.

After Joost parked the car, the two men entered the garden through the main gate. As Joost fell behind to watch for any suspicious activity, Dante approached a young woman who had her back to him, sitting on a wooden park bench.

"Hello. Are you Elise?" Dante inquired. She nodded affirmatively.

"I'm Paul Dante. May I sit down?" Elise's eyes brightened when she heard Dante's name. It was the one she wanted to hear.

"Yes, please sit down. It's a pleasure to meet you, Mr. Dante." Elise responded.

Dante began the conversation. "So one of the Pope's Swiss Guards tells me you're interested in working for the Vatican. What kind of work are you looking for?"

"Yes, Gunther is my boyfriend's brother," she responded. "He told me, in confidence I assure you, that the Holy Father needs people to work in other countries. Especially government work."

"I actually had a chance to talk with Gunther, too," Dante replied. "You understand that what you're suggesting can be dangerous. You'll be leading a double life. Is that something you want to do?" Dante eagerly awaited her answer.

"Oh, yes. I'm fully prepared," she stated resolutely.

"And what makes you so prepared?" Dante asked, impressed with the candor of the young woman as she laid out her story.

"I'm German. Both of my parents are German, as are their parents. I'm educated, as I will graduate from Zurich University in a few weeks. I've been living out of the country while studying here in Zurich. I believe I can get a job with the new German government, even though I hate the people who run it."

"What has brought on this hatred? Especially since you've been out of the country while Hitler has come into political power," Dante inquired, a keen sense of curiosity filling his mind.

"My father was an official for the Weimar government," Elise answered. "The Nazis held a protest rally and my father went to it out of curiosity." Tears began to well in her eyes as she continued her story.

"He got into a senseless argument with a Brownshirt, and he was stabbed to death. Murdered. I want to do anything I can to help overthrow the Nazis."

"Revenge can be a big motivator. I understand that," Dante said. "But you can't allow it to overtake your judgment. Your work will go on for years. Any kind of slip-up can be fatal. And you must protect the identity of the Vatican. You will have to sacrifice your life to protect the Pope and the Vatican. Are you willing to die for this cause?"

Elise dried her tears, and looked straight into Paul's eyes. "I'm not a soldier, but if I can work on the inside and help bring down Hitler and his henchmen, then I'm more than willing to die for this cause."

Dante smiled at the strength and valor demonstrated through the woman's tone of voice. Then he added, in jest, "Some people would call hatred a sin."

Elise responded, "You sound like a priest, not a soldier."

"Actually, I am a priest. And I was a soldier before becoming a priest. So you're mostly correct," Dante laughed.

"Oh, I'm sorry, Father. You didn't come across as a priest," Elise answered apologetically.

"And that's exactly how you're going to be able to fool the Germans once you get inside the Chancellery," Dante explained. "You're going to have to play a role that will endear you to your boss. You'll need to make yourself indispensable and irresistible. I have faith that you'll be able to do it."

Elise beamed at the compliment from the Vatican's handsome envoy. "I won't let you down, Father."

Dante responded. "I know you won't, Elise. Now, let's talk about some training you'll need for this work."

For the next hour, Dante talked and Elise listened to how she would be able to successfully spy on the Nazi leadership, and how she would report that information back to the Vatican. During the tutorial, Elise stopped Dante occasionally to ask a question or clarify a point. The Vatican envoy was impressed by his pupil's ability to quickly grasp the intricacies of clandestine operating tactics.

At the end of the meeting, Dante told her of the Vatican plan to compensate her for her work, and how the money would be covertly delivered to her. As they parted ways, Dante felt confident that Elise Kaufman would become a valuable asset to the Vatican.

CHAPTER THIRTY EIGHT

Kaiser Mountains – Northern Limestone Alps Austria - 1941

ENEMY bullets whizzed into and past the green-canopied German Opel Blitz three-ton grey military cargo truck occupied at the moment by the Vatican's finest covert operations team as they careened down the deserted mountain dirt road connecting the towns of Kufstein and St. Johann in the Kaiser Mountains located in the Northern Limestone Alps in Tyrol, Austria. They were aggressively fleeing from a secluded mountain warehouse they had just blown up that fronted a secret Nazi laboratory that housed incredible flying technology.

Ferrelli loved this kind of reflexive elusive driving style, hunched over and gripping the steering wheel, jerking it right and left, which made it difficult for pursuit vehicles to get a good shot at their targets. The bumpy, dizzying ride also provided a challenge of shooting accuracy for Dante, Jimmy Mac, and Ramirez as they exchanged frantic gunfire with their Nazi pursuers behind the safety of the 40-inch steel drop gate at the rear of the vehicle. While the fighting raged on, Loogie expertly loaded and reloaded the weapons for quick access, oblivious to the intense peril the Catholic group was facing.

"Goddamn it, Geno. Can't you move this thing a little faster?" Ramirez screamed while pumping bullet after bullet from his M50 Reising sub-machine gun from his prone position in the back of the truck bed. "We need to put some distance between us, for Chrissakes."

"Aw, piss on it. You just concentrate on killing those Krauts, Georgie Boy, and leave the driving to me," Geno shouted from behind the wheel. "I got this under control."

In the back corner and to the left of Ramirez, Dante was shooting his favorite M1 Garand scoped sniper rifle. Even with the enemy targets moving wildly in his line of vision thanks to Ferrelli's driving tactics, Dante was still able to drop the enemy combatants with uncanny accuracy. "Jesus Christ, I love this rifle," he yelled to Ramirez. "You did a great job updating our weapons last year. Fuck those German weapons. Give me good 'ol American fire power any day. Love that Vatican money."

Jimmy Mac had positioned himself in the right corner of the truck bed when the firefight had started about 15 minutes ago. He was the first of the Vatican fighters to hop into the bed of the commandeered troop transport truck and began laying cover fire while the others were sprinting to the vehicle. Without Jimmy's foresight to prepare the Browning M2 Heavy Machine Gun for this kind of occasion, Papa Gino would have lost every member of the team during this semi-successful clandestine operation.

Because the narrowness of the mountain road forced the three Nazi vehicles to travel in tandem, the four occupants of the lead car were the major objects for Dante's counter assault. The German BMW-manufactured army cars were much faster than Ferrelli's slower cargo truck. The combination of a faster car with the expert marksmanship of the four Nazi gunmen in each vehicle had caused Ramirez to plead with Ferrelli for more speed.

Since the dangerous chase had begun around sunset, the speeding vehicles were popping in and out of sunlight as they streaked along the tree-lined dirt road, which made most of the shots go awry. Even though the speed of their cars closed the gap with Ferrelli, the Nazi drivers were unable to successfully overtake the fleeing cargo truck.

"Paul, you gotta take out the driver of that first car," McPherrin shouted from behind his machine gun. "They're gaining on us all the time."

"That's what I've been trying to do," Dante yelled as he continued to fire. "As soon as I can get some extended daylight, I'll try something new."

Instead of aiming at standing swaying bodies in the front and back seats of the BMW 325, Dante began to take aim at the front wheels of the pursuing German car. When sunlight suddenly poked through the trees, Dante began to empty his ammunition into the path of the tires.

Suddenly, Dante heard the pop of an exploding tire. Immediately, the lead Nazi car began to swerve uncontrollably along the narrow roadway and darted up the hill toward the forest tree line. Within seconds, the car rammed into the thick trunk of a steep mountain pine tree and exploded. Remnants of car parts and body parts shot up into the dusky sky.

"Nice shot, Boss." The loud compliment arrived from Loogie, who had watched the entire scene unfold in front of him from his unscathed location behind Ramirez. "Now do it a couple more times," he shouted.

Without looking at Bellavista, Dante caught himself smiling. *"I've trained the lad nicely,"* he told himself, meaning Loogie's addressing Dante as "Boss" on all occasions, and by Loogie's increased proficiency over the past few years in loading and handling firearms.

The second Nazi car was not deterred by the crash. It quickly increased its speed to come within 50 yards of the cargo truck. At the same time, the Nazi marksmen continued to fire their weapons in rapid succession.

Suddenly, Ferrelli's booming voice echoed to the back of the truck. "Hang on, people. There's a hairpin right turn coming up in about 100 yards. I'm going to have to slow up a little to cut the corner tight. Shoot the shit out of those guns of yours because our friends are going to be right on our ass." Geno began to slowly pump the brake pedal and then deftly stomped the clutch and downshifted to slow the speeding truck before the hazardous turn.

Within the blink of an eye, the two Nazi army cars were within spitting distance of the back of the truck. Amazed and frightened by the make-up speed displayed by the German cars, Dante, Ramirez, and Jimmy Mac increased the ferocity of their gunfire.

Jimmy Mac's machine gun fire now raked across the front bumper and climbed up to the hood of the Nazi pursuit vehicle. A few bullets found themselves inching toward the exposed glass windshield as the driver quickly veered to the right to avoid the arrival of Jimmy's fatal bullets. But in doing so, the driver lost his perspective to where the roadway ended, and the long, steep cliff appeared. Before he could react, the car nosedived over the vertical cliff, rolling downward until coming to a crashing halt on the jagged rocks hundreds of feet below. The gas tank exploded within seconds of the landing, disintegrating the car and its occupants.

Unaware of the fate of the second Nazi car, Ferrelli successfully navigated the treacherous turn, and began accelerating as the third Nazi car completed its attempt to make the 90-degree turn. The Vatican team had barely a minute to catch their breath and refocus as the German soldiers closed in. As the chase continued, Ferrelli again shouted a warning to his friends as smoke mysteriously appeared from beneath the hood of the truck.

"We'll be off this mountain road in a minute, and the truck engine is starting to overheat. I've got smoke from under the hood. For Chrissakes, finish off those bastards before they finish us off," Ferrelli demanded.

Both vehicles were traveling at a high rate of speed when they reached the bottom of the mountain road. In the enveloping darkness of the night, neither vehicle saw the small earthen hill looming in front of them. Large motorized transports meeting small hill caused both to leave the ground and fly through the air momentarily. The heavy cargo truck landed with a jarring thud. The Nazi car landed less violently. The hunt resumed at breakneck speed.

"I'm getting tired of these fuckers," Ramirez shouted to the heavens. "I'm going to finish this once and for all." In his haste to address his self-fulfilling prophecy, Ramirez raised up and exposed himself to the oncoming gunfire for only a second. A bullet caught his left shoulder and whirled him around. He dropped his machine gun and fell to the truck bed, clutching his bleeding arm. *"Son of a bitch,"* he told himself. *"I am such a dumbshit."*

Stunned by the turn of events, Dante and Jimmy Mac took a quick glance at their weapons specialist. Confident that the shot wasn't fatal, the two resumed their attack on the German pursuers with increased fervor. In one final devastating volley of bullets from the Vatican truck, the Nazi driver and his three combatants were cut down savagely.

Aiming smoothly from right to left, Jimmy Mac's machine gun fire decapitated the driver and then sliced cleanly through the soldier standing in the front seat, severing the top half of his body from the bottom neatly at the waist. The two front-seat bodies instantly disappeared from view. Without explanation, the driverless car continued a straight-line pursuit, as if guided by an invisible entity.

Although surprised to see the enemy car still advancing, Dante locked on to the two marksmen in the back seat. With devilish precision, Paul deposited a bullet squarely between the eyes of each Nazi. With all four German soldiers dead, the car jerked awkwardly to the right, overturned, bounced high in the air, and rolled over several times. Mangled bodies and body parts catapulted from the out-of-control vehicle. Within seconds, the BMW 325 army car came to a rest on its side. The chase was over.

"We're good, Geno," Paul yelled to his driver. "They're all dead. Nobody's chasing us anymore." Ferrelli slowed the truck, and coasted to the side of the road before braking.

"About damn time," Ferrelli responded, a smile creasing his face and sweat dripping from his brow. "For a minute there, I thought all three of you guys were losing your touch." With the present danger rectified, everyone's attention now turned to Ramirez.

Loogie was the first to respond when George was shot. From his position nestled behind the driving cab of the truck, he had a front row seat to how the situation unveiled itself in front of him. As George spun around after being hit, Loogie immediately dropped the gun he was reloading, and dived beside his fallen friend. Tearing off his shirt and ripping it in two, Loogie instinctively balled up one part, placed it over the bleeding wound, and began to apply pressure.

"You'll be alright, George," Loogie said consolingly, noticing that the shot went clean through the shoulder. "I'm stopping the bleeding now. '*I knew that first aid training that the Boss put me through last year would come in handy,*' Bellavista told himself. Focusing back on George, he asked, "How are you feeling?"

"Other than feeling like a complete idiot, I feel just fine," Ramirez responded sarcastically.

With the truck at a standstill, Dante, Jimmy Mac, and Ferrelli soon arrived to assist Bellavista in the final stages of treating the gunshot wound on Ramirez.

"Good job, Loogie, on applying pressure to the wound. That was the most critical part in helping George." Dante explained. "I told you that you'd put that training to good use some day."

As Jimmy Mac and Ferrelli gathered gauze, ointment, bandages, and medical tape to complete their temporary wound treatment, Dante continued to chastise Ramirez.

"Now, what in the fuck were you thinking, George, when you exposed yourself to those Nazi shooters? They could have easily taken off your head. The Big Guy Upstairs was definitely looking after your sorry ass, you know."

"I'm really sorry, fellas. I screwed up like a first-year seminarian." Ramirez apologized. "I let frustration take hold of me, and it almost cost me my life. I swear it will never happen again. I won't put you guys in harm's way because of my stupidity. I promise."

While Jimmy Mac and Ferrelli administered a good-natured, profanity-laced heckling to Ramirez, Dante and Loogie completed dressing the wound. Ferrelli then examined the damage to the truck engine, and determined that the team could safely make the 15-mile trip back to Kufstein. There, they would meet up again with their Vatican network operative, get the necessary medical treatment for George, debrief the mission that took them to the Kaiser Mountains, and determine their next plan of action.

CHAPTER THIRTY NINE

HOUSED for the past eight days in the Auracher Löchl, the oldest and most regal hotel in Kufstein, allowed Ramirez to heal properly from the gunshot wound he received during the running gun battle with the Nazi soldiers following the destruction of the secret German laboratory high in the Kaiser Mountains. The respite also allowed the entire team to re-energize.

Tonight, Dante and his team sat for supper in a private ornate dining room reserved just for them. They relished a meal of salad greens, warm rolls, simmering wiener schnitzel, delectable kaiserschmarren, and several chilled bottles of the local favorite Grüner Veltliner wine. After completing the sumptuous feast, they positioned themselves around the cozy fireplace in the back of the room, where they were now enjoying a dessert of Linzer torte accompanied by some Stanz schnapps resting temptingly in Riedel glasses. Such was the lifestyle one could afford with unlimited Vatican money. Also, Ferrelli's endless flirting with the female servers added to the festive, yet relaxing, mood of the evening.

"You know, Paul, we never ate this good back in Omaha," the quickly-mending Ramirez reminded Dante. "For me, it was usually tortilla soup at my house, and I'll bet it was a lot of spaghetti at your place." He smiled as he raised his glass with his heavily bandaged left arm to toast the moment with the others in the room.

"Yeah, Georgie, you're right," Dante agreed. "It was usually spaghetti and meatballs, lasagna, Italian sausage, cannoli, and a lot of home-made bread. My mom is still a great cook. She hasn't lost her touch, even after having that stroke a couple years ago." The thought of his mother's medical crisis still pained Dante.

Jimmy Mac and Geno Ferrelli joined in the conversation, Jimmy proclaiming his mother was the best cook and Ferrelli documenting why his mother was the worst cook. The constant banter was laced with the usual profane language that these former American soldiers felt comfortable dispensing among themselves.

Loogie always thought that if someone walked in on this kind of conversation, they would never fathom that the group was a small skilled military force of three Jesuit priests and a Jesuit brother acting as covert Vatican agents with license to kill on behalf of the Pope. The salty chatter still made him cringe, and sadly, after all these years of harrowing experiences that should have bonded him with the others, Bellavista still considered himself an outsider of the group.

"Loogie, jump in any time, man," Ferrelli egged on the junior member of the team. "Looking at that undersized frame of yours, I'd bet your mom didn't feed you a lot of fattening foods." The others laughed at the subtle form of mockery.

"My mother is a saint that cooks famously," Loogie stated with pride. "Since I was the oldest in the family of six children, I only got a small portion at the dinner table. Most of the food went to my younger siblings." He lowered his eyes as he took a feeble sip of schnapps as the others looked on.

"Well, I guess that explains it then," Ferrelli exclaimed. "You sacrificed for the good of your siblings. That's admirable. I commend you for your family loyalty." Ferrelli then raised his glass to salute Loogie's story. The others joined in. Bellavista accepted the indirect compliment, but wished the focus of attention moved away from him. It did as Paul took a long satisfying gulp of schnapps, and addressed the group from the comfort of his padded chair.

"OK, let's rehash this last mission into the Kaiser Mountains again," Dante stated as he leaned forward in his chair. "Can you fucking believe what we witnessed there? I mean, that thing was levitating in the air, up and down. And it wasn't making a sound.

"We've been on the road for almost two years now, but we've never seen anything like that. The intel from our network of Vatican spies in Europe has been getting much better lately. This last mission finally gave us an opportunity to eyeball the kind of technology that Hitler is developing. And it's scary shit.

"Whatever the hell Hitler is working on that he considers is assistance from a higher power," Dante continued, "I think we just witnessed it. You can tell it's definitely something big. But it's being guarded very closely, and it's being built in pieces. Kaiser Mountain was only one part of the puzzle. Blowing up the place should set the Nazis back for a while."

"The speed of that thing was amazing. And it just flat out stopped on a dime in mid-flight," Jimmy said. "No nation that I know of has anything close to that kind of technology. But, hey, at least we got close enough for me to take some pictures of that oscillating thing, or whatever the hell it was," Jimmy added. "But it was damned impressive, if I say so myself."

Ramirez, the last person in the three-man Vatican assault team that infiltrated the secret Nazi laboratory, dialed into the conversation. "Yeah, the pictures were huge for us. Now we finally have a visual record of what some of these secret reports have been telling us.

"But, to me, the most important part of the mission was blowing that place to kingdom come. I'm not sure if anyone survived that bombing onslaught we laid on those Nazis. Hopefully, if Oberth was actually there, he met his fate. A guy like that with the knowledge he has…well, hell, you wish he was on our side, and not Hitler's."

✶✶✶✶✶✶

The incredible information that pushed the team into the mountains outside Kufstein, Austria, had been passed on to Dante's group from a highly credible network source: Elise. The coded written message had stated that the Nazis, under the direction of a German scientist named Hermann Oberth, were developing a prototype military flying attack vehicle that had a propulsion system that could make the craft go above supersonic speed. The message didn't mention levitation anywhere within its code, though.

After an extensive foot search in the vicinity of the mountain coordinates that Elise had passed along, Dante's team located the large warehouse facility hidden in the side of the mountain behind a heavy grove of scotch pine trees. Dante, Ramirez, and McPherrin infiltrated a side door after killing the two sentries guarding the entrance. Dante ordered Ferrelli and Loogie to stay behind to guard the doorway and bring the get-away truck around for a quick exit.

Once inside the large warehouse structure, Jimmy began taking pictures of the laboratory contents as they stealthily moved from room to room. When they finally reached a large open work area, they noticed a team of scientists and technicians working on a dark round object about the size of two truck wheels combined that seemed to be floating in the air. There was a lot of activity going on around this object, with a lot of loud talking and many workers coming and going.

What happened next forced the Vatican group to question their perceptions of reality. With one scientist holding a metal box and moving some dials and switches on it, the object shot straight up about 15 feet into the air and came to a dead stop in less than a second. Next, while still hovering silently in the air, the object suddenly accelerated sharply to the left for about 30 feet, and came to a dead stop again in mid-flight.

In the last dramatic part of the test flight, the object advanced slowly in the air back toward the group of scientists, mostly wobbling as it progressed. It stopped directly above the scientist who was controlling it with the dialed instrument, and then floated down gently, like a leaf falling effortlessly from a tree. It then came to rest at its original position, three feet above the floor. There was an instant explosion of applause and cheers from the scientists and technicians in the expansive room.

Dante looked at George incredulously. "Holy fuck, George, we need to do some major damage to this facility," Dante whispered to his weapons specialist while the three crouched behind some wooden crates. "We need to detonate a delayed explosive that takes out that object and as much of this laboratory as we can. Did you bring something along in your bag of tricks to do this?"

As Jimmy continued to take clandestine photos with his Minox Riga sub-miniature camera, Ramirez reached into his duffel bag and removed four sticks of dynamite, a few feet of proximity fuse, two charges loaded with a pound and a half each of plastic explosives, and a few feet of detonating cord with time pencil fuses attached. "These should do the trick," Ramirez whispered to Dante.

Ramirez quietly told Dante his improvised plan while he began cutting the detonating cord and setting the length of time on the time pencil fuses. "We'll put these plastic explosive charges over next to that machinery," he said softly, pointing to the area, "and I'll put a time pencil fuse with it to detonate in two minutes. That should destroy this entire section. As long as that floating object is still in the room, the explosion should take care of it.

"We can throw these sticks of dynamite as we're leaving the building," George stated. "The nice thing about this proximity fuse is that it detonates in the air when it nears a solid object, whether it's a man or machine. But it's all experimental shit, too. It's just starting to be developed by the Office of Naval Research. I don't know how Pacelli got his hands on this stuff. There must be a Catholic Vatican spy planted within the United States Navy."

As the magical floating object continued to be the focal point for all the scientists, technicians, and heavily-armed security guards in the room, Dante, Ramirez, and McPherrin discreetly put all the bombs in place. Working at a rapid pace, Ramirez set the plastic explosive charges next to the high-tech machinery and stuck the detonation cord with the time pencil fuses into the charges.

Sensing the major explosions were only seconds away, the team began to hasten their departure back to the Vatican-guarded entrance. Each man had a stick of dynamite, ready to throw it expertly into the crowd of fleeing Nazis. Ramirez held two sticks, leaving one to heave into the building when everyone was safely aboard the truck. The final dynamite stick would detain momentarily the band of pursuers that were sure to come after them.

Loogie held the door as a shouting McPherrin was the first person to dash through the opening when the first explosion rocked the warehouse. Seconds before, he had hurled his dynamite stick into the middle of a surprised group of white-coated Nazi laboratory technicians, causing additional disorientation, instant death, extreme fear, and burgeoning shock.

The second plastic explosive bomb detonated almost simultaneously with the first, lifting dismembered bodies and destroyed building materials into an aerial display of horrific proportions. Ramirez targeted his dynamite stick into a section of the warehouse containing clear bottles of chemical agents as he sprinted through the open door. The chemical blast spread intense heat that peeled away dripping bloody skin and burning clothing from fleeing victims.

With massive flames engulfing the building, Dante sprinted through the door, grabbed Loogie's arm, and slung the young priest ahead of him, making sure he would make it safely to the idling truck, waiting just yards away with Ferrelli eager to depart the premises. Paul then quickly spun around and threw his dynamite stick directly into the chest of the first Nazi guard coming through the door with his MP 34 sub-machine gun blazing into the dusky shadows of the evening.

The rushing Nazi guard laughed as he initially thought the stick was simply a castoff branch from a nearby tree that Dante had haphazardly grabbed to throw. Then he caught a glimpse of the protruding fuse, and sheer terror came into his eyes. Desperately knocking the stick away, the young Nazi thought he had cheated death. But the experimental fuse did its job, exploding the dynamite in mid-air within a few feet of the running sentry.

The blast, amazingly, did not dislodge the gun from the guard's hands. The aftershock of the blast, however, ripped both arms cleanly away from the broad shoulders they were just attached to a few seconds before. Screaming uncontrollably, the dying Nazi crumbled to the ground, his armless torso ending up face-down in a pool of blood-stained dirt.

Jimmy Mac began laying protective ground cover fire with his Browning machine gun the moment he dived into the back of the truck. Ramirez arrived seconds later, then Loogie, and finally, Dante.

"Get us the hell out of here, Geno," Dante bellowed to Ferrelli. The Navy flyer rapidly popped the clutch, and the lumbering cargo truck immediately pulled away from the blazing inferno around them. Picking up speed as they reached the deserted mountain road, Dante and his team found themselves fighting off three German army cars that were giving chase. The setting sun caused all the vehicles to sneak in and out of sunshine, hampering the effectiveness of the Nazi and Vatican marksmen. But Dante's team claimed victory.

Thanks to Ferrelli's deft driving skills, the 40-inch steel drop gate on the back of the truck, Ramirez's special ability to purchase the best American weaponry using unlimited Vatican cash, Jimmy Mac's foresight in planning every aspect of the mountain mission, Dante's unrivaled sniper eyesight, and Loogie's reloading and first aid skills, the Vatican team managed to act on valuable intelligence, locate a secret Nazi laboratory developing advanced flight technology, and destroy every remnant of the German operation.

******

As the team completed their final debriefing of the Kaiser Mountain mission, they all sat back in their comfortable chairs to once again enjoy the hotel fireplace flushing their faces with warmth. They also experienced the warmth in their bellies from draining the last sips of the expensive schnapps that completed the exquisite feast they began three hours ago.

"I suppose the only thing stopping us from the perfect mission would have been getting our hands on that flying device." Dante told the team. They all begrudgingly nodded in unison.

"But I'm very proud of you men," Dante stated admiringly, making it a point to make eye contact with Loogie. "Jimmy put together a great mission plan, and everybody did a great job with their part.

"It was as dangerous a mission as we've been on," Paul continued. "But there are going to be a lot more dangerous ones, especially since we've got an idea now of the magnitude of the technology the Germans are developing."

"I like our chances of kicking Hitler in the balls with this flying device thing," Ferrelli exclaimed. "But our intel is really going to have to be spot on. No more wild goose chases."

"I agree with both of you," McPherrin added. "When we finally get the opportunity to put an end to this saga, it may help put an end to this war, too. So this is huge."

"But don't forget one thing," Ramirez said. "We're on the Nazi's big radar screen now. Hitler and his henchmen are well aware of our presence. And you know we really pissed him off by bombing the shit out of that secret lab. We're going to have to be extra careful with our planning and execution."

"You're all exactly right," Dante responded after hearing the comments from around the room. "What are your thoughts, Loogie? You've been pretty quiet over there."

Surprised by the Boss's question directed to him, Bellavista cleared his throat with a quick cough.

"I, too, agree that the path ahead of us is going to become more dangerous," he stated. "I think we may need to involve more people in the future."

"OK. I'm listening," Dante responded. "Tell me more."

Loogie grew more confident explaining his perspective. "To complete our directive from His Holiness, we most likely will have to travel deep into German territory. Our targets are going be more heavily guarded. As good as the four of you are, I believe we will need more manpower. We may need to recruit some members of underground resistance organizations."

"Well, I'll be damned," Geno blurted. "Our little papal kiss-ass does have a brain above those puny shoulders." He chuckled, but not in derision of Loogie's comments. Just the opposite.

"Paul, I believe the kid's on to something here," Ferrelli stated. "We most definitely need more bodies to protect our asses in the field. Our spies should be able to assemble a team wherever we need them, don't you think?"

"Oh yeah, we should have no problem getting additional help," Dante responded. "If people don't want to volunteer to help the Pope, Vatican cash should buy us what we need, too."

Sarcastic smiles and nodding heads greeted Paul's sad-but-true comments.

"OK, it's getting late. Let's get some sleep," Dante ordered. "I'll throw some ideas down on paper, and we can discuss them tomorrow. Good job, everyone. We still have a lot to accomplish."

With the official evening activities finished, the team dispersed quietly to their separate elegant sleeping rooms. *"Loogie is starting to think like me,"* Dante grinned as he nestled under his down-filled blankets. *"He's going to be important to us down the road."*

CHAPTER FORTY

Chancellery – German High Command Berlin- 1941

GUSTAV WEBER pranced down the hallway on the creaky third floor of the German chancellery, exchanging *Heil Hitler* salutes with the unsuspecting civilian workers that populated the busy hallways of the German High Command headquarters.

Diese menschen sind so leicht zu täuschen. Weber smirked at the thought as the congested path in front of him magically opened wide as he strode through the gawking throngs. *These people are so easy to fool.*

Gustav Weber was a member of a small Nazi wartime group that played an important role for the Third Reich. The other members were Andreas Kronstaedt, Julius Schreck, and Heinrich Bergner. Their role: Hitler's doppelganger. Hitler's double. So realistic in looks and mannerisms that no one could tell the difference.

"Weber, you need to improve your theatrics," Heinrich Himmler yelled to Gustav from the open doorway to Himmler's third-floor office. "You need to practice with my doppelganger. He is more fluid in his arm movements." Weber nodded his acknowledgment as he kept walking. *Ich kann nie täuschen, dass bastard. I can never fool that bastard,* Weber lamented.

Hitler wasn't the only top Nazi official to have doubles. Himmler, Goering, Rudolph Hess, and Martin Borman had them prepared and ready to step in if they ever needed to flee Berlin. Their planned mode of escape was masterfully evil. They would all flee the city disguised as Catholic priests.

Weber and the other Hitler doubles were paid handsomely for their work. They enjoyed the notoriety that came with the position. Their primary responsibility was to make public appearances, mainly attending parties or military briefings where Hitler was not expected to have any interaction with others. But it was a sad and lonely life, too, because they were on call every hour of the day, and a personal life of any kind was strictly forbidden.

Leaving nothing to chance, all four impersonators were given body movement and voice instruction to match the Fuhrer. They all underwent facial and dental reconstruction surgery. In the most gruesome requirement, each had his spine broken in the same place where Hitler injured his while fighting in World War One.

Weber understood and accepted his fate: He would die to allow the Fuhrer to cheat death. He would die to fool the Allies and history. *"Was für ein herrlicher Weg, um das Vaterland zu dienen,"* he sighed. *"What a glorious way to serve the Motherland!"*

CHAPTER FORTY ONE

Secret Nazi Laboratory
Leitmeritz - Flossenberg Concentration Subcamp
1941

IT was an eventful morning at the secret Nazi Laboratory at Leitmeritz.

Wernher von Braun was so angry he was throwing any breakable object he could find in his office against the barren back wall. He was just informed that Hermann Goering had demoted him as the lead scientist working to back-engineer the alien craft because he and his technicians had not discovered the entry point into the craft after years of fruitless attempts.

"Son of a bitch. Er hätte mir mehr Zeit. Der Bastard hatte mich arbeiten außerhalb mein Fachgebiet, für Christus willen. Wir waren immer so nah. Ich bin krank und müde von Nazi Politik." von Braun shouted. *"Son of a bitch. He could have given me more time. The bastard had me working outside my area of expertise, for Christ sake. We were getting so close. I'm sick and tired of Nazi politics."*

******

Dr. Walter Miethe was ecstatic when Goering ordered him to replace Wernher von Braun as the lead scientist responsible for the research and development of the Nazi's greatest secret weapon, the flying disk.

"von Braun muss so sauer. Er hatte seine Chance. though. Aber er will nicht küssen genug ass. Ich werde tun, was es braucht." Miethe snickered. *"von Braun has to be so pissed. He had his chance, though. But he doesn't kiss enough ass. I'll do whatever it takes."*

******

Viktor Schauberger was deeply saddened, yet secretly joyous, when he heard the news of the bombing of the Kaiser Mountain laboratory, Hermann Oberth's unfortunate death in the blast, and most importantly, the destruction of Oberth's prototype engine.

"Ah, das ist mein größter Konkurrent Toten. Jetzt Göring muss meine Engine verwenden," he thought. *"Ah, my greatest competitor is dead. Now Goering must use my engine."*

He continued his gratuitous thought. *"Wie gut, dass Hitler nicht genug Schutz bieten, seine wichtigsten Vermögenswerte."* *"How fortunate that Hitler didn't provide enough protection for his most important assets."*

******

Schauberger and Miethe were new arrivals at Leitmeritz, while von Braun was on his way out, reassigned to Peenemunde, a seaport village on the Baltic Sea coast of Germany, to direct the development of the V-1 and V-2 rockets and missiles, armaments that would cause great destruction to London and Paris during the war in Europe. But he wasn't leaving without screaming at Miethe.

"So, Miethe, whose balls did you lick to get my position?" von Braun bellowed as he pushed his way through two security guards into Miethe's office door. "I'm sure it was Goering, and I'm sure that he enjoyed every part of it, that queer."

"Yes, as a matter of fact, it was Goering," Miethe responded, sarcastically. "You should try it some time. It will probably help your career." Miethe laughed as the two guards grabbed von Braun's arms and dragged him from Miethe's office, the profanities directed at Miethe echoing in the hall until they faded away.

Walter Miethe was the consummate "political" scientist. Born into an aristocratic family and educated with a degree in aeronautical engineering from the University of Berlin, he used family money and political guile to worm his way into Germany's society of high rollers. After meeting Hermann Goering at a Nazi fundraising event in 1939 and impressing the military leader with his theory on advanced avionics, Miethe found himself on the fast track within the secret world of Nazi military research and development.

After Hitler was given the alien craft a few years ago with no operational guidelines from Tehlri, he met secretly with Johannes Winkler, the first president of the *Verein für Raumschiffahrt* (VfR - German Society for Space Travel).

With Goering sitting next to him, Hitler addressed Winkler. "Dr. Winkler, I possess an advanced flying weapon capable of mass destruction," Hitler bragged. "But I need your help to understand how the damn thing works. You see, the little bastard I received it from neglected to give me instructions on how it works."

"Tell me more, Mein Fuhrer," Winkler responded.

After receiving just enough of the jaw-dropping details that Hitler wished to divulge, Winkler recommended that Hitler begin a campaign to compartmentalize the multiple aspects of aerodynamic design and propulsion methods with the ultimate goal of mass producing a Nazi version of the alien craft and its capabilities. But first, the craft would need to be breached, and the propulsion system back-engineered.

With unbounded excitement, Winkler eagerly accepted Hitler's direct order to manage the research and development of Nazi Germany's ultimate weapon to win the war. Goering's first directive, with Winkler's recommendation, was to move the craft to Mittelwerk, the underground factory where scientists and technicians could work without worry of bombing or discovery.

Next, he and Goering, the newly appointed head of the Nazi air forces, met to assemble a list of the top scientists to recruit into the program. They decided they would use Himmler's SS soldiers to assist the recruitment efforts if some scientists needed additional "persuasion" to join the project. Following several months of intense data gathering, Winkler announced his choices and Goering was asked to rubber-stamp a core group of specialists.

"So who are our people for this mission?" Goering asked.

Winkler read aloud his list of scientists and their specialties. "I've selected Rudolph Schriever and Klaus Habermohl for aircraft design. Then Rudolph Nebel for avionics."

Goering interrupted Winkler. "No, I want Walter Miethe for avionics. I've met him and he seems most competent in the field. We can assign this Nebel character to another area."

Understanding how political assignments were made, Winkler easily acquiesced to Goering's persuasion. "Very well, Herr Goering. Miethe is your man for avionics."

As political assignment became the topic of discussion, Winkler directed the conversation back to his list of recommendations.

"Giuseppe Belluzzo is an Italian engineer that Hitler said was recommended by Mussolini. Since Hitler is keeping Mussolini in the loop regarding this highly-classified project, I needed to pick this guy for political reasons. So he'll do work in electronics.

"For propulsion systems, I've got two of the best outside-the-box thinkers in Hermann Oberth and Viktor Schauberger. Finally, Wernher von Braun and Leo Zanssen will be the leaders of the rocketry group."

Winkler enthusiastically continued to relate his stream of thought to Goering. "This is the most profound scientific endeavor in the history of mankind. The success of this project will be determined by the degree of success of each subgroup," he said.

"To ensure the tight security surrounding this project, each specialty must work independently of each other," Winkler exclaimed. "If one part fails, we don't have to worry about it affecting the other groups directly. Only at the end will all of the pieces be put together."

Winkler finished his conversation with Goering with a demand. "Herr Goering, these men must be paid handsomely. They must have unlimited resources in what they need. They need to be supplied with all the technicians and raw materials they request. No expense will be spared."

He continued to preach. "In addition, they need to be protected personally along with their family members, and their workplace must be protected around the clock. This project now takes on the highest priority for German national security, as you are fully aware."

"Yes, yes, Dr. Winkler," Goering answered. "Adolph and I understand exactly what all of this means. Your core group of scientists and engineers will be compensated royally. In addition, all the necessary technical assistance, highly-skilled workers, raw materials, security clearances, and 24-hour protection will be delivered by the Reich. Now go out and get these people."

Feeling the full power of his administrative position firmly entrenched within Nazi high authority, Winkler began his quest to recruit the best and brightest minds to undertake the most ambitious military project in the history of mankind.

"Die Wissenschaft wird Deutschland nach Weltherrschaft wieder führen. Kein Land in der Lage sein, uns zu stoppen," Winkler prophesied. *"Science will lead Germany to world dominance once again. No country will be able to stop us."*

CHAPTER FORTY TWO

"BARYCENTRIC CONTROL." Viktor Schauberger's scream echoed throughout his secret underground lab at Mittelwerk. "I've been telling you that is our answer." The scientist raised his arms in triumphant symbolism of victory.

Barycentric control was a form of *counterbary*, another name for lofting, or the act of levitation, where gravity's force was overcome by electrostatic propulsion methods, Schauberger surmised. After Miethe's group had successfully breached the exterior of the craft using an experimental electromagnetic enhancement device, Schauberger recalled how he, Oberth, and their team of highly-skilled technicians quickly found what they perceived to be the propulsion system conveniently located directly beneath the floor of the craft's control console. But there was a problem.

"Goddamn it, Viktor," Oberth exclaimed after peeling back the final dark green rubbery floor matting, only to determine that what could be the alien propulsion system was encased in a two-foot square seamless lead box that wouldn't budge from its position, despite the fact that visually there were no fastening devices in sight.

"Wouldn't you just know this is what we would find," Oberth lamented. "The thing must be anchored to the bottom somehow."

Schauberger frowned before answering Oberth. "Shit. But we knew it wouldn't be easy, Hermann. Let's see what we can do."

Schauberger knelt down next to Oberth, and peered into the dark bowels of the craft. "We need to get this encasement out of the craft so we can examine it more closely," said the Austrian forester who espoused the philosophy that observing nature was the answer to understanding the mysteries confronting mankind.

"How do you propose we do that?" Oberth countered. "I can't see any connective materials holding it in place. And there isn't a whole lot of room to maneuver under it."

Schauberger got an idea. He ordered two muscular technicians assisting the group to lower one of their slight-framed colleagues into the black hole containing the sealed box. "Take this flashlight with you," he told the stunned technician who would be making the inverted head-first trip, "and tell us what you see beneath the box."

Despite the large contingent of scientists, technicians, and workers bunched together in the confined space, the inside of the craft became deadly quiet as the tiny technician was slowly lowered into the small hole. With the flashlight brightening his journey, the young man shouted orders to his handlers. "Lower…lower…slower…stop."

"What do you see?" Schauberger yelled. Oberth's head was literally inches away from the technician's ass as he craned his neck to view inside the opening.

"There are four long steel sleeves bolted to the bottom of the casement. You can't see the sleeves from above. But you can see them from my position. They extend from below me," he announced to the group.

"Can you see the bottom of the craft?" Oberth queried. "It would make it much easier for you to perform the extraction procedure if you can have your feet on the ground."

The young technician directed the flashlight beam away from the box to the bottom of the craft. "I can't see the bottom. The beam of light just ends in darkness."

After being lifted out of the small hole, the young technician was ordered by Oberth to gather the needed tools to separate the steel box from the bolted sleeves. He was again lowered, head first, into the dark cavity.

Schauberger ordered a floodlight to be lowered into the hole to provide the necessary light source while the technician removed the bolts. The vertical position caused the blood in the technician's head to gravitate down, causing blurred vision at times. In spite of the technician's crippling position, the final lead bolt was removed in 10 minutes, and the seamless lead box was slowly lifted from its resting position. Another technician carried the box from the craft, and laid it to rest on Schauberger's work bench.

Schauberger remembered how it took six weeks for him and Oberth to finally get the seamless box to "open". Testing a myriad of electromagnetic engineering options on the box, nothing seemed to work.

"*Dieser Vorgang testet meine Geduld,*" Oberth kept repeating. "*This process is testing my patience.*"

"Yes, I agree," Schauberger concurred. "Maybe we're on the right track, but we need to increase the voltage in the magnetometer. Let's double the Lorenz force."

"What do we have to lose?" Oberth said sarcastically.

Schauberger ordered the technician to increase the voltage meter to 2550 volts. When the extra voltage made contact with the box, a remarkable event happened. Without making a sound, the top of the lead box seemed to crack open, with a horizontal line stretching along the top. In the same movement, the lead on each side of the crack rolled away from the middle crack like a carpet being rolled up, continued down the sides, and mysteriously disappeared under the box, exposing the contents of the box. Everyone who viewed this scene was flabbergasted.

"Holy shit," Oberth exclaimed to Schauberger. "Did you just see that?"

"Yes, I did," responded Schauberger. "How do you explain it?"

"It acts with some kind of plasmonic effect," Oberth postured. "But that research is years away from actualization. We'll worry about that later. Now we need to see how this thing works."

For months, Schauberger and Oberth worked side by side each day to discover the secrets behind the advanced propulsion system. Theory after theory was hypothesized and tested.

"We can agree that we know this entire system works on some kind of anti-gravitational method, can't we, Viktor?" Oberth queried his partner.

"Yes, yes, Hermann. We can safely assume that theory," Schauberger answered. "But there has to be some key element that we're missing."

"We've experimented with superconductivity. We've experimented with magnetism, too," Oberth responded. "We've tried sound waves. My God, we've even tried using liquid nitrogen, and examined the axis of a magnet for any clues."

"What do you propose, Hermann? How can we get to the bottom of this quandary?" Schauberger asked his colleague.

"We need to experiment individually, Viktor. I need to get away and conduct my own experiments, and you need to do the same," Oberth announced. "By approaching the challenge from two different perspectives, I believe we have a better chance of unfolding this mystery."

"That's an excellent idea," Schauberger replied. "But where can you go to conduct this sensitive research?"

"There's a secluded warehouse that I'm converting into a working laboratory in the Kaiser Mountains outside of Leitmeritz. You're probably familiar with that Austrian territory, are you not?" Oberth asked without seeking a reply. "We can keep in constant communication with each other. That way, we'll know how close we're coming to developing our own version of this propulsion system. Then we can combine both our efforts into a working model."

"Yes, a splendid thought, Hermann." Schauberger agreed. "We won't be stepping on each other's toes, plus we can double our work efforts. When will you leave?"

"I'm packed and ready to go now," Oberth replied. "I've been thinking about this for quite some time. So I'll bid you a fond farewell today, my friend. I will contact you after I've arrived at Leitmeritz."

"We'll keep in constant communication, Hermann. I promise to keep you informed of my progress, and I know you'll do the same," Schauberger responded. They shook hands and gave each other a momentary affectionate hug before Oberth turned and departed the underground laboratory. It would be the last time Schauberger would see his colleague alive.

Working for months in Oberth's absence proved to be a very draining professional experience for Schauberger. "*Hermann was always the catalyst for outrageous ideas,*" Schauberger lamented to himself. "*I miss his exuberant presence.*"

Then one day, Schauberger, out of scientific desperation, began to explore the idea of quantum levitation, an idea offered by one of Viktor's young aspiring scientists during a brainstorming session. "*Can there be some kind of connection here?*" Schauberger asked himself.

Through exhaustive experimentation methods, the concept of barycentric control made its way to the forefront. Schauberger revealed this concept of combining gravitational force fields with electromagnetic energy as a way of mimicking the same kind of propulsion system effect he hypothesized when trying to back-engineer the propulsion system of the alien craft.

"Dr. Schauberger, your idea of enclosing mercury into an enclosed lead ball and forcing gyroscopic movement in an electromagnetic environment was brilliant," Schauberger's chief technician stated. "The results are magnificent."

"Indeed they are," Schauberger beamed. "I believe I've discovered the primary concept of electro-gravitic propulsion. I must tell Dr. Oberth. Write up these notes and diagrams and send them off to Leitmeritz immediately."

Sadly, word of Oberth's death and the destruction of his secret laboratory cancelled the travel plans of the courier between the German and Austrian laboratories. But it didn't stop the courier from rushing the results of Schauberger's monumental propulsion discovery into the hands of Hermann Goering.

"*Göring jetzt müssen meine Antriebssystem. Er hat keine Wahl. Ich bin der einzige mit einem Arbeitsmodell links. Die Herrlichkeit wird mein sein.*" Schauberger gushed. "*Goering now must use my propulsion system. He has no choice. I'm the only one left with a working model. The glory will be mine.*"

CHAPTER FORTY THREE

Theresienstadt Concentration Camp Secret Medical Laboratory

BLOODCURDLING screams could be heard daily throughout the eastern section of the sprawling concentration camp. The white, two-story building that housed the experimental medical facilities was off-limits to all camp personnel, excluding the stern camp commandant, Karl Rahn, who made daily visits to the highly secretive laboratories.

"Was ist die Ursache dieser elenden Lärm heute?" Rahn asked Sigmund Rascher. *"What is causing this wretched noise today?"*

Dr. Sigmund Rascher was a captain in the Medical Service of the Luftwaffe and an SS officer. Responsible for Nazi human experimentation, he split his time between the concentration camps at Dachau and Theresienstadt.

"I would like to claim my sterilization experiments are causing the commotion," Rascher snapped. "But I would be wrong."

"Well then," Rahn continued, "Let me begin the process of elimination." Rascher nodded his approval.

"Head injury experiments?" Rahn asked. Rascher said no.

"Bone, muscle, and nerve transplantation?" Rahn inquired. Rascher nodded in the negative.

"Freezing experiments? Mustard gas experiments?" Rahn kept probing as Rascher kept denying.

"Well, shit, my last guesses are the malaria, sulfonamide, or poison experiments. Is it any of them? I'm positive all of them would be painful, doctor. Am I right?" Rahn looked dazed and befuddled.

"I'm sorry, Commandant. But it's none of them," Rascher admitted. "I'm afraid all of the screams are coming from Dr. Eckhart's floor upstairs."

Rahn rolled his eyes. "Eckhart? Hell, he's only working with pregnant women. What do they have anything to scream about?" He laughed as he turned and left the building.

Rascher wondered what kind of work Eckhart was conducting on the second floor, too. The heavily-armed guards never allowed him to pass through the double door at the top of the steps, and he never talked with Eckhart because he never saw him.

I've got to get back to conduct those high altitude experiments anyway, Rascher told himself as he signed the official papers to transport the mobile pressure chamber from Theresienstadt to his laboratory at Dachau. *But I'm a little jealous. Eckhart's experimental subjects make more noise from pain than mine.*

******

Dr. Klaus Eckhart took one look at the horribly deformed stillborn male baby he had just delivered surgically from the screaming young Jewish girl, gave the experimental disappointment to his lab nurse, and told her to dispose of the body. The nurse understood that proper disposal meant jamming the dead fetus into another jar of formaldehyde, and adding the new bottle to the growing collection of other failed interbreeding experiments in a locked closet.

When Eckhart exited the room, a disinterested male lab technician wheeled the unconscious patient out of the tiny operating room, took her to an open window, and threw the body twenty feet below into an open acid pit that contained the skeletal remains of the other unfortunate female subjects that did not produce the required result.

"Another goddamn failure. That makes 24," Eckhart moaned as he shuffled from the bloody sub-standard operating room to the padded chair in his office in an adjoining room. *"Shit, they're all going to be scientific failures because Hitler doesn't want to give his space creatures anything close to a perfect hybrid. He wants me to keep using genetically-inferior hosts.*

"But I will produce a successful hybrid," he vowed. *"I'm going to start using a few healthy subjects, and see those results. It's my destiny as a German scientist. Hitler won't be upset. He'll be proud that Germany will lead the world in scientific discovery."*

As Eckhart sat with his hands over his face, he leaned back in his chair and recalled the astounding meeting he held with Hitler a few years ago. That meeting was a turning point in Eckhart's professional career.

Fall was turning to winter in Berlin when Eckhart was summoned to meet with Adolf Hitler in his private office in the German Chancellery. Eckhart was a rising star within the scientific medical community, specializing in genetic manipulation. When he entered Hitler's office, he noticed three high-ranking military officers huddled together in the back of the room.

He recognized Himmler and Goebbels. He would find out later the third person was Konrad Wolff. When Eckhart had taken his designated seat on Hitler's black office couch, the Fuhrer addressed the people in the room.

"Gentlemen, I have a plan that will make Germany not a European power, not a global power, but a universal power," Hitler pontificated. "Some of you (nodding toward Goebbels, Himmler, and Wolff) already know that I made contact with a race of outer space demons. They recognized that I was destined to lead the world and they agreed to be part of my plan. Each of you will have an important role executing your parts of the plan."

Eckhart quickly straightened up in the chair after hearing Hitler's story. "We negotiated an agreement," Hitler admitted. "They will support the rise of the Third Reich by giving us advanced technology. In exchange, we will supply them with a race of creatures. A hybrid of humans and these demons, I was told. Dr. Eckhart, that's why we need your expert skills."

"I'm honored, my Fuhrer. You can rely on me," Eckhart replied.

Hitler continued his diatribe. "These monstrous creatures came to me, of course, because they saw I would lead the superior Aryan race. I have decided the Aryan line is too pure for them. Instead, doctor, you will breed these hybrids using the inferior stock we have confined in the labor camps.

"A complete medical laboratory is set up at Theresienstadt, the SS labor camp in Czechoslovakia," Hitler exclaimed. "Female camp inhabitants will be provided for your breeding experiments. Make sure they are crippled or mentally unstable Jewish women. That should diminish the likelihood of producing a successful hybrid." Hitler laughed at his level of deceit toward Tehlri, unaware that the black communication device Hitler kept hidden in his office bookcase sabotaged any level of secrecy Hitler thought he maintained from the alien.

Then Hitler reached behind his desk, lifted a large clear bottle containing a milky-colored liquid from the wooden floor, and set it on the corner of his desk. "Here's the disgusting container that supposedly contains the demon semen that the leader of these creatures gave me to impregnate your specimens. My God, quick, take this out of my sight. Just looking at this vile fluid makes me nauseous.

"But I warn you, doctor, do not allow any knowledge of this breeding experimentation to leak out," Hitler demanded. "Your work is highly classified. Therefore, you will have armed sentries guarding access to your laboratory at all times. Only the camp commandant and your technicians and nursing staff will have access.

"Keep all of your scientific notes securely hidden and locked away. Your ultimate goal is to use your increased knowledge to breed the perfect Aryan child, not produce a perfect demon hybrid. Do I make myself clear, doctor?" Hitler motioned for Eckhart to approach him.

Feeling a sense of personal trepidation coupled with professional eagerness, a wide-eyed Eckhart quickly rose from his seat and hurried to Hitler's desk.

"Yes, my Fuhrer. I understand completely," Eckhart stuttered. "Thank you very much for your confidence in my work." Smiling sheepishly, he shook hands with Hitler, cautiously lifted off the desk the heavy jar filled with the fluid of a non-human species, and hastened his departure from the office. Hitler directed his office guards stationed outside the office door to escort Eckhart to the waiting Nazi military car that would deliver him and his liquid cargo to his new secret assignment at Theresienstadt.

Sitting alone in the back seat of the moving vehicle with the jar placed tightly between his feet on the floor, Eckhart began to imagine the unbelievable challenge he faced. But he also imagined the lasting legacy he would leave within the worldwide scientific medical community.

"Ich werde die Schöpfer einer neuen Lebensform sein. Letztlich werde ich der Schöpfer der perfekte arische Kind sein," Eckhart daydreamed. *"Ich werde ein Gott unter den Menschen sein!"*

"I'm going to be the creator of a new life form. Ultimately, I'm going to be the creator of the perfect Aryan child. I'm going to be a god among men!"

******

After Eckhart left the office, Hitler called out to his three military officers who remained standing in the back of the room.

"Do you believe Eckhart will follow his mandate?" Hitler asked the three men. "You know those damn scientists. They always have their own agendas."

"I believe you put the fear of God in him quite nicely," Himmler smiled.

"Yes, I agree," Goebbels exclaimed enthusiastically. "I believe he'll do exactly as you commanded."

Hitler now directed his comments toward Wolff. "Konrad, I'm putting you solely in charge of keeping an eye on Eckhart and his work. I want periodic reports on how his experiments are progressing. Give him two weeks to get organized. Check every month to see how many active pregnancies he's monitoring. Bring me photographic evidence of every experimental specimen he delivers."

Hitler continued. "Remember, though, I still want you and your team to keep searching for more powerful, magical artifacts that will add to my personal power. I don't trust that space beast to add to my power since he never gave us any direction on how that flying craft works. That just proves to me I need to look out for myself. I'm not helping him when he won't help me."

Wolff nodded his acceptance of his additional duties. "Anything else, sir?" Wolff asked.

"That will be all. You're all dismissed," Hitler told his aides.

As the three men walked down the long hall, Himmler gave Wolff some additional direction. "I want to know everything about Eckhart's work that you will be telling Hitler," he commanded. "You may be a favorite of the Fuhrer, but you owe all your allegiance to me and the Annenerbe. I'm the one who brought you into the fold. I'll be watching you closely."

As Himmler and Goebbels continued to traverse the hallway, Wolff veered away to the stairway to descend the steps the three floors to the street.

"That sonofabitch," Wolff thought. *"You're going to be watching me? We'll see how that works for you."*

CHAPTER FORTY FOUR

Himmler's Ahnenerbe Office Late Afternoon

"ELISE, please come into my office," Himmler yelled through the crack in his door separating his office from his secretary's.

"Right away, Herr Himmler," Elise yelled back.

When she entered, she was carrying her stenographer's pad as she always did. She quickly sat down in her familiar chair directly in front of Himmler's desk, crossed her legs, and with the pad on her lap and her writing pen ready, sat waiting patiently for any message Himmler wanted transcribed.

Himmler barely noticed Elise's arrival as he found himself immersed in piles of paper spread haphazardly across his desk. With a frown on his face, Himmler addressed Elise without looking at her.

"I am just drowning in all these damn papers, Elise," Himmler complained, his gaze still aimed squarely on his cluttered desk. "Bear with me, as I'm trying to locate some very important notes from some very sensitive meetings that Hitler has held with his inner circle these past few weeks."

After several more minutes of paper shuffling, Himmler exclaimed, "Ah, yes. Here they are." When he finally raised his eyes, he noticed Elise in her usually focused frame of mind ready to take his dictation.

"Oh no, Elise. There will be no dictation today," he apologized to his attractive and highly efficient secretary. "What I need you to do is take these pages of notes from Hitler's meetings, type up the major points, and make five duplicate sets for me."

"Yes, Herr Himmler. I'll get to it right away," she responded. She hastily rose from her chair, leaned across the desk, and accepted the seven crumpled sheets of notes from Himmler. As she turned to return to her desk, Himmler stopped her.

"It's late, Elise," Himmler stated. "There's no big rush to finish this assignment today. Since it will take you hours to sort through all the pages, you can do this first thing tomorrow morning." He smiled as he awaited her response.

"Thank you, Herr Himmler. I'll just read through them quickly and try to put them in some order so that I can get right to them in the morning." She returned his smile.

Forty minutes later as Himmler was leaving his office to attend a social function at a local hotel, he saw Elise still reading the note pages he had given her.

"I thought you would have left by now as it is well past sundown," Himmler remarked on his way out the door. "Your dedication is inspiring to me." With a quick wave, he was out the door and gone for the evening.

After Himmler closed the office door behind him on his way out, Elise slumped back in her chair, flabbergasted at the contents on some of the note pages.

"What on earth am I reading here?" she asked herself. *"Outer space fleets? Medical experiments turn humans into space creatures? I always knew Hitler was crazy. As strange as all of this seems to be, I must get this information to the Vatican immediately."*

CHAPTER FORTY FIVE

Elise's Berlin Apartment

ELISE performed the same ritual each day when she returned to her comfortable apartment following her workday at the German Chancellery. She strode to a secret hiding spot in her bathroom where she kept a vial of holy water. She dabbed a few drops onto her fingers, and made the sign of the cross. *"I need to bless myself after working with the Nazis all day,"* she told herself. *"I need to be reminded of God since I work with the godless each day."*

After replacing the holy water vial into its hiding spot, Elise walked to her kitchen table. From a hidden compartment inside her large purse, she took out a packet of secret papers that she had confiscated from Himmler's office today. It was a copy of the classified notes from Hitler's meeting with his inner circle of generals she had quickly typed up before leaving the office.

"I must get this information to the Holy Father immediately," she mumbled to herself. "I hope Paul and his team can make some sense of what I'm telling them."

She now started another ritual that she followed when preparing to send classified documents to the Vatican. She unscrewed the lower portion of one of the table legs, and removed a small Vatican medallion that Paul had given her during their meeting in Switzerland. Using an ink pad, she stamped the medallion image on the first page of the packet.

After returning the medallion to its hiding spot and screwing the table leg back into place, Elise placed the packet in a folded newspaper, and slipped the newspaper into her traveling purse. She quickly left her apartment, locking the door securely behind her. Her next critical stop: The small drug store located one block away, whose proprietor was a clandestine member of the Polish Resistance.

CHAPTER FORTY SIX

JOSEF KROL stood patiently behind the wooden counter of his small corner drug store as he watched old Gerda Saniuk, one of his favorite daily customers, agonize over which toothbrush to buy. "Take your time, Gerda," Josef joked. "I've got all night."

Elise entered the store, made eye contact briefly with Josef, and pretended to browse until Gerda completed her purchase and started to walk out. Elise then made her way to the front counter and set the folded newspaper down.

"Hello, Josef. What a grand night it is," she said.

Before Josef could respond, a Gestapo officer walked in and gave Gerda a long hard look as she left the store. Gerda scurried out to avoid contact with the officer. The officer then walked directly to the counter to grab a newspaper, and reached for the one Elise had put there. As he put his hand on the newspaper, Elise sprang into action.

"Good evening, Major," Elise said courteously.

"Good evening, Fraulein. May I see your papers, please?" the officer asked.

Fumbling around in her purse, she finally found her identification papers and handed them to the officer. Meanwhile, Josef used Elise's distractive actions to hide her newspaper under the counter and he replaced it with a regular newspaper on the countertop.

"Ah, you work at the chancellery," the young blond officer stated to Elise, returning her papers to her while oblivious to Josef's actions. "I apologize. We are ordered to be most careful when checking documents."

With a swift turn, the Gestapo officer grabbed the newspaper off the countertop, nodded to Josef, and started walking toward the front door. "Have a good evening, Fraulein," he called out as he exited the corner store.

"I have that young officer trained like a canary," Josef laughed. "He comes in, grabs a newspaper and anything else he wants, gives me a nod to make sure I understand he can do anything he wants without paying me, then he leaves with the goods."

Josef continued his story with Elise. "Sometimes, I even offer him some homemade pastry, which he never turns down."

Elise asked, "So how do you have him trained then, Josef?"

Josef quietly responded. "I've got him trained, Elise, because he has never searched my store or my living quarters upstairs. Never. And I want to keep it that way, as you well know."

Elise exchanged smiles with Josef, and turned to leave.

"Wait," Josef called out. He retrieved a makeup compact from a shelf, and set it on the counter for her.

"For saving us," he said.

Thanking Josef, Elise put the compact into her purse, and left the store.

"Let's see what we have going to the Vatican this time," he told himself.

CHAPTER FORTY SEVEN

AFTER Elise left, Josef Kroll walked to the front door of his store, flipped the "Open" sign to "Closed", turned off the store lights, and exited the store floor out a doorway located behind his countertop, the package Elise left with him securely hidden under his work apron. His destination: the secret cellar room that housed his radio transmitter.

The entrance to the secret radio room was located behind a false wall panel, nicely camouflaged behind a wash basin that rested on top of two wooden fruit crates at the back of the store room. After quickly removing the panel, Josef opened the door, grabbed the flashlight resting on the top of the stairs, and began his six-step journey to the bottom of the damp, claustrophobic radio room.

At the bottom of stairs to his right, Josef found the hanging string that turned on the dim light bulb. Because of the dimness of the bulb, the entire room was cast into a kaleidoscope of shadowy figures and objects. Josef could always count on one thing: He was always spooked by his moving shadow.

"*Przestań straszyć siebie, Josef. To tylko twoje głupie cień,*" he scolded himself. "*Stop scaring yourself, Josef. It's only your silly shadow.*" Just to be on the safe side, he peeked over his shoulder one last time before arriving at the table with the covered transmitter.

He dropped the courier package from Elise onto the corner of the table, and removed the tattered brown sackcloth sheet covering the transmitter, tossing it aside. Josef then walked to the darkest corner of the dimly-lit room, got down on his knees, and lifted a loose wooden floor board. He lowered his right hand into the dark floor abyss and grabbed from the hiding place an old leather-bound book that contained his secret Vatican codes. With book in hand, he rose from the floor, and shuffled back to the table.

When he arrived, he laid the book down, grabbed Elise's package, and slowly opened it, making sure he didn't damage the Vatican seal that Elise had attached to upper right hand side of the package. He then gingerly lifted out the single sheet containing the most unusual message he would ever send to Paul Dante at the Vatican.

Squinting hard in the eerie light to help him decipher the code contents, Josef began to transcribe the message. After completing the coding process, he began his ritual to send the secret message via Morse code to Father Roberto in the secret Vatican radio room.

"*I'm not sure he's going to believe this message,*" Josef told himself. "*I don't believe what I just read myself.*"

CHAPTER FORTY EIGHT

Vatican Secret Radio Room

MONSIGNOR PAUL DANTE was once again working late into the night in the secret Vatican radio room. Papa Gino requested that he stay as long as possible each day so that the Vatican never lost awareness of Hitler's troop locations. Since Germany invaded its European neighbors and Hitler threatened the Holy Father with public disclosure of the Nestorian papyrus, Dante thought the Pope was acting a little paranoid when he wanted hourly updates of any communication received from Vatican spies worldwide.

As Dante sat at his cluttered desk occupied with endless paperwork, Father Roberto was sitting at his radio receiver wearing a headphone. Dante noticed the young priest scribbling hurriedly on a notepad.

"What do you have there, Bobby?" Dante asked, using his nickname for the young cleric. "You look confused by the message."

"Monsignor Paul, this last transmission doesn't make any sense, and I've decoded it three times," the dismayed priest said. "Maybe I didn't hear it correctly."

"Why do you have a problem with it?" Dante asked. "What does it say?"

Reading from the notepad, Father Roberto began to repeat the strange message. "It says," Roberto slowly spoke the words, "Hitler plans outer space fleet. Stop. Medical experiments turn humans into space creatures. Stop. Packet to be delivered. Stop."

"Well, that's quite the message," Dante exclaimed. "Who sent it?"

"The operator is 27. That's Berlin," Roberto answered. "The collecting agent is number 63."

"Sixty-three you say?" Dante repeated the number. "That's Elise, our highest-placed operative within the German chancellery. If Elise collected the information, it's as good as gold. If Hitler himself held a gun to her head, she wouldn't send us false intelligence."

Dante ended his discussion with Father Roberto. "I'm looking forward to receiving that packet."

CHAPTER FORTY NINE

THE secret Vatican resistance network covertly transported Elise's private information packet from Josef Kroll in Berlin to the final stop on the trip to Rome: Banyuls-Sur-Mer, France. The tiny port city was located along the foothills of the Pyrenees Mountains, and was known mostly as the major smuggling center to and from Spain for nearly two centuries. With easy access to the Mediterranean Sea, the city was the perfect location for Vatican couriers to surreptitiously board a ship sailing to Rome.

The small grocery store on the corner of Av Mal Joffre and Rue Jean Bart was relatively calm this mid-morning. As Marcel, the owner, was assisting Mrs. LeClerc at the front counter and Francois, the 12-year-old neighborhood pickpocket, was reading silently in the back corner, a young Frenchman wearing a dark jacket with a hat pulled low over his head, entered the shop.

Nodding at Marcel, the young Frenchman opened up his jacket, revealing a courier bag slung over his shoulder. He then proceeded through the doorway leading to the back of the store. Once there, he took off his jacket, slipped the courier bag over his head, placed it behind a stack of fish boxes, and exited the shop without saying a word to Marcel.

After Mrs. LeClerc made her purchase and left the store, Marcel walked to the store window and looked warily up and down the street. Then he turned to address Francois.

"Francois, follow me to the back of the store. I have another messenger job for you."

The store owner did not admonish the street urchin as he usually did after watching him steal a small piece of candy from the taffy barrel. Marcel thought that he would owe his young delinquent much more than a piece of candy if he successfully completed his mission.

The boy jumped to his feet and followed Marcel to the back of the store. "What am I delivering this time?" the precocious youth asked. "I hope it's more exciting than just walking a couple blocks and handing it off to someone else."

By this time, Marcel and Francois had arrived at the secret drop-off location in the store. Marcel quickly moved the fish boxes to see the dark leather courier bag lying on the smelly wooden floor. He picked it up and handed it to Francois.

"This is another delivery to Rome, Francois," Marcel explained. "But it's much more important than any other delivery you've made."

Marcel continued his instructions. "You're going to meet Broussard again. Only this time it's going to be at the lake location after dark, and not down the street."

Francois' eyes lit up. "At the lake? Oh, yeah, now I can ride my bike," the overjoyed boy exclaimed.

"You must be very careful. There are more Nazi patrols than ever on the streets," Marcel cautioned. "When you leave here, go directly to the lake. Do not stop anywhere along the route."

With his final instructions to Francois, Marcel picked up the leather bag off the floor, put it over the shoulder of his young deliveryman, and helped Francois put on his warm jacket that would conceal the bag from any Nazi patrollers. Then he patted the boy on the back.

"Remember, don't stop anywhere until you deliver the package," Marcel commanded. "I'll reward you handsomely when you bring me Broussard's receipt for the package."

Francois nodded his understanding of the mission as he departed the small corner grocery store via the back alley exit. He mounted his rusty bike, which had been leaning against the building. Looking back one last time as he rode away, he saw Marcel standing in the doorway and heard the grocer's final words, "*La vitesse de Dieu.*" "*God's speed.*"

"*I don't need God's speed,*" Francois told himself. "*What I do need is some food, though. I'm starving. I'll stop at Genevieve's café. It's half way to the lake. Marcel will never find out.*" He felt proud of his cunning deception.

During the one-half kilometer trip from Marcel's store to Genevieve's café, Francois encountered only two Nazi soldiers patrolling the deserted lifeless streets. A kid riding a rusty bike would not draw much attention, he thought, as the sun began to slowly descend below the horizon. He figured he would have no problem rendezvousing after sunset with the Vatican agent Broussard at their secret lakeshore location after he had filled his rumbling stomach.

As Francois navigated closer to the café, he rode past groups of German soldiers idling away the time along street corners. He pedaled past the street entrance to the restaurant and followed the alley to the back of the brick building. Dismounting quickly, he leaned his bike against the wooden stairs that led to the back door. With the tantalizing smells of the kitchen escaping the restaurant door and wrapping their fragrance around Francois' senses, he found himself bounding up the back steps.

As he jerked open the heavy back door, ready to rush inside, he bumped into an overfed, inebriated German soldier who was leaving.

"Watch where you're going, you miserable brat," yelled the drunken soldier as he pushed Francois to the side and stumbled down the stairs. Francois knew that many of the German soldiers forced Genevieve to feed them for free. He was just happy that she also shared her leftovers with him.

"Bonjour, Genevieve!" Francois greeted the restaurant owner as he entered the kitchen. She was cooking over the wood-burning stove.

"Bonjour, Francois. Are you hungry tonight?"

"Oui. I'm starving," the youthful guest replied. "What do you have for me?" The mission for Marcel was now the farthest thing from Francois' mind at this moment.

Genevieve smiled at the enthusiasm of her young visitor. France began rationing food a few years ago, and it made life difficult for those whose livelihood depended on feeding others. Bread, meat, sugar, cooking fats and oils, cheese, and eggs were all being rationed in order to feed the French soldiers at the front lines fighting the Germans.

But because of the popularity of Genevieve's restaurant with the German soldiers occupying the small lake town, she was able to obtain many food items from black market sources, with the German soldiers surprisingly providing much of the illegal culinary contraband.

"Oh, I've got a delicious turnip and Jerusalem artichoke quiche, with apple tarts for dessert. How does that sound to you, Francois?" she asked.

"It sounds delicious," the boy cried out, climbing onto a wobbly stool at a small table in the corner of the kitchen.

Genevieve scraped the sides of the empty baking pan, collecting a small plate full of what remained of the evening's main dish. She added a small apple tart to the plate and set it in front of the hungry boy, along with a glass of water.

"I know it isn't much for you, Francois," the kind lady apologized. "But it's the best I can do today." She smiled warmly at the young boy, and caressed his dirty, but cherubic face, as she walked away. As a member of the Resistance, she knew he was on his way to rendezvous after sunset with the Vatican agent Broussard at their secret lakeshore location about a mile away. She knew her small café was the final stop before Francois began his dangerous mission. She wondered if this would be the last time she saw the heroic youngster.

After quickly finishing his meal, Francois jumped off the stool, gave Genevieve a loving hug, and hurried to the back door. Peeking outside, he buttoned his jacket up to this neck and charged down the stairs, two steps at a time. He jumped on his bike, and slowly made his way to the main street, trying not to draw the attention of the nearby German sentries.

Inconspicuously, Francois turned his bike in the direction of the lake, and started his covert journey. Suddenly, he met a German patrol vehicle driving towards him. A soldier spotted him and bellowed from inside the vehicle, "Hey, boy! Get home! You can't be on the streets after dark."

Waving a false acknowledgment to the soldier of the direct order, Francois immediately put his head down and raced away from the enemy vehicle, heading directly toward the back road leading to the lake. Two soldiers sitting on their parked motorcycle a block away noticed the unusual action.

"*Sollten wir sehen, was dieser kleine Scheiße ist da?*" "Should we see what this little shit is up to?" one soldier asked his partner.

"Yeah, he's not going in the direction of any house in town. He's heading out of town," the partner answered. "Let's find out what's going on with this kid."

One soldier jumped on the motorcycle and fired up the engine while the second soldier dived into the attached sidecar. Despite the soldier in the sidecar still clamoring to right himself, the driver took off in hot pursuit of the escaping boy.

It didn't take long for Francois to spot the two Germans and their noisy motorcycle. Knowing he couldn't outrun the speedy motorcycle, he began evasive action. He swung down a narrow alley with the motorcycle in hot pursuit. Since it was dark, he couldn't see the end of the passageway. But he kept his head down and pedaled as fast as he could.

"Stop you little bastard!" the sentry screamed at Francois. The annoyed German soldiers were tired of chasing this youthful Houdini. The closer they came to catching Francois, he was suddenly out of their reach. But they weren't about to quit the challenge.

"No way this little shit outruns us," the Nazi sentry riding in the sidecar yelled to his partner. "Let's finish this."

Francois peeked over his right shoulder as he kept his short distance ahead of the sentries. *"Ha, those Germans are idiots,"* he laughed to himself. *"They'll never catch me."*

When Francois finally looked ahead, he was shocked to see a brick wall awaiting him about 20 feet away. "Oh, no," he cried out. "I've driven into a dead end."

The screeching motorcycle was now just a few feet behind him, the engine still blasting on full throttle. "We've got you now, asshole," the driver grinned as he pictured the hunt coming to an end. His seated partner was happy that the jostling ride was at its conclusion, too.

Trapped and in despair, Francois concluded that he was not going to meet his Vatican contact tonight. He might not be meeting him again, ever, if the German soldiers took his precious package from him. Young boy or not, he figured that the Germans would probably throw him in jail after he was captured.

He feverishly began plotting his escape on foot after he was forced to abandon his bicycle. But something caught his eye as he closed in on the brick wall. The wall was broken in the center. There was a small hole in the brick foundation. And it was big enough to slide through, he thought. *"I can get through that hole! Thank you Jesus, Mary, and Joseph."*

Francois could feel the heat and smell the burning engine oil as the motorcycle was inches away from catching him. The German driver began to throttle down and lessen his speed as the brick wall loomed ever closer.

"Get off your bike now," the seated soldier yelled at the youthful rider. "The race is over, you little turd." The German duo laughed at the derogatory comment. But both soldiers were surprised when Francois did not slow his pace when he reached the wall.

Without hesitation, with his heart pounding in his chest and with a final rush of adrenaline, Francois fearlessly bolted through the small slot in the brick wall. But then he found himself airborne in the dark night. *"Oh shit!"* was his initial response. *"I'm going to die after all that work escaping the Germans. Life ain't fair."*

The wall was blocking a ledge, and the sharp drop-off jolted Francois as he was dislodged from his bike, and his body started to freefall into the dark abyss. Somersaulting backwards, he flailed his arms in desperation to stop his momentum downward during the endless fall. *"C'est elle. This is it,"* he told himself. *"Je suis hors de miracles. I'm out of miracles."*

The German soldiers had skidded to a jerky stop in front of the wall, and both now hurriedly approached the black opening to see the demise of their young nemesis on the other side.

"I guess the kid got what was coming to him," one soldier lamented as he squinted into the darkness to see where Francois' dead body was laying.

"Yeah, but I'm not going to lose any sleep over his death," his partner answered. "He was a pain in the ass. And I knew he was hiding something."

As both soldiers now peered out over the ledge, they were astounded and pissed at what they saw. The kid wasn't dead. He was alive and well, and pedaling away from the haystack that had cushioned his fall. And to add insult to injury, Francois was laughing loudly and waving at the humiliated Nazis as he disappeared into the dark night.

FRANCOIS was celebrating his harrowing escape from the motorcycle sentries moments ago as he pedaled methodically along the deserted country road on his way to meet with the Vatican messenger Broussard. His breathing was still heavy, and his skin still sweaty and dirty, following his unexpected descent into the bristly haystack. The adrenaline was still flowing as he remembered his brush with death during his freefall after leaving the ledge.

"Je vous dois, Seigneur. I owe you, Lord," Francois kept repeating the phrase when he heard a truck engine roaring ahead of him in the darkness. He quickly sprinted off the road and pulled his bicycle behind some bushes.

As the headlights flashed into Francois' eyes through the dense bushes, the truck drove past with the German guards in the back drunkenly crooning out of tune. *"Such losers,"* Francois grinned. Once it seemed safe, the boy dragged his bicycle back onto the road and continued his mission. Within minutes, Francois turned his bike off the road, and bounced down a flowery hillside toward a secluded cove along the waterfront.

Broussard, an elderly boatman, waited impatiently at the shore. Moonlight reflected off the water, the brightness making it dangerous for covert activities. The line of his small motor launch was tied to a nearby tree limb.

Hearing a rustling sound coming toward him, he crouched down to be less conspicuous. When he spotted the boy on the bicycle, he stepped out of the brush to greet him.

"Bonjour, Francois. You are late. Did you stop at Genevieve's café again before coming here?" Broussard already knew the answer, but he watched as the expression on Francois' face confirmed his hypothesis.

"Oui, Monsieur Broussard," Francois mumbled. "But there were a lot of Nazis on the road tonight. I even had to outrun a German motorcycle patrol to get here."

Broussard raised his eyebrows. "And you did this how?" Broussard inquired.

"I was able to drive through a small hole in a brick wall at the end of an alley way," Francois exclaimed with pride. "The Germans could not squeeze their motorcycle and sidecar through the hole. They were really angry." He laughed at his good fortune.

"This is a big packet of papers, so it must be important to the Pope," Francois stated as he removed his jacket, lifted the leather pouch off his shoulder, and handed it to Broussard.

"Yes, it is very important, or so I've heard," Broussard responded, taking the pouch from the young messenger and placing it over his shoulder. "I hope I can still deliver it to the boat before sunrise.

"You're doing a good job, Francois," Broussard complimented the boy. "Here's the receipt to give to Marcel so you can be rewarded for your work." He handed the boy a piece of yellow paper. "Now be careful going home."

Broussard untied his boat line from the tree limb, stepped into his motorboat, and pushed away from the shore. When he was a safe distance away, he started his noisy engine, and chugged away into the foggy mist. His destination was another boat anchored roughly a mile off shore. It was this larger boat that would make the trip across the sea to northern Italy. From there, it would only be a few days before the messenger delivered the contents of the leather pouch to Paul Dante at the Vatican.

Francois watched Broussard's boat silently disappear into the fog as he readied his bicycle for the trip back to town. He tucked the yellow receipt slip into his coat pocket, and started to push his bicycle up the short hill, retracing his steps to the road above.

A half mile from town, he again encountered the truck with the soldiers he had hidden from on his trip to the shore. This time, the truck was parked off the road, and its drunken occupants were fast asleep.

Francois slowly pedaled past the quiet Nazi truck, and made it safely to Marcel's store without meeting any other German patrols along the way. The old grocer was happy when he saw the boy climbing the back steps.

Francois eagerly handed the yellow receipt to Marcel as he slipped inside the back door.

"And everything went well for you during this trip?" Marcel quizzed the youngster.

"*Oui. Très facile. Pas de problème du tout,*" the boy muttered. "*Very easy. No problems at all.*"

Before Marcel could ask another question, he noticed that Francois was fast asleep on his makeshift bed in the corner of the backroom. He smiled at the boy as he extinguished the candle in his hand, ending an eventful day for two of the Vatican's best French resistance fighters.

CHAPTER FIFTY ONE

Dante's Vatican Office – Night

PAUL DANTE yawned as he rubbed his eyes for the hundredth time. It was past 10:00 in the evening, and he was still at his office desk. But as tired as he was, he kept reading the English translation of the pages that arrived from Elise in the courier's bag. He was still trying to comprehend the enormity of the message.

There was a crucifix on the wall, and his World War I religious medallion hung from it.

Looking up at the crucifix, Dante said, "I'm gonna need your help with this."

CHAPTER FIFTY TWO

Dr. Eckhart's Camp Medical Ward
1943

THE ward was filled with a double row of soiled military cots. Each held a young pregnant Jewish woman. One of the women was in labor. She was moved by two orderlies to a wheeled bed, and quickly pushed into the delivery room.

Waiting in the delivery room was Dr. Eckhart and two nurses. All three were wearing white masks, white surgical gowns, and all were prepped for the delivery. Lacking closet space in this room, on the walls of this sub-standard operating room were shelves holding large clear jars. Deformed fetuses in formaldehyde floated in the jars, documented proof of failed experiments.

The woman was screaming in pain. "Give her the ether," Eckhart commanded, as one nurse lowered the breathing mask onto the woman's face. Within seconds, the woman lost consciousness. One nurse raised the woman's long medical gown above her waist to expose her naked pregnant torso. The second nurse poured rubbing alcohol over the woman's round belly to decrease any element of infection during the Caesarean procedure.

"Scalpel," Eckhart ordered. A nurse handed him the surgical instrument. Eckhart only performed Caesarian section deliveries because it was a faster and more efficient method of delivery for these experimental hybrid births. He wasn't patient enough to wait for a natural childbirth to occur.

As Eckhart began his slow, deep transverse cut just above the edge of the bladder through the abdominal wall and into the uterus, he mumbled, "God, let this be the one." He took a quick glance at the jars on the wall as sweat dripped from his forehead.

As Eckhart punctured the uterine wall, blood and amniotic fluid began to gush out over the torso and down to the wooden floor. The blood loss in this patient seemed unusually high, Eckhart thought. With the nurses desperately trying to soak up the blood with towels to keep the incision as visible as possible, Eckhart quickened his slicing, finishing within seconds.

Using brute force, Eckhart pulled the incision apart, tearing the abdominal wall away to display the baby inside. Using forceps, Eckhart grabbed the baby by the head, and lifted the child upward.

Eckhart held the child up. His eyes widened. It had pink skin and a human body. The head was shaped like the aliens, and its eyes were almond-shaped like the aliens.

"My first success," Eckhart shouted ecstatically. "The Fuhrer will be so pleased."

After cutting the umbilical cord, Eckhart handed the baby to Jirina "Rina" Novak, to take it to a side room where an incubator was installed. Rina was one of Eckhart's young Czech nurses, and a valuable covert Vatican informant.

After placing the breathing hybrid child into the incubator, Rina quickly scanned the area to make sure she was alone in the room. Feeling confident, she took out a miniature camera from beneath her hospital garb that she had received from her Vatican Resistance leaders and smuggled into the camp, and snapped a photo of the grotesque creation.

Without warning, Eckhart dashed into the room to admire his work. Instantaneously, he began shouting for the security guards when he saw Rina taking the photos.

"Guards, guards, quickly," Eckhart screamed. "We have a spy!"

Rina pushed her way past Eckhart and tried to run, but two Nazi guards stationed outside the main doors to Eckhart's facility easily grabbed her as she dashed from the laboratory. The guards dragged her across the camp compound as she fought furiously to escape their tight grasp. Eckhart followed closely behind.

Konrad Wolff and his driver arrived at the camp to receive Dr. Eckhart's medical experiment updates, and noticed the commotion. Wolff exited the car, and approached Eckhart.

"Doctor Eckhart, I was in the area and I stopped to pick up your reports," Wolff stated.

"Not now, Wolff. We've caught a spy," Eckhart responded as he kept pace with the guards forcefully transporting the screaming, writhing nurse.

The guards brought Rina into the camp commandant's office, and emptied her pockets before Wolff entered. The items were on the table as Rina was pulled into a back room for interrogation.

When Wolff entered the office, he inspected Rina's possessions. There was the mini camera, some miscellaneous items, and a unique Catholic medallion on a chain. Wolff identified the medallion as similar to ones confiscated from other spies with ties to the Vatican. He palmed the medallion and deposited it into his pocket. He then pushed the remaining items into his leather satchel.

By this time, Karl Rahn, the camp commandant, came out of his office and greeted Wolff.

"You picked an exciting day to visit, Obergruppenfuhrer Wolff," Rahn boasted. "Our doctor has caught himself a nice little spy."

"Do you mind if I see her?" Wolff asked.

"I won't even charge you admission," Rahn answered sarcastically.

Wolff walked down the hall to the interrogation room. He nodded to the guard outside the door, and the guard opened the door for him.

Inside the room, the second guard stood along the back wall while a Nazi SS officer hovered over Rina, who was seated at a small table. Her hands were bound behind her, and an empty chair was opposite her across the table.

"I will interrogate this prisoner myself," Wolff told the SS officer. "She may have information important to the Fuhrer."

"*Ich glaube nicht,*" the officer protested. "*I don't think so.*"

"I outrank you," Wolff countered. "Leave immediately or I'll tell the Fuhrer about your insubordination."

"Fucker," the SS officer mumbled as he stomped from the room, slamming the door behind him.

Wolff now turned his attention to the guard standing along the back wall.

"Her information will be for the Fuhrer only," Wolff said to the guard as he directed his eyes to the door. Surprised by the order, the guard quickly left the room. Wolff secured the door, and sat down in the vacant chair.

"What were you photographing when the doctor caught you?" Wolff asked, waiting for Rina's reply. "You might as well tell me now since I'll know momentarily after they develop the film."

Rina didn't answer, but just stared defiantly at Wolff from across the table. Feeling he wouldn't get a response asking the simple questions, Wolff decided to try another approach. He lifted the unique medallion from his pocket and tossed it on the table.

"I know what this means," Wolff stated emphatically. "I know about your friends who use this medallion to identify your secret Vatican group. As I see it, the commandant will have you shot as a spy, or you can cooperate with me."

Rina's heart raced at the mention of the Vatican, but she cloaked her surprise. "Ha, is that what you Nazis call it now? Rina retorted. "Cooperate?"

"I can take you out of this camp where you'll be safe. There's no one else who can help you now." Wolff waited for Rina's reaction.

"Jesus, you sound so sincere," Rina replied sarcastically. "I almost believe you, except there's the devil's insignia on your collar."

Wolff smiled at Rina's brashness. He sat back in the chair and pondered his next move. After a silent moment, he rose, and said to Rina, "Then I'll take you with me and convince you along the way."

CHAPTER FIFTY THREE

RAHN left his office and saw the guards and SS officer standing in the outer office.

"What are you doing here?" he asked. "Why aren't you interrogating the spy?"

"That fucker Wolff said he would do it," the officer answered. "He said he's getting information for the Fuhrer."

Rahn was furious. He didn't like anyone muscling in on his territory. He quickly turned and rushed down the hall to the interrogation room.

Just as he arrived, Wolff opened the interrogation room door and he led Rina out to where the men were standing.

Seeing the anger in Rahn's eyes, Wolff interjected, "This woman is more than a common spy. She has vital information and I'm taking her to Berlin for a thorough interrogation by our experts."

Rahn shouted, "You can't just walk out of camp with my prisoner."

Wolff countered. "You've seen my papers before, commandant. I have absolute authority from the Fuhrer himself. So don't get in my way of official Nazi business."

"This won't end here, Wolff," Rahn shouted.

Wolff ignored the threat, and decided to taunt Rahn further.

"And I'll need a driver," Wolff told Rahn. "My driver says my car needs maintenance. I need to leave immediately, so I will take the prisoner to Berlin on the train. Can one of your men take us to the station?"

Wolff wanted to keep his driver out of his plan, so the maintenance diversion became a necessity.

"I can have my driver take you to Berlin," Rahn said.

"Too slow," Wolff countered. "The train is faster."

"How about a plane?" Rahn countered.

Wolff was running out of excuses. "I need to get caught up on some reports during the trip, so the train will be best. But thank you for your hospitality, commandant. I'll make sure to tell the Fuhrer of your total cooperation in this matter."

"And the prisoner won't be an inconvenience to your paperwork?" Rahn asked derisively.

"I'll have her secured. If she tries to escape, I'll shoot her," Wolff responded.

Wolff put a coat over Rina's shoulders, and the two of them walked outside to wait for Rahn's personal commandant vehicle. When Rahn's personal driver arrived, Wolff and a restrained Rina got into the back seat, and the car departed.

As a suspicious Rahn watched the Nazi vehicle leave the compound, he said to the SS officer, "Send two men to follow him."

CHAPTER FIFTY FOUR

VIKTOR SCHAUBERGER was overjoyed. He and his work team had successfully reverse-engineered the alien craft technology and built a small, one-man, disk-shaped craft that sat near the much larger alien craft inside the secret underground complex. The small craft had a backyard-mechanic look to it on the outside, unlike the polished gleam reflecting off the larger alien craft that sat nearby. But what was on the inside mattered most.

It was a big day for Schauberger. It was the day of the first test flight.

"Oh, this is grand!" Schauberger beamed. "Don't you think so, Heinrich?"

Heinrich Decker was Schauberger's technical assistant. He considered himself Schauberger's "go-for" guy, as in "Heinrich, go for some new bolts," or "Heinrich, go for some coffee." Yet, he and his fellow workers were eager to see if the craft could fly.

"Yes, Herr Viktor, it looks magnificent," Decker said half-heartedly.

Schauberger seemed like the only person showing any real enthusiasm. Decker was mostly faking his, and the other sullen workers were prisoners or locals from nearby German-occupied towns. Whatever the role they played in the construction of the test craft, each worker and technician understood that what they had built was something special.

Movable platforms with stairs surrounded the test craft's elevated dock area so workers could reach the cockpit. Schauberger and others were busy making final preparations and unhooking various wires from monitoring equipment.

A Czech painter finished his work, and removed a stencil to reveal a red and black swastika emblem on the craft. Then spinning around to notice if anyone was watching, the painter spit on the newly-painted seal of the Nazis. *"That felt good,"* the painter smiled.

When Schauberger finished checking an instrument panel, he noticed Decker on the floor working with some tools and a vintage alarm clock.

"What on earth are you doing, Heinrich?" Viktor asked.

"You told me to attach a bomb, doctor," Decker responded. "You said we'd need to bomb this craft in case the Allies got too close."

"Yes, I know that," Schauberger replied. "What are you doing with that clock?"

'It's mine, doctor," Decker said. "It was all I could find at the moment to use as a timer. We don't have anything else around here."

"All right, but hurry up," Schauberger snapped. "I need you to help monitor the test."

As Schauberger ended his conversation with Decker and began to walk away, he remembered that he should tell Decker to plant a bomb in the alien craft as well. When he turned to address his assistant, a young Luftwaffe pilot approached. At the sight of the test pilot, Schauberger forgot about his additional instructions for Decker.

Schauberger addressed the pilot. "Do you want to run through the layout of the control panel again?" he asked the pilot.

"No sir, doctor, that's not necessary," the pilot responded. "I've studied it thoroughly."

"Very good," Schauberger gushed. "For this first test, raise the vehicle fifteen meters off the floor and hover there. Then maneuver the craft ten meters to the right of center. Then move ten meters to the left. Return to the center of the pad and land. That should be all we need to see if systems are working as intended."

The pilot nodded his understanding of his duties, then added, "Thank you for this honor, doctor. It's a great day for the Fuhrer and for Germany."

Schauberger replied in jest, "Yes, yes. A great day where we hope to avoid execution orders from our generous Fuhrer if we fail this test."

The pilot shook hands with Schauberger, climbed the stairs, and squeezed into the cockpit. Once inside, he donned his aviator helmet equipped with a short-wave radio receiver so he could communicate with technicians during the test flight. Workers installed a metal dome over his strapped-in body, and bolted it into place. When the final bolt was fastened, the workers scurried down the steps, and removed all the extraneous equipment from around the craft. Now only the test craft remained in the center of the lab, resting in its docking cradle.

Schauberger and some assistants watched the unfolding scene from a raised platform about thirty feet from the craft where they had placed monitoring equipment and a tripod-mounted motion picture camera to record the event. Schauberger reached into his large lab coat pocket and realized he was still carrying something. He pulled out a small black box, identical to the one the aliens had given Hitler years earlier.

Schauberger turned to the closest assistant, handed him the device, and said, "Here, take this to my office. It's been lying loose inside the big craft. I don't want anything to happen to it." The assistant left immediately to comply with Viktor's request.

Schauberger now turned his complete attention to the test flight. He motioned to a technician near the monitoring equipment and directed him to signal the pilot to begin. The technician radioed the order to the pilot.

With all eyes glued to the center of the room, the prototype craft started to shake and an electric hum emanated from it, indicating the pilot had started the mechanism. The craft silently rose from its docking platform and floated effortlessly a few feet off the floor in a stationary position. Then it began a slow steady rise toward Schauberger's target elevation.

Suddenly, the craft shuttered, and there was a loud mechanical noise. Immediately, the craft rocketed upward at tremendous speed and blasted through the roof of the underground complex. Dirt and other debris fell heavily to the cavern floor. Workers scattered to avoid being hit by the descending rubbish. Finally, the craft stopped abruptly about 300 yards above the room.

Looking upward through the gaping hole in the roof, Schauberger and the entire room of workers and technicians were shocked at the sudden turn of events. But looks of relief returned to the faces in the testing room when the craft stabilized at its current position.

Schauberger swiftly grabbed the radio from the hands of the technician, and began to talk to the pilot.

"What the hell happened?" Schauberger screamed into the receiver, waiting to hear a response from the pilot.

Schauberger's radio initially picked up only static. Then a human voice screeched a quick incomprehensible message.

"Please repeat," Schauberger commanded. "I didn't understand you."

Without warning, the craft began to shake and gyrate violently. There was a loud popping sound, and the craft descended back through the hole in the roof as fast as it had left the room only a moment ago. When it impacted the floor, the bomb that Schauberger had ordered to be placed on the bottom of the craft for defensive purposes detonated instantaneously, sending wreckage whizzing in all directions. The bolted-down dome erupted from the top of the craft, followed airborne by the decapitated head of the helpless pilot.

Flying debris destroyed the surrounding work area, and inflicted massive carnage. Two workers near ground zero were blown backward, the blast severing limbs from their scorched bodies. A chunk of the craft burst through Schauberger's platform, grazed the doctor's head, and embedded itself in Heinrich's chest, killing the young technician instantly. The movie camera was destroyed, and the film melted and smoldered in the ruins.

Once again, like after the research facility fire, the exterior of the large alien craft was undamaged, even as large pieces of metal and heavy pipe rocketed through the air and hit the sides like missiles. Scorch marks were barely visible on the large craft from the fiery explosion.

The Czech painter did not fare well. He was lifted into the air by the blast and slammed against a pile of destroyed monitoring equipment. A piece of the broken fuselage with the painted swastika on it followed him there, landing squarely between the vocal cords in his neck, and severing an artery. *"Shitty Nazi karma,"* the painter cried as he tried to dislodge the piece of metal from his throat. He bled out within minutes.

A semi-conscious and bleeding Schauberger lay flat on his back, still dazed by the explosion and shrapnel to his head. From his prone position, he helplessly watched as pages of the craft's blueprints that were blown into the air ignited and burned as they floated down on the walkway near him. He winced when he saw the image of the test craft on the top page disintegrate before his eyes.

As one of Schauberger's assistant technicians helped him to his feet amidst the dismembered limbs, multiple deaths, and an obliterated test craft, they both looked up through the roof and saw an alien craft hovering in the sky over the hole.

"Son of a bitch," Schauberger mumbled. "Now I've got aliens and the Fuhrer's men watching me fail miserably."

CHAPTER FIFTY FIVE

WOLFF and Rina entered the busy train station just as the train was ready to depart. Rina's hands were still restrained, and Wolff held her arm. She was cooperative while they made their way to a back train car. Wolff carried his leather satchel with the papers he claimed he needed to attend to during the train trip. To Wolff, however, the most important contents were the medallion and the miniature camera.

On the platform, two plainclothes SS agents sat in separate locations, watching every step that Wolff and Rina took. Becker and Wirths, the two agents sent by Rahn, watched their targets board the train. As the train started to pull away, they nodded to each other as they both boarded, each through a different door in the car to avoid suspicion.

Wolff and Rina took seats near the front of the car, facing each other. Since the seats near Wolff and Rina were occupied, the two SS agents sat separately in seats that allowed them to watch their targets. Wolff was not aware that the SS agents were watching him and Rina.

Wolff leaned forward in his seat and addressed Rina in a low voice, so as not to be overheard.

"I just saved you from certain death," Wolff stated. "The least you can do is tell me what you photographed in Doctor Eckhart's lab."

Still feeling defiant because she was talking to a Nazi officer, Rina finally relented out of gratitude for Wolff intervening on her behalf back at the prison camp.

"Doctor Eckhart's experiments finally proved successful after all these years of failure," Rina stated in a hushed tone. "He delivered a live, breathing devil baby. It was the most hideous thing I've ever seen." The recollection alone made Rina nauseous.

"Who were you taking the pictures for?" Wolff asked.

"You already know who," Rina responded, agitation in her voice.

"The Vatican? You're working for the Vatican?" Wolff queried excitedly.

"I'm one of thousands working for the Holy Father to defeat you and Hitler," Rina responded, her voice rising with emotion.

It was an epiphany moment for Wolff. His long-held suspicions were now validated. This was the first time he officially heard the word "Vatican" confirmed by a resistance operative.

"How were you going to deliver this camera to the Vatican?" Wolff continued his questioning.

"Through a Vatican field team," Rina replied, but then quickly added, "You realize it's dangerous to try to contact a Vatican field team."

Wolff grinned, "Well, I can tell you it's not any more dangerous than what I am doing now."

Rina retorted, "I still don't trust you. But if we do make contact, you're likely to be shot wearing that uniform."

"This uniform is what got you out of that camp alive," Wolff emphasized. "I still need it if we're going to get off this train and get transportation to find your contact."

"Why are you doing this?" Rina asked forcefully. "Why are you suddenly betraying your country?" She sat back in her seat, waiting to hear Wolff's explanation.

Wolff liked this feisty nurse. He grimaced as he pondered the question he knew inevitably needed to be asked. The answer certainly foretold his future actions during the war.

"Why am I betraying my country?" he repeated the question, taking a deep breath before answering. "I love Germany, but Hitler is a madman, as are his inner circle. This war isn't about ideology regarding the German people. It's about personal ego, greed, and a terrible waste of human life and culture." Wolff leaned forward again, the inflection in his voice rising.

"My God, Hitler's eradicating an entire race of people, simply because he hates them. And because he's jealous of them, too," he added. "You know what's happening at those concentration camps. Innocent women and children are being gassed to death because they're of Jewish descent."

Rina listened intently, still trying to decide whether to trust Wolff. She was fascinated by his passionate reasoning.

Wolff continued his diatribe. "Classic art is being stolen or destroyed. Books are being burned. Hitler is having Eckhart create these genetic abominations. There are other unspeakable atrocities being done in the name of science. None of this helps the German people."

He sat back in his seat, and sighed, "I can't fight for something I don't believe in anymore." But then he looked Rina directly in the eyes.

"I see the passion that you Vatican spies exhibit," he said with emotion. "I admire your tenacity. I didn't want to see you executed. I don't want to be a part of that life anymore."

He concluded his thoughts. "I once had that passion for Hitler's ways. But the more I became aware of the true reasons why Hitler and his inner circle were doing the things they were, the more I knew I have to fight against them. And I guess doing this with you is my first act of treachery."

Wolff's gaze left Rina, and he sat back and closed his eyes, knowing he had just crossed the line from being a high-ranking Nazi officer within Hitler's inner circle to becoming a notorious Third Reich traitor with a bounty on his head.

Rina felt convinced of Wolff's defection, and stated, "We need to get off this train at the next town."

Wolff's mind was jostled back to reality. "What? Why?" he stammered.

"I don't know anything about the group you're looking for. Just that they come from the Vatican," she stated. "All I do is pass along any information I collect to my contact in the next town." Rina paused before continuing, gathering her thoughts.

"It's all the farther I could travel with papers without being arrested," she explained. "Even then, it's not safe because there are Nazi patrols all over the town."

"But you have a medallion, just like them," Wolff retorted.

"Sure. That's how we identify one another," she stated. "By the way, can I have mine back now?"

"Later," Wolff answered. "When it's safe."

Wolff needed more answers. "So what happens in the next town? Can your people find that Vatican field team I'm looking for?"

"When we get to my contact, I'll ask," Rina responded. "That's all I can do."

Wolff felt uneasy. Rina's answers weren't building his confidence in his getaway plan.

Rina snickered as she extended the conversation with Wolff. "You know, the men in that field team are ruthless. If you're lucky, they'll shoot you down the minute they see you. If you're less lucky, they'll take you prisoner. Do you know what they'll do to you?"

It didn't take long for Wolff to realize Rina was bluffing.

"I thought they work for the Vatican. You make them sound like the most fanatical Nazis," Wolff countered. "I'll take my chances that they still believe in God's commandments."

"Well, God had the devils driven out of heaven. So what chance do you have?" she asked sarcastically.

Wolff just shook his head at the audacity of his prisoner. He quickly realized that the train was slowing down as it neared the next station.

"When the train stops and these passengers start to disembark, we'll get into line with them," Wolff stated.

When Wolff and Rina got up and moved toward the exit, both SS agents were startled. "*This isn't anywhere near Berlin!*" popped into their heads. As they ran toward opposite doors in which they entered, both pulled Luger P08 pistols from holsters hidden under their dark, heavy coats. They hid their gun hands inside their coats as they neared the doors.

As Wolff stepped onto the train platform, he realized he forgot his satchel.

"Wait," he ordered Rina to stop. "I left my satchel inside."

Becker jumped down to the platform just as Wolff turned to return to the train car. As they bumped into each other, the collision jarred Becker's gun from his hand, and it fell down inside his coat and landed noisily on the platform. As both men spied the gun together, they gave each other a surprised look.

Wolff reacted first, and kicked the gun under the train. Becker pushed Wolff backward, and the two began trading punches. Wirths stepped from the opposite door, and saw the confrontation between Becker and Wolff. He pulled his gun from inside his coat, and took a quick shot at Wolff as he started running toward the two combatants.

At the sound of gunfire, the people on the platform began to scatter. Becker stopped fighting with Wolff and dropped down under the train to retrieve his gun. Wolff pulled his sidearm and fired at Wirths as the agent ran toward him. Wolff's bullet hit his target, and Wirths dropped to the platform, dead.

Wolff fired another round at Becker to keep him under the train. Then he and Rina quickly joined the fleeing crowd, and exited the train station.

CHAPTER FIFTY SIX

THE crowd fleeing the train station thinned quickly, and Wolff and Rina knew they had to find an alley immediately in order to escape. Becker, with gun in hand, sprinted out of the station gates in frantic pursuit of his targets. But he was too late to see where they had gone.

Becker feared delivering bad new to Rahn. But there was no other way to handle the situation. Becker called Rahn from inside the station.

"This is Becker," he told Rahn's secretary. "Let me speak to Commandant Rahn."

Rahn promptly answered the call. "Becker, I hope you have good news for me. I wasn't expecting to hear from you so soon."

"The suspects escaped by killing Wirths," Becker announced. "Wolff tried to kill me, too. I chased him and the nurse, but I lost them in the crowd when all hell broke loose at the station."

"So Wolff is now a traitor to the Third Reich," Rahn declared. "Take control of the local garrison, and hunt down the spy and the traitor. Shoot to kill on sight. I'll contact the High Command in Berlin, and inform them of Wolff's status."

"Yes sir, Commandant," Becker said. "I won't let you down."

CHAPTER FIFTY SEVEN

WOLFF and Rina found the alley they desperately needed. After running for several minutes, they stopped to assess their situation, and hid between some packing crates and barrels.

"I'm sure Becker has notified Rahn of the situation by now, and Rahn is most likely contacting the German High Command in Berlin," Wolff told Rina. "We are now marked for death on sight." Rina acknowledged Wolff's summation with a shrug of her shoulders.

At the end of the alley, unseen by Wolff and Rina, four village boys were hiding with rocks in their hands. A German patrol vehicle drove slowly past the alley. When it was a short distance down the street, the boys jumped out of hiding and pelted the vehicle with their rocks.

"Little shits," the soldiers yelled. The boys started to run down the alley before the last rocks had hit their target. They were whooping and hollering as they ran past the hiding spot of Wolff and Rina.

The Nazi patrol vehicle backed up to the alley opening, but the boys had disappeared. A young soldier jumped from the vehicle, and he raced into the alley after the delinquents. His run brought him to within ten feet of the fugitives' hiding place before he abruptly stopped at the sound of his squad commander's voice.

"Let them go," he ordered. "They know more hiding places than we can imagine."

"Can't I just shoot a few of them?" the young soldier asked. "I'm tired of getting hit by their rocks." The young soldier stared once more down the alleyway, took another step forward as if he intended to continue the pursuit, but relented and followed orders.

Breathing a sigh of relief when the patrol vehicle departed, Rina snapped at Wolff, "Free my hands. I can't run like this."

Wolff complied, and Rina rubbed her wrists to get back some circulation. Wolff queried her.

"We still have a short while until the local patrols know about us," Wolff stated. "Can you get us to your contact before my uniform turns into a target?"

"This isn't the usual route I take," Rina answered sardonically. "But I think we're close. This isn't a big town."

Rina and Wolff walked cautiously down the street. Some town people ducked into stores or crossed the street to avoid his German uniform. As the two stopped across the street from Rohlicek's Bakery, shouts from another block told them that the patrols were alerted of their presence.

"Let's get out of here," Wolff commanded. Hastily, Wolff and Rina slipped into an alleyway and hid behind a stack of crates until the truck of troops drove past.

Seeing a clear path to their destination, the two fugitives hurried across the street and entered the bakery. The interior was small, with counters to display the baked goods. There wasn't much on display, as supplies were short. The bakery wouldn't even be open if it wasn't a drop point for secrets to be delivered to the Vatican.

Behind the counter was Mrs. Rohlicek, an elderly, heavyset woman who warily eyed the two people who entered her establishment. She recognized Rina, but was suspicious of the German officer.

"Hello, Mrs. Rohlicek," Rina said. "How are you?"

"Never mind, missy," Mrs. Rohlicek responded. "When did you lose your senses and your good taste in men?"

Lowering her eyes, Rina apologized, "I was caught spying at the camp. This officer helped me escape. He wants to contact someone at the Vatican."

Surprised by the request, Mrs. Rohlicek stared at Wolff while speaking to Rina. "I'd like to meet the pope myself. Why doesn't your friend just wait until the Nazis kidnap Pope Pius?"

Returning her gaze to Rina, Mrs. Rohlicek blurted, "I'm not sure I recognize either of you. I'm only a simple old baker trying to stay out of the way of the jack boots of the beautiful Aryans."

Rina was starting to get anxious. "Mrs. Rohlicek, I come here every other week. Look, I have my medallion." Rina reached for the chain around her neck and realized it wasn't there.

Rina addressed Wolff. "I need my medallion."

Wolff took it from his pocket. Now the baker was more suspicious, casting a wary eye toward Rina.

"No, you don't understand," she pleaded. "It was taken from me when I was caught. This man saved it and helped me escape."

Rina then remembered an important fact. "He shot an SS agent at the train station."

They heard the engine and shouts of a German patrol driving slowly down the street. Wolff took a quick glance out the window, verified its location, and returned to the counter.

"We need to hide," he informed Mrs. Rohlicek. "Or you'll have more trouble than you can imagine."

Mrs. Rohlicek considered the request, then motioned for the two to come around the counter to hide in the back room.

"Here. Back here," she directed as Wolff and Rina darted through the door, and Mrs. Rohlicek closed the door behind them.

The same patrol that had been ambushed by the stone-throwing boys stopped outside the bakery, and soldiers jumped out to check buildings on the block. The young soldier who wanted to chase the boys earlier entered the store.

"Have you seen a German officer?" he asked Mrs. Rohlicek.

"You mean my lover? She answered. "Yes, he brings me flowers every day. He says the SS on his collar stands for Sweet Sugar."

Turning serious, Mrs. Rohlicek stated, "Does this look like a damn brothel where your officers spend their time with me?"

In the street, the patrol vehicle was hit by another volley of rocks. The soldiers outside called for those in the stores to join them.

"*Ack. Verrückte Frau.* Crazy woman," the young soldiered cried as he waved his hand at Mrs. Rohlicek.

Shouting to the others in the street, the young soldier declared, "He's not here. Let's go."

Mrs. Rohlicek walked to the window and watched the Nazi vehicle disappear down the street. She then opened the back room door and released Wolff and Rina.

"Fine example of Aryan superiority," Mrs. Rohlicek chuckled. "He took my word for it that you weren't here."

"Can you help us get in touch with the men from the Vatican?" Rina asked.

"I got a message two days ago that some of them would be in this area searching for something," Mrs. Rohlicek responded. "I was asked about troop movements and told to be ready in case they ran into trouble and needed a safe house."

She continued. "So you're luckier than you deserve. I'll draw you a map. God help me if you're lying."

Wolff interjected another request. "We're going to need transportation," he said. "Something that won't attract attention if we're seen on the road."

"You won't find many vehicles in this town that actually run, except for what the Germans have," she said. "I have a delivery truck. Promise to take care of it, and I'll let you use it."

<u>CHAPTER FIFTY EIGHT</u>

THE delivery truck was an old panel vehicle that had seen better days. It coughed and sputtered along the deserted road. Occasionally, big puffs of black smoke sneaked out of the exhaust pipes. The sides were covered with Rohlicek Bakery signs.

Rina was driving while Wolff sat on a stool in the doorway between the cab and back compartment, ready to duck inside if they passed anyone on the road. He was examining a map drawn on a white bakery sack.

"Do you know where we're supposed to go?" Rina asked as she kept her eyes on the road.

"I hope so," Wolff replied. "Our lives depend upon it."

CHAPTER FIFTY NINE

TROOPS were boarding trucks at the concentration camp to search for the two fugitives. Commandant Rahn and the platoon leader in charge of the search were watching.

"The garrison is searching inside the town," Rahn stated. "Your job is to search the roads leading out of town." Rahn quickly added, "Shoot to kill."

"Yes, sir," the platoon leader replied, hesitantly.

"Is there something else, soldier?" Rahn inquired, a tone of agitation in his voice.

"He's an officer, commandant," the platoon leader stated. "The order applies to him, too. Is that correct?"

"Absolutely." Rahn responded emphatically.

After saluting Rahn, the platoon leader turned and hurried to the truck cab of the Nazi patrol vehicle at the front of the line. He jumped in, and the caravan of fugitive hunters swiftly left the compound.

CHAPTER SIXTY

IT was deep into the night before Rina drove the truck off the road and parked it behind a grove of trees. She needed a break as they had been on the road for several hours. Wolff gripped a small flashlight between his teeth as he held and studied the hand-drawn map in his hands while seated on the stool in the back compartment. His satchel was at his feet.

"If she's correct, we should be getting close," Wolff told Rina. "There should be a side road somewhere nearby."

"Mrs. Rohlicek is rarely wrong when it comes to directions," Rina replied. "She grew up in the area. She knows everything."

"How much more of a break do you need?" Wolff asked nervously.

Rina read the anxiety in Wolff's demeanor. "I'm ready to go now," she stated.

Rina started the engine and crept out of the trees and back to the road. No more than a mile farther, she blurted to Wolff, "Wait. What was that? I think that might have been our turn."

In the darkness, she drove beyond a point in the road where vehicles had driven off the road into a field. She stopped and backed up. Wolff and Rina looked across the field and into the woods.

"Look. I see a light in those trees. Let's check it out," Wolff said.

Rina turned the truck down the grassy path. It crossed the field and then entered the wooded area.

CHAPTER SIXTY ONE

"SHIT, Paul, why can't we just meet this contact in town at a nice hotel bar?" Geno Ferrelli jokingly begged his best friend. Geno ate a candy bar while he hugged the heat coming from the warm flames of the small fire the Vatican field team built in the cramped clearing in the thick underbrush.

Dante, Ramirez, and Loogie circled the fire. Jimmy Mac drew the short straw to see who had first watch. He was thirty yards away freezing his ass off sitting high in a tree on a sturdy branch with his American-made M1 Garand scoped sniper rifle scanning the surrounding area.

"Just stop your bitching, Geno," Dante comically fired back at his pilot. "I got us out of Rome, didn't I?

"I admit, it's great to be on the road again," Geno replied.

The team was in good spirits. After being cooped up in the Vatican for over a year keeping tabs on Hitler's troop movements, collecting intelligence from Vatican spies throughout Europe, and patiently dealing with Pope Pius's extreme paranoia, Elise's packet of intriguing information helped Dante convince Papa Gino to send the team back out into the field.

"You know we've been doing this covert shit for Pacelli for seven years now," Ramirez interjected into the conversation. "I can't believe we've survived this long having Loogie along for the ride."

George leaned over and good-naturedly slapped Father Luigi on the back. Loogie still was the butt of most jokes, but he now was a valued member of the team, having performed heroically several times during important missions.

"Thank you for your nice compliment, George," Luigi stated sarcastically while loading his pistol. "At least I haven't gotten in the way of a bullet like someone I know." The entire group laughed.

"You got me with that zinger," Ramirez admitted. "You're getting much better with your comebacks, you know." Loogie grinned.

Despite the light provided by the flames, Dante sat on the ground, a small flashlight gripped between his teeth as he examined a map that he had constructed using Elise's packet of information. The team arrived in Czechoslovakia a few days ago, intent on following up on several leads from Vatican spies regarding some human genetic experimentations being conducted at a German prison camp. Then yesterday, Dante received a cryptic message from Rohlicek's Bakery about meeting a nurse who had escaped from the concentration camp where these experiments were taking place. Their present location was the designated rendezvous point.

Suddenly, Loogie stood up. "Did you hear that?" he asked the group.

The others had heard the same noise. It was the sputtering sound of the approaching bakery truck.

"Germans?" Ramirez asked.

"That doesn't sound like Hitler's well-oiled war machine," Dante answered.

The bakery truck chugged to a stop on the pathway that snaked through the trees. The trail was blocked by a fallen tree that Jimmy Mac deposited there before he climbed to his guard perch in the tree.

Wolff and Rina exited the truck. Wolff carried his satchel. After walking a short distance toward the firelight, Wolff and Rina were blinded by the beam of a bright flashlight thrust into their eyes. Jimmy Mac had descended from the tree when he spied the bakery truck driving towards the location of the Vatican team. He aimed the barrel of the sniper rifle squarely on Wolff's head when he snapped on the flashlight.

"Stop right there," Jimmy Mac ordered, his gun barrel barely 12 inches from Wolff's face. "Drop all your weapons on the ground."

Momentarily startled by Jimmy Mac's sudden appearance, Wolff complied with the directive. He first laid the satchel on the ground. Next, he removed his sidearm and holster, and dropped them to the ground.

"That's everything I have," he told Jimmy.

Rina told Jimmy she was carrying no weapons, and identified herself as the Vatican spy working with Mrs. Rohlicek. Rina explained that she and Wolff had followed the directions on Mrs. Rohlicek's map to this location. She told Wolff to show Jimmy the medallion to prove who she was. Wolff slowly dipped his hand into his coat pocket, carefully removed the unique medallion, and handed it to Jimmy.

After examining the medallion closely, Jimmy put it into his coat pocket. He picked up Wolff's satchel, and ordered both interlopers, "Get your hands in the air, and let's start walking straight ahead towards that light."

There was dead silence for a couple minutes before Dante and the others heard an absurdly familiar sound. It was hard to describe, but Dante's team was very aware of its meaning. It was Jimmy Mac's favorite "bird call" vocalization to notify the team in a "natural outdoor way" that he was returning from watch duty with unexpected guests.

Jimmy swore that he had perfected the copulation call of the adult Red-throated Loon, a bird native to his New York state. The official sound was supposedly a low-pitched moaning call. Jimmy's rendition was more like a falsetto pigeon's warble. Even though the team had heard this sound hundreds of times over the past seven years, and even though they knew the extreme importance when they heard it, there were still muffled chuckles from the other three members.

As Jimmy approached the campfire, Dante and the others drew their weapons and aimed them directly at the prisoners. As the group got closer to the fire, Dante squinted, and then mumbled, "What the fuck?"

"Hello, Monsignor Dante," Wolff stated. "I was hoping you were the leader of the Vatican team that Rina was talking about."

Still holding his pistol at Wolff's head, Dante responded incredulously, "Wolff? What the fuck are you doing with one of my spies?"

Rina spoke up. "I'm the one working for the Vatican. I was a nurse in the Theresienstadt camp and was arrested as a spy after I was caught taking pictures of an experimental devil baby."

She continued, "This German officer got me out. He said he wanted to meet the people who lead the medallion group at the Vatican. I saw him kill a German SS agent who followed us. I have the medallion to prove who I am. Your man here has it." She pointed at Jimmy.

"She's legit, Paul," Jimmy confirmed. "I've got the Vatican medallion in my pocket."

"You know those Nazis are tricky bastards," Dante countered. "Especially this one. They might shoot one of their own to get what they want." He lowered his pistol and walked slowly towards the Nazi. The others kept their weapons directed at Wolff.

"Why don't I believe a single damn thing that comes out of your mouth?" Dante accused Wolff as he stood within inches of the Nazi's face. "You were a part of Hitler's fucking inner circle the last time I saw you."

Raising his voice, Dante exclaimed, "Now, all of a sudden, you're saving Vatican spies? What are you after, Wolff? Why were you looking for my team?"

"I want sanctuary. Take me to a church for sanctuary," Wolff pleaded with Dante. "I'm a marked man because of what I did for Rina. The Nazis are hunting me down as we speak."

"I'm a Jesuit. Anywhere I am, it's a church," Dante bragged. "Why should I do anything for you?"

"Because I have information about every Nazi top secret project," Wolff blurted out. "The genetic experiments at Theresienstadt. The flying disks projects at Mittelwerk. All the information I heard from Hitler himself. Is that worth anything to you?"

Dante turned his back to Wolff and walked away slowly. *"Shit, this is everything I've been reading about from our spies for the past year,"* Dante thought. *"I need to see what kind of information he has to offer."*

"Geno, bring Hitler's friend closer to the fire so that we can hear what he has to say," Dante stated.

Ferrelli grabbed Wolff's right arm and pulled it forcefully behind the Nazi's back. He then directed Wolff towards the bright fire and pushed him to the ground.

"Let's hear what you have to say, Wolff," Dante commanded.

CHAPTER SIXTY TWO

THE German troops looking for Wolff and Rina had divided up to cover more area. One truck was driving down the road the bakery truck had used. The platoon leader was in the cab. In the distance, he saw the light from the Vatican team's fire.

"*Stoppen!* Stop!" he shouted to the driver.

Pointing to the woods, he said, "Look, over there in the woods. We need to investigate."

The driver pulled the truck to the side of the road, and the troops jumped out the back of the vehicle. They easily found the truck trail that led to the wooded area.

"Move quietly," the platoon leader commanded his troops. "No one does anything until I give the order."

Stealthily, the German soldiers began their clandestine trip down the trail.

CHAPTER SIXTY THREE

DANTE and Wolff were still talking when the first gunshot ricocheted off a nearby tree. Dante and everyone around him dove for cover. Rina pulled Wolff behind the Vatican truck.

"Holy shit, Paul. I think we've got ourselves a little skirmish here," Ramirez yelled as he flung himself behind a nearby tree. When the gunfire began, Loogie jumped into the back of the Vatican truck and began throwing additional weapons out the back to his team.

Jimmy Mac was heavily engaged with the enemy using his sniper rifle. Ramirez threw him a handful of extra ammunition magazines. He next tossed a loaded M50 Reising sub-machine gun that landed a foot away from Ferrelli. "Thanks, Loogie. I needed that," Ferrelli screamed.

Dante and Ramirez were fighting with only their Smith & Wesson pistols, and they were quickly running out of bullets. Loogie threw a Browning M1919 Medium Machine Gun to Ramirez, who quickly dropped his pistol and began rattling off short bursts of machine gun fire toward the troops hiding in the high brush. There were cries and screams as George's gunfire hit the hidden targets.

"Boss," Loogie yelled. When Dante heard Loogie's voice, he turned and saw an M1 carbine rifle flying through the air towards his location. Dante caught it mid-air, quickly turned, and shot a German soldier who began to storm the campground. Before Loogie left the truck, he armed himself with some Mk.2 fragmentation hand grenades and a Browning M2 Heavy Machine Gun.

As the firefight continued, Wolff stood out from the Vatican team because of his uniform. The Nazi platoon leader spotted him, and knew he was the fugitive the Germans were seeking. He began to circle through the trees and saw where Wolff and Rina were hiding behind the truck.

Rina and Wolff had separated themselves during the gunfire, and were now at opposite ends of the truck. The platoon leader saw that both were unarmed, and he moved in closer for a better shot. Since Rina was closest to him, he aimed his rifle at her.

Dante ran around the truck in time to see the German raise up and aim at Rina.

"Rina, look out," Dante screamed. As Rina jerked around when she heard Dante's voice, the German fired, hitting her in the chest. She died instantly.

After killing Rina, the platoon leader turned toward Dante, ready to shoot. Dante fired first, the bullet boring through the German's forehead and exploding out the back of his head. The blast drove the dead German several feet backwards and he fell into the open fire.

The cache of bullets hanging across his chest erupted as they came in contact with the flames. Exploding bullets began to fill the night air, zinging high and low. Several found their way into German troopers as they tried to dodge the spraying bullets.

When Wolff saw Dante shoot the platoon leader, he cried, "You killed him. You're a priest."

"I used to be a Marine," Dante replied solemnly. "Most of my team is ex-military. We do what we have to do." Dante then told Wolff, "Help me get her into the truck."

When the Nazi troopers saw their leader get killed, they began to retreat toward the road. Jimmy, Ferrelli, and Loogie continued firing as they chased them through the high brush, picking off several Germans when they turned to return fire with the Vatican team.

As the Germans rushed to their truck to get away, Loogie took the grenades and began throwing them at the fleeing vehicle. One grenade found its way into the back of the truck bed, exploding instantly and sending dead and burning bodies flying out the back of the truck.

Another grenade landed directly in front of the truck and detonated. The explosion lifted the front of the truck into the air. The shock wave extended to the gas tank, turning the truck into a blazing ball of fire. Screams were heard for a few seconds, and then there was a deathly quiet.

The three Vatican warriors approached the burning truck and examined the carnage that had taken place. Satisfied that no German soldier had escaped, the three turned and made their way back to the campsite.

Jimmy Mac dragged the charred remains of the Nazi platoon leader off the fire, and quickly extinguished the flame by throwing dirt on top of the smoldering branches. Loogie picked up all the weapons from the dead Germans, and threw them into the back of the truck. "You never know when you might need them," he told the group.

Ramirez finished inspecting the campsite to make sure nothing was left behind as Ferrelli jumped into the driver's seat. When all were on board, Ferrelli gunned the engine, and the Vatican team vehicle raced up the path. When they found the road, they turned in the direction away from town, and sped away into the night.

CHAPTER SIXTY FOUR

DANTE studied Wolff in the back of the Vatican truck as Ferrelli drove down the deserted bumpy road. Wolff was clutching his satchel close to his chest and looking at Rina's corpse. *"Even with her blood-soaked clothes, she still looked like she was sleeping,"* he thought.

"I take it you've never been shot at," Dante broke the silence. "And thanks for almost getting all of us killed."

"I can't believe she's dead," Wolff stammered, still in a daze. "I didn't mean for any of this to happen." Dante thought that Wolff actually sounded remorseful.

"Oh, no. I've never been shot at," Wolff answered Dante's first observation. "I've always had the troops protecting me wherever I went." He continued.

"Thank you, Monsignor Dante, for saving my life. To all of you," Wolff motioned to Jimmy Mac, Ramirez, and Father Luigi. "And I assure you, what I told you is true. Those soldiers were hunting for me." Wolff corrected himself while looking at Rina. "For us."

"Why the change of heart now, Wolff?" Dante probed. "Why are you defecting when you were in Hitler's inner circle?"

"I'm not a soldier. This uniform was only part of the job," Wolff stated. "A job I've come to hate." He continued. "I was a scientist before I was lured into the military by great lies. But being in Hitler's inner circle has proven to me that Hitler and his henchmen are only in it to profit. Their egos are destroying Germany and its people. That's why I want out. That's why I need asylum in the church."

"Yeah, well, I'll think about it," Dante countered. "I already know about the medical experiments at Theresienstadt. The Germans are trying to breed something for some creatures from another world." Dante just shook his head in amazement.

"And Hitler has scientists working to reproduce the space craft the creatures came in to help him conquer the world. My team destroyed a hidden laboratory where the technology was being tested. What more can you tell me than that?" Dante asked.

Wolff was surprised at Dante's depth of knowledge. "Your Vatican spies were very diligent," Wolff stated. "Hitler had me personally monitoring the progress of the medical experiments. But are you aware that both programs have been successful?"

"Give me the details," Dante demanded.

"I had complete access to the Chancellery. I had direct access to Hitler. I've heard about other programs that scientists are working on. I can tell you everything I know about what they're doing and where. All the work is being manipulated for Hitler's insane dream of conquering the world, and profiting from it. I want no part of that." Wolff hesitated for a moment, and then blurted, "I'll tell you everything, but I want asylum…in Rome."

Ramirez was the first to respond to Wolff's demand. "You fucking Kraut, you've got some balls demanding we take you back to Rome with us." Pointing to Rina's dead body, George continued to rant, "See that poor woman there? You're responsible for her death, asshole. So don't even think about ever getting close to Rome." Jimmy Mac concurred with George's position by echoing another profanity in Wolff's direction.

Looking at Dante, Ramirez asked, "Paul, you're not actually thinking about giving this fucker what he wants, are you?"

Dante leaned back against the interior wall of the truck and pondered his options. After a minute, he turned to the team's foil. "What are your thoughts on this, Loogie?" Dante asked pointedly.

Surprised at the request, Father Luigi took a deep breath. "I, too, question this man's character and motive, Boss," Loogie replied, looking directly at Wolff. "But the knowledge that this man possibly possesses is what the Holy Father has been seeking since the beginning of the war."

Looking at Dante, Loogie expanded his response. "I believe the Holy Father will be most pleased and most impressed if you present this Nazi officer and his exhaustive knowledge of Hitler's plans to the pontiff personally."

Dante nodded his agreement with Loogie's reasoning, and yelled at Ferrelli. "Geno, get us back to the plane. We're heading back to Rome."

CHAPTER SIXTY FIVE

Secret Flight Test Field near Prague
1945

THE dignitaries of the German High Command were slowly arriving at this highly-classified military location. Maximum security was in effect within a five-mile radius. It was mid-morning, and the sun's rays warmed the wooden bleachers that had been erected to seat the multitude of Nazi officers from the Ahnenerbe, Gestapo, and Chancellery. Behind the bleachers and framed against the cloudless blue sky was a flagpole with the red and black swastika flag unfurling in the gentle breeze.

In the center of the field covered by a black tarp sat Viktor Schauberger's newest prototype disk. All the preparations to the craft were completed before the dignitaries started to arrive. Around the craft were the movable stairs the pilot would climb and the technicians would use to attach the canopy once the pilot was inside.

It had been two years since the disastrous test flight and ensuing explosions that ripped through his Mittelwerk laboratory and destroyed both proprietary schematics and critical personnel. Schauberger himself was amazed at how quickly he and his staff of remaining technicians and workers healed the crippled saucer program.

"Ah, such a beautiful day," Schauberger said to his assistant as they both stood near the entrance to the bleachers awaiting Hitler's arrival. "If this test fails, this will be the last day I see on earth." Then he joked, "At least there is no roof to ruin our flight today."

The last car to arrive was a staff car that carried Hitler, Goering, and Himmler. Schauberger approached the car, greeted the three, and the group walked to the bleachers. When they arrived, Hitler addressed Schauberger.

"*Herr Doktor, ich erwarte große Ergebnisse bekannt.* Herr Doctor," the Fuhrer stated stoically, "I expect grand results today." He added, cryptically, "And no surprises." Schauberger smiled, turned, and walked to the equipment platform where he and his technicians would monitor the short test flight.

After Hitler, Goering, and Himmler seated themselves on the bottom bleacher seat, a motorcycle with a sidecar traveled across the field. The next Luftwaffe test pilot, Otto Lange, was riding in the sidecar. The driver stopped in front of the bleachers, and Lange got out, walked to the front of the bleachers, and gave the raised-arm salute to Hitler.

Workers removed the tarp, and the audience exploded into applause at the sight of the small prototype. Lange climbed the stairs and entered the cockpit. Technicians attached the canopy and hustled down the stairs.

Schauberger gave the signal to Lange to begin the test flight. The craft hummed to life, and it slowly rose from its launch pad.

"Here we go," Schauberger's words echoed to the technicians at their consoles. "Let's hope this is our lucky day."

When the craft reached a height of 75 meters, it carried out its practice maneuvers successfully – right, left, and back. Next, it rose another 50 meters, and performed some circular movements. "*All is going splendidly,*" Schauberger told himself.

Suddenly, there was a flash of light in the bright sky. As the crowd's attention to the test flight was momentarily distracted, another alien craft silently darted into the airspace and stopped 100 meters from the slowly-circling test craft. Without warning, the new larger craft fired a white beam weapon at the prototype. When the beam hit its target, the test craft instantly exploded and burning debris rained down from the sky. "*Son of a bitch,*" Schauberger lamented. "*Not again.*"

Blood-curdling screams and shouts of terror emanated from the fleeing crowd as they scattered like retreating ants while the hostile saucer hovered soundlessly above them. In a panic, Hitler darted straight to his staff car. Since no driver was present, Hitler jumped in, started the vehicle, and peeled away from the chaotic scene, swerving around parked cars and fleeing observers.

As Germany's Fuhrer raced away from the secret testing ground now littered with burning debris and dead bodies, the silver alien craft methodically followed his movement. As the cowering crowd watched from behind damaged bleachers, scorched trees, and upended vehicles, transfixed by the fear of what they were viewing, a golden orange light beam shot down from the bottom of the craft and engulfed Hitler's getaway car. Immediately, the engine died and the car stopped in its tracks. Slowly, inexplicably, the car, with a horrified Hitler inside, rose off the ground inside the dazzling beam.

Higher and higher it ascended. Hitler's desperate cries for help could be heard, but no one on the ground moved in his direction. When it reached a third of the way up the shaft of light, the car was quickly sucked inside the craft. The beam disappeared, and the silver craft shot away noiselessly into the distance, disappearing from sight within seconds.

Goering and Himmler watched the unfathomable abduction from their hiding place under the bleachers. Stunned, they emerged when the attack craft had disappeared.

Goering was first to speak. *"Scheiße. Ich wusste, dass dieser Tag kommen würde.* Shit. I knew this day was coming," he screamed. "Adolph had been cursing that alien leader every time they spoke. He kept asking for more technology, more weapons, just more of everything. He was insatiable in his appetite. But I think Adolph knew he was in trouble when the aliens found out they were double-crossed on that hybrid experimentation. He found out today just how much trouble he was in."

Himmler didn't care about Hitler's sudden demise. He was more interested in self-preservation.

"We need to gather all the officers and everyone who was here," he told Goering. "Anyone who saw this, no one must talk. They must swear their silence. If they don't agree, I'll shoot them myself. If it's known the Fuhrer is gone, the armies will be demoralized and the war will stop immediately. We can't allow that. For our own survival."

Goering agreed, adding, "I believe Gustav Weber just received a promotion to full-time Fuhrer." He punctuated the conversation by saying, "And at the appropriate time, he will be honored with a state funeral."

Himmler grinned, "No one will ever know about the switch."

CHAPTER SIXTY SIX

Pope's Private Vatican Dining Room

TEN days had passed since Dante and his team had returned to Rome with Wolff and Rina's body. Rina was given a private burial mass at the Vatican and interred quietly into a local public cemetery. Her family was notified, and the Vatican provided a generous untraceable stipend for her valuable undercover work.

Wolff was vigorously interrogated by Dante and his team for hours each day. On occasion, the Pontiff would step inside the isolation room and ask a probing question. At the end of the interrogations, Dante and the pope felt Wolff was true to his word. His insider information should help Dante and the Vatican to play a pivotal role in causing the downfall of the Third Reich.

Tonight, though, Dante and Wolff dined with Pope Pius XII in the Pope's private dining room. Dante was dressed in his priestly garb, and Wolff was wearing a business suit. The dinner was the pontiff's way of thanking Dante for bringing Wolff to the Vatican, and his way of thanking Wolff for the secret insider information they learned about Hitler's plans. The Holy Father recalled his appreciation of the surprise gift that Wolff presented to him upon his unexpected arrival in Vatican City 10 days ago.

"Before you start interrogating me, I have a gift I wish to present to the Pope," Wolff told Dante after the travel party arrived back in Rome. "It's my sign of good faith that I want to show his Excellency."

"I'll make sure he gets it," Dante replied, "You can give it to me."

"No," Wolff objected. "I must give it to him personally."

After confirming Wolff's private audience with the Pope, Dante escorted Wolff into the Pope's government office.

"What is so important that you need to present something to me personally, Herr Wolff?" Pius XII asked the German officer. "Giving it to Paul is like giving it to me."

"Because it's something that you've been searching for over a span of many years," Wolff responded. Wolff opened the satchel he carried with him throughout his days in Hitler's inner circle. When he pulled out an old ancient manuscript, the Holy Father's eyes widened and he let out a gasp.

"It's the Nestorian papyrus," Pius XII exclaimed, quickly grabbing the precious Vatican artifact from Wolff's hands. "How did you get this out of Germany without Hitler finding out? This was the ransom he was holding over my head, as you recall."

"I have a friend who got it for me from Hitler's secret warehouse where he kept his stolen treasures and his demonic artifacts that he thought would bring him unlimited power to rule the world," Wolff stated. "I've kept it with me for quite a while just waiting for this occasion. It was my insurance policy. Hitler never knew."

"I accept this gift, Herr Wolff, with great joy," the pontiff said. "This manuscript is vital for the preservation of the Catholic faith. I was worried sick that I may never get it back."

Despite the dour world conditions outside Vatican City, the mood of this private dinner was light and jovial. Pius always enjoyed Dante's company. Even as Paul Dante reached his mid-forties in age, his presence could always bring a smile to the pontiff's face.

"..and then the young priest says, 'I didn't know you could use a pancake for Holy Communion,'" Dante quipped as he highlighted the punch line of his joke. Dante and the pope laughed heartily. Wolff didn't understand the joke, but he still smiled to be a part of the group.

"Oh, Monsignor Paul, I should never encourage you to tell your stories," the pope declared. "They always seem to find the silliness surrounding Catholic doctrine."

After having their wine glasses re-filled by the young seminarian chosen to act as the pope's personal attendant for the dinner, Dante posed his question to the leader of the worldwide Catholic Church.

"So, Papa Gino, I wondered if you had time to think about my suggestion."

Wolff was shocked to hear Dante address the pope in what he thought was in a very denigrating fashion. "Papa Gino?" Wolff said in amazement to Dante. "What kind of name is that for his Excellency?"

"Oh, I'm not offended by that nickname Paul gave me decades ago," Pius interjected. "It is a term of endearment that I hold very special in my heart."

"You sound a little jealous to me. Do you want me to give you one?" Dante quizzed Wolff.

After thinking about it for a moment, Wolff answered, "Yes, I believe I would."

Dante's brain started working immediately. "OK, let's see what we can come up with," he mused. He took another drink of the pope's finest wine.

"Wolffie is too easy," Dante began. "I don't like easy." "Wolfmeister kind of has a nice German ring to it, doesn't it?" He continued to think outside the box. Then Dante's eyes brightened.

"You're Kon-man, with a K," Dante blurted. "Kon is short for Konrad, your first name. And you had to act a lot like a conman, a pretender, when you had to find a way out of Hitler's lair."

Pius chuckled at Dante's quick wit. Wolff wasn't sure what to think. But then he gave in to Dante's persuasion. "Very well," the German guest agreed. "Kon-man it is."

After listening to Wolff receive his nickname from Dante, Pius turned to Dante and asked, "Do you mean your suggestion regarding our dinner guest tonight?

"Yes," Dante replied.

"What's this about me?" Wolff inquired, a look of puzzlement covering his face.

"Monsignor Dante suggested that I allow you to join his team when he feels your presence would be advantageous to our cause," the pope stated. "He left the final decision to me because of your history with your former employer."

Wolff was quick to respond. "Your Excellency, I've said many times that I joined the Ahnenerbe SS only because I thought I'd be doing scientific work. It wasn't a political or a moral choice."

"I understand," the pope retorted. "That is why I'm going to agree to allow it."

"Thank you. Thank you so much, Your Excellency," Wolff said, "I won't let you down."

After all three men toasted the newly-appointed member of the Vatican covert operations team, Dante chimed in.

"Now don't go getting a big head over this, Kon-man," Dante cautioned. "You'll be working for me, remember. And you'll be low man on the totem pole, too. Even Loogie can boss you around." Pius smiled when hearing Father Luigi's nickname mentioned.

Dante continued. "Of course, we'll have to give you a new identity. It's dangerous enough without having the Nazis hunting for their former Ober, uh Uber general."

"You can change my identity?" Wolff asked incredulously.

"Sure. The Vatican is a city state. We can do everything any other independent country can do. And sometimes even more," Dante bragged.

"So who should I become?" Wolff asked Dante.

"I think we'll change your name from Mr. Wolff to Mr. Fox," Dante quipped.

The pontiff leaned over and whispered to Wolff, "Forgive Monsignor Dante. He has that distinct American sense of humor."

After the laughter subsided, the conversation turned serious, as Dante addressed Wolff.

"With the Allied and Russian troops closing in on Berlin, I think it's best to forward that list of the names of the important German scientists you compiled to some of my old military contacts I've kept in the U.S. military. They're in the best position to rescue the scientists," Dante stated.

Dante turned and addressed Pius. "I want to take my team to Mittelwerk to help retrieve that craft and any other evidence of alien technology. I don't want it falling into the wrong hands." Pius nodded his agreement.

Dante addressed Wolff again. "Are you sure that craft is still at Mittelwerk?"

"Unless something has happened to it recently," Wolff responded. "I'm certain the craft is still in Schauberger's laboratory."

"Well, we're going to need a good plan to infiltrate that facility," Dante mused. "We can't take a large group of Swiss Guards with us and just rush the place. I'm sure Ramirez and Jimmy Mac can come up with some good ideas."

Wolff pushed into the conversation that Dante seemed to be having with himself at the moment. "I'll tell you everything I know on the condition that I go with you."

Dante snapped his head in Wolff's direction. "You actually want to go back behind Nazi lines?" he asked. "You're dead if the plan fails and you're dead if you're caught. You do realize that, right?"

"I've been collecting artifacts and other valuable treasures for Hitler for years, not to mention monitoring some of his most sensitive projects," Wolff stated. "I want the chance to grab this important scientific invention away from him." He quickly added, "And how could your mission possibly succeed without me?"

Dante chuckled at Wolff's hubris as Pius leaned over and jokingly told Wolff, "Konrad, I believe Monsignor Dante is becoming a bad influence on you."

The dinner calmly ended with Dante and Wolff thanking Pius for his generosity. On the way out of the private dining room, Dante and Wolff made plans to meet the next morning with Dante's team to create the covert plan to infiltrate Mittelwerk and retrieve the alien spacecraft and any sensitive technical data they could find.

After giving the young seminarian his blessing and thanks for assisting with the evening meal, the pope quietly left for his ornate private living quarters accompanied by his two personal Swiss Guards. Dante departed for his comfortable upscale apartment within the Vatican City limits, and Wolff retired to his new modest apartment located outside Vatican City.

CHAPTER SIXTY SEVEN

March 1945

IT was an ambitious plan. Within a span of 48 hours and taking place in four European countries, hundreds of German scientists, many of them working on highly-classified Nazi advanced-weapons projects, were covertly snatched up from their homes and concealed working laboratories by troops of Marine Special Forces Commandos, transported to secret Allied airbases, herded onto American military transport planes, flown to undisclosed American cities, and delivered to agents of the Office of Strategic Services (OSS) and the Joint Intelligence Objectives Agency (JIOA).

"Who do we have to thank for getting us the names and locations of these scientists?" the Marine corporal asked his commanding officer as the young soldier attached name tags to the coats of each "prisoner" as they boarded this plane at the secret Allied airbase outside Luxemburg.

"I guess some former Marine who's a priest at the Vatican sent the information to his contact at Camp Lejeune," the officer responded. "I think he said he got the information from a Nazi officer who asked for asylum within the Catholic Church."

"I guess that's one way to get away from Hitler," the young soldier laughed.

Suddenly, a gust of wind blew the pages containing the names of Germany's top-secret scientists from the young Commando's hand. He hurriedly gathered them up again before they could escape further from his grasp.

"Shit, that's the second time they've blown out of my hand," the perplexed Marine said. "How can I keep them together, sir?"

"Jesus Christ, Marine," the annoyed commanding officer said. "Just put a fucking paperclip on them."

CHAPTER SIXTY EIGHT

**Hitler's Bunker
Late April 1945**

IN the dining area, the marriage of Hitler and Eva Braun was being celebrated. The bunker staff that included officers and secretaries, and Goebbels and his wife toasted the newlyweds with Nazi Germany's finest stolen champagne.

Gustav Weber was impersonating Hitler magnificently this day. Even Eva Braun was impressed, and she was aware of the ploy. If any others in the bunker realized the deception, they didn't let their thoughts be known.

Following the toast, Goebbels left his wife's side, walked up to Weber, and motioned for Weber to follow him. When they reached the hall, Himmler was waiting for them.

"This is a good party," Himmler announced. "The staff needed a release with the war going so badly."

"That's why we need to speed up the plan, Gustav," Goebbels whispered. "It's nearly time for you to disappear so it will appear that the Fuhrer died gloriously in battle."

"I've drawn up the personal will for the Fuhrer and written a political statement," Himmler said. "Everything is in place."

"When we tell you, Gustav, you will name Fleet Admiral Donitz to succeed you as supreme commander so he can carry on the war after your disappearance," Goebbels stated.

Weber nodded his agreement with the plan. Then he asked, "Is there anywhere besides Argentina where I can go? It's always hot there, and I don't speak the language."

"Only after we change your identity," Himmler answered. "Then you can pick a different country."

"And what about Eva?" Weber whined. "She's such a bitch. She said she still won't sleep with me even though we're married."

"You won't have to worry about Eva," Goebbels answered cryptically. "She's not a part of our plans."

"I'm relieved to hear that," Weber smiled.

"Go back to the party now, Gustav. Enjoy yourself," Himmler ordered. "We'll let you know when we need you."

After Weber left the group, Himmler turned to Goebbels. "That dumb son of a bitch has no clue what's in store for him," he laughed. "Can you fucking believe he's pissed because Braun won't sleep with him? That is fucking hilarious."

Goebbels laughed at Himmler's comment. "Let's allow Weber to play out his fantasy," Goebbels smiled. "This is his time to shine. That's why he signed on in the first place."

Himmler nodded his agreement, and the two high-ranking Nazi officers returned to the party, aware that Gustav Weber's sad lonely life was coming to a brutal ending.

CHAPTER SIXTY NINE

Hitler's Bunker
April 30, 1945

IT was a solemn time in the bunker. Weber, as Hitler, was saying farewell to his staff who had lined up in the dining hall. It was less than 40 hours ago that this same room was filled with laughter and music during Hitler and Eva Braun's wedding. The mood now was drastically different, with several secretaries crying as Hitler addressed the group.

After Weber finished shaking hands with the last person in line, he exited the room with Goebbels and Himmler. They walked through the sitting area and conference area of the bunker before ending their march in Hitler's study.

"I felt sorry for those people who have to stay here," Weber exclaimed. "They seemed genuinely sad to see me leave."

Himmler sat down on a cushioned seat while Weber positioned himself on the couch. Goebbels made his way to the fully-stocked bar where he poured red wine into three tumblers emblazoned with red and black swastikas. He delivered the drinks to each man, and then sat down next to Himmler.

Himmler took a sip of his drink and addressed Weber. "It doesn't matter now anyway, Gustav. Our plan is almost complete." Then glancing toward Goebbels while still talking to Weber, Himmler continued, "We need to wait until Eva is ready. Then we have our surprise for her."

Within minutes, Eva Braun entered the study. She was angry and agitated.

"I want to know what's going on," the 33-year-old newlywed screamed. "Why did we go through that farewell scene? Just where are we going?" Her piercing glare was aimed straight at Himmler.

"Sit down, Eva," Goebbels ordered. "Transportation will be arriving soon. You and Gustav will be flown to South America."

"Then what?" she yelled, stomping her way across the room. "I'm accustomed to a better lifestyle than a fugitive."

Then she swung around and jabbed her right index finger into Himmler's face. "Adolph would have seen that I'm well taken care of," she cried.

"We will take care of you, Eva. I promise," Himmler exclaimed to the distraught woman. "While we're waiting, let's just relax and have a drink. This is a happy day."

Himmler addressed Goebbels. "Joseph, freshen our drinks, will you please? I'll open a bottle of champagne for Eva."

Eva finally calmed down and took a seat on the couch with Weber. Goebbels refilled the three glasses from a decanter. Himmler made his way to the bar, and found an unopened bottle of champagne.

With his back to the group, he opened the bottle of champagne, with the cork making a popping sound as it exploded from the top of the bottle. "Oh, my," he turned to the group and apologized. "I hope that didn't startle anyone."

He grabbed a champagne glass from the back of the bar. Before pouring, he sneaked a vial of cyanide from his pocket, poured the contents into the champagne glass, and filled the glass half-full with the bubbly liquid. He walked to Eva and handed her the glass.

"Enjoy, Mrs. Hitler," Himmler beamed. "Let's toast to happier days for all of us."

As the three men stood, Eva joined them and took a big gulp of the champagne.

Goebbels quickly added his ending to the toast, saying "And to a quick end when our time comes."

Within a minute, Eva started showing signs of the deliberate poisoning. "What's happening to me?" she slurred. She fought to keep her balance.

Himmler reached for the glass and snatched it from her as she slumped back on the couch. Weber watched as Eva lost consciousness and her body began to convulse with seizures.

He never noticed as Goebbels positioned himself beside him.

"How long will it take?" Weber asked. "I didn't like her, but I didn't want her to…"

Weber never finished his sentence. The warm blood sprayed the air as Weber's eyes glazed over. The bullet from Goebbel's military pistol, a Walther PPK 7.65, identical to Hitler's, entered the right temple next to Weber's ear. Brain matter and shattered skull fragments exploded out the left side of Weber's head. His body collapsed on the couch, slumped awkwardly away from Eva's dead body. As soon as the body settled, Goebbels quickly placed the gun into Weber's right hand.

Looking at the two dead bodies lying on the bloody couch, Himmler took a deep breath and sighed contentedly. "I'm glad that's over." Looking at Goebbels, he said, "Excellent work, Joseph. Now quickly clean that blood spatter from your face."

Goebbels ran to the back of the bar. He snatched a clean towel, dumped a decanter full of water onto it, and hastily scrubbed his face, hands, and jacket. Peering into the long glass mirror that adorned the back of the bar, he was satisfied with his cleansing handiwork. Leaving the bloody towel on the floor, Goebbels raced to join Himmler at the entrance door.

Himmler shot a glance at Goebbels. He knew Hitler's bunker security detail along with dozens of other soldiers, would be arriving immediately after hearing the gunshot.

"Just stick to the story like we planned," he told Goebbels. "Now get ready for bedlam as soon as I open this door."

CHAPTER SEVENTY

AFTER killing Weber and Braun, Himmler and Goebbels opened the study door and rushed from the room, feigning shock in their voices, as dozens of soldiers arrived to investigate the single gunshot heard from inside Hitler's study. Pandemonium reigned.

"*Sie sind beide gestorben*," Goebbels shouted in the crowded hallway. "They're both dead."

Hitler's driver, Heinz Linge, and Hitler's trusted secretary, Martin Bormann, were the first people to enter the room. Hitler's personal adjutant, Major Otto Gunsche, hurried to the couch where he discovered the two lifeless bodies. On the floor at Weber's feet was a suicide letter that Himmler had written and put at Weber's feet after Goebbel's shot him. Gunsche picked up the letter.

"Did you see this happen?" Gunsche asked Goebbels and Himmler as he began to read the letter silently. "Both of you were in the room, weren't you?"

"Yes, we were in the room," Himmler answered. "But we had our backs turned when we heard the shot. We were shocked when we saw what had happened."

Looking at Eva's face, it was easy for Gunsche to recognize that she died from cyanide poisoning as Hitler's letter had said she took her own life. The blood from the single gunshot dripped from Weber's right temple wound, stained the corner of the couch, and pooled on the floor rug. The gun dangled from Weber's right hand.

"This signed letter seems to answer all the questions," Gunsche stated. "Hitler says Eva committed suicide by ingesting a cyanide capsule. He said he would shoot himself in the head after confirming Eva's death." Tears formed in the corner of Gunsche's eyes.

"What else does the letter say?" Bormann asked. "As close as I was to Adolph, I never knew of his intentions to write this letter and plan his demise."

Gunsche continued to read the lengthy note and disseminate its message to those in the room. "Hitler wants us to burn his body and Eva's body in the Chancellery garden. He read how Mussolini and his mistress had been hanged from their feet after they died in Italy and then were reviled by the citizens." Gunsche hesitated for a moment. "He doesn't want the German people to treat his body the same way."

That afternoon, in accordance with Hitler's instructions from the suicide note, the remains of Weber and Braun were carried up the stairs through the bunker's emergency exit. The bodies were laid side by side into a newly-dug pit in the Reich Chancellery garden near the bunker.

After dousing the fully-clothed bodies with gasoline, Heinz Linge twisted some papers into a torch. He handed the torch to Bormann, who lighted it, and tossed the fire into the pit, setting the bodies ablaze. As the bodies burned,

Goebbels, Himmler, and the other officers raised their arms to salute their fallen Fuhrer while standing in the doorway of the bunker.

The burning of the corpses lasted over two hours. During that time, a steady flow of gasoline was thrown on the flames by Gestapo guards to hasten the destruction of the bodies beyond recognition. The advancing Soviet army sporadically shelled the area around the Reich Chancellery while the bodies disintegrated, leaving a valley of bomb craters scattered within close proximity to the burn site.

The charred remains of Gustav Weber and Eva Braun were moved to their final resting place just after sunset: a deep bomb crater located near a demolished Nazi administration building. The skeletal remains were covered with dirt and then layered with tons of loose concrete blocks in order to keep the gravesite secret from the American and Russian troops that would arrive within days.

CHAPTER SEVENTY ONE

Theresienstadt Concentration Camp

THE camp was in chaos. Russian troops were within a half mile of the locked gates to the Nazi concentration camp. Rapid and continuous gunfire was heard outside Dr. Eckhart's medical ward as another young Jewish woman was wheeled toward the operating room to give birth to another attempt at perfect hybridization.

"What is going on out there?" Eckhart screamed to his nurse. "Let's get this over. I want to see what's happening."

The nervous nurse hurriedly prepped the delirious woman for the quick surgical procedure in which Eckhart would tear open her abdomen, slice into the uterus, and extract the baby. The patient was adequately sedated by placing a rag drenched in chloroform over the face of the birthing mother. After the five-minute surgery, the young mother was quickly wheeled to the second-story window that overlooked the acid pool below.

As amniotic fluid, warm blood, and ripped birthing tissue seeped off the comatose body and on to the floor, she was remorselessly pushed off the gurney. As her disposable body plunged downward to her ignominious death, she joined hundreds of Eckhart's Nazi experimental corpses disappearing into the watery skeletal graveyard below.

As Eckhart evaluated the small hybrid baby that he held in his blood-soaked gloved hands, a guard rushed into the operating room.

"The Russian army is coming, doctor," he spoke rapidly. "We're ordered to evacuate."

A disgruntled Eckhart didn't immediately answer the soldier's message. He was still judging the effectiveness of his last genetic manipulation. This naked hybrid baby, breathing in short stunted breaths at the moment, showed more elements of human characteristics and less alien characteristics, he thought. The face looked more human, even though the head was still enlarged and the tiny nose contained the enlarged nostrils. The genitalia of the baby indicated that this was a normal Jewish boy. *This is my best effort yet!* Eckhart surmised.

The shout from the soldier brought Eckhart back to reality. "Doctor, we must leave now," the guard screamed.

"Get gasoline. Douse everything in this room and burn it," Eckhart ordered the soldier. Turning toward his terrified nurse, he stated, "Take this baby and euthanize it." Eckhart dropped the baby into the arms of the horrified nurse and ran from the operating room.

As screams echoed elsewhere in the building, Eckhart rushed into his office and began to toss the research files from the cabinets into a large pile on the floor. Then he gathered the clear glass jars containing the fetuses of failed experiments from their shelf perches, and hurled them wildly onto the pile of papers. As the glass jars exploded on contact with the hard floor, the deformed baby bodies bounced and scattered throughout the room. With the smell of the leaking liquid formaldehyde from the broken jars pervading the air, Eckhart lit a piece of paper, and launched the fiery torch into the pile of papers.

The sudden blast of flames shocked and disoriented Eckhart. Feeling the effects of the deadly fumes encompassing the deteriorating room, the mad doctor continued to throw hundreds of research files into the flames, hoping the pile of paper would momentarily thwart the spreading flames and allow for his escape from the second-floor office.

The distant screams that Eckhart heard came from the women's ward downstairs. A guard wrapped a steel chain around the double-door handles to prevent the patients from escaping. Smoke was visible through the windows in the doors, and tiny flames appeared on the ceiling in the back of the room.

Terrified patients pounded on the heavy glass windows protected on the inside by bolted steel screens. Begging for help, the women futilely clawed at the screens. Realizing that strategy was fruitless, dozens began to slam into the doors, hoping the combined force would break the locked chain. That action ended when soldiers started firing shots through the locked doors, and dead bodies started to pile up at the entrance.

Commandant Rahn supervised the operation. As the guard who was chaining the inside doors came running out behind the last of the fleeing nurses, Rahn yelled to him. "Is that all the medical personnel?"

"Doctor Eckhart is still in his office," the guard shouted.

"Chain the door," Rahn commanded the guard. The guard followed his orders.

Flames were breaking through parts of the secret building's roof. Eckhart managed to flee the fiery destruction of his office and arrived at the main doors. As he tried to pull them open, he desperately looked through the windows and saw Rahn watching. Eckhart started banging on the doors.

"Open this door, Rahn," Eckhart bellowed. "I demand it, you bastard."

Looking back at the advancing flames, Eckhart cried, "Hitler will have your head, you fucker. Open up. Now!"

Unfazed by Eckhart's rant, Rahn got the attention of a nearby guard. "Shoot him," Rahn said. "But shoot low. Don't kill him."

The guard stepped close to the doors and fired through, hitting Eckhart in the abdomen. Eckhart screamed, and dropped out of sight.

As the sounds of destruction and defeat enveloped the Nazi camp, Rahn turned and calmly walked away from the burning building that had housed Hitler's dream of ruling the world through hybridization and genetic manipulation of the human race. He smiled at the lunacy.

CHAPTER SEVENTY TWO

Schauberger's Secret Lab

A chaotic evacuation of Viktor Schauberger's secret laboratory was in progress. Notification was delivered to the complex last week that the Allied troops, predominantly American and Russian, were moving undeterred toward their location as German soldiers retreated. Workers loaded boxes of research papers onto Nazi trucks. There were also many boxes containing small mechanical parts. A contingent of 20 Gestapo troops oversaw the operation.

Schauberger walked up to his assistant holding an alien device identical to the one given to Hitler by Tehlri decades ago.

"Here. This was in my office. Everything must go," he told his assistant. "I found it in the alien craft when we finally got inside the thing." The assistant took the device and placed it in a parts box.

"How much longer before the Allied troops are in range," Schauberger asked.

"We have about two more hours," the aide replied.

"Good. None of these trucks leave until they're full," Schauberger stated. "You go in the lead truck. Follow our route into Austria."

The aide nodded and both men started to walk away in different directions. Schauberger yelled back to the aide. "I'm going to set off the explosives in our prototypes and inside the main ship. We can't allow the Russian or American troops to get their hands on anything."

CHAPTER SEVENTY THREE

CAMOUFLAGED in a grove of trees on the side of a steep hill a couple hundred yards away, a man with binoculars watched the frenetic activity taking place outside the underground laboratories at Mittelwerk. Paul Dante watched Schauberger finish his conversation and walk back inside the underground laboratory. It was late afternoon, with only an hour of sunlight remaining.

Dante's team had a new member for this operation. Konrad Wolff had convinced Dante that his knowledge of the area and location of the secret lab made his presence mandatory. Everyone except Dante had their doubts.

"Are you sure we should have brought the Kraut with us on this trip?" Ferrelli whispered to Dante while they huddled in the shadows of the trees. "I'm not sold on his so-called allegiance to the Vatican."

"Geno, we'll find out soon enough," Dante replied. "He did get us to this exact location without us taking any enemy fire." Ferrelli frowned at Paul's comment.

Dante's team was dressed in battle black: black fatigues, black stocking caps, black gloves, and burnt cork on their blackened faces. Jimmy Mac also had binoculars directed on the entrance to the secret Nazi laboratory. George and Loogie were preparing the arsenal of weapons they brought along for the mission.

"Let me see what's going on," Wolff addressed Dante. "Pass me those binoculars, will you?"

Dante handed his binoculars to Wolff. As the former Nazi officer scoped the area, Dante stated, "None of those trucks is big enough to haul away the craft you described. It looks like they're only loading boxes." After a moment of silence, Dante announced, "The craft must still be inside. We need to get into that laboratory."

Wolff lowered the binoculars and said, "Maybe they already moved the craft."

Ferrelli blurted his frustration with Wolff. "Goddamn it, Paul, didn't I tell you this Nazi asshole is fucking with us." Ferrelli glared at the German and stuck his gloved finger into Wolff's face. "I don't trust you. You're going to get us all killed."

"Easy, Geno," Dante calmed his friend. "I'm pretty sure that craft is still in the lab. We didn't come all this way not to find something." Looking toward Wolff, Dante stated, "Give Konman here the benefit of the doubt. He hasn't been wrong on anything yet."

"Konman. He is a fucking con man," Ferrelli mumbled to himself.

To lessen the tension in the air, Dante asked Wolff, "By the way, Konman, in the Chancellery, did you know a secretary named Elise?"

"Why, yes. She was Himmler's secretary," Wolff responded.

"Spying for us," Dante grinned, slapping Wolff on the shoulder.

"American humor," Wolff thought. "I still don't get it."

Dante pulled the group together into a tight circle and started quizzing each member on his duties.

"George and Loogie, are the weapons ready to go?" Dante asked.

"Yes, boss," Loogie answered. "The guns are loaded. The grenades and the M7 grenade launcher are ready. The M2 flamethrower is functional." He continued, excitedly, "And we have the alphabet of explosives: TNT, RDX, and PETN." Loogie was pleased when Dante gave his nod of approval.

"Jimmy, go over the plan again," Dante requested.

McPherrin pulled out his sheet with the multi-colored diagrams. "As soon as the sun sets, we'll split up."

Then pointing at the green line on his plans, Jimmy said, "Paul, you and Wolff follow the terrain and advance to the cave opening on the left side. Loogie will be your weapons guy." Turning toward Ferrelli and pointing his finger at the yellow line on the plans, Jimmy continued, "Geno, you and I will cross the road and advance up the right side to the opening. George will be our weapons guy. We'll meet at the entrance. Take care of yourselves."

When Jimmy Mac had finished his briefing, Dante looked all of his team members in the eyes, and said, "Bring 'em in, boys." With that directive, all the Vatican warriors got up and laid their right hands on top of Dante's extended right palm in the middle of the circle. A curious Wolff mimicked the actions. When all the hands were piled together, Dante covered them all with his left hand, and started his traditional pre-mission prayer.

"Heavenly Father, watch over us as we fight for justice," Dante prayed. "Protect us and guide us. If any of us should fall, welcome us into your Holy Kingdom. Amen."

"Amen" the men repeated.

"Now, let's kick some Nazi ass," Ferrelli extorted.

CHAPTER SEVENTY FOUR

SCHAUBERGER was inside the alien craft, setting the timer for his bomb to explode in 15 minutes, when he thought he heard some noise. No one else should be inside the building, he knew. He poked his head out of the craft. The lighting inside of the massive laboratory was minimal as only one generator was functioning, providing just enough light for the evacuating workers to complete their tasks. With only one truck remaining to take Schauberger to his Austrian hideaway, the fidgety scientist did not see Dante and his men stealthily enter the secret facility as sunset turned to darkness.

Prior to meeting Paul and the others, Ferrelli and Jimmy Mac had easily disposed of the two remaining Gestapo guards and the lone truck driver at the spacious entrance, surprising the three Germans while they smoked confiscated American cigarettes.

"I hope they enjoyed their last puffs on those ciggybutts," Ferrelli told Jimmy as the two Vatican operatives dragged the dead bodies away from the loaded truck and hid them in the tall weeds next to the lab entrance. "Those were killer butts, as it turned out."

Both men smiled as they turned and quickened their pace to meet Paul and the others at the entrance to the underground lab.

When the two divided teams infiltrated the cavernous laboratory on either side of the giant steel entrance door, the dim surrounding light made the alien saucer glow in the darkness. Loogie was overwhelmed by the sight.

"Holy shit," Loogie gulped. Dante snapped his head around when he heard the second curse word come out of Loogie's mouth in over seven years of Vatican missions.

"Did you just say what I thought you said?" Dante asked incredulously. "But, yeah, I agree with your assessment, Loogie." Dante grinned.

"There's Schauberger, the lead scientist on developing Hitler's version of the alien craft," Wolff whispered to Dante as they watched Schauberger descend from the craft. "His knowledge is critical."

"Then I think we better grab his ass, don't you think, Konman?" Dante asked Wolff sarcastically. "We definitely want him in American hands after the war."

As Schauberger hastened his pace to exit the laboratory, Dante and his team jumped from their hiding places behind barrels of fuel and crates of machine parts, and grabbed the startled scientist. Even though his face was blackened by the burnt cork, Schauberger recognized Wolff.

"Herr Wolff, what is this all about?" the befuddled scientist asked. "I haven't seen you for many weeks. Who are these men and why are you dressed like this?

Ferrelli blurted out, "Let's just say that Herr Wolff was at one helluva party, Doc." Dante, Jimmy, George, and Loogie laughed at the comment. Wolff didn't crack a smile.

"I must talk with you, Doctor," Wolff said as he pulled the scientist aside. "It's very urgent." Wolff walked Schauberger a safe distance away from the craft. That was Dante's predetermined signal from Wolff that the Vatican team could begin the mission.

"Let's go, men," Dante directed. "Let's wire these things to blow to kingdom come."

As the Vatican commandos ran to their assigned duties, Dante called out, "We can't afford to let the Russians get their hands on these things."

Dante and Loogie sprinted for the steps leading up to the entrance at the top of the craft. Schauberger had kept open the entrance hatch to the craft, not thinking anyone would be coming to do the same thing he was: Destroy the craft so no one else could get it.

Once inside the craft, Loogie and Dante's job was to set multiple timed charges within the cockpit area. However, before they moved about in tandem, they paused at the sight before them. Instantly, they were mesmerized by what they saw inside.

The distance from floor to ceiling was close to 15 feet. The interior was bathed in a soft golden light, which seemed to emanate from inside the translucent walls that surrounded the room.

"This is a god-damned shame to destroy something as remarkable as this ship," Dante lamented. "But we can't have the Russians get here first and grab it." Loogie nodded in agreement.

As they continued setting the highly-explosive combination TNT and PETN charges, they noticed there were green hard polymer seats for four single occupants recessed into the back wall, with a three-foot separation between them. Huge viewing screens were mounted high on the walls throughout the cabin. There was a long circular black control panel about four feet high that stretched across the front interior of the craft, but which, strangely, included very few gauges on it. There were some indecipherable markings next to each gauge. There was no sign of any steering device next to each seat. But, again, there were mysterious markings up and down the armrest of each seat.

Spaced evenly around the interior wall were giant viewing screens and colored engravings of what Loogie identified as astronomical diagrams of the heavens. "Boss, those diagrams over there are of the planets and constellations in our solar system," Loogie exclaimed.

"Jesus Christ, Loogie, is there anything you don't know about?" Dante exclaimed as he continued his frantic work pace. Loogie ignored the question.

Looking over his left shoulder, Loogie gasped. "That's the Milky Way." But he added quickly, "Those pictures weren't taken from earth. They had to be taken from space."

Dante took a quick glance at the pictures. "Let's stop gawking, and finish this fucking job. I know your photographic memory will capture everything you see."

While Dante and Loogie were sabotaging the interior of the craft, George, Jimmy Mac, and Ferrelli were doing their part on the exterior. But George discovered quickly that the alien ship was flame-resistant as he furiously sprayed the contents of his flamethrower across the exterior walls.

"Shit, the flames are not making a mark on this fucking ship," Ramirez cursed loudly. "I'll use what's left in this thing to set the rest of the lab on fire when we leave."

He dropped the flamethrower, and ran to join Jimmy and Ferrelli. Together, the three finished their mission of taping the new experimental high-order RDX and PETN-blended explosives on the hulls of the alien ship and the smaller German prototype that rested a few yards away. They set the timers for 15 minutes, the time Dante had ordered.

When they were finished, Ferrelli scrambled up the ladder of the alien saucer. At the top, he screamed into the interior, "Paul, hurry your asses up. Our charges are set to explode in 15 minutes."

Ferrelli couldn't resist the temptation to look inside the breached craft. Without entering, Ferrelli stretched his body and craned his neck as far as he could into the open hatch. With his mouth agape and eyes widened, he could only repeat Loogie's assessment of the craft, "Holy shit."

During the time that Dante's team was wreaking havoc in and around the saucer, Wolff held Schauberger at gunpoint while he conversed with the terrified scientist.

"I'm sorry about having to hold you at gunpoint, Doctor," Wolff apologized. "But I can't allow you to try to escape."

"Herr Wolff, I had heard the rumors that you became a traitor to the Fuhrer," Schauberger stammered. "But I didn't believe them." Bowing his head in despair, the scientist mumbled, "But now I can see the rumors were true."

"Doctor, I'm sorry to disappoint you," Wolff lamented. "But the longer I worked for Hitler, the more I saw that the war became nothing more than an opportunity for Hitler and his inner circle to feed their monstrous egos and profit financially, using the German people as pawns in their quest for world domination. Plus, all of them are fucking crazy."

"But look at all the wonderful scientific discoveries and inventions we created," Schauberger cried, pointing at the alien saucer and prototype. "We wouldn't be able to do this without the direction of the Fuhrer."

"You're wrong, Viktor. The credit goes to the incredible ingenuity and resourcefulness of the German people and scientific community," Wolff replied. "Hitler directed you to use your talents to give him the weapons he needed to quench his bloody thirst to annihilate an entire ethnic race, destroy all the cultures of the world, and re-populate Germany with hybrid Aryan babies. You were simply a political pawn, Doctor. That's the sad truth to the matter."

"What are you going to do with me?" Schauberger asked suspiciously after realizing the truth of Wolff's diatribe.

"We're going to turn you over to the Americans, Viktor," Wolff stated. "Your knowledge of how to construct a craft like this and make it operate against all the known laws of physics is too valuable to fall into the hands of the Russians." Wolff quickly added, "You will be the leader of a new world order after the war."

Empowered by Wolff's cryptic prophecy, Schauberger shouted, "Then we must leave immediately. The bombs are set to explode any minute."

"No, we have more time than that, Doctor," Wolff replied confidently. "We're setting our charges for 15 minutes. We have at least a couple of minutes left."

"No you don't, "Schauberger cried. "I set my charges for 15 minutes, and your group didn't start deploying theirs until a few minutes later. You're working with an inaccurate timetable."

Stunned, Wolff grabbed Schauberger by the arm and immediately started running and screaming in the direction of the two booby-trapped flying craft. "Everybody out," Wolff yelled at Jimmy and George, the only two people he saw near the saucers. "Schauberger's bombs are ready to explode."

Instantaneously, Jimmy yelled to Ferrelli, who was still at the top of the alien ship, "Geno, get Paul and Loogie. Schauberger's bombs are set to go off any second."

Dante heard Wolff's loud warning inside the craft while he and Loogie scrambled up the inner stairway after completing their job. Before Ferrelli could respond to Jimmy's directive, Dante pushed him out of the hatch opening. Ferrelli tumbled backward, losing his balance. But before falling, he grabbed the handles of the ladder, locked his feet on the outside of the ladder steps, and slid down without touching a rung. Dante and Loogie followed, using the same innovative descending procedure.

Within seconds, all six men were dashing breathlessly toward the gigantic entrance doors over a hundred yards away. "I forgot the flamethrower," George called to Dante as the Vatican team and German scientist sprinted away from the massive impending detonation.

"Don't worry about it, Georgie," Dante yelled over his shoulder. "Nothing is going to be left of this place anyway."

As the weary group was within 50 feet of their front-door destination, they heard the first explosion erupt. Quickly turning around, they saw debris raining down in all directions from the exploding German prototype. Covering their heads with their bare hands, they continued to hustle towards the heavy steel door. When they heard the first explosion resound from inside the alien craft, there was no flying debris. But a strange electronic humming sound started to resonate.

Reaching the door, they turned and watched the scene unfold as the humming sound increased in volume. Suddenly, they witnessed an eerie pulsating blue light ooze ominously out of the open hatch at the top of the craft. The light slowly floated around the hull until it enveloped the entire outside of the craft.

"What in the hell is happening here, Doctor?" Wolff bellowed at the bewildered scientist. Dante and his team locked their gazes on Schauberger for his answer.

"I have no idea, Herr Wolff," the scientist screamed, clasping his ears to decrease the volume of the hum, which now escalated to an excruciatingly painful pitch level. The others mimicked Schauberger's defensive movement, crouching down and covering their ears with their gloved hands to save their eardrums from the shattering sound.

Inevitably, the timing mechanisms on the Vatican bombs activated, joining the German bombs in a cacophony of destructive fireworks. However, with each ensuing explosion, the blue light expanded outward. With each detonation booming milliseconds apart, the bewildered ambushers watched incredulously as the pulsating blue light grew darker in color and spread like an angry cloud closer to their location.

"Shit, Paul, we need to get the hell away from here, pronto, buddy," Ferrelli screamed into Dante's face. "It ain't looking good."

Dante focused on Ferrelli's wild eyes. It was no surprise when Paul yelled his response. "Evacuate!" he commanded. At the sound of Paul's direct order, the group jumped to their feet, stumbled momentarily in their haste to escape, and didn't stop running until they reached the document-laden Nazi truck, parked thirty yards from the entrance.

Shielded safety behind the large sturdy vehicle, each man cautiously stretched his head around the corner of the back of the truck to determine if the evil blue cloud was still pursuing them. They saw that the blue light had not breached beyond the entrance to the underground lab, but the intensity of the pulsating light had increased dramatically.

Wide-eyed, each man surveyed the group members, looking for any sign of injury that may have occurred during the treacherous ordeal that seemed to last much longer than the five minutes that Jimmy timed on his watch.

"No way, Jimmy," George reacted to Jimmy's declaration of how long the entire sequence of events had lasted. "Our explosives went off, so that's at least 15 minutes!"

"Yessir, partner, but the watch doesn't lie. It says five," Jimmy answered. "But it was five minutes of hellfire, if you ask me."

Relieved by their good fortune, the interlopers were quickly startled back to reality when the ground around them started to shake. The heavy truck began to rock on its wheels, causing the men to jump away in fear. As the light pulsated more rapidly, it began to extend out of the cave entrance.

When the alien blue light collided with the natural blackness of the night, Loogie envisioned himself looking at the Gates of Hell.

Inside the deserted lab, the pulsating blue light was forming a rapidly-whirling vortex around the alien craft and the remains of the German prototype. Faster and faster, the spinning vortex resembled the eye of a hurricane. There was no movement of the two flying discs and surrounding debris as they sat stationary on the lab floor despite the unearthly activity surrounding them.

The speed of the funnel-like air movement was increasing exponentially each second. Suddenly, the debris on the ground and the German prototype began to rise and swirl around the alien craft. When the vortex speed reached its zenith, the pulsating motion suddenly ceased. The ear-splitting electronic humming sound faded away. The blue glow remained. Then there was a loud snapping sound, like raw electricity crackling angrily along the ground.

In the blink of an eye, the alien saucer and nearby German prototype and all scattered disc debris vanished from the interior of the lab. Gone in a flash. Swept clean. Only two small craters remained where each vehicle had stood in the lab. But the powerful residual effects of Tehlri's mysterious alien technology that was activated to rescue discs under attack were just beginning.

Outside, intimidating shadows in the tree line appeared through the flickering moonlight. Instantly, each man realized that something had dramatically changed. The truck stopped rocking. The earth stopped shaking. The terrible humming noise stopped. A moment later, the light stopped pulsating, but the blue glow remained. There was an eerie calmness settling in the area.

"I don't like what's going on here, Paul," Ferrelli cautioned.

Dante was satisfied that the group had survived the strange experience without any adverse effects. "I think we're okay, Geno," Dante responded. "Let's see what's going on in there now," he told the group as he began walking towards the entrance.

It came out of the blue. Fifty feet from their destination, the massive invisible shock wave generated by the aftermath of the alien technology from inside the lab, blew the men off their feet, lifted them ten feet in the air, and catapulted them backwards into the dense grove of trees and shrubs thirty feet away.

"*Hurensohn. Nicht schon wieder.* Son of a bitch. Not again," Schauberger yelled as he tumbled head over heels backwards ten feet in the air and landed upside down against a bent dark oak tree, nearly uprooted by the effects of the sound wave. "I'm too old for this shit," he lamented as he noted the bloody gash on his leg.

The German truck was lifted five feet off the ground, with the shock wave blasting through the interior of the truck, ripping apart boxes containing the sensitive scientific notes and valuable materials, and scattering the contents of half the boxes in the cargo throughout a half-mile radius. No evidence of the blue light remained.

"How's everybody doing?" Dante moaned loudly as he slowly rolled onto his back after landing face down in a large pile of prickly tree twigs. Finally sitting up after a few minutes, he spit out and dusted off the twigs while mentally identifying the voices of his team members without actually seeing them as they answered his call for injury assessment. "So this is how it feels to be molested by the power of science," Dante thought.

Thirty minutes later, after slowly recovering from the effects of the blast and mending Schauberger's gashed leg, Dante and his team lumbered to the ruptured entrance door of the secret laboratory. When they looked inside, they were dumfounded.

"Where is all the debris?" Loogie asked, completely amazed at what he was seeing. "A blast of that magnitude should have caused extensive damage."

"Everything's the same, except that all the flying craft are gone," Ferrelli stated in amazement. "It looks like nothing unique existed here."

George, too, was amazed. "I found the flamethrower," he announced gleefully, finding it in the exact location he had dropped it.

Dante and Wolff tried to make sense of the scene. They turned to Schauberger for the answers.

"It looks like a giant vacuum cleaner came through here and sucked up only two things in this room," Dante told the German scientist. "There's only a crater where the prototype and the alien craft were sitting. And only the disc debris on the ground is gone." He shook his head in wonder.

Wolff chimed in, "Even some of your equipment is still sitting on the work bench undisturbed. How in the hell do you explain any of this, Doctor?"

Schauberger put on his scientist face. "Quite possibly the explosion caused each craft to implode on itself, turning all the debris into microscopic pieces that are now imbedded deep in the ground."

"Aw, piss on it, Doc. You know that explanation is a boat load of shit," Ferrelli pontificated.

Looking embarrassed, the scientist quickly added, "Or they simply vanished into that blue light. Maybe this was some kind of defense mechanism built into the craft by its creators. We'll never know for sure."

After unsuccessfully combing the inside of the lab for five minutes for any remnants, Dante and the group returned to the truck with their flashlights and salvaged the scientific contents of the boxes that lay scattered around the area. Schauberger's leg injury prevented him from actively participating in the salvage work. He assisted while standing against the side of the truck and informed the team which papers and materials needed to stay together. Packing the remaining boxes into the cargo bed, Dante declared the mission a success.

"What do you want to do with the truck we came in?" Jimmy asked Paul as he jumped into the cargo hold to join Loogie, George, and the resting Schauberger.

"We'll just leave it behind, Jimmy," Dante answered. "Everything we need is with us in this truck anyway." He had one more order before he moved to the front seat. "Now, you guys try to keep the old guy as comfortable as possible. He got banged around pretty good in that silent explosion." Jimmy nodded his understanding.

It was nearly midnight when Ferrelli jumped into the driver's seat of the heavy German cargo truck and turned the ignition key. The truck engine groaned for a second, but then sprang to life. "Ya gotta love that German technology," Ferrelli quipped.

Dante and Wolff joined Ferrelli in the cab. Schauberger rested in the back of the truck under the watchful eyes of Jimmy, George, and Loogie.

"Let's get going, Geno," Dante ordered. "We've got some valuable cargo to deliver to the Americans."

CHAPTER SEVENTY FIVE

Allied Forces Camp of General Dwight Eisenhower 1945

TEN Nazi trucks carrying Schauberger's notes and materials were commandeered on their way to Austria by U.S. Rangers and driven into the Allied Forces camp. The Rangers attached U.S. flags to the sides to counter the German insignias painted on the cabs. However, five Nazi trucks with the same ultra-sensitive contents were commandeered by the Russian forces before the Rangers arrived on the escape route leading to Austria.

American soldiers were removing boxes from the Nazi trucks when Dante and the Vatican team arrived at Eisenhower's battlefield headquarters. The truck was temporarily detained at the camp entrance by a swarm of armed troops who saw the swastika painted on the side of the cab as the truck drove up. It took Dante ten minutes to explain the situation before the sergeant-in-charge allowed the group to pass after receiving Eisenhower's personal consent.

"Nice job explaining our predicament to the sarge, Paul," Ferrelli quipped. "For a minute there, I thought we all were going to be shot." Dante grinned at Ferrelli's forced humor.

Eisenhower and his commanders stood outside the command tent as the German truck with the Nazi secret cargo and Vatican commandos on board rolled to a stop. As personnel exited the truck, Eisenhower stepped forward to greet his unexpected guests. Dante was at the head of the line.

Extending his right hand, Eisenhower addressed Dante, "Should I call you 'Father'?" Dante stopped and saluted the Commander-in-Chief of the Allied Forces before shaking his hand. "No sir, General. You can call me Paul." Eisenhower grinned as he invited the Vatican group and two Germans into the large canvas tent.

"Can I offer you a cold beer?" Eisenhower asked. Ike directed his aide to supply each man with a Budweiser lager served in the non-reflective olive-colored cans reserved for the military.

For the next two hours, Dante answered a bevy of Eisenhower and his commander's questions, clarified the Vatican's clandestine role during the war, and explained how Wolff and Schauberger were in their custody. Eisenhower was impressed with Dante's briefing.

"Lieutenant, please escort Doctor Schauberger to the processing tent," Eisenhower ordered his aide. "Make sure he's properly interrogated and prepared for the trip to the States." The aide gathered up the coveted scientist, and they made their way toward the entrance.

Before leaving, Schauberger addressed Eisenhower. "Thank you, General. I hope we meet again." Eisenhower nodded in reply.

Eisenhower turned away from the entrance, and while addressing Dante, expressed his admiration for the work Dante and his team had accomplished during the war.

"Paul, I still find it hard to believe that a unit like yours is working for the Pope," Ike stated. "You're all priests, Jesuits no less, yet you're fighting like American G.I.'s, killing enemy soldiers." He smiled, then quickly added, "There just seems to be a little bit of irony here, don't you think?"

"His Excellency felt that the perils of war dictated desperate measures," Dante answered. "He told us when we started our mission that the war was a classic battle between good and evil. He told us that the only way to deal with evil is to destroy it in any manner possible."

Dante then gave Eisenhower the answer he was probably looking for. "General, I assure you that our consciences are clear." Ferrelli, Jimmy, George, and Loogie all agreed with Paul's summation by giving their own audible affirmation to Eisenhower.

"Well, men, thank you again for all the bravery and courage you've exhibited," Eisenhower motioned to the entire Vatican team. "It's been a long night and I'm sure you'd like to get some food and rest before you head back to Rome. And, Paul, tell the pontiff that I'm in his debt." Dante nodded as Eisenhower ordered another aide to get the group some warm food and provide bedding and blankets.

While the group shuffled towards the door, shaking Ike's hand on the way out, Ike stopped Wolff. "Well, Mr. Wolff, I would be remiss if I didn't thank you for supplying us with the names and locations of the German scientists. The Russians got some of them, but we feel we got the best ones."

"It was the least I could do, General," Wolff responded as he walked out the entrance.

Eisenhower followed Dante's group out the entrance, and sauntered to the back of Dante's truck. As the Rangers continued to unload the German trucks in the early morning light, Ike picked a box to examine the contents. When he opened one box, he spied the alien device that Schauberger's assistant had hurriedly placed in the box while packing up the contents of Schauberger's lab.

After examining the device and returning it to the box, Ike addressed the Ranger commander. "Major, see that this box is fully secured, tag it along with all the Nazi files and materials as my personal property, and ship it back to the states immediately," Eisenhower ordered.

CHAPTER SEVENTY SIX

**Oval Office
September 1947**

"WHAT IN THE HELL IS GOING ON HERE?" an exasperated President Harry Truman vented to the 12 members of his secret committee (Code name: Majestic 12) that had been summoned hastily to the White House and were now gathered in the Oval Office. The group that included scientists, military leaders, and government officials had been assembled through Truman's classified Executive Order only weeks ago.

Their task was to investigate the reports of "flying disc" sightings that were pouring into U.S military intelligence sources. But the most pressing issue at the moment was the preliminary findings regarding the recovery of debris and bodies from a saucer crash that was discovered outside Roswell, New Mexico, two months earlier. Truman skipped the niceties and got right to the point.

"General Twining, what is your assessment of the Roswell craft?" Truman asked his chairman of the Joint Chiefs of Staff.

"Mr. President, from our initial analysis, we believe the craft was some kind of reconnaissance vehicle," Twining said. "Just by the size of it, we think it was likely used for short-range missions."

Truman moved on to question Dr. Vannevar Bush, the chairman of the recently-created Joint Research and Development Board and chairman of the wartime Office of Scientific Research and Development. He was highly involved in the Manhattan Project, the super-secret scientific project that developed and tested the nuclear bombs that were dropped on the two Japanese cities.

"Dr. Bush, where do you think this craft originated from?"

"We're in complete agreement that no country on earth has the capability of constructing this kind of craft," Bush exclaimed. "Maybe it came from Mars. Our telescopes have picked up strange activity on the surface of that planet in the past."

"I think the source is outside of our solar system," interrupted Dr. Donald Menzel, the Harvard astronomer who worked as a cryptologist during the war. "Those beings we found at Roswell prove we're looking at some sort of life form outside our solar system."

Truman picked up on the topic of the four dead bodies that were recovered a couple miles from the actual Roswell crash site, and directed his next question to Dr. Detlev Bronk, the chairman of the National Academy of Sciences and the only medical physicist on the secret committee.

"Doctor Bronk, what did you discover after performing autopsies on the occupants of the craft?"

"Mr. President, they're very short in stature, a little less than four feet tall," Bronk stated. "These creatures looked human-like on the outside, even though they only had four fingers on each hand. But once we got inside, it was remarkably quite different than a normal human being."

"How so?" Truman inquired.

"Their biological systems were quite different from our own," Bronk replied. "Their hearts were on the opposite side of the chest cavity of the normal human. Their lungs were under-developed. It was quite evident that the evolutionary processes of these creatures are much more evolved than homo-sapiens." He added quickly, "They may be a hybrid race. Certainly, they are of extraterrestrial origin."

"What were you calling them, Detlev?" asked James Forrestal, Truman's Secretary of Defense and former Secretary of the Navy.

"For now, we're calling them Extra-terrestrial Biological Entities. Or EBE's for short," Bronk replied. "We'll keep that designation until we come up with something more definitive."

Truman wasn't impressed with the identification tag. But he moved swiftly to question Dr. Jerome Hunsaker, the aeronautical engineer from the Massachusetts Institute of Technology.

"Dr. Hunsaker, what can you tell me about the propulsion system of this damn saucer?"

"It's the damnest thing, Mr. President," Hunsaker began. "It had no wings. It had no propellers. It had no jets, or any other kind of conventional propulsion system that we could identify."

Hunsaker's frustration began to surface. "On top of that, we found no wiring, and no vacuum tubes. Sir, we found no metallic components of any kind in the wreckage. In addition, there were no electronic components, so we couldn't detect any kind of guidance system. The craft is a total mystery in the aeronautical field at the present time."

Truman grew more agitated with the answers he received from this elite group. "What else didn't we find, goddamn it?" The rhetorical question garnered a response from Dr. Lloyd Berkner, a physicist with expertise in radio communications, and a colleague of Vannevar Bush at the JRDB.

"We found no method of radio communication, obviously," Berkner announced. "That should be expected since we found no electronic components of any kind." He shrugged his shoulders in frustration.

Truman turned to his director of Central Intelligence to get some answers.

"Didn't we find some form of writing in the wreckage?" Truman asked Rear Admiral Roscoe Hillenkoetter, the director of the newly-formed Central Intelligence Agency.

"Yes, Mr. President, we did." Hillenkoetter quickly glanced at Rear Admiral Sidney Souers, a colleague at the Central Intelligence Group. After receiving an affirmative nod from Souers, Hillenkoetter swallowed hard before continuing. "There was some form of the letters of the Cyrillic alphabet that were stamped on some materials inside the craft."

"Cyrillic? Are you shitting me?" Truman exploded. "You mean to tell me that the goddamn Russians are behind this advanced technology?"

"Let's not jump to any conclusions yet, Mr. President," interjected General Hoyt Vandenberg, the director of the Central Intelligence Group. "Russian scientists were all locked up in gulags during the war. Stalin didn't trust them. There was no scientific program in Russia capable of producing this kind of technology. They got help from somewhere else, or somebody else."

"Maybe their German scientists are better than our German scientists," quipped General Robert Montague, the guided missile expert who headed the nuclear Armed Forces Special Weapons Center production facility at Sandia Base outside Albuquerque.

"What do you mean by that statement, General?" Truman shouted as he stood up behind his desk and whipped his head in Montague's direction.

"I mean, Russia got their share of the German scientists after the war, and we got our share of them," Montague stated, referring to America's Operation Paperclip. "Maybe their Germans are better than our Germans. Maybe their German scientists were working on these types of projects and our Germans weren't as involved."

"For Christ sake," Truman yelled, "We got Wernher Von Braun and Ernst Steinhoff. You people told me they were two of the most critical German scientists we needed to get to America after the war." Truman shook his head in amazement. "So now you're telling me that these two Germans aren't the guys we wanted? That the best scientists got funneled to Russia?"

"Montague has his opinion. It's not necessarily the correct one, Mr. President," replied Gordon Gray, the Secretary of the Army. "But we better find out in a damn hurry which German scientists are behind the creation of this new technology. We know for sure that they do not currently reside on American soil."

Over the next two hours, Truman and the members of Majestic 12 debated the immediate course of action. It was decided that scientists Robert Oppenheimer, Albert Einstein,

Karl Compton, and Edward Teller would be sworn to secrecy and brought into the workings of the group. It was also a unanimous decision by the group that a state-of-the-art research and development facility under the command of the military and intelligence communities needed to be designed and made operational as quickly as possible.

"We need to centralize all of this data, research, and development into a top-secret military facility that the public will never know about," Truman expounded. "Hoyt, what are our options?"

Vandenberg looked at Twining, Montague, and Souers. "Gentlemen, don't you think our Nevada operations would be the best site for this facility?" he pondered.

"Yeah, the area around the Nevada Test and Training Range encompasses over 4600 square miles," Montague stated. "Hell, we should be able to hide any facility in that desolate part of the country."

"Groom Lake is a good location," Souers added. "We've got it plotted out on our surface maps as Area 51. I've always liked it because it's surrounded by mountains and the lake bed is dry. The ground is conducive for all the tunneling we'll need to have to keep topside movement to a minimum. Plus, Nellis Air Force Base is right there to use for cover stories if we need them."

"Mr. President, I concur with my colleagues," Twining stated. "The Groom Lake area on the Nellis Air Force Range in Nevada is our best site for what you want to build."

"Very well," Truman responded. "Let's get the plans moving on this. Remember, this is top secret. Everyone involved will be sworn to secrecy. I'll write up another Executive Order stating that people will be prosecuted for treason if they talk about any of this in public." The president wiped his brow and massaged the back of his neck as he pondered his next statement.

"Goddamn it. This has to be another subject that Congress will not be told about," Truman lamented. "I took a lot of shit when we dropped the bombs on Japan, and members of Congress found out only from news reports." He continued to bemoan his disdain for the majority of American senators and congressmen.

"But those bastards can't keep their mouths shut," Truman stated deploringly. "They either tell their mistress or their wife or their girlfriend, and those people blab it in public, and then it hits the newspapers, and I'm screwed again for being the nice guy." He finished his diatribe.

"But the buck stops here," he announced proudly. "National security trumps the people's right to know. That's the way it's got to be."

CHAPTER SEVENTY SEVEN

Paris, France 1951

DWIGHT DAVID "IKE" EISENHOWER took his favorite solitary evening walk southeast along L'Avenue des Champs-Elysees after completing another hectic day in his official duties as the first Supreme Allied Commander of the North Atlantic Treaty Organization. It was the best way of clearing his head and relieving the stress associated with occupying the newly-created international politico-military leadership position.

He only arrived in Paris with his family a few months ago. The appointment to the post came quickly after he resigned his three-year presidency of Columbia University in New York City in 1950. Ironically, after three years in academia, he became disenchanted with the political demands expected of a college president.

Tonight, it was a gorgeous early summer evening. A wispy east breeze tickled his sun-parched skin, and the sunset spilled golden light as far as the eye could see. *"Paris is a beautiful city at night,"* Eisenhower marveled. The young branches on the decorative crab-apple trees lining the famous Parisian street were recently pruned. The sidewalk was cluttered with young lovers, busy shoppers, and tired workers making their way home. His stroll to the secluded garden that overlooked the Seine River had a calming effect on him.

As he walked, he unloosened his tie, unfastened his top shirt button, took off his military suit coat, and reminisced about the exciting life he was living. "*Graduating at the top of my class from West Point was quite an accomplishment for a kid from Abilene, Kansas, who worked at the Bell Springs Creamery,*" he proudly recollected.

After a mile down the cluttered Champs-Elysees, Eisenhower turned south on to quieter Rue de Courcelles. He didn't notice the shadows forming around him as daylight faded to darkness. "*Working for General Fox Connor in the Panama Canal Zone was fortuitous,*" Ike remembered, as it was Connor who encouraged Eisenhower to apply to the Command and General Staff School at Fort Leavenworth, Kansas, the Army's prestigious graduate school. "*Graduated first in my class again,*" Ike recalled with pride. "*But the best part of Leavenworth was driving to see my family in Abilene every weekend. That made it special.*"

Lately, Eisenhower began receiving daily communiques from Republican Party leaders in the States. The topic was always the same: Become the Republican nominee for President of the United States. It was an intriguing idea at this point in his career, he mused.

"*Jesus, Senator Kenneth Wherry, the Senate Minority Leader from Nebraska, just won't stop contacting me,*" Ike recalled as he left Rue de Courcelles and turned east on to deserted Cours la Reine. His destination loomed ahead.

"But the guy that's incessant about this whole presidential thing is that senator from New Hampshire, Styles Bridges," Ike lamented. *"God, what kind of name is Styles, for Christ's sake?"* Eisenhower laughed at his observation.

Within minutes, Ike arrived at his favorite relaxation location. The secluded garden, about the size of an American football field, was hidden behind a grove of trees less than thirty feet from the Seine River, which snaked its way around and through the city. He settled into his favorite small wooden bench seat, dropped his suit coat next to him, stretched out his legs, and inhaled the amazing fragrances that overwhelmed his senses.

This fertile patch of land was the pride of Paris. Hundreds of species of iris flowers and lilies dotted the landscape. The most prevalent flower was the hybrid fleur-de-lis iris that Louis VII adopted as the national symbol of France in the 12th century. Lilies colorized the grounds in their myriad of white, pink, plum, yellow, orange, and red hues.

Eisenhower was captivated by the minty smell of nearby rosemary bushes. The purple Gourdon wildflowers grew naturally in the area, and the abundance of perfumery cabbage roses made the experience a sensual and visual delight for all visitors to this blissful haven.

On this cloudless evening, the moon cast its image on to the rippling Seine water, giving Ike a mirror image on the water of what he was actually seeing in the sky. Ike always appreciated how Mother Nature displayed her beauty.

As he sat in deep thought pondering his interest in running for political office, his attention was diverted to the image of a bright white light moving on the water. Except, it wasn't on the water, it was in the sky. As his eyes drifted from the water to the sky, the light unexpectedly blinked out. *"That's certainly odd,"* Eisenhower thought at the time.

Without warning, Eisenhower felt a tingling sensation run through his entire body. As he tried to make sense of what was happening, his mind was invaded with a clear, but strange message…

"Dwight Eisenhower," the ethereal voice announced, *"We have been observing you at a distance for many of your earth years. We know of your ambitions. We are here to help you attain those ambitions. We come as friends."*

CHAPTER SEVENTY EIGHT

Eisenhower Presidential Campaign Headquarters 1952

THE Commodore Hotel sat next to Grand Central Station on East 42nd Street in New York City. The 2000-room hotel, which opened in January 1919, was developed as part of an aggressive city modernization project called Terminal City, a grand plan to build a complex of palatial hotels and offices and connect them to Grand Central Terminal. The hotel, which boasted about having "The Most Beautiful Lobby in the World" along with a waterfall on property, acted as Eisenhower's headquarters during the 1952 presidential campaign.

The joyous celebration began in the mammoth ballroom immediately following Eisenhower's victory speech to the crowd of faithful followers. The newly-elected 34th President of the United States had defeated Democratic opponent Adlai Stevenson in a landslide vote. America liked Ike.

The five-star Army general would leave a lasting legacy of innovation during his two-term presidency: the launch of the Interstate Highway System; the creation of the Defense Advanced Research Projects Agency (DARPA), one productive output being the birth of the internet;

the establishment of the National Aeronautics and Space Administration (NASA) to encourage peaceful exploration of space; the passage of the National Defense Education Act to foster strong science education; and amendments to the Atomic Energy Act to promote the peaceful use of nuclear power.

Exhausted from the proceedings of the evening, Eisenhower decided to leave the boisterous party and return to his quiet private suite which overlooked the ballroom from the next floor. After arriving at the deserted room, he loosened his tie, grabbed a liquor bottle and glass from a cabinet, and poured himself a drink. He plopped down in his cushioned chair behind his desk, and sipped his soothing beverage.

There was a light tapping on the door. "What is it?" Ike asked.

Henry Cabot Lodge, Eisenhower's campaign manager, opened the door and walked to the front of the desk.

"Sorry to bother you, Mr. President." he stated, "There are two men who want to talk with you."

"Goddamn it, reporters again?" Ike responded disgustingly. "I've been talking to them all night." He instructed Lodge to send them away.

"Tell them it's late, and I'm tired," he commanded. "Tell them to come back tomorrow and I'll give them all the quotes they want."

Lodge hesitated for a moment, and then addressed the president-elect.

"They're dressed in all black and they have Vatican credentials," Lodge emphasized. "They say it's important."

Eisenhower was not happy. "Damn it," he exclaimed. After a moment, he said, "OK. Show them in."

Lodge nodded, returned to the open door, and motioned for the two visitors to enter. The campaign manager stepped aside as Dante and Wolff hastily strode into the room. When the two Vatican emissaries were in the room, Lodge left and closed the door behind him.

Ike immediately recognized Dante. "You again?" Ike complained. "I've more than evened the score for the Vatican's help during the war. Why do you keep harassing me?"

"The Holy Father is indeed thankful for your assistance in helping in the return of the stolen artwork and statuary from Catholic churches throughout Europe that the Nazis tried to hide and sell after the war," Dante explained. "It amounted to tens of millions of dollars restored to the safety of the Vatican bank."

"See there, I made the Vatican rich again," Eisenhower bragged. "You helped America get those important German scientists after the war, and in exchange, America helped you get back your valuable and expensive Vatican artwork. That's an even trade in my book."

Eisenhower continued to vocalize his unhappiness with Dante and Wolff's presence. "The best part of being president will be having Secret Service agents who will keep pests like you away from me."

Dante smiled at the veiled threat, but continued his dialogue.

"But General, I mean, Mr. President, you haven't lived up to your part of your agreement with the Vatican," Dante stated emphatically. "We gave you the names and locations of those

Germans so you could rescue men of science from death. But now you're using their knowledge and expertise for personal and professional gain."

Eisenhower's rage was beginning to surface. His face turned red, and he slammed his fist on the desk. "Who the hell do you think you're talking to?" Eisenhower shouted. "And how in the hell am I benefitting personally and professionally from those German scientists?"

Dante responded calmly. "Mr. President, we know that you have a device that you're using to contact certain otherworldly individuals. That device was taken from the Nazi materials and documents you had shipped back to the United States for your personal curiosity immediately following the end of the war."

Eisenhower looked stunned. "What do you know about that?" he snapped at Dante.

"We also know about your Cosmic Top Secret security designation you started while you were at NATO for that short period of time," Dante preached. Eisenhower's face registered the look of a kid caught with his hand in the cookie jar.

"The arm of the Vatican stretches throughout the world, Mr. President," Dante stated. "Our reach extends into the depths of the American intelligence bureaucracy."

Eisenhower sneered at the revelation as Dante proceeded with the conversation.

"Frankly, we don't care if you keep these unworldly individuals a secret from the American people," Dante commented. "The Vatican has been aware of their presence for quite some time." He quickly added. "But you're aware that Hitler tried to exploit his relationship with them, and you know how that turned out."

Eisenhower fired back. "Well, I don't see there's much you can do about anything now, Father. What's done is done."

Eisenhower pointed his finger at Dante and Wolff and stated vigorously, "You can tell the Pope that he's meddling in the affairs of the United States of America, and you have no business doing that."

Eisenhower left his standing position behind his desk and started moving towards the closed door. "I held the Allies together during the war and I'm going to hold this country together during my presidency."

He added his parting words as he rumbled out the door, "Now if you'll excuse me, I have a ballroom full of people who want to congratulate me." Ike chugged the remainder of his drink and handed the empty glass to Wolff as he quickly exited the room.

CHAPTER SEVENTY NINE

AS Eisenhower stormed out his office door, he nearly ran over two of his top aides. Henry Cabot Lodge and Pat Loomis, another campaign staff member, saw Ike barreling towards them, and quickly jumped apart as the president-elect burst between the two talking men.

"Whoa, look out!" Loomis screamed at Lodge as the agitated Eisenhower didn't stop his rapid getaway gait from the two unwelcome Vatican visitors who still occupied Ike's private suite.

"What's got him so pissed off?" Loomis asked Lodge.

"It's those two guys from the Vatican," Lodge began his explanation. "Every time they show up, it drives Ike crazy."

"You said that Ike knows them, though, doesn't he?" Loomis asked.

"Yes, Dante, the taller one, was the person who contacted the Marines during the war, and gave them the names and locations of German scientists who were working for Hitler," Lodge said. "Dante personally delivered one of the scientists to Ike in Germany, an important guy who was working on some kind of flying machine that defied the laws of physics."

"So Dante was responsible for helping the Americans bring these scientists to the States after the war," Loomis stated. "So why is Ike pissed at him?"

"Over the past few years, Dante has showed up where Ike was working and reminded him that Ike was not living up to the spirit of some agreement that they made at the end of the war," Lodge stated. Then Lodge kidded, "Ike calls them the Men in Black because every time they show up, they're wearing all black and the message is ominous."

Loomis laughed at the characterization. "Well, after tonight's argument, I don't think we'll be seeing Dante and his buddy any time soon."

CHAPTER EIGHTY

"THAT didn't go well," Wolff quipped as he and Dante left Eisenhower's presidential celebration and the extravagant décor of the Commodore Hotel.

"It might have gone better if I could have busted his chops," Dante countered. "But that wouldn't have been a good idea."

As the two Vatican emissaries walked briskly to their parked car, Wolff addressed Dante.

"I've been meaning to bring this up," he stated hesitantly. "I appreciate all that you and His Excellency have done for me these past several years. And working with your team has been most enjoyable and educational, to say the least." He continued his comments.

"I appreciate the chance to work all over the world, and actually practice my first occupation of science. But this emissary work and covert operations isn't my cup of tea, as you Americans would say. I just want to concentrate on the science."

Dante laughed. "So you're after my job, Konman? Oh, is that a knife that I feel in my back?"

Wolff stammered, "No, I didn't mean…"

"Take it easy, Konman," Dante replied. "I'm just messing with you." After a moment of silence, Dante added, "Actually, there's a chance you may be taking over my job."

Wolff was dumbfounded. "What? You mean as head of the Pontifical Commission for Sacred Archeology?"

"Yeah, but promise me that you'll shorten that name," Dante joked. "Oh, and one more thing: You may get my old job, but you won't get my team. They stay with me. Even Loogie."

"Yes, I assumed that would be the case," Wolff stated. "They enjoy your leadership."

Wolff wanted more answers. "Then what will you do? I can't see you leaving the Vatican and your team and retiring to a little Catholic parish in Nebraska."

Dante replied sarcastically, "That ain't going to happen any time soon." He added, "Papa Gino has been hinting about starting some kind of Vatican intelligence agency, something patterned after the American CIA, and he wants me to run it."

Wolff was ecstatic at the news. "Well, congratulations are in store," he said as he gave Dante a long and clinging hug.

"You too," Dante countered. "I know you'll do better than me. I liked the adventure and excitement, but I was never any good with the science. That's why I picked good team members. I hope you do the same."

The two men reached the parked car as they concluded their conversation. As they opened their side doors, both looked up at the night sky. They saw a large bright light hovering in place a short distance away.

CHAPTER EIGHTY ONE

Pope's Private Library
December 1953

"SERVIZIO INFORMAZIONI DEL VATICANO," Dante repeated as he nibbled on his warm chocolate chip cookie and washed it down with sips of cold milk. Pius learned early in his friendship with the Nebraskan that cookies and milk was the best way to keep Dante's attention. Pius made this tasty combination his permanent choice of refreshment whenever he and Dante met in the pope's private library.

"Vatican Information Service." Dante chuckled. "Quite the understated name for a secret intelligence agency, isn't it, Papa Gino?" He waited to see how the pontiff would reply to his sarcastic comment.

"Yes, I guess it is, Paul," Pius XII answered matter-of-factly. "But the code name for the Vatican Intelligence Agency will be S.I.V. That sounds a little more cloak-and-daggerish, don't you think? Right up there with CIA, MI5, and FBI?" Pius couldn't help but smile at the absurdness of the present conversation with his newly-appointed director of the Vatican's ambitious goal to build a worldwide secret intelligence-gathering operation that would rival the world's best agencies.

For the past hour, Dante listened intently to the fantastic story of how Pius XII forged this blossoming idea into a definitive reality. He was still stupefied at the grand nature of the venture.

"You've got to tell me again how you put all of this together," Dante requested. "And, frankly, I'm a little disappointed in myself for not having a damn clue that you were planning this for years." He shook his head in dismay. "And if I can't read your overt actions to gather covert insight, then how can I possibly become a good intelligence agent, much less teach others to do it?"

"Now, Paul, don't be so hard on yourself," the pontiff replied. "Your personality is perfect for this job because it entails handling people properly. You can relate to all groups of individuals. Remember, you recruited Elise and others during the war. And with the political power of the Vatican behind you, I see nothing but great advances in building our network of clandestine agents."

Pius added proudly, "I've cultivated the assistance of several high-ranking officials within the U.S. intelligence community over the past decade. I'll give you those names shortly."

Dante nodded. "Now when did this all start? Did you say even before you became pope?" Dante began his interrogation of the leader of the worldwide Catholic Church.

"Yes, it was during my two-week trip to America in October and November of 1936, when I was performing my duties as Cardinal Secretary of State and Camerlengo under my predecessor," Pius began. "You and your team were chasing down those Illuminati thieves at the time."

"Your trip to D.C, New York, Boston, and Chicago was planned out well in advance," Dante interjected. "Who did you talk with, and how did you find the time to divert away from your busy schedule?"

"Oh, there was always unplanned time built into my schedule," Pius laughed. "When I met with President Roosevelt in Hyde Park in New York, I privately broached the subject. Since I had an inclination of what Hitler might do because of my time in Berlin, Roosevelt thought I should talk with Naval Intelligence and the FBI. So he was directly responsible for setting up all my meetings."

Pius continued. "So I had the opportunity to meet with representatives of the Office of Naval Intelligence and the FBI. It so happened that the idea of the Office of Strategic Services was beginning to take shape even though that office was not officially established until Roosevelt did it by a Presidential military order in 1942. So I met with them, too."

Dante was intrigued by Pius's guile and foresight. "So who did you talk with?" he asked.

"Colonel William Donovan was doing preliminary studies before the OSS was sanctioned, so I spoke with him," Pius related. "I also met with Captain William Puleston at Naval Intelligence. Finally, I met with J. Edgar Hoover at the FBI."

"What did you ask them?" Dante asked eagerly.

"I just wanted to know how they gathered intelligence within their respective organizations," Pius responded. "And I asked them if they would be willing to quietly share that information with the Vatican."

"And all of them agreed to do that?" Dante asked incredulously.

"Yes, with two caveats," Pius stated. "The Vatican needed to share any secret intelligence we obtained."

"And the second caveat?" Dante asked.

"The second caveat was that if any of the Vatican intelligence did not prove to be truthful, that the relationship would be terminated," Pius said.

Dante was impressed. "Well, I guess all of the intel you gave them during the war must have been worthwhile if the relationships are still going on," Dante exclaimed.

"The majority of that worthwhile intelligence came through the efforts of you and your team," Pius was quick to compliment. "And then when Mr. Wolff came into our purview, that intelligence became even more valuable."

"So who are you working with now within U.S. intelligence?" Dante inquired.

"Hoover is still with us," Pius stated. "Rear Admiral Carl Espe is our contact at Naval Intelligence. The Central Intelligence Agency has been onboard since its inception. Our present contact is Allen Dulles, although Walter Bedell Smith supplied us up to his departure."

"We're establishing S.I.V. for a specific reason, though, right?" Dante inserted. "It's because of the flying saucer sightings and the presence of life forms from other planets."

"Yes, that's correct, Paul," Pius admitted. "As you know, the discovery of the Nestorian papyrus verified the presence of extraterrestrial life as far back as the time of Jesus. So we've been aware of that fact for centuries."

Pius took a deep breath before continuing. "But ever since that crash in Roswell, New Mexico in 1947 and the discovery and recovery of the four small bodies from that crash, it has become imperative that the Papacy knows everything about this alien technology and especially knowing the purpose behind these sightings and contacts."

"Yeah, well you saw the pictures of that alien ship that Loogie took when we captured Doctor Schauberger in Germany," Dante recalled. "I agree that we need to keep tabs on everything associated with this mystery."

Dante followed up with another philosophical question. "Papa Gino, wouldn't the Vatican be interested in extraterrestrial life simply because it's another manifestation of God's presence and power?" he stated. "Isn't it another unbelievable example that God has created intelligent life throughout the universe? Plus, it's another opportunity to save more 'souls', right?"

"Well, yes, of course, you're right, Paul," Pius stammered, awed at Dante's innate sense of Christian morality. "I'm sure the Vatican will send the first religious missionary into outer space."

Dante took his final gulp of milk and finished the last bite of the two dozen cookies he had eaten during the meeting.

Pius looked on in amazement. "Can I get you more cookies and milk, Paul?" Pius inquired, sarcasm dripping from his lips.

"No thank you, Papa Gino," Dante answered sheepishly. "I'm trying to cut back a little."

Pius resumed his conversation. "The CIA has been very forthcoming with their information," Pius stated. "Interestingly, President Truman established a secret committee after the Roswell incident called MJ-12, or Majestic 12. It was a group of 12 military, government, and scientific experts who looked into the crash and recovery. The CIA had representation on that committee."

"Didn't Truman decide that the American people should never know the truth behind the flying saucer mystery?" Dante remarked.

"Yes, Truman's part in setting up the veil of secrecy has never been publicized," Pius stated. "But he and MJ-12 were behind all of the intelligence-gathering on this topic from the beginning." Pius hesitated for a moment before continuing. "Plus, a new secret facility in the Nevada desert is being built just for research into saucer technology and the quest to ascertain the biology of these alien creatures."

"What do you know about it?" Dante inquired enthusiastically.

"It's being built in the Area 51 sector of the Nevada Test Range, and it's rumored that the majority of it is being built underground," Pius said. "I've heard there are hundreds of miles of tunnels connecting various parts of it. The buildings that are visible on the surface are used mostly for storage and to hide test craft from public view."

"We know Eisenhower is a part of this," Dante stated with certainty.

"Yes, he's made sure that the funding keeps flowing on this project since he became president. I think this is one of the projects that are described as Black Operations," Pius commented. "I heard that he's also having all captured and crash evidence from around the country being shipped to this central location." The pontiff had more to tell Dante.

"When I received word of the reality of this facility, I transferred my Archbishop of New York, James Francis

McIntyre, to Los Angeles in 1948 to keep a Vatican presence close to the situation," Pius related.

"You sent a guy from New York to L.A.?" Dante wondered. "Why this guy?"

Pius was uncomfortable with the question. McIntyre had a reputation for harboring racial and cultural prejudices, as did Pius, whose animosity was directed toward the Jews. But McIntyre had a forceful personality, and Pius felt he needed a strong, albeit controversial, figure for this covert element of McIntyre's assignment.

"McIntyre was a take-charge individual," Pius admitted. "His work was exemplary for the first few years. But lately, he was becoming less committed to this part of his assignment."

"So how did you motivate him?" Dante asked.

"I made him a cardinal last January," Pius smiled. "As a matter of fact, along with that designation of Cardinal Priest of *Santa Anastasia*, I named him first cardinal of the Western United States. At my personal meeting with each cardinal following the ceremony in the consistory, I emphatically told him why he was receiving this new title."

Pius believed strongly in his philosophy of utilizing Church hierarchal titles as his means of both honoring and bribing members of the clergy.

"So with Nevada being a part of his territorial responsibilities, it's been easier for him to visit the state often and gather as much information on Area 51 as he could," Pius stated.

"Yes, you do enjoy conferring those clerical titles on us," Dante said humorously. "So what kind of protocols do you want this Vatican Intelligence Agency to work under?"

"I'm designating the term *Secretum Omega* as the highest classification of secrecy in the Vatican," Pius stated firmly. "All information that you gather for this agency will be classified under this security level."

"That's it?" Dante responded. "We stamp every S.I.V. Vatican file with *Secretum Omega*?" He continued without interruption.

"Or do you want levels of secrecy?" Dante asked. "American intelligence uses *Confidential, Secret, and Top Secret*."

"Yes, I see what you mean," Pius stated. "What do you suggest?"

"Well, let's have three levels of secrecy, too," Dante exclaimed. "How about *Secretum Omega Level 1, Level 2, and Level 3*, with *Level 3* being the highest level?"

"That sounds reasonable, Paul. Good idea," Pius praised Dante's insight.

"So when do I go to work?" Dante inquired.

"Very soon," Pius confirmed. "Cardinal McIntyre has informed me of an extraordinary event that is going to take place in February."

"What is this event?" Dante asked eagerly.

"First, I want to tell you that your suspicions that President Eisenhower has been having an ongoing dialogue for years with this Tehlri creature are correct," Pius exclaimed. "McIntyre has informed me that these multiple meetings have escalated to the point that Eisenhower is contemplating signing some kind of treaty with the aliens."

"Holy shit. Oh, pardon my French, Papa Gino," Dante caught himself expressing his true feelings. "That decision can't be very popular with U.S. military or intelligence people."

"No, I'm sure it's not," Pius replied. "But McIntyre was approached by Eisenhower's people to be a part of this meeting as a representative of organized religion. But I'm sure he picked McIntyre because he knows the Catholic religion is the only true religion."

Dante witnessed Pius's smug reply. "Ike is Presbyterian, I believe. But you're right. There are more Catholics in the world than Presbyterians. He got it right by choosing McIntyre."

Dante continued his questioning. "When and where is this meeting supposed to take place?"

"The third week in February. And I think it's going to take place in California somewhere," Pius replied. "Every element is classified as Top Secret according to McIntyre."

Pius gave additional instructions to Dante. "Your team will fly to California a few days before the event. But only you will join Cardinal McIntyre at this meeting. He is supposedly bringing you along at the last minute as the Vatican's official envoy."

"I guess I should be honored, right?" Dante exclaimed. "But I can tell you now. Eisenhower will not be thrilled to see me there."

"At the time, he won't have anything to say about it," Pius stated. "He'll be too busy worrying about other things."

"The boys will be excited for the road trip, Papa Gino," Dante said exuberantly. "They've been pretty bored since the war ended. Not enough excitement in their lives, including Loogie."

"Well, they're not just going along for the ride," Pius interjected. "I have another job for them that will be just as important as yours."

"And what about Wolff?" Dante asked the pontiff.

"Mr. Wolff has been busy assembling his new team, I understand. But since I think you'll need him for this assignment, I'll pull him away just for this trip. But this will be his final mission with you and your team," Pius stated, "before he officially assumes your old position." Dante nodded his agreement with Papa Gino's decision.

CHAPTER EIGHTY TWO

Muroc Air Field, California
February 20, 1954

"**WELL,** are you ready for this, Sherm?" Eisenhower asked Sherman Adams, his White House Chief of Staff, as they both stood in the darkness on the deserted back tarmac of the isolated Air Force Base. Chilled to the bone, both men realized it wasn't the weather that was causing them to shake. It was the realization of what was about to happen.

At the moment, other top administration officials were huddled within close proximity of Eisenhower, including Secretary of State John Foster Dulles, Secretary of Defense Charles Wilson, Attorney General Herbert Brownell, Jr., and Secretary of the Interior Douglas McKay. All were deep in private conversation. The entire scene was the result of months of secret coordination between members of Eisenhower's administration, the American military, and the American intelligence community.

"Are the cameras in place?" Eisenhower asked Secretary Wilson.

"Yes, Mr. President. We have three 16mm cameras using color film set up in three different locations within 25 yards of our current position," Wilson replied. "We've made sure that the cameras have spring-driven motors. We were afraid that electric motors would not function properly in the presence of the aliens."

"Is our group of 'wise men' in place to witness this event?" Eisenhower addressed Adams again.

"Yes, Mr. President," Adams responded. "Doctor Norse, Mr. Light, and Mr. Allen are all present and accounted for. However, Bishop McIntyre is late in arriving."

Dr. Edwin Nourse was the chairman of the Council of Economic Advisers. He was asked to attend to provide his expertise on the economic impact of first contact with extraterrestrials. Mr. Gerald Light was known as a gifted writer and lecturer, and a prominent leader within the Southern California metaphysical community. His presence was requested to test public reaction to the presence of extraterrestrials.

The third member of the "wise men" group was Franklin Winthrop Allen. Allen was an 80-year-old former reporter for the Hearst Newspaper Group who had written a textbook instructing how reporters should cover sensitive Congressional Committee Hearings. His presence was requested to determine how confidentiality could be maintained by the press with knowledge of an extraterrestrial presence on earth.

"Goddamn it," Eisenhower cursed. "How in the hell can the religious guy be late to this incredible event?"

Before Eisenhower could finish his derogatory statement, a black car drove up and parked within 10 yards of the group. Out stepped James Francis McIntyre, the 67-year-old Catholic Archbishop of the Los Angeles diocese. He was dressed in a black suit with his priest's collar. McIntyre's presence was requested to get a reaction of religious leaders to the presence of extraterrestrial life. He walked briskly up to Eisenhower.

"Hello, Mr. President," McIntyre greeted Eisenhower with a handshake. "Thank you for your invitation."

"Good evening, Bishop," Ike replied while shaking McIntyre's hand. "For a moment there, I thought you weren't going to make it."

McIntyre smiled at the sardonic comment. "I hope you don't mind that I invited a Vatican envoy. I thought it was imperative that I do so."

Eisenhower furrowed his brow and glared at the Roman Catholic cleric. He hated surprises, and this was one he didn't see coming.

Before he could voice his distain to McIntyre, another black sedan drove up and parked parallel to the group. Dante, dressed in his black priest suit, emerged from the front passenger-side door.

"Oh hell," Pat Loomis said to another White House aide standing nearby as both watched as Dante moved closer to Eisenhower's group. "Ike's gonna shit bricks when he sees this guy."

"Why? Who's this guy?" the unaware aide asked.

"I'm not sure what his name is. We just call him and the guy who's usually with him the Men in Black," Loomis responded. "This guy can really rile up the president."

Eisenhower shouted his unhappiness with McIntyre when he saw Dante.

"This is the goddamn envoy from the Vatican?" Ike shouted to McIntyre. "This is the best you could do, for Christ's sake?"

"No need for the profanity, Mr. President," McIntyre scolded Eisenhower.

Dante arrived amidst Eisenhower's rancor. "Mr. President, thank you for the invitation," Dante exclaimed while extending his hand toward Ike. "I really didn't expect it." Eisenhower ignored the gesture.

"I guess you were successful in sneaking out here and passing it off as an emergency visit to the dentist," Dante commented smugly. "And it looks like your friends have arrived." Dante pointed down the tarmac.

Hearing that, Eisenhower snapped his head back and gazed out to watch a large opaque flying saucer as it settled quietly on the tarmac a short distance away. A doorway on the side of the craft magically appeared, and a dazzling white light burst from the interior of the craft. Tehlri and another short Grey alien emerged from the blinding white light and began their approach down the tarmac towards Eisenhower. From a distance, it looked like they were walking quickly. As they neared Eisenhower, it was discovered that the alien visitors were floating above the ground.

Confusion and terror gripped the area at the initial sight of the extraterrestrials. A group of armed military police started walking swiftly towards the two short figures, but Eisenhower motioned for them to stop. Secretary McKay vomited, while AG Brownell got lightheaded, and sunk to his knees. The mechanical humming sound of the three 16mm cameras in the distance indicated that the film crews had turned on their devices as the craft descended to the ground.

Dante spoke to Eisenhower. "I strongly warn you not to do what you're planning," he stated firmly.

"Stay the hell out of this, Father," Ike snapped. "That's what's best for you." Eisenhower spun around and walked to meet the two alien ambassadors.

Dante moved to where McIntyre was standing. "Do you think he's going to do it?" Dante asked McIntyre. McIntyre shrugged his shoulders without answering.

While pandemonium reigned on the tarmac, covert activity was taking place in two locations nearby. The pope's secret plan to film the clandestine meeting between Eisenhower and the extraterrestrial visitors had begun. Pius didn't trust U.S. intelligence to provide copies of the exact footage their cameras were collecting.

"Loogie, you got that thing turned on?" Wolff asked his diminutive companion while both huddled behind the darkened windows in the back seat of Dante's sedan. "Is that camera working?"

Loogie cracked the back window slightly as he pointed his hand-held 16mm camera in the direction of Eisenhower and the aliens. "Yes, I've got it working," Loogie whispered to Wolff. "Everything's under control." In the front driver's seat, Ferrelli remained motionless.

One hundred yards away to the east, Jimmy Mac parked his car behind a grove of trees located off the narrow dirt access road that circled around the base, and he and George quickly unloaded their camera equipment. Hidden perfectly by tall California jubatagrass plants, Ramirez adjusted the zoom lens on his 16mm camera while Jimmy Mac tightened the screws on the legs of the tripod.

"Are you picking everything up, Georgie?" Jimmy asked. "Make sure you get some good footage of that saucer and of those two little uglies. The pope really stressed that when he talked to us before we left Rome."

"I've got the little bastards and Eisenhower squarely in my focus, Jimmy," Ramirez responded. "I hope Loogie is getting some good footage from the back seat. It's got to be tense for him and Wolff since they're right in the middle of the action and they have to remain invisible to everyone at that location."

The encounter between Eisenhower and Tehlri lasted less than 15 minutes. Cameras picked up Eisenhower's mouth movements when he spoke, but no audio was heard on film. There was no discernable movement of any kind from the aliens on film. Communication was via telepathy, as Eisenhower had told his inner circle. At the end, all recording cameras witnessed what they perceived as Eisenhower and Tehlri making a gesture similar to shaking hands.

Within seconds of the conclusion of the bizarre encounter, Dante had separated himself from McIntyre's company and jumped in the front seat of the sedan. Ferrelli expertly guided the car away silently from the chaotic scene.

Jimmy Mac and Ramirez left their hidden location a few minutes after Dante. Ramirez was burdened with the responsibility of filming the aliens as they returned to their ship, and filming the ship as it rose and disappeared instantaneously into the dark moonless sky.

Both teams rendezvoused at the private Palm Springs airport thirty minutes later, stowed their valuable gear, and boarded the Vatican plane for the trip back to Rome.

"We've got a hell of a story to tell His Excellency when we get back," Loogie announced excitedly.

As everyone settled into their comfortable seats, Dante remarked, "And I have a feeling it's only the beginning of the story."

CHAPTER EIGHTY THREE

Florissant, Missouri
August, 1918

"JESUS CHRIST, where in the HELL is this fucking place?" Paul Dante asked himself for the hundredth time. He was now entering his eleventh hour of a lonesome and boring drive from his home in Omaha, Nebraska, to Saint Stanislaus Society of Jesus seminary in Florissant, Missouri. He had departed Omaha at sun-up, knowing the trip would take him at least to sundown to complete, which would make it almost 16 hours on the road.

He figured he was presently about 50 miles from St. Louis. When he arrived in downtown St. Louis, he would need to get directions to Howdershell Road, and then travel another 20 miles northwest to finally reach his destination. *"What in the hell did I sign up for?"* Dante again queried himself, second-guessing why he was going to make his post-war career a religious one.

Dante was feeling sorry for himself at the moment. The long trip was finally taking its toll on the young war hero, as each mile seemed to take forever to traverse. The August heat in the Midwest was the hottest at this time of year. And it didn't help matters that the scenery along the way looked the same to him. Along the north-south Capital Route from Omaha to Kansas City, Missouri, there was nothing but farmland and a few small towns along the way. Once in Kansas City, he had to catch the east-west Ozark Trail to continue his journey to St. Louis. For countless hours, he saw only farmland, grazing cattle, wayward cattle, lost and wayward sheep, barking dogs, a few wandering skunks, corn fields, bean fields, hard-working farmers and their families doing chores, and a few cars and horse and buggies going in the opposite direction.

He did enjoy stopping in small towns to eat and show off his brand new 1918 apple-red Chevrolet Series FA Roadster, a gift from some Omaha businessmen that was secretly arranged by the archdiocese of Omaha. He was proud of the nice comments he received on the two-door, closed body auto while gassing up at the town filling stations. And he liked talking about the car to the attendant at the gas pump.

"Chevy really made a nice car here. Did you know lengthening the stroke of the four-cylinder engine enlarged its displacement to 224 cubic inches," Dante proudly told the uninterested attendant. "This little adjustment boosted horsepower to 37. Wow!" Dante's knowledge of new cars was legendary in his old neighborhood. Of all the classes he took at South High School during his abbreviated two-year stay before forging his mom's signature to enlist in the Marines at the end of his sophomore year, the car shop class was his favorite. And Mr. Caffrey, the shop teacher, was his favorite teacher.

Between necessary stops for gas, food, and rest, Dante had plenty of time during his long trip to recall how his life had progressed to its present state. And it seemed like all the important conversations were with his mother. The first critical incident was telling his mom that he had enlisted in the Marines on his 16th birthday.

"Son of a bitch, Paul, you did WHAT?" Jo (Josephine) Dante had blurted out. "Did you say you enlisted in the Marines? Why would you do that? How in the hell DID you do that? You need a parent signature. And since your father has been lying peacefully in his grave for the past five years, I'm the only parent who can sign for you. What did you do, forge my signature, you sneaky little shit?"

Jo Dante could swear with the best of them. She was old school, having made the long trip from northern Italy to America with her young husband, Leo, when they were barely out of their teens. The marriage, "made in heaven" as she used to tell her three young children, was the foundation for their happy family life up to the day that Leo was freakishly kicked in the chest by a cow while inspecting a herd at the Omaha Stockyards as a part of his job for his commission company. Within minutes, the virile, handsome, and healthy 40-year-old man had collapsed in the cattle pen, and died. A subsequent autopsy indicated that the kick had ruptured a heart vessel, causing a massive heart attack. The sudden death of the well-liked family man known for his sense of humor sent shockwaves through businesses and homes in the compact community.

Paul, barely 11 at the time, remembered the funeral at his parish church, St. Francis of Assisi. The pastor of the church, Reverend Michael Gluba, had only arrived at the small parish a year before. Paul recalled Father Gluba stating that Leo Dante's funeral mass was the most heavily attended that he had ever conducted. Hundreds of family members, relatives, friends, and co-workers from the Yards filled every pew and spilled outside the quaint South Omaha Catholic Church.

Although the neighborhood was made up of predominantly Polish-speaking immigrants, there were several families of Irish, Italian, Greek, German, and Mexican ancestry living among them. It was a tight-knit community where neighborhood spirit matched ancestral pride. No sooner had Leo Dante been laid in his grave at St. Mary's Cemetery than Josephine Dante quickly added a patriarchal approach to her matriarchal leadership role. And a patriarchal approach meant cussing up a storm when she wanted to make a point.

"Tell me again what you just told me," Jo Dante ordered her 16-year-old son as both of them stood in the small, sun-soaked kitchen. "I want to make sure I have all the facts before I knock the holy hell out of you."

"Ma, I'm sorry, but it was time for me to step up and act like the man of the family, which I became after Dad died," Paul Dante began his story. "Ever since Dad died, you and Margie have been running my life for me. When Dad died, his dream for me to attend Creighton High School disappeared because your savings barely paid for the funeral. We couldn't afford for me to attend Creighton.

"Even though I got into South High, I felt I was letting everyone down. So I thought the only way to make some money for the family would be to enlist, and I'd send the money home to you and Margie and Patrick. My heart was in the right place, Ma." He bowed his head, took a step backward, and steadied himself for the verbal onslaught and head slap that he was positive was going to follow.

"God damn it, Paul. You may have thought your heart was in the right place, but your head sure as hell wasn't," the immensely-upset mother began her tirade. "You're too young and scrawny to enlist. I just need to go talk to that dumbshit Marine recruiter, and I can nip this little piss-ass stunt of yours in the bud. Plus, me and your older sister and younger brother don't want to get word that you've been killed in action overseas somewhere. We couldn't handle another death." She took a deep breath before continuing her tirade.

"I'm upset because it was a very selfish thing to do, Paul. You obviously were never thinking about your family's feelings when you did this. What's the name of that dumbshit Marine who allowed you to sign up? And when did you get this asinine idea in your head, anyway?"

Dante held his composure while listening to his mother's emotional rant. He didn't feel he was being selfish at all. He thought he was doing the right thing to help out his financially-strapped family. But it was time to continue his side of the story.

"Sergeant Gomez is not a dumbshit Marine, Ma. He's a nice guy." Dante rebutted. "On my way home from South, I'd walk past the Marine recruiting office on the corner of 24th & L. I'd usually wave to Sergeant Gomez, but just kept walking. Then a couple weeks ago, he waved me inside, and we started talking. We just talked about things. Nothing about signing up or anything like that.

"Then one day he asked me how old I was. I lied, and told him I just turned 18. He said I was eligible to sign up, but that I'd need a parent's signature. He told me how the Marines would make me a man, and he said I could pick the job I wanted to do. He told me he could get me ranked as an E-2 Private First Class instead of just an E-1 Private when I enlisted. He told me how much money I could make. Plus, he said the government would help pay for any schooling or job training I wanted after I was honorably discharged." Paul felt confidence building inside him as he continued his story.

"I told him I wanted to be a sniper since Dad had taught me how to shoot. I wanted to make Dad proud. And I wanted to make you proud. I got tired of hearing the neighbors talking behind my back that I wasn't doing my part as the man of the family after Dad died. This was the way I wanted to take care of things. So I took the papers home with me, signed your name to them, and gave them back to Sergeant Gomez." Now he was starting to feel remorseful.

"Please don't embarrass me by taking me out after I've already signed on. I want to do this, Ma. I can do this, and I won't get killed. I promise. I need to do this."

Paul remembered the conversation like it was yesterday. He remembered his Mom sat down at the kitchen table after he concluded his remarks, and buried her face in her hands and sobbed lightly. Paul remembered sitting down at the small red table directly across from his mother, and fighting to hold back the tears that were forming in his eyes.

At the sound of their mother's rising profanity-laced voice, 18-year-old Margie and 13-year-old Patrick crept silently to the edge of the doorway separating the living room and dining room. The two siblings huddled nervously just out of the line of sight from their position and the kitchen. Both knew what the argument was about as Paul had told them a day before, but had sworn them to secrecy so he could tell his mother first. Both were ready to jump to Paul's defense if Jo made the final decision to rectify her forged signature that Paul had skillfully placed on the enlistment form, and rescind Paul's enlistment. But, to their surprise, it didn't come to that.

With a sudden movement, Jo Dante got up from the table, and dabbed her eyes with the dish towel she still held tightly in her right hand. She slowly walked around the table and stopped directly in front of her son. "Get up, Paul," she ordered.

Feeling very nervous, Paul slowly rose from his seat. By the time he stood fully erect, his mother had thrown her arms around his shoulders, held him tightly for a long time, and, finally, kissed him gently on the top of his head. Pulling away slowly, she cradled Paul's face in her hands while saying, "Alright, Paul. If this is what you want to do, you have my blessing. But so help me God, if you do make it back in one piece, you will do what I tell you to do. Is that clear?" Paul nodded in agreement, while Margie and Patrick raced into the room and embraced their brother. He left for boot camp two days later, and to Europe two months after that.

For the past twenty miles, a stiff southern breeze had been blowing through Dante's windows as he made his way to St. Louis. As it was getting later in the afternoon, the breeze seemed to calm itself as the sun was slowly plummeting toward the western horizon. He did notice some thunderheads in the distance.

The next mental image to find its way into Dante's mind was his glorious return from Europe with his Distinguished Service Cross award. He was just happy to be home. He was not ready for the reception he received from the city upon his return to Omaha just a couple months ago.

He first remembered that upon his return to the States a week before his trip to Omaha, he had a private lunch meeting with Nebraska Democratic Senator Gilbert Hitchcock, who congratulated him on his honor, and thanked him for his service to his country. He was then flown by the Marines to Chicago, where he was honorably discharged with a bump in rank to an E-7 Gunnery Sergeant in a formal ceremony. Then, per Dante's request, he was given a train ticket to Omaha. He wanted the 10-hour trip to relax and gather his thoughts before he reached home.

Paul fondly remembered stepping off the Chicago, Burlington, and Quincy Railroad car at the Burlington Train Station in downtown Omaha wearing his dress blues on that late May afternoon. What first caught his attention wasn't what he saw, but what he heard. A small high school band that was wearing the identifying colors of South High School was standing on the railroad platform about 20 feet away playing a rousing John Phillip Sousa march. He then quickly spotted his mother, brother and sister running feverishly toward him, arms outstretched and wide smiles on their faces. When all four bodies met, Paul needed to steady himself as the momentum of the familial collision almost caused him to tumble to the ground.

After lots of hugs and kisses from his family, Paul noticed another group of individuals that he did not recognize. But from the looks on their faces, they seemed to recognize him. Upon closer inspection, Paul noticed that a couple of older men not wearing business attire were wearing priestly apparel.

"Mom, who are these people coming towards us?" Paul inquired. "I recognize two of them as priests, but I don't recognize the other guy."

"Paul, dear, the taller priest is our new archbishop, Jeremiah James Harty. He was named the new bishop of the Omaha diocese right after you left for boot camp. I don't know who the other priest is with him.

"The gentleman in the blue suit behind the bishop is our new mayor, Edward Parsons Smith. He was elected just a few weeks ago. Both of them are eager to talk with you."

Turning back to face Paul, Jo Dante couldn't contain her pride in her oldest son. "Oh, honey, we are so proud of you," his mother exclaimed, the smile on her face showing how happy she was to see her son return home in a healthy condition.

"Are you fully healed from your gunshot wound? We all were so afraid when Sergeant Gomez came to our house to tell us you had been wounded in battle in France. But he said you were healing up just fine. And then he told us about the Distinguished Service Cross award you received for your bravery. He wanted to tell us before we read about it in the paper. You were right. Sergeant Gomez is a fine man."

She gave him another kiss on his forehead as Paul became aware of the presence of the photographer from the Omaha newspaper, snapping his pictures in rapid-fire execution. The young female reporter accompanying the photographer was standing close by, pen and pad in hand, ready to ask questions. But she first waited to hear the welcoming speeches from the two local politicians, one representing the physical plane and one representing the spiritual plane.

When the two Omaha dignitaries completed their short walk along the train platform from the band's location to where Paul stood with his family, it was the man from the secular world that spoke first.

"Paul Dante, on behalf of the citizens of Omaha, I want to welcome you home and congratulate you on your tremendous honor that has surely captivated and energized our community," Smith bellowed as he grabbed Paul's right hand and gave it a long and vigorous shake. "I want to tell you that this city is so excited and proud to receive back one of its own war heroes.

"We have a lot of public events planned for you, young man. Tomorrow morning, you will be the guest of honor in a ticker-tape parade around South Omaha. Then after the parade, you will be taken to Aksarben where a lunch reception in your honor will take place, and I will present you with a symbolic key to the city." The beaming mayor concluded his remarks.

"Again, welcome home, Paul. Archbishop Harty here wants to welcome you, too. So get a good night's sleep because tomorrow is going to be a busy day for you." Smith again shook Paul's hand, and then gracefully backed away as Bishop Harty moved to the front of the congratulatory line.

The 65-year-old archbishop slowly made his way to meet the young American warrior. The Irish prelate had just completed two years ago a 13-year term as Archbishop of Manila in the Philippines. Following Manila, and knowing he was nearing retirement age, he had sent word to Rome to request that he complete his administrative duties in his hometown of St. Louis, Missouri.

The Vatican did move him 7916 miles to the middle of America. But it was to Omaha, Nebraska. Harty knew this would be his last administrative assignment. And even though it wasn't to his beloved St. Louis, he welcomed his new assignment in Omaha. And he truly enjoyed talking with young war heroes who may be persuaded to join the religious life.

Extending his right arm to continue the manly ritual of shaking the hand of the young war hero, the archbishop began his words of welcome with gusto. "Gunnery Sergeant Dante. That is your Marine rank, is it not, sir?" Harty asked. Paul nodded affirmatively, and gave the religious leader a firm handshake.

"Son, I also bring you greetings, not only from the Roman Catholic population of Omaha, but from the Holy Father in Vatican City," Harty exclaimed. "When I relayed the information to him that one of the sheep in my flock was returning home from the war as a Distinguished Service Cross recipient, His Holiness directed me to tell you of his happiness for your health and good fortune. He proclaimed that you are living proof that God looks most favorably upon those who bear the cross of the Catholic faith."

It was obvious to Paul that Archbishop Harty considered himself an insider when it came to his relationship with the Pope. How else could Paul receive a special welcome from the Holy Father if Harty didn't have a close relationship with Pope Benedict XV?

After giving Paul the official Papal welcome, Harty put his left arm around Dante's shoulders and motioned with his right hand that the two of them should take a walk to guarantee the privacy of the next conversation. Jo Dante had a look of excitement as the two distanced themselves from the crowd. About 30 feet down the long wooden platform, the two stopped their walk. Harty removed his arm from Paul's shoulder, took a step back, and began to speak softly to the young Marine.

"Thank you, my son, for allowing me to have this private conversation with you. Your mother did not want me to bring this to public attention."

Before Harty could utter another word, Dante quickly interjected. "Wait a minute, Archbishop. Are you telling me that you already had this conversation with my mother?"

Paul felt the anger rising within him. *Goddamn it. This feels like a shitfaced set-up, if I ever heard one.* Harty quickly noticed the discomfort invading Paul's body language, so he hurriedly replied.

"Yes, Paul, I have previously had this conversation with your mother. We had it last week. In fact, both your brother and sister listened in. It's not a bad thing, by any means. May I proceed?" the stoic churchman asked.

"Sure. Sure, sir. I mean archbishop. Since you already talked to my family, I felt a little set-up here. Like I didn't have any say in what you're going to tell me. I don't like it when I can't control the situation. I guess I got that from the war." Feeling humbled and embarrassed, Dante quickly gave his full attention to the message from the archbishop.

"Thank you." Harty replied. "I really have two rather ambitious items to discuss. And you will benefit from both topics, I'm sure of it.

"The first thing I want to discuss with you is a conversation I had a few weeks ago with Alexander Burrowes, the provincial superior for the Jesuit order in St. Louis. Are you familiar with his name?" Harty waited for a reply.

"Yes, I vaguely remember that name. It was told to me by an Army chaplain who visited me in the hospital in France. Matter of fact, it was the same day that General Pershing gave me and another soldier at the hospital the Distinguished Service Cross. I think that chaplain's name was Duffy. Francis Duffy. Quite a talker, I remember that," Dante responded.

"You are correct. The chaplain's name was, indeed, Frank Duffy. And the story goes that after Duffy left you that afternoon, he sent a Western Union telegram to Al Burrowes informing him that he had spoken with a young wounded soldier from Omaha who had just been presented with a Distinguished Service Cross who would make a perfect candidate to join the Jesuit order."

Dante laughed loudly. "Oh, did he now?" Paul stated. "How did he come to that conclusion?"

Harty continued with his story. "Well, he came to that conclusion from a number of factors. One factor was that you were wearing a St. Ignatius medal around your neck. Duffy said that you called it your lucky charm because it saved you from a German attack." Paul felt a tinge of embarrassment.

"The second factor was your fascination with Jesuit life and the many questions that you posed to Father Duffy while he was giving you the story of Ignatius of Loyola. Duffy thought you possessed great insight into religious life. He especially enjoyed your comment that you classified yourself more superstitious than religious. But most of all, he was impressed with your leadership characteristics. And the first quality that the Society looks for in its candidates is leadership instincts." Paul felt honored by the compliment.

"In any case, Duffy was impressed enough to put your name into nomination to enter the Society of Jesus. Burrowes agreed with Duffy's recommendation, and I am happy to inform you that Provincial Superior Burrowes eagerly awaits your response to his invitation."

All of a sudden, Paul Dante felt a chill of panic run up his spine, and it made his body shudder for an instant. It wasn't the invitation that scared him. It was the realization that he needed to respond to the invitation. And then he thought of his mother and brother and sister.

"I'm certainly flattered by all the fuss that people have gone to to welcome me home," Paul said. "And I'm truly humbled by the invitation from Father Burrowes. But I want to take some time to weigh all the different options that I will have presented to me before I make a final decision. I'll give the Jesuit invitation some thought. But I can't give you an answer now. I hope you can respect my wishes on this. By the way, what did my family have to say about it?"

Harty was quick to reply. "I must say, your mother was thrilled when she heard of the invitation. She wants you to live a life free from danger, and one that you can serve mankind. And what life is safer and more helpful to mankind than a life in a religious order. And what mother doesn't want to have a priest in the family?" He smiled while delivering his last comment.

"And what about my brother and sister? What did they say?" Dante inquired.

"Both of them were rather quiet to begin with," Harty stated. "They didn't want to see you leave again so soon. They want you to stay around for a while longer. But both of them said they would back you up no matter what decision you made regarding your post-war career."

Dante wanted to leave the Jesuit invitation topic as quickly as possible, so he jumped at the chance to ask about the second topic of discussion.

"Archbishop Harty, what is the second thing you wanted to discuss with me?" Paul asked.

The elderly man seemed to gain new energy with the new inquiry, and his eyes started to sparkle. He took a deep breath, dusted off some imaginary flecks of lint on his priestly garb, and once again put his arm around Dante's shoulder. Only this time, it wasn't to walk again. This time it was to whisper into Paul's ear.

"Well, my son, I think you're really going to enjoy this news," he said with a widening smile on his face. He once again removed the arm from Paul's shoulder. But this time, he latched onto both of Dante's arms with a tightening grip, pinning them to Paul's sides.

"Uh, Archbishop Harty, your point is taken," Dante responded. "You can release the death grip on my arms now." Dante smiled, while Harty's eyes displayed shock and embarrassment at Paul's comments. He quickly released his grip.

"Oh my. I am so sorry, dear fellow. I guess my enthusiasm got away from me for a second there." Harty straightened his posture and cleared his throat with a quick cough. Dante pursed his lips, gave the Catholic leader an inquisitive look, and waited for the information that Harty seemed overwhelmed to deliver.

"Paul, you know the auto that you will be riding in for the parade around the city tomorrow is a brand new Chevrolet Roadster. It is quite attractive," Harty stated.

Dante raised his eyebrows and nodded. "That's very nice. I didn't know how that parade deal was going to work. So a new Chevy, huh? Well, that's great. Thanks for telling me." With that, Paul began to walk away from the elder churchman.

"Oh, Gunnery Sergeant. I am not finished with my message," Harty interjected as he extended his arm to stop Paul's departure. "There's more to tell you."

Dante quickly stopped, and turned his attention back to the archbishop. "Oh, sorry about that. I thought that was the end of the story. I apologize. Please continue."

"There is more to the Vatican's wishes for your health and good fortune," Harty exclaimed. "His Holiness also directed me to procure a welcoming gift for you. He left it up to me to decide how to make the appropriate choice." Harty became more animated with his hands.

"When I was informed by Mayor Smith of the parade, I asked him how you were going to be transported. He told me that someone in his office was going to contact Henry Gering, the president of the United States Carburetor Company in Omaha, and ask him to supply the car. Since Gering's company works closely with the auto industry, he procured the Chevy Roadster to be used just for the parade.

"I then took the liberty to contact the successful owners of the four breweries in Omaha. That would be Krug, Storz, Willow Springs, and Metz. Since the citizens of Omaha have been very supportive of their products over the years, I thought it would be a nice gesture for them to give back to one of their own. When I told them it would be given to the local war hero, they were eager to participate. So as a personal favor to me, I asked them if all four could contribute to the purchase of the parade vehicle. They quickly agreed to pay the $1,475 sticker price.

"So, my dear boy, at the conclusion of the parade tomorrow, your riding vehicle will become yours to keep permanently, as a gift not only from the Vatican, but from the business leaders of the city. I hope you will accept this symbol of the generosity shown to you by the Omaha community and the Vatican hierarchy." He stepped back to gauge Paul's response.

Paul was absolutely dumbfounded when Archbishop Harty finished his message. The look on his face told the story to everyone in attendance at the train station that day. His exuberance was overshadowed only by his "jumping for joy" at the news. The sight of watching Dante spring into the air with arms outstretched and yelling "All right!" at the top of his lungs was eventful, especially for Jo Dante. *See*, she thought to herself, *I knew Paul would be thrilled when Archbishop Harty told him about the Jesuit offer.*

A steady rain began to fall as Dante passed an Ozark Trail obelisk telling him that he was 16 miles from St. Louis. Even though the roadway was little more than a rutted dirt path that allowed passage for a single vehicle in either direction, the Ozark Trail Association in 1913 had begun an aggressive public campaign to improve the road infrastructure along this major east-west route. It was the idea of the founder of the association, William Hope "Coin" Harvey, to build cement obelisk-shaped markers to assist travelers. Dante was thankful of the progressive thinking of a volunteer organization to improve travel conditions in the Midwest. He had passed a similar structure about 75 miles back.

With the weather-proof roof already in place, Dante decided to pull his new car to the side of the road in order to close his side curtains with the Bair brackets so that the rain wouldn't harm the interior made up of mahogany woodwork and French-pleated leather upholstery. The future Jesuit couldn't believe his luck with the cushy ride his red Chevy provided. The eight-cylinder and valve-in-head engine was revolutionary for its time, and the entire foundation was made of pressed steel. Chrome Vanadium heat-treated steel gear shafts that ran on Hyatt roller bearings along with the self-lubricating clutch collar allowed the three-speeds-forward and reverse-type transmission to operate noiselessly as he drove.

The starter switch was located on the toe board, which was conveniently located next to his accelerator pedal on the floor. The dash board instrument panel included an ammeter, electrically-lighted oil pressure gauge and speedometer. When it got dark, he knew his two 16-candle-power headlamps and four-candle-power dimmers would sufficiently light his way. While out of the car, he made a quick check on the quantity gauge of the 20-gallon gas tank located at the rear of the car, and felt confident he could make it to St. Louis on what gas was left in the tank.

The demountable 34-inch Goodyear non-skid tires with the external contracting service brakes and the internal expanding emergency brakes made his trip as comfortable and safe as a 16-hour trip could be. Even though the cruising speed by design for the Roadster was well over 60 miles per hour, Dante rarely attained a speed of 40. Because of road and weather conditions, he was content to stay in the 25-35 mile per hour range.

When he got back into the car five minutes later, he grabbed the 17-inch steering wheel and engaged the wipers on the nickel-plated windshield to clear his view of the road. He figured he had about three hours of daylight left, and he wanted to be at his destination before darkness fell on his journey. He took the final bite of his country ham sandwich that had been lying idly on the passenger-side seat that he had bought during his last stop for gasoline.

With the constant rain and challenging road conditions, Dante didn't do any more reminiscing the final 16 miles to St. Louis, forcing himself to concentrate on his driving skills so that he didn't slide off into a deep roadside culvert.

Arriving on the western edge of the city around 6:15 in the evening, he drove into the first filling station he saw. This station, owned by the Automobile Gasoline Company, had two gasoline pumps open for use, a rare sight since every station on the trip so far had only one pump. Dante parked next to a pump, got out of the car, watched as the attendant filled his tank, and then he followed the attendant into the wooden building to pay his five-dollar bill. He also asked the grizzled, middle-aged attendant behind the counter wearing a St. Louis Browns cap for directions to St. Stanislaus Seminary in Florissant.

"Headin' up to the priest farm, are ya?" the bearded man asked. "Hell, they're up there all by theirselves all the time. Some crazy sons-a-bitches live up there, too, you know. Do some really weird shit, too. You're pretty young, so you better watch out for yourself." The old man gave Dante a long stare and a head nod to strengthen the importance of his message before he took another swig from his half-empty whiskey bottle.

"Weird shit? Like what?" Dante asked.

"I mean grown men huggin' and kissin' and feelin' each other up. Weird shit like that. Didn't know that was part of becoming a priest. Did you?" The old man waited for an answer.

Paul gave the man an inquisitive look and said, "Who told you this stuff anyway?"

"It's just common knowledge in these parts," the accusatory man replied, his words beginning to slur. "These stories been around as long as the seminary's been up there. Over 100 years now. Supposedly some of those missionaries that started the place used to do things to those little Injun' boys they were teachin'. No proof. Just stories that have been passed down from generation to generation." The man took Dante's money and put it into the old crank-handle cash register.

Paul did his best to conceal his widening grin. "Well, sir, thanks for the warnin'. I'll make sure that nobody's huggin', kissin', or feelin' me up while I'm there learnin' to become a priest." He thought mimicking the man's speech pattern would have a bonding effect with him. He was wrong.

"You're a cocky little shit comin' in here with yur big fancy car and makin' fun of what I'm tellin' ya." The angry old man wasn't slurring his words anymore. "Seems to be that bein' cocky is what they want up there, I guess. So you'll fit in just fine, asshole."

Before Dante could apologize, the offended attendant screamed some abbreviated directions to Howdershell Road and told him to get his scrawny ass out of his station. Paul darted from the building, quickly started his car, pointed it northwest, and zipped out of the station, not looking back.

After a few tense miles, Paul finally began to relax. He first chided himself for acting "un-Christian-like" with the old man. But then he exploded with laughter at the unbelievable tale spun by the liquored-up proprietor. *That guy was so full of shit*, Dante told himself.

By the time Paul had fled the tirade of the old geezer, the rain had stopped falling and daylight was waning. Dante's route was taking him directly into the setting sun. Lucky for him, the route was completely lined with tall, majestic-looking oaks, maples, walnuts, and cottonwoods that allowed only fleeting bursts of sunlight to escape through the camouflaged branches. Even though he could easily see the narrowing roadway in front of him, the sky was turning an orange-blue, and dusk was less than an hour away. As he was getting closer to his destination, he couldn't help but think back to the last conversation with his mother that set this God-forsaken journey into motion.

"Goddammit, Paul, we've been over this a million times. Don't give me any more lip about this. It's a done deal," Jo Dante yelled. "You promised me before you trudged off to war, illegally, I may add, that you would do what I said when you got back home. I'm holding you to your promise. You can't go back on your promise. I didn't raise you to not live up to your promises," Jo Dante preached, making sure she pounded in feelings of guilt into her rebellious son.

"Geez, Ma, I've got better offers than becoming a priest. Mr. Dennison said I could work for his trucking company. And Mr. O'Malley said I could work for him at the Yards for Interstate Commission Company. They're both, you know, safe jobs," Dante pleaded.

"Oh, no, you won't, young man. Dennison is nothing but a crook, and I don't want you anywhere near the stockyards. The stockyards killed your father. It'll kill you, too," Jo countered, her agitation building with the level of her son's insolence.

"But it takes 13 years to become a Jesuit. That's way too long to be studying for something. Plus, you don't get paid anything. I won't be able to help you out at all," Paul replied, grasping on to the "no money" excuse to wear his mother down. He knew how important money was to her.

"Money is not an issue anymore, Paul, so you can just put a lid on that crap," Jo Dante countered. "When you got that promotion to Gunnery Sergeant before you were discharged, the pension benefits on that, along with the small retirement savings your father had set up at work, will take care of your brother, sister, and me. Plus, my new job cooking for the Archbishop now will help some, too." Jo Dante took a step closer to her oldest son's face.

"So no more whining, you hear me? You get your ass over to the Archbishop and tell him you graciously accept the invitation. You tell him that you'll become the best Jesuit that ever came out of Omaha." She wasn't done emasculating her son.

"You're doing this, Paul. Not just to make me and your father, *rest his soul*, proud. But Margie and Patrick will be proud of you, too. Don't you want to make your brother and sister proud of you?" Jo ended her lecture with her favorite guilt-inducing argument, the kids. She knew how Paul adored his sister, and that he would never willingly let his little brother down.

Both siblings had pledged their loyalty and support to Paul during the mother-led, one-sided family discussion of the invitation from St. Louis. They said they would be sorry to see him leave so soon, and the time commitment would be so extraordinarily long. But they would see him during breaks and over the holidays. Plus, they thought that having a priest in the family guaranteed the entire family eternal salvation in heaven when they died.

Paul remembered being exasperated after the "discussion" ended. He may be a war hero and the man of the house, he thought, but he was still only 18-years-old, and he really felt compelled to keep his promise to his mom. *Mom does a good job of making you feel guilty*, Paul thought. But he wasn't going down without a fight either, he told himself.

As soon as Paul told Archbishop Harty that he accepted the Jesuit invitation, things started to move at lightning speed. Paul needed to provide proof of two things to Provincial Superior Burrowes. He needed to have a medical release indicating that he was in good health. Burrowes told Dante he would accept the results of his physical when he entered the Marines.

The second prerequisite to enter the Society of Jesus was a high school diploma. Dante realized there was no way of getting around this requirement as he did with the physical. But Harty came to his rescue.

"Paul, by waiting until the middle of July to declare your intentions, you will need to work hard to meet the educational requirement before you report to St. Stanislaus Seminary in August," Harty stated. "But let me see what I can do to expedite the process for you."

Within days, Dante received a letter from the office of the superintendent of the Omaha Public School system, informing him that he needed to report to the principal's office at South High School in one week to complete a general education equivalency test. With a passing grade, the letter indicated that Dante would receive his high school diploma.

The letter specified that the superintendent, John H. Beveridge, had received a personal request from Archbishop Harty asking for help in assisting Dante to meet the educational requirements for acceptance into the Jesuit order. Beveridge said that he was fully aware of Dante's status within the community, and that the school district would do what it could to assist him. Beveridge also stated that Dante was among a group of former soldiers from Omaha who had returned from World War I, and were interested in earning a high school diploma.

Beveridge told him that the test would include questions on reading, writing, social studies, science, and mathematics. He also gave Paul a list of teachers with whom Dante could contact to help prepare for the test. Paul chose Mr. Gerry Caffrey, his favorite shop teacher, to assist him. Caffrey spent one hour each day up to test day quizzing and teaching Paul on the test subject matter. At the end, Caffrey chuckled and wished him luck, expressing his doubt that he had assisted Paul in any way. Dante felt overwhelmed with information.

Dante remembered the special written test he had to pass just to get into South High School. This general equivalency test seemed much more difficult to him, especially the science questions. *Well, it should be harder. It's to graduate*, he surmised. He was given three hours to complete the test. His test administrator, Miss Bevins, the guidance counselor, gave him a five-minute break half-way through the test. Dante was the only person in the principal's office taking the test that day. With the door closed and no windows in the office, the temperature easily reached 100 degrees that July afternoon. Paul was sweating for several reasons.

He vividly recalled not finishing any sections of the test. He asked Miss Bevins for clarification of some questions at least twice for each subject being tested. She gave him very minimal assistance, telling him that was the best she could do. Miss Bevins timed each section and yelled "Stop" when the allotted time had passed. When she yelled "Stop" for the fifth and final time, Dante had a sinking feeling in his chest.

Bevins smiled at Paul as she collected the final section answer sheet from the former student. "How do you think you did on the test, Paul?" Bevins asked.

"Ah, Miss Bevins, I don't think I did very well at all," Dante answered. "You saw my answer sheet for each section. I never finished all the questions for any of them." Dante was wiping the sweat from his brow as he spoke.

Bevins gave Paul a small smile and wink. "Don't fret too much over this, Paul," she stated. "This test is relatively new, so the grading on it will be a little different than for a regular test. Plus, you only have to get a little over half of the answers correct in order to pass. I think you'll do just fine."

As Paul rose from the desk and began to leave the overheated office, Bevins told him that he could expect a letter from Superintendent Beveridge within a week informing him whether or not the scores were good enough to earn the diploma. He thanked her, and waved as he left the brain-draining room.

Miss Bevins was wrong. It took only three days for the letter to arrive. But along with the letter came another package. When Dante opened it with his mom, older sister, and younger brother all peering over his shoulder, he discovered that it was something enclosed in a frame. Upon closer examination, Dante realized that it was a high school diploma with his name on it.

With his heart pounding and a huge smile on his face, Paul lifted the accompanying letter from the envelope, and read it to his family.

"Dear Paul:

Congratulations on meeting and exceeding the minimum requirements on the Graduate Equivalency Test of the Omaha Public Schools. As a result of your scores, I am proud to inform you that you are now officially a graduate of Omaha South High School.

Please accept the congratulations of the entire faculty and staff at South High School and the entire office staff of the Superintendent of Schools. As a gift to you, the faculty and staff at South High School encased your diploma in a handsome frame so that you can proudly hang it in the Dante home. I'm sure your family is thrilled with your success.

Again, congratulations on earning your high school diploma, and best of luck on your future career as a Jesuit priest. Please keep all of us in your prayers, and don't hesitate to come visit us here in the Superintendent's Office any time you're in town."

The letter was signed by the Superintendent of Schools, John H. Beveridge.

"Oh, Paul, I am so very proud of you," Jo Dante exclaimed after checking the letter to make sure Paul had actually read what was on the page. "Now you can tell Archbishop Harty that you graduated from high school, and everything should be all set for St. Louis."

Margie and Patrick also gave their sibling congratulatory hugs. Jo Dante easily located the most suitable location for hanging the diploma. It would go on the living room wall right between the picture of the Last Supper of Jesus and his disciples and the special crucifix blessed by the Holy Father himself that Jo Dante had received from her relatives in Italy after Leo's death. *Paul's life will be safe resting between these two religious icons*, Jo told herself.

The descending sun was pricking the sky with brilliant red-orange daggers that were swiftly finding their way below the horizon as Dante spied the last road sign pointing him to the seminary of St. Stanislaus. *God damn, I made it here*, he rejoiced. As the isolated road was still flanked on both sides by the towering rows of leafy trees, Dante decided to turn on the headlights of his Chevy Roadster to help him navigate the final mile to his destination.

As he slowly maneuvered his vehicle down the gutted pathway, the gleam of his headlights caught some movement in the dark trees to his left. As he neared the location that he thought the movement had occurred, he glimpsed two men, one heavier than the other, about 20 feet back from the road, naked from the waist down, lying on the ground on a dark blanket, entwined in passionate kissing and groping. They were oblivious to the sound and sight of Dante's approaching vehicle.

Dante slowed the Chevy to a crawl as he gazed with incredulity at the shocking sight he was now viewing. Nothing in his short lifetime had prepared him for such a sickening spectacle, he thought. Not even the gruesome images of war, with blood and dismembered bodies strewn around him. *Jesus Christ, I think I'm going to barf*, Dante told himself. He also thought that this was something he need not divulge to anyone, lest they think he was delusional. *Who at the seminary would believe me anyway*, he presumed.

As he discreetly passed the scene and slowly increased the speed of his vehicle, he realized that he was still holding his breath from the initial shock of the horrendous encounter. He quickly took a couple deep breaths to resuscitate, and a couple more deep breaths to come to terms with the putrid images still rolling around in his mind.

As his clouded consciousness regained normalcy, he began to notice the dim lights of the seminary entrance a short distance ahead. As his fancy new Chevrolet Roadster was delivering him to a new segment of his life, Paul Dante realized that he should be prepared to face some strange and unexpected situations at this Catholic outpost.

Then he chuckled to himself. *I'll be a son-of-a-bitch. That old bastard at the gas station WAS telling the truth after all.*

Unknown to Paul as he slowly drove toward his new life, the heavyset lover suddenly sensed an unwanted intruder, released the clinching grip on his younger partner, and arose from his prone and compromising position to glare at the tail lights of the shiny red automobile. *There will be hell to pay for this intrusion*, the heavy man declared.

CHAPTER EIGHTY FOUR

Office of the Vatican Intelligence Agency
April 1954

AS the Pope's newly-appointed Director of *Servizio Informazioni del Vaticano* (S.I.V) – Vatican Intelligence Agency – Dante decided to establish his office in a secluded corner in the basement of the Vatican Apostolic Library. He picked this location for one reason: It was only steps away from the entrance to the Secret Archives, the resting spot for all of the *"Eyes Only"* documents, artifacts, and other Top Secret confidential files and materials that the Vatican had procured over a span of 1,800 years. It would also become the resting place for all the reports that his new agency would generate over the next several decades. Quick and easy access to the archives was paramount for Dante and his team.

Geno, Jimmy Mac, George, and Loogie were the backbone of Dante's new S.I.V team. In the near future, though, Dante anticipated that the needs of the agency would dictate that the team split up, with each original team member recruiting and leading their own group and branching out to different parts of the globe. The nature of each mission would dictate the role of each group. Dante clearly understood that this spy business he was embarking on would be both dangerous and addictive.

The time was slowing creeping up on 10:00 P.M., and Dante rested comfortably in his favorite leather chair behind his huge mahogany desk. Much had happened over the past 18 years in his life, he mused. All of the excitement, intrigue, and deadly skirmishes with Nazis, the Illuminati, and American Secret Service agents had prepared him well for this assignment.

Papa Gino had made his life interesting, for sure. And it all started on that cold, misty morning in the Vatican Garden back in the spring of 1936. His Holiness Pius XI had notified his top Vatican confidante, Pacelli, of a heinous crime against the Vatican. To address the crime, Cardinal Pacelli had handpicked his young American Jesuit protégé for an assignment that would culminate with a new department that answered only to the Pope himself.

Archbishop Paul Dante (he smiled to himself about the "new" bump upwards in Church hierarchy the Pontiff gave him with his new S.I.V. position, while the pay remained the same as the first day he arrived as a young seminarian at the Vatican decades ago) sat back in his chair, closed his weary eyes, and recalled the extraordinary information he was given that day from Papa Gino.

The unbelievable story that started the whole adventure: the mandate to locate and return the stolen Nestorian papyrus, the most sensitive Vatican manuscript in the history of man. This story was the reason why Papa Gino bestowed upon him and all those who would work with Dante on future sensitive projects within S.I.V, with the controversial "Secretum Omega", the highest Papal secrecy level within the Vatican. The new wardrobe of all black suits sans the priestly white collar would add to the mystery and confidentiality of the new S.I.V. agents.

But first, the recollection of that bizarre, but true story, from long, long ago…

CHAPTER EIGHTY FIVE

DANTE leaned forward on the brown Vatican Garden stone bench, laid his arms firmly on the top of his black cassock-covered legs, and slowly clasped his hands together as if to pray. The cool early morning air made him shiver slightly. The way the slumping Pacelli was talking to him, however, also made him shudder.

"Papa Gino," Dante stammered, "you have been my mentor, friend, and teacher since I arrived in Rome to continue my studies. I owe you my life many times over. You know I will do whatever you ask of me. You really don't need to tell me this embarrassing information if it makes you feel uncomfortable."

In a calm, but determined voice, Pacelli stated, "Paul, I must tell you this information, regardless of the level of embarrassment and sadness it gives me. You may not think as highly of me or the Church after hearing this, but you will grasp the tremendous importance it has for all of humanity."

Straightening up to listen, Dante responded, "Then, by all means, tell me what I need to know."

With a tenuous tone of voice, Pacelli implored, "This knowledge you must take to the grave with you, Paul." Dante nodded in agreement.

Pacelli began his remarkable, and unbelievable, story.

"During the early years of Christianity after Jesus was no longer around, there was much infighting among the apostles and disciples as to what direction this new religion should take. Peter wished to go his way, whereas Mary Magdalene and James, the brother of Jesus, wanted to take a different approach. Then Paul also became a dominant figure after his sudden conversion to Christianity. But after the assassinations of Peter and Paul around A.D. 67, there was much chaos for the next hundred years." Pacelli continued his extraordinary story.

"Papal leadership was not very strong during those early years. However, the Papacy itself grew in wealth, stature and power worldwide. With this wealth and power came the need to keep secret any historical artifacts that could harm the burgeoning power of the Vatican," Pacelli stated.

"For centuries, the Vatican has been the repository of the world's greatest archeological discoveries. Some of these have been obtained in less than honorable ways. All of these discoveries have been chronicled in meticulous fashion in several secret documents entitled the Pope's Book of Secrets. These secrets are most heavily guarded, and have come with a tremendous price of loss of life and much bloodshed, all in the name of keeping the Pope as the most powerful religious and political figure in the world." Pacelli gained more energy as he spoke.

"As you would imagine, the Vatican has developed a long list of enemies over the centuries whose single purpose is to discredit the Church and Holy Father in any way possible. Those enemies have determined that the best way to accomplish this goal is to gather, steal, and reveal the scientific archeological discoveries of ancient manuscripts containing information damaging to the credibility of the Vatican," Pacelli stated.

"To prevent this from happening, and to justify the use of deadly force, Pope Pius IX, in January of 1852, quietly established the Pontifical Commission for Sacred Archeology. This secret organization within the Vatican was given all the discretion and resources to make sure that any archeological discoveries of magnitude would find its way to Vatican archives only," Pacelli said.

"And since these archives have become so immense over time, it was decided that secret archives would be established in various locations worldwide, such as Istanbul, Cairo, London, and Paris, and with all the necessary security precautions put into place. But it seems that our security in Istanbul has been breached, and a critical file is now missing."

Dante suddenly interrupted Pacelli.

"But Papa Gino, you have told me nothing that will cause me to lose my faith in you or the Church."

Pacelli paused for a second to allow Dante to complete his thought. He then proceeded with his story.

"This is very painful for me." There was yet another long pause. Finally, Pacelli pierced the eerie silence that had overtaken the somber scene.

"We know that Jesus WAS NOT the Son of God," Pacelli blurted out. "He was from a royal bloodline, and was the most highly evolved mystical human being ever created, but he didn't possess any level of divinity. He never professed to have any. He actually argued against it. We, meaning the administrative structure of the Papacy, MADE him into a divine being."

Dante was stunned. "But how can this be?"

Pacelli immediately felt the pain in Dante's voice. However, he could not stop now.

"At the Council of Nicea in A.D. 325, the Roman emperor Constantine, a late convert to Christianity, needed to quiet the infighting among the Catholic bishops regarding the Arian controversy. This controversy, started by a priest named Arius, stated that there were human elements to the Father and the Son in scripture. To put an end to this heretical thinking, a dogma was written, proclaimed, and voted upon by the majority of those bishops in attendance, making the divinity of Jesus a part of canon law within the church. The bishops VOTED Jesus to be divine in nature, something Jesus never proclaimed to possess during his lifetime."

Dante, still reeling from this faith-shattering pronouncement, cried out, "That's unbelievable! Is this the information that the stolen manuscript contains?"

With his eyes cast downward, Pacelli stuttered, "No, but there's more for you to digest."

Pacelli paused again, stood up next to Dante on the bench, and took a deep breath before resuming. Staring straight into Dante's eyes, the Pontiff's chief confidante dropped another bombshell.

"Paul, Jesus was married…to Mary Magdalene. From our archeological discoveries, we know Jesus was brought up in a mystical Essenic community, and Magdalene was his mentor from a young age.

"The Essenes were a very loving, very humane group, with a deep passion and unique knowledge of the biological sciences, astronomy, archeology, metaphysics, and technology. The Essenes also held learned women in high esteem. Mary was one of these very intelligent, very caring individuals with the position of Master Teacher within the community. This story literally had the student falling in love with the teacher.

"Also, you recall the story about the wedding feast at Cana mentioned in the scriptures? That was the wedding of Jesus and Mary. As far as we can tell, Magdalene was about eight years older than Jesus, and they had three children."

Dante, inquiring further, said," There's more you want to tell me, isn't there, Papa Gino?"

Pacelli slowly nodded his head in agreement.

"Yes, my son, there's much more to tell you."

The magnitude of what he was telling Dante was taking an incredible emotional toll on the cardinal. But he would not allow himself to stop without telling Paul everything he needed to hear. With that thought in mind, Pacelli unloaded more startling news on Dante.

"The story of the death, burial, and resurrection of Jesus, the story and belief that is the foundation of the Catholic Church, did not happen the way you and I were taught."

Dante was now incredulous. "What exactly do you mean by that?"

Speaking softly, Pacelli carefully considered his words.

"Jesus was an historical, deeply human, deeply mystical being with a political agenda to accomplish during his lifetime.

He WAS the so-called Messiah in the scriptures that was to come and save his people from the oppression of the Roman dictatorship. Six of his 12 apostles were religious zealots, ready to fight and die at any time. The other six were his brothers and members of his Essene community.

"Magdalene mentored Jesus to be a preacher, spreading an elevated, spiritual concept of peace and harmony. He had a magnetic personality that drew crowds wherever he spoke. He spoke the common language of his listeners, often using simple stories to punctuate the importance of his message," Pacelli related.

"But something went terribly wrong that caused his own inner circle of zealots to turn against him. It was an innocent remark to a simple question during one of the many conversations Jesus had with the Pharisees who routinely followed him wherever he preached."

"What question was that? Dante interrupted.

"Scripture noted the question to Jesus: Should the Jews pay taxes to Rome? This was a loaded question because the zealots wanted nothing less than the complete removal or destruction of Rome's hold over Judaea, and would fight to the death to stop paying any kind of taxes to the Roman emperor. Paying taxes was one of the major fighting points that the zealots used to justify using deadly force against Rome, and would be the battle cry when the war between the Jewish zealots and Rome began," Pacelli stated.

"What angered Jesus's followers?" Dante asked.

Pacelli took another deep breath before answering. "Jesus answered, 'Give to Caesar the things that are Caesar's, and to God the things that are God's.' This answer incensed Judas, the most passionate of all the apostolic zealots following Jesus. In the mind of Judas, Jesus had just given Rome justification for keeping the Jews subservient, and crushed the zealot's major reason for battle. This is the real reason why Judas betrayed Jesus."

Dante was troubled and confused by what he had just heard.

"Papa Gino, my heart weeps at this incredible disclosure. What more could you possibly say that could shatter the image of the Church beyond what you've already told me?"

After hearing Dante's question, Pacelli became even more determined to explain.

"Jesus was tried, tortured, and crucified as a political prisoner. Crucifixion was how political extremists were killed according to Roman law at the time. The Church does not want to admit this, but it is true."

Dante continued to question Pacelli's candid story.

"So you say that Jesus was killed as a political prisoner. That's not surprising. That still doesn't explain how the rest of the story changes."

Pacelli continued without interruption.

"The Jewish scriptures said that the Messiah would be killed, buried, and rise from the dead in three days. Because Jesus was not divine, and his metaphysical and paranormal powers could not defy death itself, he could not be allowed to die. He had to survive the crucifixion. And he did, but it took extraordinary means of cunning and bribery."

Astounded, Dante asked, "And how did this occur?"

Pacelli was quick to answer.

"One person orchestrated this entire sequence of events: Joseph of Arimathea. History describes Joseph as a rich man who was a silent believer in what Jesus preached. But he was so much more than that," Pacelli stated.

"Joseph was one of the elders of the Essene community that nurtured Jesus from infancy. His stature afforded him much wealth and influence with both the Jewish and Roman authorities," Pacelli said. "After Jesus was ordered to be crucified, Joseph, quickly and quietly, approached Pontius Pilate, the Roman magistrate who announced the death sentence for this political prisoner, and, through bribery, arranged to not only be given the body of Jesus, but also cut short the time Jesus had to hang on the cross. This act of humanity and cunning by Joseph is what saved the life of Jesus that day."

Dante still needed clarification.

"But the Bible says so much more happened to Jesus that day," Dante argued. "He was lanced in his side, not to mention the loss of blood from being nailed to the cross. How did he survive that trauma to his body?"

Pacelli elaborated.

"Again, Joseph used his cunning, bribery, and esoteric knowledge of metaphysical chemistry to keep the secret plot on target." Pacelli continued.

"The wine that Jesus was given by the centurion at the cross to quench his thirst contained a drug that hastened his unconscious state. That same Roman centurion had been given a sizeable bribe by Joseph to place the required lance mark in a precise location under the ribcage of Jesus, and to only penetrate the skin superficially. To those watching this scene from afar, this political crucifixion was being played out exactly according to Roman law."

"What happened then?" Dante asked.

Pacelli, despite the coolness of the pre-dawn breeze, dabbed his sweating brow with his silk handkerchief.

"After all official elements of the crucifixion had taken place, and because Jesus appeared to be dead on the cross, time now was becoming a huge factor in order to carry this uncanny plot through to completion," Pacelli recounted.

"As the sun was beginning to set and early evening approached, Joseph and the other Essenic disciples at the scene gently lowered the body, placed Jesus on a wooden pallet, and quickly rushed him to a burial cave nearby that Joseph had purchased only days before. Once within the confines of the cave, Essenic doctors were already there to administer medical treatment to keep Jesus alive."

Dante was in total amazement when he asked, "If Jesus survived the crucifixion as you say he did, how did the resurrection play out as it did?"

Pacelli, who had returned to his seat beside Dante only moments earlier, leaned forward on the bench.

"The unbelievable events that occurred surrounding the resurrection story are contained in the Nestorian papyrus that was stolen. I've asked you here tonight to give you a Papal directive, through the power of the Pontifical Commission for Sacred Archeology, to hunt down the thieves responsible for this brazen act against Holy Mother the Church, retrieve this valuable document by any means necessary as quickly as possible, and return the document to me personally here at the Vatican," Pacelli directed.

He continued, "We know the Germans will be hunting for these criminals, also, because for years they have been searching the same archeological sites for the same precious manuscripts and artifacts that the Vatican covets. So you will not be alone in this quest."

Dante was now very eager to begin his mission.

"Papa Gino, as a Jesuit, I have pledged my loyalty to the Holy Father. As a former soldier, I am equipped with the necessary skills to carry out this dangerous mission. Thank you for giving me this responsibility."

In a grave voice, Pacelli firmly addressed Dante.

"Paul, before you go, I need to tell you why you're risking your life to accomplish this holy mission."

Pacelli bit his lower lip, and then gently released his toothy grip with a slight exhalation.

"The Nestorian papyrus holds the most incredible and most damaging information to not only the Roman Catholic Church, but to all organized religions. This document holds the secret that the Vatican has been hiding for millennia. If the information contained in this ancient manuscript ever became public knowledge, the total collapse of civilization as we know it will begin."

Dante wrinkled his forehead and clenched his jaw.

"What information can cause such a calamity to occur, Papa Gino?"

Slowly rising again from his side of the bench, Pacelli looked Dante squarely in the eyes.

"The presence of extraterrestrial life on earth. This stolen file documents the existence of a group of highly-evolved superior beings not of this earth, and how they have created and manipulated the human race for tens of thousands of years. And especially the role they played during the resurrection of Jesus."

Rising quickly from the bench, Dante gave his mentor another stunned look of incredulity.

"I don't believe it! I can't believe this!" he cried.

Extending his right arm and placing it on Dante's left shoulder, Pacelli spoke almost apologetically.

"I, too, was overwhelmed when I learned of the contents of the Nestorian papyrus. But it's true, and this document can never be exposed. The possessor of this information truly holds immeasurable power; but keeping it quiet holds an even greater responsibility to mankind."

Dante needed to know the incredible details surrounding the Resurrection. He pumped Pacelli for more information.

"So how did these superior beings affect the resurrection of Jesus?"

Pacelli straightened his venerable crimson cassock, ran his fingers through his short thinning hair, adjusted his bifocals, and folded his arms across his chest.

"These superior beings, both male and female, very human-like in appearance except for their lightly-colored skin, elongated foreheads and tall stature, well over six and a half feet for the males and six feet for the females, were intricately involved within the Essene community, and exposed the inhabitants to the wonders of science and technology. They chose the Essenes because of their docile nature and passion to help humans attain a higher level of consciousness." He continued to elaborate.

"This was the philosophy that Jesus openly preached, to attain a higher level of peace and harmony, to ascend spiritually to a 'Father' in heaven, to become like 'sons of God.' Jesus never claimed to be THE Son of God. He preached that people should reach a level of consciousness that likens them to be 'sons of God.'"

The cardinal paused to breathe in the sweet smell of the myriad of wild and exotic flowers that flourished in the Vatican Garden throughout the year.

"The Nestorian file explains how Mary and Joseph, the parents of Jesus, were carefully chosen from royal bloodlines, Joseph from the royal bloodline of David, and Mary from the priestly bloodline of Aaron, to form a dynastic marriage.

"Barely in their teens, the file revealed the story of how Mary and Joseph were transported together off the planet in some kind of flying machine by the beings to a facility the beings said they established on the dark, far side of the Earth's moon. There, in a medical procedure that took place in a sterile environment, Mary was artificially inseminated with Joseph's sperm. Thus, an immaculate conception did actually occur, leading to the birth of Jesus. The story goes on to state that the birth of Jesus was the only time artificial insemination was used with Mary for conception. Mary and Joseph had seven other children through natural childbirth," Pacelli recalled.

"The file stated that the alien influence on Jesus was overwhelming. During what the scriptures call 'the hidden years of Jesus' life,' much speculation has arisen that Jesus went to Egypt, India, or China to learn from master teachers. But that's not completely true," Pacelli noted.

"The file states that Jesus was instead transported to the moon base for weeks at a time, and taught mind-enhancing techniques that would allow him to not only read people's minds, but also to be able to put himself into a self-induced trance that would allow him to reach a higher level of consciousness. From this higher state of consciousness, he was able to perform all of the 'miracles' that are mentioned in scripture. It was these skills that Jesus used when he began his public life of preaching and teaching."

Dante was now beginning to show some impatience with his Papal father figure.

"Papa Gino, this is all extraordinary! But how did the aliens influence the resurrection?"

Pacelli, realizing that his young ward was growing a little weary of the winding tale, made a concerted effort to finish the improbable story.

"Yes, I need to conclude this story so you can be on your way. I don't want to delay you much longer. But the resurrection account, according to the papyrus, is the most fantastic story of all."

Pacelli proceeded to tell the ending to his cathartic tale.

"The Essenic doctors in the cave waiting for the arrival of an unconscious Jesus were actually alien physicians. When Joseph of Arimathea and the brothers of Jesus carried the body of Jesus into the cave, the alien doctors quickly took charge. The file said that they stopped the loss of blood almost immediately. But it still took almost two hours to fully revive Jesus to where he was alert and out of medical danger," Pacelli stated.

"Jesus then was secretly moved from the cave after darkness fell late that night, and taken back to a secret underground Essene community near Qumran. After a few weeks of recovery, Jesus and two of his brothers were taken by flying machine to France."

Pacelli stated, "The file contains incontrovertible evidence that Jesus was still alive in A.D 45, almost 12 years after his supposed death and resurrection. It goes on to say that Mary and their children arrived by flying machine months later, and they lived a secret, but happy life around the mountainous village of Rennes-le-Chateau, with Jesus finally dying of old age around A.D. 73."

"However, the resurrection ruse had to play out to fulfill the scripture promises. What happened next was ungodly, but the manuscript says it happened this way."

Pacelli took a deep breath before he continued.

"After Joseph and the others had moved Jesus safely away from the gravesite, a new group of aliens arrived, and replaced Jesus with a perfect duplicate body they had created through cell experimentation and gene manipulation at their moon-based laboratories," Pacelli related.

Pacelli added excitedly, "The Shroud of Turin was created as a side effect of this alien process."

Dante was stunned by this revelation. "You mean the Shroud of Turin is really the burial cloth of Jesus?" he asked.

"Technically, yes," Pacelli responded. "Only it was the burial cloth of the duplicate Jesus." Pacelli quickly turned his focus back to his running story.

"This body double of Jesus was then left in the burial cave, along with two alien guards, and the stone was rolled over the entrance. The Roman centurions that Pilate ordered to guard the cave didn't arrive until mid-morning the next day. They only took a quick peek inside, stayed a few hours around the grave site, then deserted their post, feeling they had done enough since they weren't being paid for their time that day anyway.

"Plus, no one had come by to examine the grave or inquire into its inhabitant, the centurions thought. Most importantly, no one had stolen the body of Jesus on their watch, they told each other as they walked away." Pacelli breathed in the night air for a second before he continued.

"On Sunday morning, according to pre-arranged plans, Mary Magdalene and Jesus' mother arrived at the cave at sunrise and found the stone already rolled away from the entrance to the grave. They were initially shocked to find no one in the grave, as they were led to believe a body would be inside. They thought their plan had gone excruciatingly wrong.

"The two alien guards, dressed conspicuously in long white flowing garments, had awakened the sleeping duplicate only a few minutes earlier before the arrival of the two women, telekinetically maneuvered the stone a few feet to allow Jesus to walk outside, and returned to their sitting positions at the top and bottom of where Jesus had laid. They also had been informed to tell both women that Jesus was not there. Everything was following the written scriptures," Pacelli remembered.

"While walking outside the grave, both women noticed a hooded figure standing alone a short distance away, but didn't think to ask him what happened to the body inside, thinking it might be a Roman official waiting to report any suspicious behavior.

"As they slowly walked away from the grave, they were deep in thought as to what they were going to tell the disciples about the missing body. Then they heard a voice say "Mary." They both turned, not knowing which Mary was being addressed. The figure then lowered his hood to reveal his face, and both Mary's cried out in shocked surprise. It was Jesus!"

Pacelli related, "Mary Magdalene walked up close to the duplicate, but the duplicate Jesus told her not to touch him, as his body was not yet ready to function normally, thus fulfilling the scripture, "Mary did not recognize him after he called out her name."

"This is where the manuscript abruptly stops its dialogue, Paul," Pacelli said. "But as I told you, the contents are explosive in nature. So you understand the enormity of this situation."

Positioning himself in front of Dante, Pacelli stated, "You must go, now, my son. Let me give you my blessing, and wish you God's speed."

Dante dropped to his knees while Pacelli prayed over him and gave him a papal blessing, gently touching the top of Paul's hair and then cradling the young American's head. Dante then stood, and Pacelli embraced him and kissed him on his forehead.

As Dante moved away from Pacelli to run to his apartment to gather his belongings and prepare for his adventure, he quickly turned and yelled to the elder Italian priest, "I won't let you down, Papa Gino."

Pacelli, in return, yelled to Dante, "And take Father Luigi with you as one of your helpers." Dante wished he hadn't heard that last request.

"*Jesus Christ*," Dante thought as he hurried to his apartment, "*How in the fuck is Loogie going to be able to help me?*"

As Dante opened his eyes and stretched his arms, he turned his head to note the time. His clock read 11:43 P.M. His mental recollection had lasted over 90 minutes. He slightly grinned and told himself, *"Papa Gino, I did not let you down. And surprisingly, Loogie didn't let me down either."*

CHAPTER EIGHTY SIX

Underground Alien Complex
Antarctica

UNFORGIVING is the word most commonly used by unwitting visitors when describing the degree of coldness in Antarctica. The searing frigid winds act like frozen razor blades when making contact with human flesh.

The flat, snowy surface in a camouflaged crevasse in the mountains of Neu Schwabenland, Queen Maud Land, Antarctica, began to shake. The ice, at some places hundreds of feet deep, suddenly cracked, and an opening appeared. As the parting steel sliding doors of the underground alien complex continued to spread wide, a glimmering silver oblong UFO slowly emerged, floating silently upward out of the hole until it reached a couple hundred feet into the sun-soaked, ice blue sky.

The gleaming disk accelerated for a short while until it arrived at a watery tributary filled with floating ice chunks that were bouncing freely against the frozen banks of the river. Stopping suddenly, the silent ship opened its sliding hatch doors at the bottom of the craft, and a dark object fell away from the cargo bay, plunging quickly and disappearing instantaneously into the frigid waters below.

As the craft reversed its course to return to the underground base, the slowly-sinking object kept on a trajectory that would have it hitting the bottom of the Antarctic Ocean in a matter of minutes.

CHAPTER EIGHTY SEVEN

**Vatican Intelligence Agency Repository
Secret Archives**

AN open file laid unattended on the small wooden table in the S.I.V. room in the Secret Archives about 30 feet from Dante's subterranean office. A figure was casually walking the semi-lit passageway holding a manila envelope in his left hand. Hand-stamped horizontally on the top half of the envelope in bright red capital letters was "SECRETUM OMEGA Level 3." He stopped when he reached the table.

The name on the file was ADOLPH HITLER. The black-suited delivery man stood above the table, carefully opened the envelope with his right hand, and eased out the contents. He stared at the picture with a blank expression on his face.

For several minutes, he gazed at the color 8 x 10 photo showing Hitler's black staff car with the specially-designed gold swastika hood ornament submerged in dark, murky water, having found its final resting ground in a watery grave thousands of miles away from its homeland. A note attached to the photo simply stated Antarctic Ocean. He methodically placed the photo back into the envelope, sealed it, and placed it firmly into the thick HITLER file.

He turned and carried the confidential file a few feet to the entrance of the high-security vault where two of his top Swiss Guards protected the silent-alarm encased entry 24 hours a day. The two young guards were dressed in newly-designed black S.I.V military combat uniforms instead of the obnoxious ceremonial garb they wore in public when they protected the pope or guarded public-access buildings. The S.I.V medallion patch prominently adorned the upper left arm on their dark shirt. They lowered their automatic rifles to their sides, and stepped away from the vault entrance as he approached the Secret Archives that contained all Top Secret files, manuscripts, and artifacts from S.I.V. investigations.

He unlocked the steel-enforced vault door with his gold-plated Vatican key, and walked to a large metal safety deposit box located toward the back of the gigantic vault. He placed the entire file folder into the open safety deposit box marked "NAZI LEADERS". He then closed the box, locked it with a different smaller key, and exited the vault. A few steps down the hallway, he heard his guards slam shut the heavy vault doors.

The two Swiss Guards resumed their positions in front of the vault doors as Dante's shadow faded into the dark passageway.

Epilogue

Dante's Apartment – Vatican City Late Evening

SHE met him at the door, surprising him with a glass of chilled *Vittorioso* wine and provocatively dressed in a short silky red LaPerla negligee. Her ample breasts and shapely long legs captured Dante's undivided attention. After he entered, she playfully kicked the door shut with the back of her right high-heeled red-feathered pump.

"Hello, sweetheart!" she exclaimed, kissing him softly on the lips. "I thought I'd give you your anniversary present at the door, and I don't mean the wine. Do you like it?" She quickly twirled to give him a full view of how little coverage the gown gave a naked body. She giggled, giving him her sexiest smile as she took another sip of Italy's finest wine.

Dante was mesmerized by the sight of her gorgeous body sensuously exposed from beneath the flimsy but expensive lingerie. He quickly dropped his attaché case next to the black leather sofa in the spacious living room, took a healthy gulp of his cool enticing drink, and eagerly pulled her to his chest.

"After all these years, you're as beautiful as the day I met you on your dad's farm," Dante whispered, smothering her with a long, passionate kiss. "I can't believe we've been together for 20 years."

"Time has passed by so quickly," she smiled, leading him by the hand to the small kitchen table where a candle-lit dinner was waiting. The dinner was their special moment, an anniversary practice that started nearly a generation ago after Dante had saved Pacelli from imminent death.

Papa Gino had turned a blind eye to the connubial arrangement after Dante approached him with the request long ago. After listening to Dante's reasoning to break several commandments, ignore numerous Catholic religious traditions, and brazenly disregard some unwritten pontifical rules, the future Pope Pius XII simply nodded his consent. He figured that he had allowed much worse actions to take place within the confines of Vatican City, and far beyond. Unofficially sanctioning a common-law marriage between a woman and his favorite Jesuit seemed inconsequential in the mind of the future Pope.

Following their traditional buttermilk pancakes, sausage and eggs dinner, the two ageless lovebirds took their unfinished bottle of wine into the bedroom. Stripping each other naked with lustful energy, foreplay consisted of pouring droplets of wine onto each other's exposed bodies and licking dry the fruit of the vine off the seductive flesh. They then made passionate love, experimenting with new sexual positions that enhanced their erotic experience.

After climaxing simultaneously, both lovers rolled onto their backs exhausted, sweat covering every inch of their satisfied bodies. After a few minutes of controlled breathing to create relaxation, they rolled over into each other's arms. The long embrace included short, poignant kisses that brought a smile to their faces.

"I love you so much," she whispered. "I always have, and I always will." Dante gently caressed her face, pushed back her long blonde hair, looked deeply into her sky blue eyes, and kissed her lightly on the forehead.

Still entwined with her life partner on their conjugal bed, she stated softly, "Good night, my love."

Dante closed his eyes to hasten much-needed sleep after his long day and very eventful evening. He spoke in a hushed tone.

"Thank you, sweetheart, for the nice surprise at the door and for the great meal. And making love to you just gets better all the time." Then he spoke his last words for the night.

"I love you, honey. Sweet dreams, Laura."

Selected Bibliography

Acharya, S. (1999). *The Christ conspiracy: The greatest story ever sold.* Kempton, IL: Adventures Unlimited Press.

Andrews, R., & Schellenberger, P. (1996). *The tomb of god: The body of Jesus Christ and the solution to a 2000-year-old mystery.* Boston, MA: Little, Brown and Company.

Baigent, M. (2006). *The Jesus papers: Exposing the greatest cover-up in history.* New York, NY: HarperCollins Publishers.

Baigent, M., Leigh, R., & Lincoln, H. (1983). *Holy blood, holy grail.* New York, NY: Dell Publishing.

Bull, S. (2009). *Special ops 1939-1945: A manual of covert warfare and training.* Minneapolis, MN: Zenith Press.

Collins, M. (2008). *The Vatican.* New York, NY: DK Publishing.

Cori, P. (2008). *No more secrets, no more lies: A handbook to starseed awakening.* Berkeley, CA: North Atlantic Books.

Cornwell, J. (2008). *Hitler's pope: The secret history of Pius XII.* New York, NY: Penguin Books.

Cornwell, J. (2003). *Hitler's scientists: Science, war, and the devil's pact.* New York, NY: Penguin Books.

Crowe, M. J. (1999). *The extraterrestrial life debate, 1750-1900.* Mineola, NY: Dover Publications, Inc.

Driver, J. M. (2006). *The Vatican: Conspiracies, codes, and the*

Catholic Church. London, England: Kandour Ltd.

Ehrman, B. D. (2009). *Jesus interrupted: Revealing the hidden contradictions in the bible (and why we don't know about them)*. New York, NY: HarperCollins Publishers.

Ehrman, B. D. (2011). *Forged: Writing in the name of god – Why the bible's authors are not who we think they are*. New York, NY: HarperCollins Publishers.

Farrell, J.P. (2010). *Roswell and the Reich: The Nazi connection*. Kempton, IL: Adventures Unlimited Press.

Gardner, L. (2005). *The Magdalene legacy: The Jesus and Mary bloodline conspiracy: revelations beyond the Da Vinci code*. New York, NY: Barnes & Noble.

Gomes, M. (2009). *The secret doctrine: the classic work by H.P. Blavatsky*. New York, NY: Jeremy P. Tarcher/Penguin.

Hart, S., & Mann, C. (2012). *World War II secret operations handbook: S.O.E., O.S.S. & Maquis guide to sabotaging the Nazi war machine*. Guilford, CT: Lyons Press.

Hopkins, B, & Rainey, C. (2003). *Sight unseen: Science, UFO invisibility and transgenic beings.*New York, NY: Atria Books.

Jacobsen, A. (2011). *Area 51: An uncensored history of America's top secret military base*. New York, NY: Little, Brown and Company.

Jenkins, P. (2010). *Jesus wars: How four patriarchs, three queens, and two emperors decided what Christians would believe for the next 1,500 years*. New York, NY: HarperCollins Publishers.

Kasten, L. (2010). *The secret history of extraterrestrials: Advanced technology and the coming new race*. Rochester, VT: Bear & Company.

LaViolette, P. A. (2008). *Secrets of antigravity propulsion: Tesla, ufos, and classified aerospace technology.* Rochester, VT: Bear & Company.

Lo Bello, N. (1998). *The incredible book of Vatican facts and papal curiosities: A treasure of trivia.* New York, NY: Gramercy Books.

Martin, J. (2010). *The Jesuit guide to (almost) everything: A spirituality for real life.* New York, NY: HarperCollins Publishers.

Martin, M. (1987). *The Jesuits: The Society of Jesus and the betrayal of the Roman Catholic Church.* New York, NY: Simon & Schuster.

Medawar, J., & Pyke, D. (2012). *Hitler's gift: The true story of the scientists expelled by the Nazi regime.* New York, NY: Arcade Publishing.

Norwich, J. J. (2011). *Absolute monarchs: A history of the papacy.* New York, NY: Random House.

Patrick, B., & Thompson, J. (2009). *An uncommon history of common things.* Washington, DC: National Geographic Society.

Pawlicki, T. B. (1981). *How to build a flying saucer and other proposals in speculative engineering.* Englewood Cliffs, NJ: Prentice-Hall.

Picknett, L., & Prince, C. (2008). *The masks of Christ: Behind the lies and cover-ups about the life of Jesus.* New York, NY: Touchstone Books. New York, NY: HarperCollins Publishers.

Proud, L. (2013). *The secret influence of the moon: Alien origins and occult powers.* Rochester, VT: Destiny Books.

Russell, L. (2008). *The scourge of the swastika: A history of Nazi war crimes during World War II*. New York, NY: Skyhorse Publishing.

Sharpe, M., & Westwell, I. (2007). *German elite forces*. London, England: Compendium Publishing, Ltd.

Smith, R. H. (2005). *OSS: The secret history of America's first central intelligence agency*. Guilford, CT: The Lyons Press.

Stevens, H. (2012). *Hitler's flying saucers*. Kempton, IL: Adventures Unlimited Press.

Stevens, H. (2011). *Dark star: The hidden history of German secret bases, flying disks, & u-boats*. Kempton, IL: Adventures Unlimited Press.

Stone, D. (2009). *Hitler's army: The men, machines and organization 1939-1945*. Minneapolis, MN: Zenith Press.

Temple, R. (1998). *The Sirius mystery: New scientific evidence of alien contact 5,000 years ago*. Rochester, VT: Destiny Books.

Thomas, G. (2012). *The pope's Jews: The Vatican's secret plan to save Jews from the Nazis*. New York, NY: St. Martin's Press.

Vesco, R., & Childress, D. H. (1994). *Man-made UFOs 1944-1994: 50 years of suppression*. Stelle, IL: Adventures Unlimited Press.

Vining, M. (2008). *Jesus the wicked priest: How Christianity was born of an Essene schism*. Rochester, VT: Bear and Company.

Warner, P. (2004). *Secret forces of World War II*. Yorkshire, England: Pen & Sword Books Limited.

Zuk, B. (2001). *Avrocar – Canada's flying saucer: The story of Avro Canada's secret projects*. Ontario: Boston Mills Press.

ABOUT THE AUTHOR

Jerzhy Knuteman is the pen name for the owner of a Midwest education and motivation consulting company. The former college basketball coach holds a doctoral degree in performance and health psychology, and is an adjunct professor at a Midwestern university. He has been a practicing sport psychologist for over 25 years.

He has extensive writing experience, authoring 14 books on the psychology of sport and coaching education topics. He published an online subscription email newsletter for college coaches for five years.

This is his first fiction novel. He and his writing team have written the script for The Vatican Files: The Movie.